MW00880891

BRAINS & BRAWN

BRAINS & BRAWN

A Novel of Suspense

Annie Gottlieb & Jacques Sandulescu

iUniverse, Inc.

New York Lincoln Shanghai

BRAINS & BRAWN

A Novel of Suspense

All Rights Reserved © 2003 by Annie Gottlieb & Jacques Sandulescu

No part of this book may be reproduced or transmitted in any form or by any means, graphic, electronic, or mechanical, including photocopying, recording, taping, or by any information storage retrieval system, without the written permission of the publisher.

iUniverse, Inc.

For information address:
iUniverse, Inc.
2021 Pine Lake Road, Suite 100
Lincoln, NE 68512
www.iuniverse.com

ISBN: 0-595-29872-9

Printed in the United States of America

For the Pearsons:
Warren, George, Ralph & Robyn,
and especially Margaret

CHAPTER 1

▼

"Why don't we get married?"

For once, it was Sunny who suggested it. The meeting at *Metro* had gone better than she'd hoped; she had the assignment letter in her purse, and she was feeling grand and reckless. Besides, it was their anniversary. She could never remember the exact date, but she knew it was around late March or early April that they'd met. And she always felt a special rush of affection for Sasha when she got back from uptown.

Sunny could dress and act just as urbane as the other writers who worked for *Metro,* but she lived for the moment when she could scrub off the suffocating makeup, get down from the high heels, take off her clothes, and sit cross-legged on their big bed in one of Sasha's double-extra-large T-shirts, letting the cats crawl into her lap and waiting like a baby bird to be fed. She was home.

Sasha stood by the stove, his broad back turned, fixing dinner with motions incongruously delicate for his size. When he broke an egg, both his thick pinkies lifted like an orchestra conductor's, and the yolk plopped into the bowl intact. People saw Sasha as a giant, a pro wrestler or truck driver—an impression reinforced by the movie "heavies" he played for a living. He was six two, but his small, boxer's bullet head, broad Slavic face and powerful body made him look even bigger. Sunny, a diminutive five three, could remember looking way up at him the first time he'd visited her little studio apartment. The contrast between them still drew stares on the street, yet she hardly noticed the size difference any more, just as she no longer heard his accent, she was so used to him. She knew what he was going to say now, because he always said the same thing. She even chanted it along with him:

"We're better than married!

"What's the matter with you?" Sasha had turned around, waving a big spoon for emphasis. "Look at your sisters and brother. All three of them get married, have a couple of fat kids, and get divorced. And we've been together now, what? Six months?"

"Twelve years," Sunny said.

She knew he didn't like being reminded of the passage of time. To Sasha, cats were "kittens" and women were "girls." It wasn't condescension, but a way of keeping what he loved as far as possible from death. "You're fulla shit," he grumbled. "I know you six months. And we've got more going for us than most married people. You want to give City Hall twenty dollars? You know how much tuna fish salad I can make for twenty dollars?"

It was Sasha's obsessive theme. He had been taken prisoner in a Soviet labor camp at the age of sixteen. When he'd escaped in winter two years later, he'd been as tall as he was now, and he'd weighed 120 pounds. And so food had become, for life, the measure of all things. Sunny had once taken the est training—out of curiosity, the same relentless drive that made her a good reporter and, Sasha said, a pain in the ass. Est still made him mad whenever he thought about it. "Two hundred fifty dollars to listen to some con man call you an asshole?" he'd bellow. "Do you know how many boxes of corn flakes I can buy for two hundred fifty dollars?" Sunny had to admit she'd never thought of it that way. Living with Sasha changed your perspective on a lot of things.

"Ah," she said now, in a tone of discovery. "You're too cheap to get married."

"Definitely," he said. "Open your mouth." He came towards the bed with one big hand cupped under the spoon.

"What is it?" Sunny asked.

"Have I ever given you anything bad? Close your eyes and open your mouth!" She obeyed, and the spoon slid in. It was Sasha's Japanese-Transylvanian fried rice, with egg, green pepper, lots of garlic and soy sauce, and the bean sprouts still crisp. Sunny groaned with bliss.

It was reason enough to marry the man. God, what a cook he was. He loved cooking; no doubt nearly starving to death had something to do with that. But you had to have the talent, and Sasha had inherited his from his kind, big-boned mother, a traditional Transylvanian household manager of awesome skills. Sunny adored and admired this 78-year-old woman who could spin a lace tablecloth from a single thread and coax a perfect pound cake out of a wood stove. From her own high-strung mother, she'd inherited mainly her intellect. If she hadn't met Sasha, she supposed she'd still be living on canned tuna, coleslaw, and Entenmann's coffee cake from the deli across the street, picked up in a break between paragraphs.

Like many of her generation's female high achievers, Sunny sometimes felt guilty for not serenely serving her man something different every night. But in fact both she and Sasha were simply being true to their natures. Sunny was a walker on air, so wrapped up in her ideas and ideals that she had to be reminded to eat. Sasha was a born nurturer who loved doing the reminding. When he was "between thugs," as he called his movie roles, taking care of Sunny was his main activity and pleasure. *"I need a wife"* had become the career woman's lament, and it was Sunny's ironic secret that she *had* one, when her friends took one look at this huge ex-boxer and bar owner and assumed he was Rambo's old man. Only Darlene, Sunny's best friend as well as her editor at Metro, had Sasha pegged as "a male earth mother."

The trouble was, he overdid it.

Sunny spread a towel on the bed for a tablecloth as Sasha brought over two mountainous bowls of fried rice. "Jesus, Sash," she moaned. "You forget I'm half your size. I can't eat all that."

"I thought you said you were hungry."

"I *am* hungry, it's just—"

"Then shut up and eat!" Sunny gave in and started picking bean sprouts and peppers out of the rice, one of her desperate stratagems for living with Sasha and not weighing two hundred pounds. The most important was the strenuous karate workout they did together three or four times a week. Daintily-built, Radcliffe-educated Sunny seemed an unlikely prospect for karate, but when Sasha had first told her about his friendship with Japan's greatest karate master, she'd insisted on watching him work out. Then, being Sunny, she had to try on a *gi* and see how those strange movements felt. Twelve years later, she was a first-degree black belt, and karate's shouts and punches had transformed a shy, pudgy girl into a woman with a strong will, a firm voice—and a knockout body. Sarah Randall was far better-looking at 37 than she'd been at 25. It was just one more way that Sasha had revolutionized her life.

"Let me count the ways," Sunny had confided in Darlene over a beer in Jimmy Day's one Saturday afternoon when she was feeling sentimental about Sasha. Darlene, who had heard a darker side after some of Sasha and Sunny's titanic fights, studied her friend's bright face while Sunny numbered the good things. Without Sasha, would she ever have come to love jazz, or really *hear* flamenco? Traveled to Transylvania or Tokyo? Learned how to curse in five Balkan languages? Gotten to have as many cats (nine) as she'd always secretly wanted? Learned to live in her body as much as her head? Would she ever have found a man who wasn't afraid of commitment? Darlene knew Sasha was almost *too* committed, and possessive and protective: he didn't ever want Sunny to go out dancing at night, because, as he said darkly, "I know what's out there."

"Sounds to me like things are really good between you," Darlene said with a wry little edge of envy in her voice. Darlene was four years divorced, a survivor of the singles scene and very tired of it. She wouldn't have minded having Sunny's problems. When you were near forty, going out dancing at night wasn't so much to give up.

"Oh, yeah," Sunny sighed. "I used to be kind of intimidated by him. I stand up to him much more now, and you know what? He *loves* it!" She leaned over and touched her friend's arm. "We have a fire axe in our apartment—a friend of his once stole it from a movie theater or something. Well, the other night I got so mad at him, I picked up the axe and said, 'I'm going to murder you in your sleep!' And he *creamed!* Oh, I don't mean it turned him on sexually. He just got this blissful look on his face and said, 'Ahhhh. Now I can die in peace, because I've created a monster. I know you can take care of yourself.'" Sunny clenched her fists and growled in imitation of Sasha. Darlene recognized the portrait and laughed.

"He loves you," she said. "And he loves you strong. Come on." She leaned forward. "When are you going to marry him?"

Sunny's face suddenly had a closed, stubborn look. Darlene saw the warning and swerved into lightness. "It's the patriotic thing to do these days," she said. "People are dropping like flies, and most of them don't have half of what you two do. So why hold out? Sasha wants to get married, doesn't he?"

"I think so," Sunny said reluctantly. "He'd never admit it, but…yeah, I think it would make him happy."

"So what's the problem? What's the difference, even? You *are* married. You know that, don't you?"

"That's exactly it," Sunny said. "What's the difference? If *we* feel married, what business is it of the State's?"

Oh, Christ, Darlene thought, her friend's Sixties roots were showing again. Remind her to have her vocabulary touched up. Sunny seemed to lack the postmodern survival skill of hopping from decade to decade, cheerfully changing one's spots. Come to think of it, being with that outlaw giant was kind of a Sixties thing to do. You couldn't fit Sasha into a three-piece suit, or an episode of "Thirtysomething." Or, for that matter, into a nice postmodern mom-and-pop, two-career marriage.

"I guess you two are just the last Bohemians," Darlene sighed. She had given up a precarious career as a cabaret singer for her prestigious office job. As much as she appreciated the steady income, the power and perks, her secret sympathy with the freelance life was one of the reasons she and Sunny were friends.

"Bohemian? *Sasha?*" Sunny picked up a fried mozzarella stick and dunked it in marinara sauce. "His role model for the perfect haircut," she said with her mouth full, "is George Patton."

But she had to admit to herself that it was true.

Sunny had often puzzled over what bound her and Sasha together, when they came from such different worlds. One of her better theories was that they had both been uprooted in adolescence. "I was arrested on my way to school," Sasha's stark autobiographical book, *The Seventeenth Level,* began. From the moment he saw the Russian soldiers with machine guns, he could never go home again. Sunny had merely had the certainties of her Fifties childhood dynamited out from under her by the Sixties. But in a sense she, too, could never go home again. Both of them had learned to live in the whirlwind, and they took pride in that skill even now, when most people were scrambling back to the *terra firma* of tradition. Let others have their weepy white weddings; Sasha and Sunny would laugh and shudder together at the words "wife" and "husband," "honey" and "dear." They were fond of their odd-shaped relationship, wary of corseting it in convention. "If it ain't broke, don't fix it" was one of Sunny's standard replies to questions like Darlene's.

"Three strikes and you're out" was another, for in fact Sasha had already been married three times. "Once for U.S citizenship," he said, "once for an air conditioner"—it had been a hell of a New York summer, and the girl wouldn't let him move into the cool without a license—and once to a Radcliffe-educated mathematician who'd won his heart by explaining a card trick. While this proved to be insufficient basis for a marriage, it had crystallized Sasha's taste in women, for which Sunny had to love him: he wasn't the least bit interested in blondes, dumb or otherwise—he went for brunette brains. Sunny was only his second serious attempt, and this time it was working. *Don't fix it!*

But Sunny knew better. Deep down, she didn't think getting married would hurt her and Sasha's relationship at all. It would probably make it better. The fact was, after twelve years they were still shacked up like teen-agers because Sunny Randall was afraid of marriage. Sasha wasn't the problem. She was.

She'd never said this even to Darlene, because she couldn't explain it very well to herself. The closest she could come was to say, "I have to write a book before I get married," or "I have to make my name." It was as if she was afraid of disappearing. Wife and mother had been her mother's whole identity, and Sunny had been raised for the same. Her own will had been hard to carve out, a frail pillar still marked by the discarded chisel of feminism, a barrier island challenged daily by the rough sea of Sasha's personality. Single status, even if in name only, was the symbol and sea wall of her independence. To get married might be to give in and go under.

Tonight, though, basking in Sasha's warmth, eating his cooking, bantering with him, she wondered what she'd been resisting. He was her family, her home base. Why not declare it to the world? What a dumb idea, to wait till she was famous. That was almost a *fait accompli* anyway. She could feel the assignment letter glowing like a little power source in her purse.

Landing the campus drug-plague story was a coup in itself. It was a cover story, for sure. It meant that *Metro* felt she was ready for a lead investigative piece. Here it was at last, the coveted prize of name and reputation—maybe even the Pulitzer—almost within her grasp. Sunny knew she could do a bang-up job on this piece, because she had a resource that most writers didn't. A largely middle-class, college-educated bunch, they were out of their element on the street. So was Sunny. She wasn't sure she could spot a pusher, much less walk up to one and get him to talk to her. But she had her own personal Virgilian guide to the underworld.

She had Sasha.

"So what's this new assignment?" he was asking. "What'd Darlene say?" He'd already finished eating. Sasha still shoveled food into his mouth like the starving teen-ager of forty years ago. He had a great mouth for it, too, supple and childlike on the outside, absolutely cavernous on the inside. Sunny liked to tease him that his mouth was like a loading dock. She also liked kissing it. Right now he had a toothpick cocked at a jaunty angle, and he leaned forward on his chair, forearms on thighs, ready to hear about her day.

Sunny suddenly wanted to put off telling him about the assignment. The little worm of doubt she'd had in her mind all afternoon was growing into a dragon. This was the opportunity of her life. What if Sasha didn't like it? He was usually very supportive, but if he thought an assignment was a waste of time, or dangerous, he could make it very hard to work. Remember the punk club story? God. And the suicide story! She'd come close to giving that one up. And this time, she needed more than just his support. She needed his help.

She felt something like stage fright.

"Tell you after 'the Wheel,'" she stalled.

To her relief, Sasha immediately got up to make coffee. Watching "Wheel of Fortune" was one of their rituals. Sunny clicked on the TV remote control. While the audience chanted "WHEEL! OF! FORTUNE!!" and Pat said "Oh, Vanna!", she soothed the cats' sibling rivalries, letting Blueberry the Siamese (named for his nearly purple eyes) nest in her crossed legs, tucking Ollie with the crooked tail (named after the dragon in "Kukla, Fran and Ollie") up against her left hip, and granting Harley the teen-ager (named for his loud purr) her right thigh.

When Sasha brought her coffee, she was gazing intently at the first puzzle, two blank rows with a few scattered N's and E's. The contestants on the screen looked blank, too. One of them asked to buy a vowel.

"'ELEMENTARY EDUCATION,'" Sunny announced.

"*Je*-sus Christ." No matter how many times she did this trick, Sasha always acted admiringly stunned. "You're dangerous."

"It's an idiot-savant talent," Sunny said dismissively. But she was beaming. When you were held to Olympic standards in your professional life, it was nice to come home and be treated like a genius for solving a silly puzzle.

"All right, that's it. You've got to get on this show," Sasha declared. "If you have luck, you could bring home forty, fifty thousand dollars *and* the His and Hers Cadillacs." His face was bright with what Sunny called the Big Score Dream. Some version of it, she knew, had sustained him as early as the prison camp in Russia. Then he had dreamed of glorious meals, and gleaming marmalade jars lined up in his mother's pantry. Today it might be a movie deal for his life story, a suitcase full of cash misplaced by the Mob, a friendly hacker with the key to a multinational bank's computers—even a small killing on "the Wheel." Whatever it was, for the moment it could be more real than reality. He looked as happy now as if Sunny had already won.

The Wheel spun, the audience clapped and screamed, the contestant asked for a T and got three of them.

"How much did he land on?" Sasha called from the stove.

"I don't know," Sunny said absently.

"You don't *know!*" Sasha exclaimed, coming back with a two-cup Pyrex measuring cup full of milky coffee. It was what he always drank from; regular mugs were too small. "What's the matter with you?"

"I was looking at the puzzle."

He groaned. "What have I been trying to teach you for the last twelve years? Has a word of it sunk into that Radcliffe head of yours? If you take that puzzle to the supermarket, what will it get you?"

"'PEANUT BUTTER'!" Sunny said triumphantly. The TV audience clapped and cheered.

"I give up," Sasha sighed. "What can you do? You grew up with a full refrigerator and an allowance from Daddy. How can I expect you to understand *in your gut*"—roughly grabbing his own belly for emphasis—"what that gangster in 'Body and Soul' said—"

"'It's a question of addition and subtraction,'" Sunny recited dutifully. "'The rest is conversation.' Look!" She pointed at the new puzzle, hoping to get Sasha off the sore subject of her priorities.

Even "Wheel of Fortune" could reopen this deepest rift between them: life had forced him to think in numbers, while allowing her to be a woman of letters. A common sight was Sunny lost in the *New Yorker* while Sasha scanned a supermarket sale sheet. No amount of financial security could break his habit of elation at finding a can of tuna for fifty cents, a pint of sour cream for .89.

He was always trying to make Sunny aware of the raw girders of money that had upheld her carefree childhood and education like silent steel beams under a superhighway. He'd told her over and over that her idealistic desire to "make a difference" with her writing was a luxury. In the real world of power, there was only one way to make a difference: to "be somebody," to "have substance." Then and only then would your words carry weight. So he wanted her to want something more substantial, like a million dollars, first. Sunny was an earnest pupil, and understood in principle, but in moments of excitement she would invariably forget and follow her interest instead of her self-interest. She hated being hollered at, so she tried distracting Sasha: "I know this one already. 'IF YOU HAVE YOUR HEALTH YOU HAVE EVERYTHING'…"

He took the bait, and "the Wheel" rolled peacefully to its conclusion, Sasha commenting that the bonus-round player was a dumb son-of-a-bitch for taking the $25,000 cash instead of the $62,000 Porsche and selling it. "Bye-bye," chirped Vanna, waving.

And reality came crashing back in.

"Good evening. I'm Dan Rather, and this is a CBS news brief. A new front opens in the war on drugs; once again, the casualties are our children.

"We finally thought we were winning. Crack abuse—down for the first time in a decade. Crude methamphetamine 'crank' labs—successfully shut down across the country. But now, a sinister new synthetic drug called hexamethylene—known on the street as 'hex'—has triggered an epidemic of abuse on college campuses, and has been reported in high schools as well.

"'Hex' is a 'designer drug,' a brainchild of the laboratory that combines the thrill and the addictiveness of cocaine with the mystical rapture reported by some LSD users in the 1960s. It's been called 'the strongest kick since crack,' and at four to six dollars a capsule, it's almost as affordable. As police and the Drug Enforcement Agency race to find the underground labs that are flooding campuses with the drug, two student deaths have already been reported, one from a brain seizure, and one when a student jumped out a sixth-story dormitory window, believing..." Dan looked fifty million people dead in the eye..."that she could fly. I'm Dan Rather. More news at eleven on this CBS station."

Well, now was as good a time as any. Sunny took her cue. "That's my new assignment." She waved a casual hand at the screen, but her chin was up, a sure sign of readiness for battle.

Sasha was alert. "What do you mean?...You going to interview Dan Rather?" Sunny saw calculation, then satisfaction cross his face, swift as sun after shadow. "He's got a lot of clout," he said, nodding approval. Her heart sank.

"No, dummy. The drug story." She wasn't looking straight at Sasha now, but she saw his face change out of the corner of her eye. She plunged ahead. "This new drug is one of the biggest stories of the year, and I get to do my own investigation! Interview the cops, Dar said. Interview DEA agents. She wants me to work from both ends, and see if I can trace the drug back to its source. Poke around some college campuses, talk to the kids, try to find out who they're getting the hex from. I can pretend to be a psychedelic relic from the Sixties, they'll trust me. And talk to some drug dealers, too, check out the rumors in *that* world. That's where I'll need you. I know you know some of those people from the after-hours club. And those mysterious Italians who always greet you with such respect around the Village—you can't tell me *they* don't know about it. You could introduce me to them…and…" In Sasha's silence, her willed exuberance drained away. She heard herself sounding lame. She stopped.

"Yeah. And knowing you," Sasha said with heavy sarcasm, "you're going to take the drug, so you can write about how it feels."

"I am *not*," Sunny protested, furious at the childishness in her voice. In fact, she had been trying to figure out how she could do just that without Sasha knowing about it. Shortly after they'd started living together, he had found a Zip-Loc bag of pot in her stocking drawer. "What's *this?*" he'd roared, holding it dangling from thumb and forefinger. And then he'd ordered her to flush it down the toilet. Sasha's boast was, "I can get high on a glass of water." And he could.

"It's out of the question," he said, sitting back. His big arms were folded like Mr. Clean's.

"What's out of the question?"

"This assignment. What's the matter with Darlene? She's supposed to be your friend. Where does she think she's sending you, to the supermarket?" One of Sunny's bigger stories had been on the tri-state milk-price scandal. "Does she have any idea what's out there?" Sasha reached and put the telephone in front of Sunny. "Call her up right now at home. Tell her you won't do it."

"I will not!" Sunny was fizzing like a shaken Coke bottle. Sasha had hassled her about assignments before, but he'd never actually tried to *forbid* one. It was a breathtaking violation of her sovereignty. The tanks were in her streets. "How dare you tell me what I can and can't do! You think you can make me turn down the biggest break in my career? This piece could lead to the Pulitzer"—oh, shit, he couldn't care less about the fucking Pulitzer—"it could lead to a book, a movie deal—"

"And it could lead to you being dead."

"Oh, Sasha," Sunny wailed. "Don't be melodramatic."

"Melodramatic?" The gleam in Sasha's eye was dangerous, the light before thunderstorms. "Was it melodrama when Charlie Shaw turned up in the East River? Was it prime-time soap opera when they found Fast Eddie in the trunk of a car? Hah?"

Sunny remembered foxy little Charlie, with his silver-white hair, black brows over sharp bright eyes, zipped-up windbreaker and discreet diamond pinky ring, greeting Sasha at the Washington Square chess corner on a chilly gray day. Sunny had been introduced, as she always was to Sasha's killer, cop, gangster and thief friends, and as always, a story followed. Sasha explained that he and Charlie had once been partners in a Village coffee shop, and that since then Charlie had supported himself as a "second-story man"—a skilled burglar—tithing himself by contributing generously to wildlife-protection organizations, his great love. He was always talking about retiring to Miami, but a restlessness like a compulsive gambler's kept driving him back into the deals. When Charlie was found in the river a few years later, Sasha had commented tersely, "He got greedy," and had deplored the fact that Charlie—so cocksure in his luck he felt immortal—had died intestate, leaving over a million in ill-gotten gains to the state, not even to the Sierra Club.

Sunny remembered Fast Eddie, a young black hustler, mainly for his handshake. Introduced, she'd reached out with naïve eagerness, and he'd let his hand lie in hers like an inert, scaly object, emptied of himself. It was a tactile lesson in street paranoia. But his wariness hadn't kept him alive. So now Sasha was saying that both these deaths were "drug-related." Sunny wondered what that had to do with her. "Sasha, they were *dealing,*" she said. "They probably burned somebody. I'm a reporter."

"Reporters got killed in the Vietnam war," Sasha said. "And believe me, this is a war, just as deadly as Vietnam." He sighed. "Sunny, Sunny. The best times in my life have been spent in this little apartment. This is my haven. I don't want to bring the shit from the street in here. But I see I have to explain the facts of life to you, since they obviously don't teach them at Radcliffe."

Sasha got that far-seeing squint that meant he was looking into life's bleaker realities. Deep lines appeared beside his eyes, crevices carved by Russia's cold winds into his sixteen-year-old face when he'd worked on the mine-slag tower. Even as she braced for a buffeting lecture, Sunny marveled helplessly at the way his face could change. It could be as round and warm and harmless as a teddy bear's, then as harsh as a golden eagle's.

"Take cocaine," Sasha said, settling into his subject. Sunny opened her mouth to protest, but he held up a warning finger, and she subsided. "If you make some friends in Bolivia or Colombia, you can buy a kilo of pure coke for as little as $5,000. Smuggle it up here to New York City, and you can sell it for $100,000. Or step on it twice, and on the way down to street level it gets stepped on again, and it could bring in $350,000 or $400,000—from a $5,000 investment! When did Wall Street ever see that kind of profits? And you don't need a Harvard MBA. All you need is basic intelligence, good sharp instincts, and street sense.

"If you deal in larger quantities, ten or twenty kilos, you can make millions on one deal." Sasha could put his whole body into his words. He drew out "millions" as if he were Midas, spreading heaps of gold voluptuously under his hands. "A few deals, and you'd be a multimillionaire"—another word given heft and gusto. "If you were still around. Because that big, fast profit draws the cowboys and crazies like blood attracts sharks. And you know sharks in a feeding frenzy. They'll tear anything apart"—he bared his teeth—"including each other.

"You think you know everything about me, Sunny. You've been to my home in Romania. You've read my stories and watched me wake up from nightmares. You know more than I've let anyone else see. But there are a few things even you don't know." Sunny suspected there were more than a few. Her curiosity had met its match in Sasha's Piscean secretiveness. In his rough, resourceful life, he'd been what he called "washed with all the waters." He claimed to have been in jail in an unspecified number of countries. There was a hint that he had been in the Foreign Legion—and gotten out. He wouldn't talk about it. After Sunny had known him for eight years, he'd casually let drop that he once swam the English Channel, in exchange for all he could eat. Sunny still didn't know what he'd been doing for a living when they met. She didn't want to know how close it was to what he did on screen for a living now. "Your boyfriend loves you very much, but, dear, *don't* ask him about his past," a psychic had once told Sunny "He won't tell you."

"I've been right up to the edge of the drug business," he was saying. "I've known guys who had millions of dollars in their apartments, brown paper bags and suitcases stuffed with hundred-dollar bills. On the surface it looks like easy money. And I've given it a lot of thought. There's only one way to do it. Get in and out in a year. Don't let greed suck you into one more deal. And most important, never touch the stuff. There was one smart operator who almost did it that way, Frank Matthews. Black guy. Made himself a nice little fortune of twenty million dollars, and disappeared. They say he's living somewhere in the Caribbean. I was terrible disappointed when I heard that he started sniffing a little towards the end." Sasha shook his head with real sorrow, as he did whenever his faith in brains was betrayed. "But he was still the exception. He stayed in control. Most of them go off the deep end.

"I probably could have done it. You know I don't have the slightest interest in coke, or any drug. I had more opportunities than I can tell you. You know why I didn't get into it?"

"Because it's a dirty business, and deep down you're a clean guy," Sunny said.

Sasha scowled. He didn't like having his hardened pragmatism seen through so easily. "Nah. People want to put shit in their bodies and kill themselves, fuck 'em. There are too many people on this poor little planet already. I stayed out of the drug business for *me.*" He jabbed a finger at his own powerful pectorals. "'Sasha's' was one of the hottest jazz bars in the Village. I sold it because of the hassle. Eighteen hours a day, up till four in the morning, dealing with drunks, fights breaking out, bartenders stealing from you, cops giving you summons…What kind of life is that? The drug business makes it look like a vacation.

"Supposing the stuff is delivered to your apartment. Then you sit there and sweat, waiting for raids and rip-offs. You're smart, you stay in the background, far away from the street. Your distributors bring suitcases full of cash to make the exchange. Maybe it's funny money. Maybe it's numbered bills from the DEA. Maybe they're going to stick you up and take off with the money *and* the stuff. Around that kind of payoff there's no such thing as 'trust' or 'loyalty.' The only way to control people is fear, so you've got to be ready to set an example if somebody burns you. You're constantly surrounded by violence, coming at you from all sides and going out from you in waves.

"All your senses have to be on the alert all the time. That's one reason why most dealers end up on coke. You have to *listen* as if your life depended on it. It does. At the moment when a transaction starts to go bad, it's like a wrong note in jazz. It's not too loud, but it's there for the hearing. And on the other side is that suitcase, fat with hundred-dollar bills. Do you listen to your instinct or your greed? Choose wrong and you're dead, or worse than dead."

"What's worse than being dead?" Sunny challenged him. She wasn't sure she wanted to know.

"The Colombian cartels have always been the suppliers, but when they started getting into distribution up here, things got a lot bloodier. When the guineas want to make a point"—Sasha slipped easily into the ethnic epithets of the street—"they usually use guns. You've seen those *Post* pictures, some big shot on his back in a family restaurant with his cigar still in his mouth and blood all over the tablecloth. Or they might use a baseball bat in a soundproof basement, break some arms and kneecaps, or shatter the hands." As he spoke Sasha's big body flinched in sympathy, like it did when he watched boxing or pro wrestling. For such hard-earned intimacy with blows and pain, Sunny didn't know whether to pity or fear him.

"The spics are more into knives and razors, cutting off body parts, stuffing them into other body parts. They leave grisly messages. I heard about a Colombian outfit that caught some Italian gangsters muscling in on their territory. They taped a guy's mouth, sawed his legs off with a chain saw, and left him to bleed to death. He was found bled white, with his eyes wide open.

"The Colombian cocaine cowboys are the most feared, for good reasons. They're fucking maniacs—unpredictable, hair-trigger tempers, no conscience, no fear. Jaguars straight from the jungle. They dominate the drug business now. If I let you go near them, *I* should be shot."

Sunny couldn't keep her mouth shut any longer. "I've read the books and the *Times* articles. I know all this stuff—"

"—you *think* you know it. To you it's just words. I want to make it *touch* you—" Sasha wrapped his huge hands around Sunny's upper arms with a grip that hurt—"before you go on one of your crusades and get yourself in real trouble."

"Ow, Sash, let me go!" Sunny struggled helplessly until he did. She rubbed her arms and glowered at him. "This is *not* cocaine we're talking about! What do Colombians have to do with hex? You heard Dan Rather—it's a sophisticated designer drug! It probably comes from some lab in California. I'll bet it's being sold by a bunch of balding old hippies who think they're bringing in the Millennium! It's a whole different thing!"

"You still haven't learned." Sasha pinched the bridge of his nose with professorial weariness. Sunny suddenly remembered him reading her German poetry on their first date, his reverent expression, his scholarly little half-granny glasses perched incongruously on his broad face. "It's *exactly* the same thing," he explained, as if to a slow child. "Big money, tax free. I'll bet you this drug is made from ordinary, cheap chemicals. Once the lab's set up, it can't cost more than a few cents a dose to make. Sell it for a few dollars, and you've made a hundred times your investment. Same profit margin as coke. Less risk—there's nothing to smuggle across borders.

"If this drug catches on with the kids, and it looks like it is, it's cutting into the crack pushers' market, number one. Number two, it's going to look attractive, and the Mob and maybe even the Colombians are going to want to move in on it. Then whoever's been pushing it is going to defend their territory. Bang, the shooting and the cutting starts. And there's little Sunny right in the middle, going up to some gunsel with her microphone and saying, 'Wow, this is exciting! Can I interview you?'" Sasha's voice rose in an infuriating falsetto, then dropped as he pointed commandingly at the phone. "Call Darlene!"

"No way," Sunny hissed. Her eyes flashed, and she seemed to grow taller. Sasha had committed the one unpardonable sin: he had condescended to her.

"I'm not your child, Sasha. And I'm not your pet. Just because you're bigger and stronger and you've lived through more, you think you can push me around and say it's 'for my own good'! How the hell do you know what's good for me? If I choose to go out there and risk my neck to make my name, that's my choice, and it's my business!

"You don't want to protect me, you want to own me! You'd like to lock me away from the world and keep me to yourself! You're a bully, Sasha, a...a dictator!" She was standing in front of him now, electric with outrage. Her next words rang with the triumph of an Einstein who's found his proof:

"You see? That's why I'll never marry you!"

CHAPTER 2

▼

Sasha strode through the predawn streets of Greenwich Village, through streetlights the color of cheap pink champagne, toward the Bleecker Street subway station. In the country, in his childhood, this hour would have been the beginning of morning: roosters crowing, the clank and creak of people starting their chores in the dark. In New York, five A.M. was part of the night. A few fanatical joggers pounded around Washington Square Park, but the streets still belonged to the other, nocturnal population. Like night creatures in any jungle, they would scuttle and struggle and feed until the tide of weary daylight washed them away, leaving a spoor of broken glass, spit globs, and crack vials. Sasha granted the night creatures neither fear nor interest. He plowed through their writhings with the grand indifference of an ocean liner in a sea of snakes. Yet he knew without looking what each one was high on, what he wanted and what lengths he would go to to get it. The awareness was effortless, automatic. Sasha breathed the street.

On Washington Square Park South, a tall black man in a bulbous leather hat hissed "Sin, sin" at the passing joggers, who stared puritanically straight ahead. Near Thompson and Third, two Spanish boys sat on a stoop, their big radio blasting, passing a joint back and forth to a blonde girl with a black eye. The girl looked about fifteen. A dirty yellow pup on a string lay beside her, chin on paws, endless patience in its eyes. Sasha felt a pang of pity for the dog. *So innocent…those kids have a choice…the parents' fault…ahh, people suck.* He scraped and spat his bitterness out.

Further down Thompson, five young men with long, lank hair and heavy eyelids clustered around a bottle in a brown paper bag. They swayed like clowns on a high wire, balancing between violence and unconsciousness, their voices slurred and rising. Sasha could calibrate the precise moment when shoving would break out, glass would smash, and one would chase another into the street in rubber-legged slo-mo, with the jagged upraised end of the broken bottle. By then he would be in the next block. When he passed them, the boys swayed apart, feeling a breeze of authority, peered at him with bleary respect, and mumbled, "Howaya, sir!"

A few blocks behind him, safely five stories above the street, Sunny slept in a nest of blankets, with a cat curled in every crook of her body. Sasha had hated getting out of that warm nest, and he'd done it for her. In the early part of the night Sunny had been mad at him and had scrunched over by the wall, withdrawing every inch of her body from the stealthy peace overtures of his forearms and knees. But in her sleep she'd relented and melted into him, fitting perfectly, like a small spoon inside a big one. He'd willed himself not to get a stupid hard-on and spoil the coziness. No snake in this garden, not tonight. Now, with every step, sanctuary receded. Sasha was going back into a world he had meant to put behind him. He was going, he told himself, to protect Sunny. He knew that he was also going because he couldn't say no to her. And perhaps he was going, finally, because he couldn't stay away. Can a fish escape its element?

He hurried down the steps into the Bleecker Street station, past two homeless men lying curled on their sides on sheets of cardboard. Sasha could never be prepared for this sight, and it hit him with the force of a flashback. The soles of their shoes looked so unprotected. He saw himself in the rubble of postwar Hanover, happy to have a pair of cracked leather boots to rest his cheek on. Thank God it wasn't a cold night, spring was coming and the poor bastards would have it a little easier for a while. He dropped a token in the slot. A train was just rattling in, an old one, deafening. There were more ragged, dirty people sleeping on the plastic benches in the bright light. He wasn't sure which was worse, the cold or the dirt.

Sunny would say he was taking the subway because he was too cheap to take a cab, even though—in between sleepy, surprised thanks—she'd promised unlimited reimbursement by Darlene. No, Sasha had taken the subway because he needed time to think. This errand was embarrassing. He already knew what Brooklyn Georgie was going to say: "What the fuck's the matter with the cunt? Why can't those people mind their own business?" And of course he was right, though he had no business calling Sunny a cunt. But Georgie called all girls broads and cunts, it didn't mean anything. Sasha just had to steel himself. That was the other reason why he wanted this time on the train. He had to "suffer a sea-change"—the words startled him, from that beautiful poem Sunny had read him. He had to get back into the after-hours-club frame of mind.

A few years ago, after he'd sold his jazz bar and before the movie roles had really started rolling in, Sasha had been Brooklyn Georgie's partner in the club on East 75th Street. The silent partners, who put up most of the money, were major Mob guys, shadowy figures who were mentioned in murmurs of reverent discretion, but rarely seen. Sasha was a working partner, which meant that for two years of his life he had gotten out of bed at 3 A.M., washed, dressed, kissed Sunny in her sleep, and taken a cab up the empty canyon of Third Avenue.

At 4 A.M., as the legal bars closed, the after-hours clubs opened. Serious night people were just getting up to speed, and the feverish energy they'd built up could not be contained by the flimsy dam of closing time. The descendants of Prohibition speakeasies caught the spillover: bartenders and bar owners, hard-core drunks, revved-up cokeheads, dope dealers, big-spending thieves and torpedoes, compulsive gamblers, pimps, call girls. The clubs were dens, but they weren't dives. At six dollars a drink (a profit of at least $120 a bottle, tax free), they didn't cater to the destitute, the derelict, the street hooker or street dealer. They drew a better class of criminal, and they had their own code of glamour. For members in good standing of low society, they were the place to show off your bankroll or your new breast implants to a jury of your peers. For high society, they were the place to roll your shoulders in some high-smelling sleaze, the way lions roll in elephant dung. The crowd always included a sprinkling of Wall Street types with surreptitious addictions or young mistresses to impress. And the cherry in the sundae was the occasional celebrity: Sasha had personally greeted Mick Jagger, Robin Williams, John Belushi in his free-fall.

Sasha had worked the door. It was the most important post in an after-hours club, because the doorman was the intelligent valve the controlled the mix upstairs, allowing in enough volatility to keep the money flowing, but not so much that the place would blow up and bring down a raid. The doorman had to know at a glance who was connected and who was blacklisted, who was carrying a piece, who was high and edgy, who was a rat, a troublemaker, a plainclothes cop, a freeloader, a spender. In the case of an unknown quantity, he had to make a snap judgment based on instinct: let them up, or turn them away. And he had to have the personality and force to make his decisions stick. Up to thirty thousand cash on a good gambling night could depend on it.

In all respects, Sasha was supremely qualified. His knowledge of humanity was encyclopedic, and it didn't come from books. By nature he was a keen observer, and a little psychic; experience had honed that endowment to near infallibility. In addition, he had inherited the presence of his father, an officer in the Austro-Hungarian cavalry, and his grandfather, who had owned nine villages and had the power to hang and marry. Even bums on the street responded to that aura without quite knowing why. Of course, it didn't hurt that he was very large, and as powerful as he looked.

The train rattled northward with what felt like inevitability. Fourteenth Street, eighteenth, twenty-third…It wasn't electricity powering this trip. It was the pull of the underworld, that gravitational force Sasha could not resist no matter how hard he tried. At sixteen, guilty of nothing more than looking big enough to do a day's work (well…not counting the black-market sale of his birthday bike to a Russian officer), he'd been arrested like a criminal, and dragged across the line that separates good citizens from the outcast, condemned, and suspect. It seemed he'd spent the rest of his life trying to get back across that line, not because he had such respect for the respectable—he'd lost *that* naïveté early—but just because he was, after all, *not guilty!* It was useless. Legitimate people gave him the fish eye. Gangsters and thieves embraced him.

It had always been that way. He remembered his terrible discomfort as a young fighter in Chicago, boarding with a nice American family, trying to go out with their son and two girls on something called a "blind date," explaining earnestly to the mother why his top dresser drawer was full of soap: "When the rationing comes…" She had stared at him with incomprehension verging on disgust, as if he came from another planet. Same with the business owners he'd approached for a job busing dishes or mopping floors while he trained for his first U.S. fight. They'd looked him up and down, this big young bruiser with the thick accent, baby face and ancient eyes, and their own eyes had hooded over like shop-window shutters slamming down. What did he say his experience was? Prisoner in Russia? *Killer, Commie agent, or both.* Sorry, we're full up.

And then one day, after his workout, he'd been having a cup of tea at the coffee shop across the street from the gym, and a hand wearing a diamond pinky ring had reached over and picked up the check.

"It's OK, kid, I'll take care of it." Looking up, Sasha recognized a man who sometimes lounged by the ring and watched the fighters train. He had on a fine dark overcoat and a dark hat tilted at a jaunty angle. He threw a handful of change on the counter, spun around on his stool and stood up. "Wanna go for a ride?"

The man had led him to a sleek dark car and opened the back door. Sasha got in, and they drove a long way. When they stopped and got out, the man ushered him into a dim, empty nightclub—dim and empty except for one table that had a spotlight trained on it. At that table, a man of about forty was eating a thick, juicy steak, with a beautiful girl on either side of him. The girls had on show costumes, and their creamy breasts were popping out of their red satin tops, and their long legs in black net stockings crossed and uncrossed under the table. Sasha took it all in with one hungry look.

The man who'd brought him had taken off his hat. "This is the kid I was telling you about."

"Hi, kid. Howya doin'?" The man at the table measured Sasha with keen black eyes. He had a small hawk nose, and sallow skin; his hair was black as patent leather, slicked back and impeccably barbered. He wasn't tall, but he was broad and solid, and Sasha felt power coming from him. It was a sensation as familiar as his own father, and suddenly this jumbled new world made sense, as if the planets were circling the sun again.

His eyes dropped inadvertently to the steak, and the man didn't miss it. "Hungry, kid?" Sasha nodded, bashfully but factually. The man raised one hand in an imperious come-here gesture. A tall, balding waiter came running out of nowhere, almost falling over himself in his desperation to please. "Bring another steak for the kid. And a Coke." The waiter bobbed and backed away. "Siddown, kid."

Sasha took a chair from the next table and sat down. The two girls giggled and rustled and cooed, and he felt himself blushing all over his body. He looked at the tablecloth.

"Sally tells me you take a punch real good, and you got a left hook like a mule's kick. I won't beat around the bush. We're interested in picking up your contract. Where you from, anyway?"

"Romania."

"Rom*a*nia," the man said, in a that's-very-interesting-what-ever-the-fuck-it-is tone of voice. Just then, a huge steak was set down in front of Sasha's eyes. He didn't know what else to do, so he picked up the knife and fork and dug in.

"Whew! You eat good," the man said a couple of minutes later, as the last of the steak was vanishing. "You really *were* hungry. Don't your manager feed you?"

"I am always hungry," Sasha said.

"Oh yeah? Why's that?"

Sasha told him. His English was elementary, but so were the facts: cold, hunger, work, coal, snow, cave-in, escape.

The man had stopped eating and was gazing at him with total attention. After Sasha had finished, he was silent for a full minute. Then he made another one of those commanding gestures and said, "Show me your legs."

Sasha swung his feet around to the side and hitched up his trouser legs. The girls oohed and ahhhed when they saw the scars on his shins.

The man half stood, leaning forward for a look. He sat down again, shaking his head. "Son of a bitch." He signaled, and Sasha's driver and another man waiting in the shadows sauntered forward.

"You see this kid?" the man said, with a flourish of his hand. "He's got a lotta heart. We're gonna have a little talk with his manager. In the meantime, don't let nothing happen to him. Here, kid." He leaned forward, brought out a bulging bankroll, and peeled off four bills. "Put this in your pocket. Whenever you wanna eat, eat."

Sasha slipped the bills in his pocket without looking at them. He started to say thank you, but their eyes met, and the man nailed him with a look so direct and forceful that there was nothing left to say. The look said *I understand you,* and it said, *Count on me.*

When Sasha took the bills out of his pocket later, they were hundreds.

And that was the beginning of his lifelong relationship with the underworld, which had led by a roundabout route to his partnership in the club on 75th Street.

Forty-second already. The train was slowly filling up with working people, mostly black, the night shift going home, the early shift going out, everyone doped with fatigue. When the train jerked, heads lolled; mouths hung open in sleep. Sasha averted his eyes from the unguarded faces, the painfully neat, shabby clothes, the death struggle between dignity and exhaustion, like hyenas dragging down an antelope. Shit, he should've taken a cab. All this honest futility depressed him. The nether world of the gangsters might be sordid, but at least it had defiance, vitality. Its denizens refused to play by the rules and get ground down. You might think they were nuts, but you didn't have to feel sorry for them. They took what they wanted and paid for it.

Somehow, Sasha had managed to be in that world but not of it. "Just like a Pisces," he liked to say to Sunny, "to crawl through the garbage cans of the world and come out clean." The Chicago mobsters had delayed making their move on his contract because of his immigration problems. Then the Korean War had intervened—funny how your immigration problems cleared up when they needed you for cannon fodder—and Sasha, who'd had enough of war, had contrived to get himself sent to France as an army interpreter. One thing had led to another, and after putting himself through the Sorbonne's literature and philosophy course by dealing on the Paris black market (and getting along fine with the Mafia's Algerian equivalent), he'd landed in New York as a Greenwich Village coffee shop proprietor.

Around the corner from the Café Flamenco was a storefront with its windows painted over, a blind, inscrutable maroon. On summer days Sasha saw old Italian men in shirtsleeves sitting out front on wooden chairs, fanning themselves with the Daily Racing Form, drinking orzata, watching. The storefront was a social club, one of those inconspicuous command posts tucked away around the Village and Little Italy. Sasha, the son of a feudal village, could feel the invisible kingdom submerged under the city's innocuous streets, like an undersea mountain range. It was a place where he felt at home, and he was soon on friendly terms with the men in shirtsleeves, greeting them by name on the street, exchanging nods of mutual respect and tacit understanding.

On occasion, Sasha found opportunities to do small favors for them. He donated some extra chairs to the social club. He tipped them off when he learned that the D.A.'s office was watching the storefront. And when he was getting ready to open his jazz bar, he agreed to buy all his liquor from a local heavy's nephew, who had just gone into business. "I appreciate it," said Rocco, the kid's uncle. "I won't forget this." And they were as good as their word. Sasha knew instinctively not to get in any deeper, not to take their backing for his bar. Because he observed the unwritten laws, they honored his independent status. He was an equal and an ally, not a contender in their hierarchy. He never had a problem—until his bar opened, and was a success. Then the stakes went up, and the truce was tested.

The first week after he got his liquor license, "Sasha's" did a booming business. Right away the sharks moved in. A couple of freelance hitters came in one early afternoon, unsmiling, and demanded their cut. It was the classic ten percent shakedown: these goons thought they could come around every Saturday and collect three, four, five hundred dollars for nothing. Sasha told them he didn't want any deadweight partners. "We'll talk to you later," one of them had said, hinting at baseball bats and lead pipes wrapped in newspaper. Sasha knew he wouldn't be easy to hurt, but who needed this shit? Disgusted, he mentioned it to the pizza-shop proprietor next door.

A couple of hours later he was summoned. Two unfamiliar younger soldiers, dressed in gray suits and ties, came into the bar looking for him. They took off their hats, and one of them said almost formally, "There's somebody who wants to see you." Sasha understood from their religious demeanor that it was not just somebody, but Somebody. He signaled the bartender to take over and went with them. He could as easily have refused a shogun or a khan.

Inside the social club it was cool and dim. The two messengers ushered him into the back room and stopped in the doorway. The man sitting at the table over a cup of espresso just moved a finger, and the two men melted away. He motioned Sasha closer. Sasha had instantly recognized him: Carlo Visconti, Don Chaluch', the acting head of one of New York's major crime families (the aging *capo* was doing time for tax evasion). Sasha had seen Don Chaluch' on the street, always closely attended by two or three bodyguards, but he had never spoken to him. Two members of the usual entourage, jackets off, ties loosened, were playing pinochle at the next table. They nodded warily to Sasha.

"Please, sit down." The Don's voice was quiet. He made a graceful gesture of hospitality, and Sasha sat down opposite him. Chaluch' sat with his back to the window, so that his face was in shadow. Sasha felt sure this was deliberate. It gave the Don a chance to read him, while he could not quite fathom the expression in Chaluch's eyes. But he caught the gleam of intelligence, the concentrated awareness, at once animal and aristocratic, and the rich, sensual twist to the mouth, which could be cruel or generous.

"I hear those two assholes bothered you," he said.

Sasha inclined his head in uncomplaining acknowledgement.

Chaluch' studied him keenly for a moment. Then he sighed, a sound somewhere between world-weariness and the rumble of a dynamo releasing excess steam. "Don't worry about it." He waved one hand as if brushing away a fly. "The word is from the street that you're all right. Go on out there and make money. And from now on, if you got any kind of problem, you come to me. You understand? Ask for Chaluch'." And he nodded dismissal.

"I very much appreciate it," Sasha said, standing up. "I will not forget it. Thank you"

He knew that he had just received a benediction, one far more potent in these precincts than the Pope's. Indeed, no sooner had he gotten back to the bar than two chastened protection peddlers hurried in to apologize. In the weeks, months, and years that followed, Sasha rarely saw Don Chaluch', but he sensed an invisible protective umbrella over him. Cops and robbers alike were friendly and respectful. He was not hassled as long as he ran "Sasha's." And after he sold the bar, it was Chaluch' who had introduced him to Brooklyn George, and told Georgie to take him in as a partner on 75th Street.

Leaving Fifty-ninth now…almost there.

He hadn't seen his "rabbi" for a couple of years now, but knowing Chaluch' was there if he needed him gave Sasha the same sense of security he'd had so long ago at that table in an empty Chicago night club. He had not availed himself of Chaluch's offer of help; that was something to be called on only in the direst need. He would never dream of approaching Chaluch' about this little business of Sunny's. You didn't bother him with trivia like this.

Sunny had once met Chaluch' on the street with Sasha, when they hadn't been going together very long. *The Seventeenth Level* had just been published, and Sasha had sent one of the first copies to his godfather with an inscription. He and Sunny were coming back from the cleaner's when Chaluch', passing on the other side of Sullivan Street with his bodyguards, sent one of them over for Sasha. The two men shook four hands, and Chaluch' kissed him on both cheeks, sending ripples through the entire Lower East Side and recharging Sasha's invisible shield with a few thousand volts.

"Don Chaluch', I'd like you to meet my girlfriend, Sunny."

Chaluch' took her hand and graciously inclined his head. "It's a pleasure to meet you." Sunny had blushed, unaccustomed to courtliness. She hadn't yet been in Romania, where every male over the age of eight actually *kissed* your hand.

Chaluch' turned to Sasha. "I am very impressed with your story. My friend used to work for a book company, and she read it in one evening. She told me all about it." He jabbed one of his bodyguards in the chest. "Hey. You. You think you did hard time upstate? What the hell do you know? This guy did time in Siberia." He turned back to Sasha. "We'll have dinner some time, and you'll tell me more about it."

And to Sunny: "You got a man there. Take good care of him." It was an order. The little group moved away.

"Who was *that?*" Sunny had asked when they got around the corner.

"A friend," Sasha had said tersely. Sunny had looked at him, her blue eyes huge with unasked questions. Today, not much was sacred to Sunny. She'd irreverently refer to Chaluch' as "your Vito Corleone" just to get his goat. But in those days, her awe of her new boyfriend and his world had been as unbroken as new snow.

It was around that time that she had proudly shown *The Seventeenth Level* to her parents. And here was the irony: Chaluch', a killer and racketeer, who hadn't even read the book, had praised it with real understanding. Causwell Randall III, Yale man, New Hampshire banker, modest heir, had read it and said…nothing. Caus Randall, who could be so loquacious in praise of John Cheever and John Updike. "He doesn't say anything because he doesn't know what to say," Sunny had interpreted with desperate inventiveness. "This isn't a book you can make small talk about. You've struck Dad dumb. It's a compliment." Compliment, my ass. Sasha knew the hollow sound of America's front door slamming in his face when he heard it.

Let's face it. He'd been welcomed to this country by hoodlums, mobsters, black fighters, Jewish promoters—outsiders who'd made it by their bare fists and guts and wits. Straight people, safe, respectable people like Sunny's parents shied away from him. And why shouldn't they? What on earth did he have in common with Caus Randall? Everything about the man was modest, cautious, privileged, discreet— everything Sasha was not and never could be.

What could you do? You followed the law of life, like water seeks its own level. You went where you were appreciated.

You went back to 75th Street.

The trouble, Sasha thought—getting up as the train screeched into 77th—was that he didn't really belong there, either.

Taking the stairs two at a time, he strode eastward under awnings, past drowsy doormen. It had happened again and again: Sasha would be drawn, like a moth to a flame, by his underworld friends' primal energy, but then he would find himself repelled by their morbidity. The fucking guineas were obsessed with death. They dealt it, they courted it, they feasted in its shadow. Sasha couldn't understand them. He had come very close to death himself, and meant to spend the rest of his life as far away from it as possible. And then there was their illiteracy. Oh, they could read the racing form all right, or an Italian menu. But that was the limit. And again, Sasha parted company with them. He didn't understand how anyone could live without books, literally. Books had saved his life.

He'd had books in Russia—the ones in his head, the books he'd read as a kid. Karl May's fantastic Westerns, Sherlock Holmes, had lifted him out of his exhausted, shivering body and transported him far away. Those flights of the spirit had saved him from deadly despair. And in lonely years in America, books had been his best friends, letting him escape to better worlds in fantasy (he loved happy endings) and distilling his bitterness at this world into healing words (he loved the great cynics: Dostoevsky, Nietzsche, Celine). Sasha's biggest secret was that he lived in his imagination, a vast inner world that no one looking at his rough exterior would suspect. A few of the jazz greats who'd played his bar had had a hunch. But he had never opened it up to anyone—except Sunny.

God, being with Sunny was a relief. When they met, he'd been sick to death of people whose whole life was booze, blows, bucks and broads—and she'd been sick of the conversation of intellectuals. "You got me out of the salon," she liked to joke, "and I got you out of the saloon." Together they had made a world of their own where ideas had flesh and blood and facts had wings, where they shared belly laughs and soaring speculation. It was the world Sasha wanted to live in, and since then he'd withdrawn from the rough-and-tumble of his old life. He'd let himself get soft. But life never let you get away with that for long. Some situation would come up that forced you to be hard: a friend in trouble needed a nasty favor, some asshole tried to pick a fight, somebody threatened your girl. This time Sunny herself, with her dumb assignment, was sending him back into the fray. He'd needed the train trip and the walk to grow his crusty shell again.

Seventy-Fifth Street east of First gave no sign of the secret world behind its walls. The place was so well soundproofed that not a whisper of the booming disco beat leaked out to the street. The block was silent and deserted, except for one man in a trench coat walking a Doberman. How many spring nights Sasha had sat on a chair right here, reciting Schiller to himself and watching the faint city stars—until the next Cadillac drove up.

A black door, 475 on it in chrome. Sasha knocked, and the little window slid back. Right away he heard and felt the pulsing beat. The suspicious eye of Salvatore the doorman darkened the slot, and then the door clicked and opened.

"Hey, Salvi, who loves ya?"

"Sasha, my man!!" Salvi grabbed Sasha's big hand and shook it like a terrier. The warm greeting was genuine, but Sasha saw fear in the stocky little gunsel's eyes—fear for his job. Any time Sasha wanted the door back, it was his.

"Just dropped by to see how things are going. Georgie upstairs?"

"Yeah, yeah. The whole gang's up there, Georgie, Joey. The joint's packed. Go right on up."

Sasha started up the red-carpeted stairs. They vibrated under his feet as the driving disco music throbbed and throbbed, growing louder with each step. It reminded Sasha of the pumping heart of a great beast, always hungry for more, more, more. But there was something heartless and mechanical about the rhythm, too, like the thud and suck of pumps on the Texas oilfields. It was the sound of an illegal money machine in overdrive. It was relentless, and your whole body had to get used to it before you could hear again.

Entering the club, Sasha passed the source of the noise, the packed dance floor, where bodies writhed like furious maggots in red light. It was a good night, his eye told him—and it was night in here, oblivious to the dawn outside. Sasha saw flashy fabrics, glints of gold, lots of bare female skin. He heard the roar of two hundred people stoking the furnace of their desires: drinking three deep at the bar, necking on low leather couches in the lounge, gambling in the back room—he got a glimpse of the crowd as someone went through the door—and sucking up lines of coke in both bathrooms. The babble of voices rode the crest of the beat like foam on surf. Sasha had a moment to take it all in before the whole room turned towards him and opened to him.

"Heyyyy, Sasha!"

"If it ain't the big man himself! Hey, big man! Howya doin'?"

"I thought you went to Hollywood!"

"Well, honey! Where have *you* been?"

"Hey, baby, welcome home!"

"My maaaaan!! Saw you in a fuckin' movie!"

Male hands grabbed his hand, women's arms twined around his like serpents. Sasha said hello to Uptown Tony and Downtown Tony, Spanish Eddie who'd been in on the Brink's job and his barmaid girlfriend Patty, Fat Joey with his belly slopping over his belt, sexy Remy who'd won her name by putting away a whole bottle of cognac, Charlotte the elegant black madam, and dozens more. The boisterous welcome warmed him. Why had he stayed away so long?

He spotted Margie's pale, freckled face and straight black hair behind the bar. So his protégée was still working here. Sasha excused himself from the stone-faced killer shaking his hand and worked his way towards the bar to surprise her.

"Pick a card, any card!"

Sasha turned and met the bright black eyes of C.J. East, the magician. He grinned—he'd always had a soft spot for the kid—and drew a three of clubs out of the proffered fan of cards.

"What the eye sees, the heart must believe!" C.J. shuffled, making a little dancing bridge of the cards. He thrust the deck out, and Sasha slipped his three in face down. The cards whirred again.

C.J. was never far from Margie, Sasha remembered. It had been a standing joke around the club: the young magician's hopeless hang-up on the barmaid. Margie could do a lot worse. C.J. was what you'd call a "strapping lad": around thirty, over six feet tall, with big limbs and raven hair, sweet-tempered, and so healthy he literally had roses in his cheeks. He hardly drank; aside from Margie, what brought him to this den of passions was his sleepless passion for practicing his magic after a dreary day of adjusting insurance claims. He always plied his tricks right by the bar, where he could keep an eye on Margie just in case somebody bothered her. Yet he'd never made a move himself, and he'd once laid Fat Joey out for making a crude suggestion. In this unlikely setting, C.J.'s devotion to Margie resembled the gallantry of the troubadors. To deepen the mystery, he wore a wedding ring.

"Is this, by any chance, your card?" Out of the middle of the deck, C.J. produced the three of clubs with a flourish. "And the crowd went wild!" Sasha, an eternal child for magic, howled and slapped C.J. on both upper arms. The flesh under his hands was as solid as rock. When he wasn't feathering cards, the magician must be pumping iron. Sasha was glad that in his absence, Margie was protected.

Sasha saw her face turned toward him like a startled deer's, a half-poured Heineken's suspended in her hands. She'd heard his bellow of delight through all the noise. "My cousin!!" he roared, arms outstretched.

"We-e-e-ll! If it ain't the Transylvanian maniac!" Margie said in her husky voice. She put down the beer, wrapped her arms around his neck, and smooched him lingeringly on each ear, clinging with what felt to Sasha like relief.

"Georgie been hitting on you?" he said in a low voice when she unwound herself.

"No-o-o way! Ever since you put in the word, he's been a prince. Not only does he keep his hands off, he won't let anybody else touch me. Between him and C.J., I'm the only virgin in the place." She squeezed Sasha's arm. "Thanks for being such a good cousin."

It was their code word for Sasha's patronage, without which Margie could neither have gotten the job nor endured it for long. A barmaid in the club could make $300 and up a night, so the spots went to girls who were well-connected, mostly the girlfriends of made guys. That status also served to protect them from the boss, who considered any unattached, attractive female fair game.

Sasha had once gotten another aspiring actress in as hat-check girl. He'd told Georgie she was a special friend, to look out for her. Then Connie, more reckless and naïve than he'd known, had started sleeping with the Puerto Rican blackjack dealer. She'd believed she was in love. Georgie saw it differently. He'd taken her into the hallway and demanded a blowjob. She'd given him a hand job and come weeping to Sasha. He held her till she cried herself out, then scolded her for forfeiting his protection, indulging her hippie romanticism in this primitive world where the unwritten rules for women were ruthless. He'd never have that problem with Margie. She'd been a dancer in Vegas. She knew the ropes.

She leaned towards him to make herself heard over the roar. "What are you drinking? Wait—don't tell me. Ginger ale." She shoved a glass under the spout. "How's Sunny?"

Sasha spread his arms in a what-can-I-tell-you gesture. "She's great."

"Give her my love, will ya? I miss her. God, I miss the dojo, too. With this and auditions and dance class, I just don't have the time any more. But I still remember. See?" She threw a little side kick behind the bar. The way she did it, it looked hopelessly feminine and frivolous. Sunny was five inches shorter, but she could kick like a mule.

Margie had met Sasha and Sunny when she joined their karate school. She had come from Vegas to try her luck as a legitimate actress. She was working in Jersey as a go-go dancer, and without the high-level protection she'd been used to, she felt the need to learn some self-defense. Sasha had immediately been drawn to her. He was settled happily with Sunny, he wasn't looking, but he wasn't blind either, especially not to a pair of long dancer's legs. Margie was the sexiest dancer Sasha had ever seen on the disco floor. And she had a mixture of tomboyish directness and natural seductiveness that drove men crazy.

She was a runaway from a big, poor family, bright, tough, self-reliant but vulnerable, that combination of survivor and waif that always got to Sasha, maybe because it reminded him of himself. In some ways he had more in common with her than with Sunny, who'd never had to struggle. Sunny sensed that, and she was sullenly aware of Margie's sex appeal, but she knew Sasha was much more of a rescuer than a womanizer. She couldn't stop him from picking up stray kittens *or* lost girls. So Margie had become friends with them both. She'd turned out to be a good friend to Sunny, because like so many women in the flesh trades, she was a natural feminist, with a strong sense of loyalty and affectionate sisterhood.

"Any luck with the auditions?" Sasha asked her.

Margie sighed. "Not yet. A few jobs modeling for catalogs, that's it. You should see those cattle calls. I'm competing with every waitress and model in town. But I'm hangin' in there. At least I don't have to dance to make decent money any more." She picked up his hand and kissed the rough karate knuckles. "Thanks to my cousin again." When they'd been friends a few months, Margie had confided to Sasha how much she hated men's eyes crawling all over her. That was when he'd gotten her the barmaid's job. He wanted to do more, get her big break for her. He wanted to make a movie of his life and put all his struggling actor friends in it so they wouldn't have to struggle any more. He felt like Noah without an ark, and the cold rain falling.

"I've got an agent now. I'll set you up with him today."

"Oh, *yeah!*" she shrieked. "I saw you in 'Trading Places'! I jumped out of my seat and yelled, 'I know him! I know him!' Everybody was going, 'SSHHHHH!' You're working a lot, huh?" She looked wistful.

Sasha shrugged. "I'm a type. When they need a Bulgarian bruiser, they call me. You seen Georgie? I want to talk to him."

Margie jerked her thumb in the direction of Georgie's office. "He's in there. He's—"

But Brooklyn George had already gotten the word. He came rolling like a tugboat through the crowd, a short, fat, balding man with a weary-wise face.

"Well, whaddaya know. I ain't seen you in a while. What's cookin'?" He shook Sasha's hand and smiled tiredly. And that was the extent of his greeting, after more than two years. Sasha had never seen Georgie get excited. He had robbed banks and done time. His appetite for women was large, callous, and casual. He was an addicted gambler, chronically in debt, and constantly hiding out because the shylocks were after him. Yet he had an air of detachment that could be called philosophical. He looked at the world through a lizard's eye; if he had a motto, it would be "There is nothing new under the sun." Sunny had met Georgie once, and had marveled to Sasha afterwards at a lack of illusions and attachments so total it was almost Zen. She'd dubbed Georgie "the Thoreau of the underworld." She didn't know the Georgie who would hide behind the car of someone who'd screwed him and shoot the guy in the leg.

"How's your mother?" Sasha shouted over the noise. When he wasn't hiding out, Georgie lived with his mother in Crown Heights. Her great Italian cooking accounted for his shape.

"She's good, God bless her," Georgie shouted back. "How's your girl? You still with that writer broad, or you had four or five more since I seen you?" He winked at Margie. Sasha's domestic contentment had earned him a lot of ribbing around the club. The guys saw him as 150% man, and couldn't understand why he didn't act accordingly. Some had privately concluded that Sasha's girl must either have some outstanding anatomical feature or some exotic and tireless talent. They wouldn't have believed it if they'd seen Sunny in glasses and business suit, but they were right on both counts.

"What's the matter with you?" Sasha pretended indignation. "Sunny's fine, she sends her best. Listen, there's something I want to talk to you about. You got a minute?"

"Funny, I was gonna call you," Georgie said. "You musta read my mind. C'mon inside, I got something for you." He started to lead the way to his office, then turned back. "Hey Marge, you tell him about Dracula?"

"Oh! I forgot." Margie's hand flew to her mouth. "Sasha, you're not gonna believe this. We had a creep in here a couple of weeks ago who said he was from the Romanian—" She frowned and shrugged. "Something about the U.N. But was he slimy! Yuggh!"

"What did I tell you about Romanians?" bellowed Sasha, who was not sentimental about his native land. "Bottom of the barrel! Stay away from them!"

"I *tried!*"

"The scumbag was all over her," said Georgie. "Tall, kinda yellow looking, like Dracula in the movies. I hadda peel him off her, and then I hadda peel C.J. offa *him*. He says, 'I am from da Roo-manian position.'" Drawing himself up to his full 5'6", Georgie put on his version of a haughty face and a thick Balkan accent.

"The Romanian *mission,*" Sasha managed to get out through his laughter.

"Missionary position, what the fuck do I care. So I says to him, 'I don't care if you're the king of fuckin' France, leave the girl alone or get the fuck out of here.'" Georgie shrugged. "Haven't seen him since. He was a pretty good spender, right, Marge?"

"Yeah. He had this big bankroll he wanted everybody to see. He kept trying to buy me drinks. He gave me the creeps." She laughed unhappily. Margie didn't scare easy. But the Romanian mission to the U.N. was run by the *Securitate,* the Romanian equivalent of the K.G.B., and they could be very sinister and sleazy. Sasha wondered what one of *them* was doing in an after-hours club—*his* after-hours club. For an instant of crazy paranoia, he wondered if they were looking for him. Of course not, just wallowing in capitalist decadence. They scared Sasha, too, when he was on their territory. But in New York the shoe was on the other foot.

"Next time he comes in, tell him your cousin wants to talk to him." Sasha polished one big fist in his other hand. "I've always wanted to get my hands on one of them. They killed my father. Give him to me for twenty minutes." He mimed breaking the Romanian into little pieces, and Margie's laugh came freer, reassured.

Sasha followed Georgie through a gauntlet of grabbing hands and greetings to Georgie's "office." It was more like a storage closet: no books or papers—in this cash business, accounts were kept in heads—just stacked boxes of liquor, a Penthouse calendar on the wall still featuring Miss January, a bucket and mop, and a desk with overflowing ashtray, phone, and the intercom to the door downstairs. The closed door filtered the throb of the music. Sasha and Georgie sat on metal folding chairs. Georgie reached under the desk, brought up a bottle of Dewar's and two glasses, and raised his eyebrows. Sasha shook his head. Georgie poured a shot and tossed it down. Then he unlocked a drawer, took out a fat envelope and skidded it across the desktop to Sasha.

Sasha picked it up. It felt like money. He looked at Georgie quizzically. Georgie waved a hand. "Stick it in your pocket. Business was good when you was on the door. Don Chaluch' says 'Give him the envelope,' I give you the envelope. What am I gonna do, argue with him?"

Sasha slipped the envelope into his inside pocket. He was surprised and pleased that his godfather had thought of him, as much as for the money. He'd count it later.

"How is Don Chaluch'? Is he in good health?"

"Yeah, he's goin' strong. Comes by every coupla months, makin' his rounds." Georgie chuckled. "The place gets real quiet. Think you were in a fuckin' church, the way these gaboons behave themselves."

"Well, give him my respects. Tell him I appreciate him thinking of me."

They were silent for a moment. Georgie cocked his head, listening like a doctor to the muffled heartbeat of the club. It was preventive medicine: Georgie had to be able to detect and treat trouble in its early stages. Apparently satisfied, he nodded, and raised a questioning eyebrow at Sasha. Sasha mentally cursed Sunny and forged ahead.

"I got a problem you can help me with." Georgie lit a Lucky, nodded, and sat back to listen. "You know my girlfriend Sunny—"

The intercom buzzed.

"Aahhh, shit," Georgie growled. "Wait a minute." He stabbed the intercom button. "Yeah?"

"Vinnie the cousin is here!" The high, excited voice of Salvi the doorman came through noisy static. "He's a little high, I didn't know whether to let him in or not, but he got in and he's coming upstairs."

"Sal, you're an asshole." Georgie released the intercom button before the doorman could reply. "See what I gotta put up with? 'He got in,' my ass. He palmed Salvi a sawbuck, is what he did. Now we're gonna have a problem, mark my words."

More than once in his nights on the door, Sasha had turned away "Vinnie the cousin," a hothead whose only claim to fame was his kinship to the mastermind of the JFK Airport heist. That was enough to make it a delicate transaction for the doorman; you couldn't just say "No" to Vinnie, you had to say "You can't go up there because so-and-so is there," or "there's a couple of cops upstairs." Salvi didn't have the knack, let alone the character to resist a little green persuasion. If Vinnie started mixing it up, Salvi's ten-dollar tip could cost a whole night's revenues.

"You sure you don't wanna come back on the door," Georgie said wistfully.

"Georgie, in a pinch you know you can count on me. But on a steady basis I wouldn't do you any good. I work two weeks, then they call me away on a movie job."

Georgie shrugged. "Yeah, all right. But, shit, we never had a problem with you down there. You know…" He smiled. "When I first met you, I took a look at you, you big galoot, and I thought you were stupid. Then after a while I realized *I* was stupid. What you wanted to ask me?"

"You know my girl Sunny, she writes for the big magazines. Well…she got an assignment to find out about this 'hex' thing the college kids are going nuts over. You heard about it." Georgie nodded. "They want her to try to find out where it's coming from, who's—"

He stopped. Georgie had raised one hand in a "hold it right there" gesture. "I can't believe my ears," he said. "She's your girl. Don't you tell her the score?"

"Georgie, what do you think I've been doing all night? She's got her mind made up. She's going in there whether I help her or not."

"So rap her across the mouth! She'll come into line," Georgie said, wide-eyed, as if this were the commonsense solution.

"Georgie," Sasha said reproachfully. "Sunny's not the type you can rap."

"Yeah, I know. Dumb cunt." Georgie sighed. "What the fuck is she, a writer or a narc?"

"She's an investigative reporter." Sasha felt an unfamiliar shame, what he imagined was the emotion of the informer. Sunny had asked him to violate a code of discretion that was written in his bones.

"Yeah, a scoop snoop," Georgie said contemptuously. "They dig around in things that are none of their business, they name names, and the cops make the arrests. That's how Tony Marco went down, that asshole from the *Post.*"

"That's why I want to 'help' Sunny," Sasha said with sudden ingenuity. "If it's something she should stay out of, I can steer her away, tell her some bullshit so she doesn't hurt herself or anybody else. On the other hand, maybe it *is* just some old hippies dealing this stuff, like she thinks. I thought maybe you heard something. You know who's who in this business." He played another hunch. "Sunny wants me to ask you for help. To her this is some kind of romantic adventure, and you're this mysterious wise man who has all the answers. She said, 'Ask Georgie. Georgie will know.'"

It got to him. Georgie chuckled. "Wise *man* or wise *guy,* d'she say?"
His belly jiggled, and he shook his head. "Smart cunt."

"So ask around, would you? I'll see that there's compensation. Of
course, no names—"

A splintering crash of glassware and male shouts came through the
door. In one practiced motion Georgie was out of his chair and, throwing Sasha a "What did I tell you?" look, yanked the door open and
plunged into the crowd. Sasha followed, saw the knot of struggling
bodies by the bar, and saw Georgie dive straight into the middle of it,
fearless as a pit bull.

The fight was stupid, like all drunken brawls. Four or five guys were
involved, with Vinnie-the-cousin at the center and a dozen spectators
getting ready to jump in on both sides. Sasha saw swinging and grappling and thought of a melee between cartoon cats, a brainless whirl
with fur and curses and drops of sweat flying out. He sighed and waded
in to help pull them apart. Just then, Georgie came flying out of the
center as if by centrifugal force. He crashed into the wall, turned, and
dived right back in again. And then, somehow, he stopped it. Vinnie-the-cousin and a stick-up guy named Joey from Jersey stood panting and glowering at each other, shirts torn and noses bloody. Georgie,
winded but unscathed, held them apart with a hand on each heaving
chest, keeping their allies at bay by sheer force of personality. "All right!
All right, you guys! What's the matter with you? Hey! What's your
problem?"

"This guy comes in, Vinnie," Joey panted. "I don't care who his
fuckin' cousin is. I turn my back for a minute, and he buys my broad a
drink. The douchebag." He was drunk enough to be slurring his
words. "Nobody buys my broad a drink."

"All right. Cut it out. That's it," said the street diplomat. "Joey,
keep your mouth shut. Vinnie, go down to the end of the bar. I don't
want to hear any more of this shit. Come on, break it up, break it up."
The combatants were obediently subsiding and separating, touching
handkerchiefs to bloody lips, studying torn clothes with the comically

slow comprehension of drunks. People crowded around the bar ordering doubles, as if the fight had turned up the flame of their thirst. The music pulsed louder, the money flowed faster. Disaster had been averted.

Georgie mopped his face with a big handkerchief and rolled back toward his office, beckoning Sasha to come with him.

"Whew." He plopped down behind the desk, poured another Dewar's, and drank it in two gulps. "I'm getting' too old for this shit." Georgie was forty-eight, but he looked sixty. High-pressure Wall Street traders didn't know from stress. "Where were we?"

"Hex."

"Oh yeah. I gotta talk to Dominick. He might know something." Georgie was still breathing hard. "We ain't seen none a that in here yet. It's coke up the ying-yang, and then we got the pillheads. But I heard a little talk, and what I heard is like, 'What *is* this shit? Where the fuck's it coming from? I smell money.' Like it ain't in the usual channels. But you can bet some people are gonna find out. I'll see what I can pick up." He stood up with an effort. "Wanna go out for breakfast? I'm hungry. I'll come back and close up."

Sasha looked at his watch, surprised. It was after seven already. When they went out into the club, he detected a thinner note to the noise. There were still close to a hundred people drinking, arguing, and dancing, but by eight or eight-thirty the place would be empty. When it happened it happened fast, like the tide rushing out of the Bay of Fundy. Sasha waved to Margie and the magician. Near the door, a little thief from the Bronx was haranguing a tall, weathered-looking man who wore tooled leather cowboy boots and a fancy belt buckle. This guy was from out of town. *Way* out of town. As he and Georgie started down the stairs, Sasha heard the stranger say with dangerous patience in his voice, "Don't you understand, man? I'm from Butte, Montana, Evel Knievel's home town."

Outside the light was blinding, disorienting. All around them, men and women in suits were already striding purposefully to work. Sasha and Georgie ambled toward their favorite diner, moving to a different drummer.

"Well. My favorite eater! It's been a long time." The pretty blonde waitress slapped down two plastic-covered menus.

"Take care of my boy Sasha," Georgie said grandly. "Half a dozen soft-boiled eggs, a stack a toast yea high, and when he finishes that, I want you to bring him another one. Oh yeah, and a quart a milk." For himself Georgie ordered a serenade in cholesterol: three fried eggs, sunny side up, with bacon and sausage.

During Sasha's years at the club, this had been a ritual, eating breakfast with Georgie at the Green Kitchen. Georgie always insisted on paying. The tubby little bank robber took a motherly pleasure in feeding his big friend's bottomless hunger. Not even in front of Sunny could Sasha eat so unselfconsciously. He hunched over the food with total concentration, sucking the rich liquid eggs into his mouth and squashing slices of toast in after them two at a time, exaggerating his greed a little bit for Georgie's benefit. His hunger finally muffled—it was never gone—he finished the last of his milk and wiped his mouth. "You doing O.K., Georgie? Not gambling too much?"

Georgie made a gesture of disgust. "Aahh, you know me. I'm a degenerate. I stay away from the tables two weeks, it starts to itch me. You know what my problem is? I got nothing better to do." The fact was, Georgie was very bright. Even Sunny had picked up on it. Sasha imagined how bored he must be by his life—the repetitive cycle of lulls and thrills, the relationships limited to pursuit and orgasm. In a city where the treasures of thought and imagination were piled to the skies, Georgie was a prisoner, because he couldn't read.

It was time to go home.

C H A P T E R   3

▼

"Put your hands on my feet," Sasha said in the voice of a sleepy child.

"Let me catch my breath first, okay?"

Sunny unslung her pocketbook, heavy with the tape recorder, stripped off her maroon cape and threw it on a chair. She'd bounded upstairs two at a time, eager to tell Sasha her news and to hear his. She'd found him sleeping, arms wrapped around himself, a huge, lonely mound under the covers with two cats curled up on top. Now he wanted comforting, and she was still in work mode, bright, bustling and impersonal. Exasperated, she kicked off her shoes, threw back the blanket, and grabbed hold of his size-fifteen feet.

"You don't have to rub them," Sasha murmured. "Just put your hands on them. Ahhhh." He closed his eyes. "I don't know what you've got in your hands." Sunny didn't know either, but she too felt the current of soothing start to flow between her hands and Sasha's big, battered feet, without her will. She could feel what his feet were feeling, share the easing ache as the poison of fatigue drained out of them. She began to relax, coming down from her nervous work high.

"My feet are so ugly," Sasha said plaintively

"You shut up." Sunny flowed her palms over his soles, insteps, his swollen ankles speckled with coal tattoos and broken capillaries. "Leave your feet alone. They're innocent." She sometimes felt she had a relationship with Sasha's feet that was more direct and uncomplicated than her relationship with Sasha. He could be bullying and bitter, devious and envious, but his feet were naked, dignified and shy, like his writing style in *The Seventeenth Level.* Those were two places where she could touch the sixteen-year-old boy buried alive inside the man, mostly hidden even from her. She loved his feet and found them beautiful, large and gnarled as they were. They had carried that boy out of Russia.

"I forgot about your stupid interview," Sasha grumbled. "I come home with a big surprise for you, and you're not here."

"Well, I'm here now," Sunny said, pressing her thumbs into his soles. "Tell me. Does Georgie know something? Because the head of the New York Joint Task Force on Narcotics sure as hell doesn't."

"Georgie's gonna ask around. I have to call him back in a few days. No—this surprise I got to show you." Sasha struggled to get up. Sunny pinned his legs to the bed.

"Just hold it a minute. I'm not finished here." Once she started something, her concentration was even stronger than her curiosity. She ran her hands from Sasha's ankles up his legs, over the brown spot on his shin like a bruise on an apple, and the shiny scar the shape of a capital I branded into his calf. Right beside the I, a bulging vein left its river-like course down his leg and made three tight loops, as if it had diverted there long ago to feed the healing wound. Sunny traced the loops with her finger, fascinated by this evidence of the intelligence of life. Sasha's legs were a geography of survival, a battle map of his victory over death.

"Oh. Margie sends you love," Sasha said. "You ought to call her up, get together for lunch sometime."

"Margie's still there? How's she doing?" At the mention of Margie's name, Sunny's hands had paused imperceptibly. They immediately resumed their soothing stroking, but wandered casually higher. If the female animal in Sunny had had words, she would have said, *He saw Margie, did he? He'll forget all about that in a minute.* But Sunny was hardly conscious of rising to a challenge. One thing just led naturally to another: shins to knees, knees to thighs…

"What are you *doing?*" Sasha sounded startled.

"That's a pretty dumb question." Sunny's breathing had deepened. "Somebody here knows exactly what I'm doing and wants to help."

"Come on up here," Sasha growled, with what sounded like menace, but wasn't. He grabbed Sunny's arms, hauled her onto the bed, and lifted all 115 pounds of her into the air above him as if she were a 50-pound barbell. The big bow of her silk blouse dangled in his face, and he moved his head from side to side sensuously, so it teased his cheeks and mouth.

"Let me down!" Sunny squealed, kicking and struggling. His arms were iron pillars; she felt stranded like a kitten in a tree "Let me get these stupid clothes off! God, you're so strong it's ridiculous." That made him laugh, and he let her collapse on top of him, still dressed in her business skirt and jacket. She pulled the skirt up around her hips and felt him harden at the sight of the stocking tops and garters she wore to feel secretly feminine underneath her suit. Sasha claimed his father had taken him to the local whorehouse at age 11, "after he caught me chasing the maid with a hard-on that would derail a train." Maybe that accounted for his susceptibility to fancy lingerie. Whatever turned him on turned her on. She began to rock and sigh as Sasha unbuttoned her blouse with big, clumsy fingers and freed her breasts from her brassiere. They were the part of her body she was surest of, not too large or too small. She leaned forward, letting them brush his face, and then put her mouth on his. He had a mouth like a newborn calf's, muscular and innocent, fresh as milk and grass. She thought he could suck her soul out with it.

Sasha was very private about sex. "If you ever write a book about us," he'd warned her, "don't you dare say anything about what we do when we're alone together. It's nobody's business." That was old-fashioned European, she thought—privately uninhibited, publicly prudish. Coming out of an era when sexual frankness had been *de rigueur*—

Sasha had been horrified to hear that Sunny's *mother* had once asked her, "What's sex like on grass?"—Sunny had slowly learned to keep her mouth shut even with her close girlfriends. She found this habit of discretion surprisingly refreshing.

"I'll bet a lot of our friends wonder how we do it without me getting squashed," she'd once giggled to Sasha.

"Let them wonder," he'd replied curtly.

So a movie camera at this point would pan bashfully to the floor, where it would observe various pieces of clothing fly onto the rug, followed by several cats, fleeing as if from a familiar earthquake. Sasha's big feet might descend from the bed to fill the frame; after a while perhaps Sunny's little ones would come to face them. Then both pairs of feet would be drawn back up, and the bed would cry out at its lively burden. Among other noises, the sound track would prominently feature laughter. Sunny and Sasha's passion was not solemn.

The next thing Sunny knew, it was raining money.

She had drifted to sleep, one arm and one leg slung over Sasha, consciousness dissolving in the rainwashed warmth after orgasm. Sunny was not a natural early riser. She was still suffering dream deprivation from having gotten up with the alarm at seven. So she was not aware that Sasha had eased out of bed, quietly hanging up her clothes and then reaching into his inside jacket pocket. She was on a beach in Florida, waiting for a message in a pill bottle to float ashore and wondering why there were two moons in the sky, when something started pattering on her face. She frowned, rubbed her nose, opened her eyes—and saw a hundred-dollar bill in her hand. Her eyes focused on the deep drift of bills strewn around her.

She sat bolt upright.

"What *is* this!!!"

Sasha was beaming as he released the last few hundreds to flutter down on her. "I always wanted to wake you up this way."

"But where did you get it?"

"A little bonus from my share in the club."

"But this is—how much is it?" Sunny started raking the bills together. "No, Blue!" She grabbed Blueberry, the sleek Siamese, just as he was about to jump off the bed with a hundred-dollar bill in his mouth. Sunny gently rescued the "prey."

"Just ten thousand."

"Just ten—"

"See? That's your problem," Sasha roared. "To you, ten thousand dollars is a lot of money! You think like a cockroach!"

Sunny threw a fistful of hundred-dollar bills at him.

"Ah-ah-ah. Be nice," Sasha warned, giving her a baleful look as he bent to pick up the scattered bills. Treating money *that* casually was sacrilege. Once again, Sunny realized, she'd betrayed her scandalous lack of reverence for the stuff. She started gathering and piling it neatly as penance.

"Count it," Sasha commanded.

So Sunny sat cross-legged on the bed, counting money, while Sasha, wearing nothing but his T-shirt, vacuumed, a daily chore for anyone with nine cats and two litter boxes. It was probably a funny sight, this half-naked giant so domestically occupied, but to Sunny it was merely normal. The money was something else. She'd never seen so much cash at one time. It came to exactly ten thousand—a thick, faintly greasy wad in her hands. This money had been around. It needed laundering, literally. It could even be drug money, Sunny realized with an uneasy little thrill. She could hardly wait to get it into the bank and turn it into nice, disinfected, interest-bearing numbers.

She already knew what she and Sasha would do with the money. They'd talk about buying a car, or going scuba diving in Bonaire, or building new closets into the apartment. But when it came right down to it, they'd wind up taking most of the money on their next trip to Romania, changing it on the black market—where dollars were wildly in demand—and giving it to Sasha's mother, to Omar, hero of *The Seventeenth Level,* who'd dug him out of the Russian mine cave-in, and a couple of dozen others in his impoverished village whom Sasha felt obliged and proud to help. That was what always happened to Sasha and Sunny's extra money, and it was fine with Sunny. She made a lousy yuppie. No material thing could give her as much pleasure as Sasha's pleasure in his largesse.

Sasha was looking at his watch. "Come on, Sunny!" he suddenly barked like a drill sergeant. "We can still catch the three o'clock class at the dojo, but you got to *move!*"

She stepped into the hot bath Sasha had run for her. Ten minutes later, they were leaving the apartment. When she wasn't going uptown, Sunny turned tomboy and could dress with the speed of light. She just jumped into a pair of Norm Thompson "unjeans," an old white sweat-shirt and running shoes, pulled a brush through her thick black-and-silver hair, and was ready to go.

It was one of those early spring afternoons when the sunlight seems to blink with shy surprise at its own warmth, and the people who come out to bask in it look pale and convalescent. Sasha strode toward Washington Square Park, cutting a swath through the strolling crowd: spike-haired punks from New Jersey, young mothers pushing Aprica strollers, red-eyed drunks jingling coins in paper coffee cups, slow-walking, waxen old men in black overcoats, disheveled psychotics haranguing invisible enemies, shiny-faced NYU students clutching spiral notebooks, tourists speaking German, sashaying transvestites from Christopher Street—there went a six-footer in a full-length mink. A normal sample of the Greenwich Village population. "Brother, please, gimme a quarter for something to eat," a wino pleaded with a long-haired student.

"I'll give you a dollar if you promise to be *my* bum. Okay?"

"Hey, brother, you got spirit! You all right!"

The park looked like a swarm of bees. People clustered thickly around the central fountain where the sexy young Chinese fire juggler performed. Smaller knots surrounded a variety of musicians and magicians. Blue, red and yellow Frisbees skimmed above the crowd, and

Sunny heard the throb of boom boxes and faint snatches of guitar chords.

"Sin, ss-ss, sess," somebody breathed in her ear. "Hex."

Sunny froze. Every nerve in her body thrilled to attention. Ahead of her Sasha strode on, unaware that he'd lost her.

"Yes! I'm interested," she said to the lanky black dealer. Her heart was pounding. "How much?"

"You gotta tell me what you interested *in*, sista."

"Hex," Sunny said, feeling self-conscious. She was way out of practice at this.

"Five dolla' a cap for you, pretty lady." The dealer ambled casually along beside her, his voice low and intimate. "You havin a party? I get you all you need."

Sunny thought fast. How much would be more than he'd have on him? "A *big* party. Can you get me, um…thirty caps?" Now if she could just watch him, see where he went. But Sasha was looking back, his angry eye rolling like a stallion's.

The dealer whistled. "Hey, baby, what, you dealin' to your friends? I get you the stuff, sure, but you got to meet me at—Oh, 'scuse me, sir." The dealer melted away. Sasha's big hand clamped on Sunny's wrist, like fate.

"Don't you ever, *ever* embarrass me like that again," he growled, walking so fast he was almost dragging her. "Everybody in the Village knows me, and they see my girl buying drugs from a scumbag street pusher? What if got back to Chaluch'?"

Sunny struggled to pull free. "Everybody in the Village knows *me*, too, and they see me being dragged along like a dog on a leash? Let me go, you fucking Stone Age bully, you—"

Sasha suddenly let go. He stopped, doubled over with his hands on his knees, and wheezed and staggered with laughter. Sunny stood there rubbing her wrist, glaring. Even at his maddest, Sasha often found her temper funny. She could threaten to kill him, and he'd crack up. It made her feel totally powerless.

"All right. You go to the dojo alone," she announced when he came out of his spasm.

"Oh, no you don't," Sasha wiped his eyes, looked at his watch, and started walking fast. "I'm not letting you out of my sight until the article is finished."

"How am I supposed to write with you blocking me every step of the way?" Sunny danced furiously alongside him. "I might've been able to follow that guy to his source. Or I could've asked to make a bigger buy, and met the next guy up the ladder. Then at least I'd know—"

"Are you a trained narcotics agent? Do you carry a gun?" Sasha didn't wait for an answer. "If the DEA hasn't broken the ring that way, what makes you think you can? Because you've read a few Elmore Leonard novels? You're the worst kind of amateur. Let the pros do the dirty work. You be a reporter and interview them. And please, let Georgie look into this thing from the top. Stay away from these street-level—"

He was interrupted by a rumble as the evening shift of hot-dog sellers rolled their carts out of the garage on Thompson Street, heading for the park. "Oops," Sasha said. "Here come the Romanians."

Sunny looked straight ahead, too angry for her usual quip. It was a running joke between them that all the hot-dog vendors who worked Washington Square Park seemed to be Romanians, mostly gypsies. Sasha had spotted them first, pointing out to Sunny the coarse, sly look that comes out of inbred Balkan villages. And sure enough, they'd been arguing in staccato Romanian. Sunny had joked that they were *Securitate* plants, stationed on this block to report on Sasha's movements to the supermarket and the dojo. Romanians were one of those nationalities you'd never even heard of, and then once you became aware of them you started seeing them anywhere—cab drivers, sales clerks, elevator operators, doctors, hot-dog sellers. Like you didn't hear the drug dealers whisper "Hex" till you had a reason to.

When Sunny had been punitively silent for two blocks, Sasha said, "Tell you what. I'll do something else for you. Boston's a big college town. Right?"

"Mmm."

"This drug is big on college campuses, right?"

"Mmm."

"Gary might be able to find out who's running it up there for you." Sasha had a strategically placed friend in nearly every major city. "And then there's Bo-bo—he'd know what's going on in Buffalo. Maybe I could get him to come down to Boston, and we'll all meet at Gary's. Like a reunion of the old after-hours crowd. I'll call them tonight. Okay?"

As peace offerings went, it wasn't bad. "Okay," Sunny said. Boston and Cambridge were her old stomping grounds. While Sasha pumped his friends, she could find out what was going on among the students, even better than at Columbia or NYU.

Their karate dojo was in SoHo, in a converted industrial loft below Houston Street. Sunny reached the top of the stairs ahead of Sasha and took off her shoes, Japanese style. Pushing the heavy door open, the saw the gleaming blond wood floor and white walls that gave the place such a clean, welcoming feeling. Sensei was sitting behind his desk, scowling as he always did before class to create the properly sobering atmosphere. After class he'd talk and giggle with his students—Japanese, no matter how macho, are great gigglers—but this was a time for seriousness, even a little fear. Sunny bowed and said, "Osu!", the karate salute. And what do you know, the first student she saw was Pierre.

That gave her another bright idea.

"Sun-*nee!* 'Ey, Sa*sha!* Osu!" Pierre Coquillon came forward to shake their hands, already wearing his white cotton *gi* and brown belt. He was a tall, handsome, effusively friendly Haitian in his early thirties. He was also a small-time coke dealer in Brooklyn. To Pierre, this was not incompatible with studying karate for spiritual strength, consecrating himself to the voodoo goddess Erzulie Freda, or giving as many women as many babies as he could, sowing little golden-brown tiger lilies of the field. Sasha was fond of the good-natured Haitian, and had tried to talk him out of dealing, but for Pierre, the swagger and risk were part of his manhood. So was his claim that the drug proceeds went to support a revolutionary force in the hills of Haiti, a romantic story that had assisted in the conception of more than one little Pierre, Jr. Sunny couldn't help liking Pierre. As drug dealers went, he was more absurd than sinister. And Sunny was his *senpai,* his senior in the dojo. If she asked him a question, he'd be eager to help find the answer.

But not now. Talking before class was a no-no.

Sunny went into the women's dressing room and unrolled her *gi.* Slipping into the heavy cotton jacket, wrapping and knotting her faded black belt, she felt the mysterious sustenance of the natural materials and the ritual. Somehow you were stronger making these stark, archaic moves in a cotton uniform on a wooden floor than doing aerobics in Spandex on a polyester carpet, or pumping machines made of chrome and Naugahyde. Sunny bowed and ran barefoot onto the floor where the students were assembling in a silent line, taking her place second, between Sasha and Pierre. They knelt and closed their eyes, facing Sensei, and started class with a long minute of meditation.

Early in class Sunny's mind often wandered, escaping the relentless repetition and the body's unpleasant climb through first and second gears by returning to whatever had occupied it that morning. Today, while her body dutifully did warm-ups, stretches, and eight kinds of punches, Sunny's mind was back in the office of New York Joint Task Force Chief James T. O'Brien, mercilessly reviewing her own performance. He'd been a tough old silver-haired cop from a generation that didn't take women seriously, and Sunny had been stung by his patronizing manner. She'd fought hard to impress him with her competence, and she wasn't sure she'd succeeded.

She shouted and punched and replayed the interview, rubbing at the rough spots, shaping a stronger, wittier Sunny. She had broken out in a sweat. By the time Sensei growled *"Keri no yoi"*—get ready to kick—

her mind had begun to come home to her body. About twenty minutes into class, it happened: the nauseating monotony broke through into refreshment, the fantasies faded, and the position of her arms and knees became the most interesting thing in the world. By the end of class, it would be the only thing in the world. Everything else would be gone, washed away on the clean flood of effort.

All through the class, Sunny was fondly aware of Pierre training beside her. He tried so hard, sweated so much, and made such funny noises that she had to stop herself from giggling, especially when she caught Sensei's eye and saw a gleam of amusement behind the samurai mask. Most karate schools were either ruled by fear and intimidation, or they went to the other extreme and were little more than dance classes. This one struck just the right balance of challenge and affection. In Sasha's old friend Mas Oyama's Kyokushinkai schools, the fighting was serious enough so people occasionally got hurt—"Which more important," Sensei would admonish a white belt cradling a jammed knuckle, "your finger or your spirit?"—but there was also a lot of humor and love. It never ceased to astonish Sunny what a strong bond you could form with people by punching and kicking them. In today's *kumite,* her freestyle sparring partners were Sasha—like hitting a redwood tree—Pierre, so amphibian-slippery by now that her fists slid off his chest, and a timid new woman white belt whom Sunny encouraged, "Go on, punch me as hard as you can!"

After they had meditated and bowed three times—to Sensei, each other, and the dojo—Sunny ran to be the first to wipe the floor. She wanted to get to Pierre before Sasha finished dressing. She was dressed and waiting when Pierre came out of the men's cubicle, tucking a leather amulet into the open V of his tropical shirt.

"Pierre! C'mere a moment, I want to ask you something." Sunny beckoned, stepping into the hallway, out of Sensei's earshot.

"Osu, Sempai Sun-nee!" Pierre presented himself as eagerly as a junior officer to his colonel. Sunny felt an odd pang of guilt.

"Pierre, you may be able to help me."

"Anything I can do for you or Sasha, Sempai!"

"This new drug, hex? I'm doing an article on it. I need to find out where it's coming from, who's dealing it. Don't go out of your way, just let me know if you hear anything, okay?" She dropped her voice even lower. "I can pay you."

"Don't worry about that, Sempai Sun-nee. Pierre do it for you, because you my karate sister."

"Do me one more favor. Don't tell Sasha yet." A pained little frown crossed Pierre's face. Did this request compromise his loyalty to Sasha? "He'd just tell me not to bother you," Sunny ad-libbed craftily. "He thinks some Italian friends of his can find out for me, but I have a feeling you know at least as much as they do."

Pierre's chest rose to the challenge. "You know true, Sun-nee. Nobody know de street like Pierre."

"SUNNY!" came Sasha's familiar bellow.

"Thanks," Sunny whispered to Pierre, and then yelled, "I'll be right there!"

On the way home, Sasha chattered about the World Karate Tournament coming up in Tokyo in the fall. Sunny answered absently. She was plotting. When they got to the park, she coaxed, "It's so beautiful out. Let's stop and watch the juggler for a few minutes, okay?"

Sasha gave her a look of withering suspicion. She tried to make her face open and innocent, but it was no use. He saw right through her. "You watch the juggler," he growled. "I'll watch *you.*"

Sunny shrugged. "Be my guest. C'mon." She tugged Sasha toward the fountain, darting her eyes around in search of her dealer. Damn. So many people. It was impossible to pick out one individual in this crowd. She had an inspiration.

"I'm too *short,*" she wailed. "I can't see anything. Pick me up on your shoulders."

"With pleasure," Sasha said with grim satisfaction. *Now you can't wriggle out of my grasp!* He bent down, ducked his hard little head between her legs, and lofted her into the air. Ouch! Perfect. Sasha was pacified—and Sunny had an eagle's-eye view.

In the circular arena of the fountain the longhaired Chinese juggler passed flaming torches between his legs, joking about his posterity in a falsetto voice. The crowd screamed and laughed. Sunny scanned the crowd for the dealer. How many black men in brown leather jackets could there be in this little park? This guy had had a funny Afro, shaved close on the sides, tall and square on top. Wait…that looked like him. Yes, there he was! Strolling slowly up one of the paths, leaning aside to murmur to people who passed him. Sunny craned to follow his progress, and Sasha, thrown off balance, swayed under her. "What are you *doing* up there?" he hollered, giving her ankles a yank.

Sunny grabbed his head and centered her weight, keeping her eyes riveted on the dealer. There—he had a sale! Not a student, a bearded fortyish man with an attaché case, looked like a professional or a professor. Maybe he was only buying marijuana, but he *could* be part of the hex network. Sunny tried to fix him in her mind: bulky body, blue suit, full reddish beard, black-rimmed glasses. The two men were off by the side of the path, in the shadow of a tree, dickering. They exchanged something small. The beard strode rapidly off, and the dealer ambled on. He stopped to buy a hot dog and sat down on a park bench to eat it, crossing his long legs in the sun

"Let me down," Sunny whispered in Sasha's ear. "You head's too hard. It's hurting me!"

Please, God, give him a location movie job for just a week or two, she pleaded silently as they walked home. She missed him painfully when he went away—you didn't know how empty life could be until someone that big and warm and loud went out of it—but it was the only time she had real freedom of movement. Sunny had done some of her best and nerviest reporting when Sasha was off shooting a movie. Unsupervised, she'd been known to skip meals, ride the subway at night, venture alone into the South Bronx with her notebook, and in general, revert to the defiant recklessness of her East Village youth. The dark side of that freedom had been loneliness—not to mention danger—and she knew Sasha clipped her wings because he cared. Still, she saw herself as a she-wolf, not a lap dog, and when she was turned loose, she ran like hell. Occasionally she even went dancing.

When they got home, Sasha cooked and Sunny tapped away on the computer. She wrote to a neurochemistry professor at Berkeley who'd published important papers on designer drugs, and to the author of a history of LSD who had interviewed other members of the "better living through chemistry" network—a bunch of brilliant eccentrics, all protected by aliases. After what Chief O'Brien had told her, Sunny was surer than ever that that was where hex was coming from. It was too late to transcribe O'Brien's interview. She'd do it tomorrow on the train to Boston. Sasha had called his two friends, and both of them were up for the meeting at Gary's. Sasha had punched the speakerphone button so that Sunny could hear Bo-bo, "that crazy Polack" from Buffalo, rejoicing at the prospect of the reunion: "Get me a fuckin' barrel, I'm gonna go over the fuckin' falls!"

The 9:33 A.M Patriot jerked into motion exactly on time. Five minutes into the ride, Sasha had taken out a bag of Granny Smith apples and his pocketknife, and Sunny plugged in the earpiece of her tape recorder and settled down with pen and legal pad. The frank, flat voice of New York Joint Task Force Chief O'Brien filled her ear.

"Please sit down, Miss—?"

"Randall."

Sunny heard the rustling of papers on O'Brien's desk, phones ringing, voices shouting, and she was no longer on a train to Boston. She was back in police headquarters, looking at drab green walls that reminded her of elementary school, smelling stale cigarette smoke and the steam from old, clanky radiators. "'Scuse the mess," O'Brien was saying. "We got over thirty investigations in progress here, and they all land on my desk." It was a cop voice, a blend of Irish warmth and urban disillusion. When Sunny had first heard that voice on Darlene's phone, she'd imagined him stereotypical—big gut, red nose, bleary eyes. She'd been surprised to find him small and physically fit. She had always liked talking with blue-collar men: cops, plumbers, truck drivers. They struck her as "real," down-to-earth, in a way that men of her own class did not.

On the other hand, men of her own class had been trained not to talk down to women.

"You're the girl from *Metro,* right? What can I do for you?" A squeak as he'd sat down in his old brown swivel chair, jiggling his crossed leg, fixing her with a neutral ice-blue stare. *Get to the point,* his body language urged her. A lot of cops hated humoring the media. Sunny guessed he'd been asked by Public Affairs to grant this interview, and considered it a waste of his time. There was a war on.

Sunny fast-forwarded through her questions. She clicked back to "Play" and heard O'Brien blow a long-suffering sigh. "All right. Let's take those one at a time." He began to recite with the enthusiasm of a taped bus schedule. "Where is it coming from. We don't know yet. It's too new. The leads we've got, I'm not at liberty to discuss because it could compromise an ongoing investigation. That answers your second question. Yeah, we're investigating. Not on the scale I'd like, but you got to realize, we've got a manpower shortage. Crack is still the number-one problem."

At the mention of his main enemy, O'Brien's voice unwillingly warmed to its subject, and Sunny's pen speeded up. The shaking train made it jerk like a polygraph needle.

"It's not just the Colombians and the Italians any more. Everybody wants a piece of the action: blacks, Hispanics, Jamaicans, Palestinians, Russians—we even busted a ring of Israelis in Brooklyn. Two-thirds of the PD's narcotics division is on crack full-time and they aren't making a dent. They're just getting shot. Then there's been a big upsurge in China White—Southeast Asian heroin. The Chinese gangs are bringing it in, eliminating the mob middlemen so it's hitting the street 50% pure. Those two drugs account for 90% of the violent crime in this city. All the signs say kids on hex don't kill.

"On the other hand, it has started killing them. And *who* is it killing? The middle—"

"Open your mouth." Sasha's voice broke through O'Brien's, and a cold slice of apple pressed against Sunny's lips, yanking her back to her seat on the Patriot. "You gotta have something in your stomach, or in an hour you'll bug me to go to the club car and buy you a three-dollar hot dog." Sasha shoved a second apple slice into her mouth

"Mmf!" Sunny protested. "'M vegetarian—I haven't wanted a hot dog in ten years! Now will you *please* let me work?" She stopped the tape and ran it back to catch what she'd missed.

"Communist," Sasha muttered.

"—it killing?" O'Brien's voice resumed. "The middle-class kids, the so-called yuppie puppies. What crack is at DeWitt Clinton High, hex is rapidly becoming at Music and Art, Trinity, Bronx Science…and the college campuses are rotten with it. So we're getting pressure from influential people whose sons and daughters are involved to nip this thing in the bud. If you ask me, it's already too late. I think this summer is gonna make the Summer of Love look like a picnic." *Bingo! Great quote!* Sunny underlined it twice. If the mystery of hex remained unsolved, at least she had the last line of her piece.

"Can you name names, any of those 'influential people' whose kids have a problem with hex?"

"No." A long pause while O'Brien stared at her incredulously. Then he relented a little. "Whyn't you try calling up some of the big names who signed that ad in last Sunday's Times? What'd they call themselves—KOKOH, Keep Our Kids Off Hex, something like that. Stallone, I think, was on it, Senator—"

"'Scuse me, Chief, I need you a minute." A short, sweating detective had stuck his head in the door. Sunny fast-forwarded through their discussion of a three-ton cocaine seizure from a Brooklyn stash house. Afterwards, O'Brien had explained to her wearily that yes, it was a major bust, and no, it would not make any difference. Sunny picked up the thread of the hex discussion with difficulty.

She remembered O'Brien turning his palms up. "What else can I tell you?"

"I suppose you have undercover people on campuses and in high schools?"

"Yes, we do."

"Both DEA and NYPD?"

"That's correct."

"Would it be possible to interview a few of them? I'd disguise their identities, of course."

"I'm afraid not, at this sensitive stage of the investigation."

"Have you found any labs yet?"

"No. This drug is not being made on every street corner, like crack—at least not yet. We think it's still a centralized, tightly controlled operation."

"Why?"

O'Brien had sighed, resigning himself to actually telling her something. "Because, first of all, our usual sni—informers haven't been able to pick up anything on it." Sunny scribbled frantically, pausing the tape from time to time to catch up. "Say you lean on a student dealer, or a street dealer. The trail stops there. They got it from somebody who left town." O'Brien hesitated. "All right, I'll tell you about one lead that led nowhere. They had us looking for a transient name of Randy Flagg." Sunny heard her own surprised snort of laughter. O'Brien had smiled back humorlessly. "Right. We were chasing a character in a Stephen King novel. We still don't know if that was a distributor's alias, or just a joke. This thing's well protected, very professional.

"Second, there have been 'famines,' times when you can't buy the drug. That suggests a few major sources. Given the history of designer drugs, of course we're looking at the West Coast. But it's only a matter of time before local chemists figure out how to copy it.

"See, people underestimate the danger of synthetic drugs. They're cheaper to make than botanical drugs, and more potent. Amateur chemists can make most of them in labs at home. If we could interdict one hundred per cent of the cocaine and heroin at our borders, this country would be flooded with synthetic drugs in two months. I'm told hex has a twist that makes it harder to duplicate than some. But you'll have to get a chemist to explain that to you."

Silence while Sunny had scanned her list of questions.

"Have there been any shootings or killings in connection with the hex trade?"

"Not as far as we know."

Sunny stopped the tape and backed it up. Beside her Sasha was snoring gently. She elbowed him. "Listen to this." She played the last exchange with the volume turned up. "See? You can stop worrying. No violence. Just intelligence. There's a brain behind this drug."

Sasha looked at her with disbelief, like O'Brien. "And you think because they're smart, they're not dangerous?"

"No! I mean they're not cowboys, they won't be shooting guns off in all directions! *You* taught me that—very bright criminals avoid violence unless it's absolutely necessary. Like karate masters."

"Don't you think it could be 'absolutely necessary' to get rid of a very bright reporter who was poking into your business?"

"Flattery will get you nowhere," Sunny said. "Go back to sleep."

She flipped through the jittery handwritten transcript with excitement. This assignment really was right up her alley. All signs—okay, there weren't that many yet, but all signs so far pointed to the mastermind of hex being an old hippie or radical, maybe one of those Berkeley chemists. Sunny's imagination fleshed him out: a wild-eyed guy with long gray hair dangling from a bald spot and a bedroll on his back. Or he could have gone straight on the outside and look just like a Republican. But somebody with an old grudge against the System and fresh rage at its triumph starting with Reagan in 1980, someone who wanted to get revenge and get rich in the process. "Randy Flagg," indeed.

Flagg had been the "dark man," the "Walkin Dude" in Stephen King's apocalyptic novel, *The Stand.* Not a man at all but a demon, tirelessly striding the back roads of America, sowing destruction—a Johnny Appleseed of death. Sunny felt a little chill. The in-joke could be straight out of Sixties drug culture, except it was darker. Not the Garden, but Armageddon; no new beginning, but The End. Sunny thought of an eighteen-year-old girl diving out her sixth-floor dormitory window. She wasn't sure she wanted to take this drug, after all.

But she did want to talk to some of the kids who were taking it. She'd told Sasha she planned to spend the afternoon with Willa Rosenstein, her old college roommate, who lived on a shady Cambridge street and was an English professor at BU, an expert on the Victorian novel. Sunny had dressed casually, in khakis, a turquoise necklace and a denim jacket, not hippie enough to arouse Sasha's suspicions, but not yuppie enough to turn off the kids. She'd ask Sasha's friend Gary to drop her off at Willa's, and as soon as Sasha and Gary left to do whatever men friends do, she'd head for the Yard and Harvard Square. She was sure she'd learn something there.

CHAPTER 4

▼

The train finally pulled into South Station at a quarter to two. Boston was breezy, sunny and cool—a perfect spring day. Sasha and Sunny stood on State Street, puzzled, looking up and down the row of cars and limos waiting by the cub. Gary's maroon Lincoln was nowhere in sight.

"Maybe he got stuck in traffic," Sunny said. "Boston's is the worst in the world."

"Hey, you guys, over heah!" The familiar voice with its broad Boston Irish accent was coming from a long, gleaming white stretch limousine. The door opened and Gary Field bounded out. Sunny smiled at the way his movements declared him—generous, expansive, humorously self-important. Gary had been a fast-living liquor company representative when Sasha had told him to get out of the after-hours life, go home, and go into a daylight business. Gary had taken the advice, and now the cop's son was a real estate multimillionaire in his hometown outside Boston. But unlike so many of the successful, Gary believed money was for living and giving—it was in character that he'd picked them up in a limo. He was simply incapable of being small or tight. Everything about him was grand and magnanimous: his blunt, flushed face, his ample, friendly St. Bernard body, even the way the tail of his suit jacket flounced and flew as he came toward them. Sunny ran to meet him and kissed him on the cheek.

"How ya *doin'?"* Gary asked, arms outspread, as Sasha came up and kissed him on both cheeks. Sunny had noticed that Gary was one of the very few American men who didn't recoil from this Eastern European expression of male affection. In his early thirties, he regarded Sasha almost as a father. His own father, who had also been in a prison camp—a German one—had died in his forties.

"What's *this?"* Sasha indicated the limo, whose white-gloved driver stood at attention.

"I've got a limousine company now! We've got three cahs, and I'm lookin' at a fourth one this week. This is one of my drivas, John Merlino. My friend, Sasha. You might've seen him in 'The Pope of Greenwich Village,' 'Moscow on the Hudson'..."

"Pleasure, sir. Please." The driver stood aside, and Sasha pushed Sunny in ahead of him. She giggled with delight at the red plush interior. It was like being in the womb—a womb with a wet bar, stereo and color TV. Sunny dived for the radio and found her soft-rock station before Sasha could insist on jazz. She gave Willa's Cambridge address to the driver, and then leaned back. She hated road-hogging, show-offing, gas-guzzling limos—but this was *sensuous.*

"Something to drink? Can I offer you a Captain Morgan?" Gary knew Sasha's sweet tooth made him a sucker for rum and coke. Sasha put on the comic shamefaced look that was his way of saying yes. Sunny asked for a vodka on the rocks and pressed the cold glass against her cheek, hot with excitement.

"We'll drop Sunny off and then go pick Bo-bo up at the airport," Gary said. "Jesus, that crazy bastid. Tonight's gonna be just like old times."

"You better be back by seven, or the shit will hit the fan." Sasha shook his finger at Sunny.

"Don't worry," Sunny said, for the millionth time in her relationship with Sasha. "Willa will drive me."

It was always a shock, going from Sasha's world to any of her other worlds: *Metro,* Radcliffe friends, her family. Sunny was a chameleon who could take on the coloring of any environment. Sasha and his friends were larger than life, so with them she felt like a giant among giants. With others she had to scale herself down, like Alice in Wonderland. As she stood on Willa's porch and embraced her old roomie, with Sasha looming beside her, she felt herself helplessly shrinking down and away. Willa invited Sasha in for coffee, but when he excused himself with Old World courtesy, she didn't understand him. Sunny heard his accent thicken, and she didn't know whether he had mumbled—he wasn't comfortable around her intellectual friends—or whether it was a treachery of her ears, already hearing from Willa's point of view. It was a relief when he left—with a final "Seven o'clock!"—though she felt the emptiness.

Willa led her inside, through a little foyer where a telephone sat on a telephone table on a little Oriental throw rug on the blond wood floor. God, it was so neat, and so *quiet! I could have wound up living like this,* Sunny thought, visualizing her own chaotic ménage. *I would have died of the quiet.* In the living room, where Willa's 'cello poised on its stand like a nude mahogany woman, the roommates turned to face each other. It had been over a year.

"You look wonderful," Willa said. "You've been working out."

"Yeah, and I haven't been raiding the refrigerator, either," said Sunny, and they both cracked up.

Freshman year, Sunny and Willa had discovered that if they wandered down to the dorm's dining room at midnight, the Irish night watchman would take pity on two homesick seventeen-year-olds and unlock the kitchen door. (Seventeen. Sasha had been a hungry prisoner at seventeen. What do I know about homesickness? Sunny thought in a flash of guilt.) They would make themselves heaping ice-cream sundaes and leave brazen finger marks in the whipped cream. For the first time in her life, that year Sunny got fat; in those not so diet-conscious days, she'd been surprised to find these funny rolls around her waist.

But she and Willa had gotten fat together, just as they'd had their first intense discussion of ideas together, and talked all night about each one's first heartbreak—and first time in bed with a man. The diverging paths their lives had taken couldn't erase those memories.

"You look good, too," Sunny said. "You never change." Willa's beautiful skin was almost as unlined as it had been in college. It was their old joke that with her long blonde hair, china-blue eyes, and softly curving body, like her 'cello, Willa should be the WASP, while dark, intense, vivacious Sunny was the one who looked Jewish. They stood there now like day and night, admiring each other, friends.

"Well—I've got about four hours to get into trouble," Sunny finally said, looking at her watch. "Think that's enough?"

Willa burst out laughing again. Sunny loved the way that delighted, sensuous laugh broke free of the fine restraining nets of her friend's mind. "Sunny, you can get into trouble faster than anyone I know," Willa said. "Come on, have a cup of tea with me first."

Sunny was eager as a bird dog to get going, but she sat down at her friend's kitchen table and gulped a cup of hot herb tea and told about the assignment and tried not to look at her watch while Willa talked about her book-in-progress on Jane Austen. The gulf widened again between the scholar and the front-line reporter, between Willa's placid academic pond and Sunny's turbulent urban ocean. But when she got up to leave, the split was healed by their hug.

"See you around six-thirty," she called back to Willa, waving from her porch as if Sunny were a departing ship.

Willa's little side street, with its bumpy brick walks and frame houses, ran into Garden Street, the main drag between Harvard and Radcliffe. Sunny remembered walking back up this street, feeling strange and sore and new, the morning after losing her virginity. She didn't know which had changed more, herself or Cambridge. The Common was the pastoral park it had always been, but powerful highways plunged around it, and major urban buildings shadowed Harvard Square. Sunny, too, was a different person. The tidal wave of Sasha had swept her away from this safe shore, and she'd survived by developing strong new muscles. Willa's life had unfolded predictably, with logic; Sunny's was so starkly Before and After that the memories from Before felt like someone else's.

That was what made it so eerie walking into Harvard Yard. Because the Yard hadn't changed at all. From the torrent of traffic and construction around the Square, you stepped into an island of timelessness. The noises of the world died away, and there were the paths, familiar as the lines in Sunny's own hand, the buildings furred with ivy, the statue of John Harvard, the sharp white steeple of Memorial Church. The cast of characters seemed just as unchanged: undergraduates strolling to class, grad students clustered in intense discussion, the occasional solitary professor, the colorful carnival of long-haired kids sprawled on the library steps—

Wait.

Sunny's eye had taken this scene in too easily, as if twenty years had simply disappeared. She shook her head and blinked. For a moment she'd thought she was back in the late Sixties. Those anarchic kids sunning themselves on the stairs—when she'd been here last year, they had not. All she'd seen then was suits and purposeful striding, a lot of straight arrows aimed at the bull's-eye of business school. *Somethin's happenin' here,* Sunny thought, walking towards the library, her heartbeat quickening. Was it just the new Nineties fad for Sixties nostalgia? The last time such a wave of chaos and color splashed the Yard, it had signaled the presence of a drug.

A girl and two boys moved politely aside to make room for Sunny. *Weird,* she thought. *I'm almost old enough to be their mother.* The sun was warm, but the cement step was cold under her thighs. Pretending to gaze around at the sights of Harvard Yard, she covertly studied the kids.

They all had the incredibly smooth, blank faces of the young, like paper waiting to be written on. Close up, they weren't really hippies, despite the long hair and the tie-dye mandalas on their T-shirts. These kids were too clean, for one thing. Their hair was immaculate and shiny, their fashionably torn jeans looked fresh-washed, and Sunny didn't see any black fingernails or grimy necks. *Well, that's progress!*

There *was* one odd thing, Sunny realized after a few minutes. Quite a few of the kids were talking nonstop. The whole crowd hummed like a hive of bees. Sunny strained her ears to pick out individual voices:

"And then he said to me, he said, it's over, and I said you can't do this to me, not now, when we're just—" (A dark thin girl.)

"See, it all goes back to Schopenhauer,

"A philosopher who was kinda sour,

"He said, Nietzsche was a favorite student a mine

"And the next big dude was Wittgenstein—"

(A tall, pimply boy.)

"The Dead have sold out, man, Jerry sold out, too many of them at the concerts now, just tourists—" (A beautiful boy with long dark-blond hair and beads.)

Broken love affairs, intellectual enthusiasms, rock'n'roll—nothing new, except the rap rhythms woven into the mix. It wasn't what these kids were saying. It was how they were saying it—intense, rapid-fire, without pause for breath or punctuation. Sunny had the impression that every third or fourth kid on the steps was delivering a jittery monolog. And now she noticed something else: a familiar look on the faces of the kids around a talker—at once tolerant and vigilant. Sunny had seen that expression at every acid-rock concert she'd ever attended. It was the face of someone who is, for the moment, straight, and is humoring and protecting a tripping friend.

She was in the presence of hex. She was sure of it.

The steady murmuring was starting to get to her. It created an unpleasant contact high; she felt her own nerves being wound tight, whining like high-tension wires in the wind. Sunny remembered the first time she'd taken mescaline. (She'd only had time to take it twice before she'd met Mr. Clean.) Walking towards Central Park with a friend, waiting for the visual show to start, she'd become aware of a deep, inconsolable craving, an unscratchable itch in the marrow of her bones. It made her need to toss and turn and whimper, like someone with a high fever or a searing desire. It felt as if it had been there all along, and the drug had simply drawn back the veil of superficial contentment to reveal the relentless longing at the core of life. Sunny felt that unappeasable hunger in the hive-like humming all around her now.

Funny she'd thought of a hive, because there was a picture of a bee on the blond boy's T-shirt! A big, vivid, black-and-yellow bee, posed at an angle over a golden honeycomb cell. Several more hexagonal cells clustered in an asymmetrical pattern. With a start Sunny recognized the molecular structure of hexamethylene. There was no mistaking the wit of a drug culture.

"I like your shirt," she said to the boy, a little too loudly.

The humming stopped, and all eyes turned toward her. How could she have mistaken this for a gathering of healthy young people? Eyes burned like hot coals in faces that were almost anorexic: cheekbones sharp, skin translucent as candle wax. It was creepy the way they *all* stared at her, like a herd of deer that have scented a lion on some PBS nature program. Sunny had a feeling that if she said the wrong thing, the steps would empty in moments. She lowered her voice and spoke casually to the blond boy, who seemed to be vibrating at an ultra-high frequency.

"Where'd you get it? I'd like to buy one like that."

"At-at-at the head shop, you know, Randy's, on Kennedy Street." *Randy's!* Her hunter's heart gave e leap. The murmuring had begun again tentatively all around them, shielding their conversation like rain. "But you're not, you're not with us, are you," the boy said. "I mean, you know, I can't feel you."

Small hairs stirred on the back of Sunny's neck. "No, but I…" She winged it. "I want to be."

The boy stared at her and into her, as if he were trying to read her entrails. His eyes were hurt and fanatical, in the grip of prophecy or pain. Sunny had an absurd urge to tell him everything was going to be all right, the way an adult lies to a child caught in a nightmare. Finally the boy nodded as if he'd come to a conclusion. He dug into his pocket, reached out slowly and clasped Sunny's hand. A small hard lump muffled in tissue paper pressed into her palm. His hand was ice-cold.

"Thank you," Sunny said, cradling his cold hand in both of hers for a moment. *Where did you get it?* The question jumped up behind her lips, dying to be let out, but she held it firmly by the collar. Somehow it seemed like a betrayal of trust. Besides, she was willing to bet they got it at "Randy's."

The boy was staring at her expectantly. It suddenly dawned on Sunny that he meant for her to swallow the pill, or whatever it was, right now, right here. Her heart began to pound in her throat. Here it was, the ultimate challenge of reporting, research, life itself: Were you willing to put yourself on the line to find the truth? *Do you dare? Or are you scared?*

Sunny thought of it as the Spallanzani principle. The eighteenth-century Italian scientist, one of the heroes of her childhood book *Microbe Hunters,* had studied digestion by swallowing hollow wooden blocks with meat inside them, then forcing himself to throw them up. To the seven-year-old Sunny, this had been the awesome epitome of courage: what could be worse than throwing up?? Knowledge must be a wonderful thing, to be worth so high a price.

She had tried ever since to live by the Spallanzani principle, experimenting on herself, forcing herself through each of her fears—of the dark, escalators, and horses, later of marijuana, sex, mescaline, hitch-hiking, and finally Sasha—for the prize of experience. As a reporter, she constantly had to push past her own shyness and fear to get The Story. Pride was involved, as well as curiosity. To motivate Sunny, all you had to say was, "Scared?"

On the other hand, she knew that was an adolescent attitude, no older than this beautiful boy staring at her with hot evangelistic eyes.

As you got older, prudence set in like farsightedness, and you realized that there were things worth being scared of. Would she shoot heroin for a story? No way. So why take this drug, about which she knew even less? Sure she was scared. (Though the same dry mouth and knocking heart could signal love, or adventure.) Most of all, she was scared of returning to Sasha three hours from now in a detectably altered state.

Sunny sighed. Her heart slowed down; the precipice receded. "Is there anything I should know first?" she asked the boy, one hand surreptitiously fishing in her purse for her notebook. "What happens? Can you tell me what it's like?"

The expectant light went out of the boy's eyes. Down slammed the shutters. "I thought so," he crooned to himself, shaking his head back and forth, back and forth. "Too old" His eyes stopped on Sunny again, and narrowed with suspicion. "Who are you? What do you want?"

Sunny felt a pang of schoolyard shame, but she swept it aside with the broom of professionalism. "I'm a reporter," she said. "I'm writing a story. Here's my card. If you or any of your friends would be willing to talk to me, I promise to keep it confidential." She knew she'd lost him, but she went on. "And thank you for this," She raised her fist with the little wad of tissue clenched in it. "You may be right—I can't write about it without trying it. I'll seriously consider it. But not now."

If not now, when? echoed mockingly in her mind as she slipped off the steps and walked towards the exit from the Yard to Massachusetts Avenue. But as soon as she got out of that net of humming, she felt released from a spell. The beauty and normality of the day burst in on her. She'd been straight around stoned people before, and all she'd felt was left out and superior, as if the stuff they were giggling about was so dumb that the real joke was on them. This was different, in a way she couldn't quite pin down but didn't like. At the gate of the Yard she looked back and had the sense of a narrow escape. She wanted to throw the little wad of tissue paper away, but she put it in her coin purse. She'd need to describe its contents. That might be a good way to start the article.

The smell of sauerkraut hit her with the wave of relief as she came out onto Mass Ave. She hated to admit it, but Sasha was right: she should have eaten something. If hot dogs smelled that good, she was *really* hungry. She stole a reformed junkie's sidelong glance at the cart. Fortunately, the young Latino vendor chose that moment to pick a pimple. Sunny hurried across Mass Ave, bought a vegetarian pita sandwich at a Middle Eastern place, and walked toward John F Kennedy Street munching.

Now that her eyes were open, she kept seeing little signs of the latest chemical change in the culture. Rock-concert posters wrapped around lampposts advertised groups called Weird Sisters, Sorcerer, and Big Brother, minus the Holding Company. The posters had an aggressive new visual style: abstract circular patterns in bright, hard-edged colors that vibrated at their contrasting borders, making them hard to look at and impossible to ignore. A couple of kids passed Sunny at an intense lope, wearing T-shirts printed with the same kind of vibrating mandala. The long, clean hair and near-anorexia she'd noticed in the Yard were coming into fashion for both sexes; some kids wore their hair in a tight ponytail or bun, giving them a severe, ascetic look nothing like the defiant sloppiness of the Sixties. There was a compulsiveness to this drug, a driven quality. But Sunny knew she couldn't piece the puzzle together from the outside; all these clues referred to an experience she had not had. Yet. The key was in her purse. Could she refuse to use it?

Near Harvard Square Sunny recognized the gray concrete pillars of Holyoke Center, the ugly modern administration building, new in her time. She'd gone there to see a Harvard Health Services shrink sophomore year, the year she first smoked grass and had sex. She'd had the feeling that the world was coming apart, or maybe it was her. *Somethin's happenin' here.* "Can you study?" the shrink had asked her. She said yes. He'd sent her back to her dorm. They'd wised up since then. In front of the building, a public bulletin board fluttered with flyers for drug counseling and self-help groups. Anorexia/bulimia, suicide hot line, cocaine…the words HUNG UP ON HEX? jumped out at Sunny.

"Sobriety takes support," she read. "HA 12-step groups forming. Join us now." HEXORCISM, promised another. "HHS Substance-Abuse Programs Can Help You Break the Spell." Sunny tore off paper tabs with both phone numbers and slipped them into her coin purse, where they bracketed the little wad of tissue like two cops guarding a perp.

As she snapped the coin purse shut, a hand closed on her elbow from behind.

Sunny nearly jumped out of her skin. She jerked around, expecting a Sasha-sized cop—her guilt in uniform—and saw, instead, the slight dark girl from the library steps, the one who'd been babbling about a love affair.

"I-I'll talk to you," she said. "If you'll just throw those numbers away. You won't need them. Honest. Everything will be okay."

Sunny saw that the girl's black bangs were quivering. Her eyes oscillated rapidly, as if she were dreaming awake, or maybe just anxiously speed-reading Sunny's face. "I'm s-sorry about Ralph," she went on, so low and fast that Sunny had to lean in to hear her. "He always says, you know, never trust anyone over thirty. But we got good vibes from you, we wanted you to have the chance, so hey, some people have to process it through the left hemisphere first." She shrugged and gestured, arguing with someone not there. "I'll *talk* to her, if it helps her come to us!"

Sunny was getting the creeps, and turning them into questions. Who was this *we, us?* "The chance" at *what?* She'd better slow down, play this girl like a skittish fish. "What's your name?"

The girl smiled. It was a smile of pity and amusement, as if Sunny were a kindergartener who'd asked, "Why are trees green?" "You can *call* me Maria," she allowed finally, pronouncing it Mar-eye-ah. *But what? But I'm far, far beyond all that?*

"Hi, Maria, I'm Sunny." Sunny thrust out her hand with resolute normality—and jumped at the girl's touch as if she'd grabbed a joke electric buzzer. This kid was really wired. "Is there someplace we can go to talk?"

"We can talk at Randy's, if talking is what you want." Maria took Sunny's hand again and towed her toward Kennedy Street, chattering away. "Talking is what you want but talking won't—"

"Maria, I told your friend—Ralph?—I'm a magazine reporter," Sunny broke in, not liking the feel of her hand in the girl's cold quivery one. "I'm doing an article. I want you to be clear about that."

"You to be clear about that," Maria chanted, as if it were "Follow the Yellow Brick Road." "You to be clear about that's what brought you to us. You'll see! You'll see it so clear!" She laughed merrily. "So many roads, and they all go home to Rome!"

"Maria, why do you keep saying 'us' and 'we'?" They had turned into John F. Kennedy Street—Boylston Street in Sunny's day—sloping gently downhill towards the Charles River. "How many of you are there?" There hadn't been more than thirty kids on the library steps.

"Oh, I don't know." Maria frowned, as if thinking about it for the first time. "A hundred thousand? Numbers aren't important when you're One."

"A hundred *thousand?* What is this, some kind of movement? Or do you mean—"

Maria stamped her foot and yanked her hand away "Oh, it's so *hard* to talk to you singletons!"

A block down from the Square, three-story frame buildings lined the left side of the street, craft shops, ethnic restaurants and tiny cafés tucked into every story. Sunny saw Randy's from half a block away. You couldn't miss it. The big yellow banner featured an R. Crumb "Keep On Truckin'" character, with a blue-black face and big white choppers bared in a grin of apocalyptic glee. *I am become Death, the destroyer of worlds,* that grin said to Sunny, *and I'm loving every minute of it.* Maria scampered down the four steps to the basement entrance as if she lived here. Bull's-eye! Sunny followed through the door with its tinkling bell, and found herself encircled by grinning skeletons.

They were only Grateful Dead T-shirts: tie-dyes with the skull in black-and-white, black ones with the skeleton in glitter. Randy's was a tropical forest of T-shirts, a complete iconography of underground culture: the Dead's trademark skeleton, the five-pointed marijuana leaf, the Zig-Zag Man, the upside down Hanged Man from the Tarot deck, Mickey Mouse as the Sorcerer's Apprentice, the head of Bob Marley, the head of the Joker from "Batman," the head of a UFO alien with its big insect eyes, the bee poised on its hexagonal honey cells, a hexagram from the *I Ching*—"Revolution, or Molting"—the "Keep on Truckin'" demon, those bright round patterns Sunny had seen on the street—of course, they were Pennsylvania Dutch hex signs!—and the large handsome head of a man Sunny didn't recognize. The proprietor, a big-bellied middle-aged man in a faded tie-dye T-shirt, leaned both hands on the glass counter and stared noncommittally at Sunny. Maria had vanished through a curtain of clicking beads.

"Who's *that?*" Sunny pointed at the T-shirt with the man's head.

"Big Brother," said the proprietor, unbudging, inviting neither a conversation nor a purchase. He had a hillbilly accent, a graying red beard that split in two like Yosemite Sam's, and a blurred tattoo on his upper arm. Hell's Angel? Vietnam vet? Nasty customer. Sunny wished Sasha were beside her.

"Ahh! Big *Brother*, as in *1984*," she said out loud. She studied the little pipes and rolling papers in the display case, trying to figure a way around this guy. He wasn't the type to confide in a magazine writer. Why'd she have to blow her cover to the kids? "An attack of the honests," Sasha would call it.

"Maria said we could talk here," Sunny said. "Where'd she go?"

Yosemite Sam jerked his head. "Café in the back." But when Sunny started forward, he held up a hand like a school crossing guard. "Private club."

Sunny felt like a lioness seeing her quarry bound away. She had to restrain herself from pacing in frustration. She'd had so many questions to ask the girl! Well, maybe there was another kind of information to be gained here. Sunny strongly suspected that Yosemite Sam was the main local distributor of hex. She wondered how he'd managed not to get busted when this shop virtually shouted its real merchandise. He had to be a wily old survivor. He was looking at her with expressionless little eyes, no doubt reading her agitation and running it through his street computer for possible reasons. Sunny had to do something or leave.

She put her palms on the glass case and leaned forward. "I need to see Randy," she said in a low, urgent voice.

For the first time something moved in the proprietor's eyes. He looked startled. His face shifted. And then, to Sunny's consternation, he roared with laughter.

"I think," he wheezed, his belly shaking, "I think you would fahnd the conversation a trahfle one-sided."

The line sounded funny in that redneck accent, but Sunny got it. "You mean he's dead!"

Yosemite Sam shook his head. "You ever seen Wile E. Coyote die?" he bellowed on a fresh wave of laughter. "No, he just gits right back up again! Lady, you can't see Randy 'cause there ain't no Randy. But maybe I c'n introduce you to Fred Flintstone." He doubled over in a falsetto howl at his own humor.

"You don't understand," Sunny said coldly. "I want to make a buy."

The laughter fell off of Yosemite Sam like the shabby traveler's cloak off Death in a medieval tale of the Plague. His face went stone cold, and Sunny knew she had made a bad mistake. Fear climbed in her, along with mortification: twelve years with Sasha and she wasn't any more streetwise than she'd ever been. She took an involuntary step backwards, but controlled the urge to look towards the door. Too late anyway: Sam, quick for his bulk, came round the end of the counter, pinioned her wrist, and twisted her right arm behind her back.

Sunny knew how to get out of it. Many times it had been Sensei back there, faking a mugger's stupid strength against her growing knowledge of torque and angle. But she didn't want to squander the surprise value of her skill. If she escaped Sam's grip now, he'd know what she knew, and she'd still be in his store and a lot smaller than him. So she just whimpered as he unslung her purse from her shoulder with his free hand, dumped its contents on the counter—her lipstick rolling, falling on the floor—and pawed through them. He picked up her tape recorder, looked at it, and tossed it behind the counter with a thud that made her flinch. Then he flipped through her identification. Apparently not finding what he expected, he ran his hard hand down both her inner thighs, under her armpits and around each breast, letting it linger, looking into her face with a rapist's intimate contempt. Sunny lowered her eyes and concentrated on relaxing all her telltale muscles. It was the hardest thing she'd ever done. Every cell screamed for action.

"Hey, Eddie, what're you doing?" came a plaintive voice. The beaded curtain snicked, and Maria stood in the rear doorway. "She's *my* catch."

"Catch, my ass," Eddie drawled. "She didn't know Rule One, that nobody buys in. She's the Man."

"No, she's not," said Maria. "She's a writer. And she already got her in-gift from Ralph. Just give me an hour with her. She's a goodie, I can feel it."

"Yeah? I *feel* things pretty good myself," Sam/Eddie said sarcastically. "I feel that she is looking into things that are none of her business, and I feel it would be very interesting to know why." His eyes followed the trail blazed by his hand. "And I can think of some more things I'd like to feel. So you give *me* an hour with her. When I'm through, she's all yours." He released Sunny's arm and gave her a rough shove towards the counter. "Get your shit together, cunt. We're gonna have a talk."

He'd fallen for it! He took her for unarmed and helpless. Sunny's mind started to move, fast and smooth and silent as the Niagara right before the falls. To the naked eye, she was all cowed humility, stumbling forward to scoop pens, keys and identification into her purse. She started to stoop to retrieve her lipstick, lying near Sam/Eddie's boots, then hesitated and looked up at him meekly. He nodded curt permission. She bent, picked up the lipstick and, rising out of her crouch, in one continuous, fluid, accelerating motion, kicked him hard in the groin with pointed toe and hardened instep—WHAP!—a *kin-geri*.

"*Aaauuuuggh!!*" Yosemite Sam doubled over, gagging. Sunny felt a flash of wicked tenderness for the male anatomy, a girl's best friend.

"*Eeeeeeeeee!!*" Maria was screaming excitedly.

The little bell tinkled as Sunny yanked the door open and sprinted up Mount Auburn Street.

She slalomed around startled pedestrians. At the first corner, halfway to the Square, she made a skidding right turn and ran between the heavy gray pillars of Holyoke Center. Through the glass door in the dim concrete lobby, an elevator's doors were closing. Sunny ran for it and stuck her arm into the rubber jaws. They rebounded, and she pushed her way in and pressed against the car's back wall, panting. The neat young administrative types in the elevator gave her queasy looks. Now the doors wouldn't close. Sunny reached forward and viciously jiggled the CLOSE DOOR button. Just as the doors slid together, she saw a tie-dye slice of Yosemite Sam come hobbling through the glass doors.

The elevator rose too slowly. How fast could a man in Sam's condition climb stairs? With shaking fingers Sunny snapped open her coin purse and fumbled out the two paper slips she'd plucked off the posters on Mass Ave. Above the phone number one said "HHS Drug Program, Holyoke Center, 9th Floor." The slips fluttered to the floor. Other passengers had punched 3, 4, 6, 8. Sunny pressed 9 and shrank back, expecting to see Sam waiting each time the elevator doors slid open. Three was clear.

On four, the stairwell door squealed open just as the elevator doors were closing. Sunny's heart leapt into her throat. She wondered if Sasha could feel her fear, like Vincent in "Beauty and the Beast." *Oh Sash, if only you could jump on top of a subway car and be here.*

When Sam didn't appear on six, Sunny thought the elevator was winning. Then a tall, colorless man got in and pressed seven. Sunny had always hated perfectly healthy people who took the elevator one floor. She wished the tall man the cardiovascular disease he deserved.

The doors opened on seven and there was Sam. He bulled his way in, gave Sunny one gun-muzzle look, and turned around so his back blocked the door. He stank, and he was breathing in great wheezing heaves. He was as out of place as a wild pig in this elevator full of yuppies. Sunny's only hope was to stay with them. Sam was too smart to make a scene and call attention to himself. He couldn't do anything unless he got her alone.

Sam was smarter than she gave him credit for.

The elevator doors slid open on eight. The last of the office workers drained out, parting around Sam's bulk. Sunny tried to go with the flow. As she slipped past him, Sam clamped a hand on her upper arm. Before she could scream, he said in a loud, sorrowful voice, "Come on, Martha. You know you got to take your meds, or you get crazy. Don't make a scene. Let's go home."

The nerve of it knocked the breath out of Sunny. Her mouth opened, but nothing came out. The yuppies were edging away, eager to avoid the tawdry drama of domestic conflict and mental disturbance unfolding behind them. Sunny had aroused their suspicion by running into the elevator, disheveled and out of breath. Now whatever she said or did would only reinforce the impression Sam had deftly created of her—and of himself as her long-suffering caretaker, entitled to take control. But she had to do something before they all got out of earshot. She chose the simplest thing: play the role to the hilt.

"I want to see my doctor!" she screamed. "I have the right to see my doctor!"

Sam was trying to drag her back into the elevator. She drove the edge of her shoe down on his shin in a *kansetsu-geri* and took advantage of his pain to lunge for the safety of the floor. "Help me! He's going to hurt me!"

Doors opened and heads stuck out. "What's going on?"

"Old hippie type says his wife won't take her medication. Says she's a crazy."

"Probably took too much LSD back in the Sixties. A lot of them are still schizophrenic, you know."

"Maybe somebody should call her doctor."

"Call the police!" Sunny screamed, furious that Sam's story was being believed. Did she *look* like a dope dealer's crazy old lady?

A clear-faced, well-dressed young black man was coming towards them. Sunny felt a split-second's indecision in Sam. For a moment she thought he'd let her go and be swallowed by the elevator. But he stayed and bluffed it out.

"What's the problem here?" said the young man. "Don't you think the lady has a right to see her doctor?"

Sam/Eddie turned confiding, man-to-man. "Private business between me and her. Just let me take her home before she makes any more trouble. She's sick." He glared at Sunny. "She sees things that ain't there."

The man hesitated and looked at Sunny. She gave him the full blast of her blue eyes, beaming messages of sanity and urgency. "I've never seen this…man before today," she hissed. "I'm a writer. I was working on a story, and I…" It sounded like delusions of grandeur. "You've got to believe me! I'll show you my card."

"See what I mean?" Sam said sadly.

The good Samaritan shook his head. "I'm afraid if you don't let her see her doctor, I'm going to have to call building security. Where's your doctor, hon, up on nine?" Sunny nodded, and he said to Sam, "Whyn't you just be a nice guy and take her up there?"

"All right, sure, I'll do that," Sam/Eddie agreed too quickly, trying to suppress a smirk of triumph.

"NO!!" Sunny gasped, grabbing her rescuer's arm. "Don't leave me alone with him!"

The black knight looked startled. "Well, all right," he said reluctantly.

Sunny clung to his arm while they waited for an elevator. Yosemite Sam dug his fingers into her other arm, causing her as much discreet pain as he could. Sunny prayed for an elevator full of people. She did not want to be alone in a car with this kind young man and a wised-up, pissed-off Sam. He'd take care of her protector in two seconds, and she'd be his.

The elevator arrived, not full, but bearing two precious witnesses. The threesome got in and rode in grim silence up to nine, Sam's threatening stink filling the car. A quick glance at the floor directory and Sunny said "This way," tightening her grip on her hero's arm, no longer trying to explain. If he thought she was a terrified, abused wife, fine. She just wanted to get away from Sam.

The door was marked "Harvard Health Services Drug Abuse Program." Beside it several molded plastic chairs were lined up along the wall. "I'll wait for her right here," Yosemite Sam said, and sat down. He gave Sunny the look that a mean and patient hound gives a treed raccoon.

"Thank you *very* much," Sunny whispered to her rescuer. Someone would have to call security, but he'd done enough. She squeezed his hands and pushed through the door.

She was in a bright waiting room, with more chairs lining the walls and a gray-haired nurse behind a desk near the doorway to a corridor of consulting rooms. Three kids fidgeted on the chairs, two very thin boys and a tiny, frightened girl. Sunny wondered if this sterile room was as cheery a refuge to them as it was to her.

"Can I help you?" asked the nurse in a pleasant voice. Then she frowned. "Are you all right?"

"Yes, thank you, I'm fine," Sunny snapped, angry that she was shaking. She clicked her business card down on the desk. "I'd like to talk with the program director, if she or he is available. I'm with *Metro Magazine* in New York, and I'm writing an investigative piece on hexamethylene." It felt so good to be herself again, to shed the tawdry role Yosemite Sam had trapped her in. Her upper arm ached and throbbed from his grip, but she felt manhandled in some deeper place.

"Do you have an appointment with Dr. Goodman, Ms. Randall?"

"I'm sorry, I don't. I...didn't have a chance to call."

"Let me buzz her. I don't think she's left for the day."

While the nurse murmured over the phone, a kind-looking man in a three-piece tweed suit leaned out the inner door and said, "Come on in, Franny." The tiny girl got up and tiptoed in, clutching her large bag to herself. She looked as lost and scared as a three-year-old just awakened from a nightmare. Was that what hex did to these kids? Or—worse—was that what getting *off* hex did to them? Maria hadn't seemed lost. She'd seemed all too found, like a Moonie or a Mansonette.

"Dr. Goodman would be happy to see you now," the nurse said. "Just go down that hall to your right. Her office is straight ahead, at the end of the corridor."

Sunny passed several closed doors. From the sounds behind one, an intense group session was going on. Dr. Donna Goodman's door was open. Her office was full of light, its big window looking out over the Charles River and the white steeples of the Harvard Houses. Shelves overflowing with books, an orange-and-brown shag rug, diplomas framed on the walls, kids' and dogs' pictures in Lucite cubes on the desk. The small, clear-eyed, sympathetic woman behind the desk got up.

"Whew." Sunny collapsed in the comforting leather chair opposite Dr. Goodman, as if she was at home with a friend. "You don't know what I've just been through. I need you to call building security, or the campus police."

"What happened?"

Sunny told her about Yosemite Sam. "As far as I know, he's still out there. I must have stumbled into something big, for him to come after me like that. On the other hand…" She shrugged wearily. "Maybe he's just pissed 'cause I kicked him in his…dignity."

Dr. Goodman wasn't smiling. "Do you want him arrested?"

"On what grounds? He didn't actually *do* anything to me, except follow me. And make it very clear what he *meant* to do to me." Sunny shivered. "No. I just want him far away from me."

Dr. Goodman picked up the phone and relayed Sunny's description of Yosemite Sam to security.

"They'll show him out," she said, hanging up. "Unfortunately, I know who that man is. His name is Eddie Cole, and his store is one of the places where the 'hexies' hang out. They could be getting the drug from him. I don't know, the kids aren't telling. What I do know…" She leaned forward. "This is a violation of confidentiality, so please keep it off the record. One of my clients, a seventeen-year-old freshman, was raped by Eddie Cole." Sunny sucked in her breath. "She was high on hex and completely defenseless. The incident was extremely traumatic for her. I tried to persuade her to press charges. She refused."

"*Why??*"

"Fear. And loyalty, if you can imagine those two emotions together. Think of Charlie Manson and *his* girls. Eddie Cole is small-time by comparison, but he is a kind of Svengali-big brother figure to the hex users. And he likes to hurt girls, the younger the better."

"But why would he try to hurt me, if he thought I was a cop? That would be the dumbest thing he could do."

"When he searched you and didn't find ID, a wire, or a gun, he probably thought that you were deep undercover, and he could get to you before you got to a phone." Dr. Goodman caught Sunny's surprised look. "I know, I sound like a cop myself. If my clients could hear me, they'd go up the wall. We had a seminar on the hexamethylene crisis with the law-enforcement people. They gave us the rundown on what they're doing and asked for our help. If we learned anything about where the kids get the drug, or if we found one who'd be willing to talk to them, to help other kids…We gave them the rundown on professional confidentiality, and how crucial trust is to successful therapy, and said we'd do what we could, but the client's interest and the healing relationship come first."

"Way off the record, have *you* ever heard anything?" Sunny covered her ears in a hear-no-evil gesture. "Don't tell me what."

"Occasionally somebody mentions getting hex from a friend. Period. Press the point, and you could lose months of work building trust. These kids are so paranoid. They have an 'us versus them' mentality"—Sunny nodded in recognition—"that you have to dismantle very slowly, very carefully. Anyway, they're just the cannon fodder in this war. I'm sure they don't know or care where the drug is coming from."

"But 'Sam' knows. And he didn't want me to find out."

Dr. Goodman shrugged. "Maybe. The police got a warrant to search his store, and they didn't find anything. He threatened to sue the city for harassment. The *Phoenix* blew it up into a major civil-liberties story: 'Small-Business Owner Harassed for Hippie Dress.' You could say that this man knows how to cover his ass." She said it with perfect professional diction, and then winked. She couldn't have been more than forty-five. "What else can I tell you?"

Sunny rummaged in her purse. "Dammit! He took my tape recorder. I'll have to use this." She took out a tiny spiral notebook and a pen. "Tell me about the kids, what hex does to them, and what it does *for* them. I got some very creepy vibrations. Almost like it's a cult."

Dr. Goodman rested her chin on steepled hands. "What do you know about MDMA, also known as Ecstasy?"

"Well…that it combines some of the qualities of speed and mescaline…that there are no hallucinations, just a strong feeling of trust and empathy, an ability to share emotions without fear…that some therapists are upset that it was classified, because it seemed to accelerate therapy…side effects are sweating and rapid eye oscillation…and some University of Chicago researchers found permanent brain damage in animals." She winced. "Why do they have to do that to animals?" Sasha would have said, "The fucking bastards, I'd like to break their legs."

"I'm inclined to agree with you," Dr. Goodman said. "I've got two dogs at home, and they're like my kids. Well, you've done your homework. But you never tried Ecstasy?"

"No, my drug-dabbling days are over," Sunny said resolutely. She wondered if Dr. Goodman had taken Ecstasy, and decided not to ask. Because if Dr. Goodman said yes, Sunny would have to ask her what it was like. And there would go the interview, bounding down a side path like an undisciplined hound.

"It would have given you the bare beginnings of an idea of hex. MDMA is a drug that temporarily lowers interpersonal boundaries. Hexamethylene dissolves them. A child on hex literally doesn't know where she leaves off and others begin. For instance, like some schizophrenics, she loses the distinction between thoughts experienced inwardly and thoughts spoken out loud. People high on hex tend to babble whatever comes into their heads."

"I've heard them!"

"Secrets come out, and what's more, suggestions go in with extraordinary ease. If it were legal just for medical uses, this would be a terrific drug for weight-loss and stop-smoking hypnosis programs. It would also be an ideal drug for interrogation and brainwashing. Eddie Cole wouldn't have needed to hurt you." *(No,* Sunny thought, *he just wanted to.)* "All he'd have had to do was force you to swallow a capsule—"

"—and he'd have found out that I was exactly what I said I was."

"And maybe planted a suggestion that would have scared you off the story. Some image or idea that would've given you nightmares or panic attacks if you even thought about hex. You'd have had to give the assignment up, or feel like you were having a breakdown. That kind of suggestion is built into the hex subculture, part of the set and setting in which people learn to use the drug. I've seen young adults frightened for months that because they'd left the 'hive,' as they call the community of users, something terrible was going to happen to them. A common belief is that their flesh is going to rot on their bones, like living corpses, because they 'aborted the process of evolution.' Treating 'hexies' has been unfavorably compared in the literature with treating brainwashing victims and deprogramming cult members. I'm not exaggerating when I say that this drug could destroy a generation. Hex is the worst thing to hit this society since crack or AIDS."

"It sounds absolutely terrifying." Sunny shook out her right hand and picked up the warm pen again. "Why does anybody take it in the first place?"

"Because it creates the same feelings of 'trust and empathy' that MDMA does, only much stronger. 'Bliss and fearlessness' were the words one articulate young man used to describe it to me. It creates a feeling of oneness with others. Chronic users believe they share a 'group mind,' that they can read each other's thoughts—'like dolphins,' one girl told me—and more and more come to have the same thoughts. A lot of them actually believe they're the next step in evolution, and that when this planet is destroyed—not if, when—by nuclear war or ecological devastation, they'll be rescued by aliens in UFOs. Arthur C. Clarke's *Childhood's End* is one of their cult books; Whitley Strieber's *Communion* is another. But do you know what they remind *me* of? That Fifties movie, 'Children of the Damned.'" Sunny remembered the movie. Solemn little mutant children of all races who shared one genius mind. They could control and punish nasty adults with a stare of their white-hot eyes.

"Would you say that hex is addictive?"

Dr. Goodman sighed, took off her glasses and pinched her eyes. Then she put her glasses back on and looked straight into Sunny's eyes, her own steady green ones slightly magnified. "Is an end to loneliness addictive?" she said. "Is certainty addictive? Remember, this is not a generation with a lot of hope. We had hope. In retrospect, 1960 was a good time to be young—the world still was. Fast-forward a few decades. A recent survey shows that more than half of all eighteen-year-olds don't believe they'll live long enough to have children. They just don't see a future. More than half their parents are divorced. These are the kids who were doing drugs and committing suicide in junior high school. The successful ones, who make it to a place like Harvard, have a thin veneer of ambition over the fear and despair. They try hex and those other truths break through. The trouble is, they *are* truths. You can't lie to these kids and tell them the human race is going to make it. We don't know that for sure.

"That's what makes it so bloody hard to rehabilitate these kids. You have to take away certainties and replace them with some very humble maybes that call for a lot of hard work in the dark. You have to rebuild personal boundaries that isolate as much as they define. You take them out of their cozy 'hive' and put them in therapy groups where they have to communicate with the clumsy tools of words, instead of reading each other's minds. It looks like a bad bargain, doesn't it? There's a very high risk of relapse. And of suicide."

She was silent for a long time while Sunny wrote. Finally Sunny looked up from her notebook and said, "Whewwww."

"You got it."

"Is there an answer?"

Dr. Goodman gave a short sharp laugh, and then went on as if she hadn't. "Some researchers are looking for a chemical antagonist that would block the action of the drug. I think that's a Band-aid approach. I think the only antidote is hope. And that means therapy isn't enough. Therapy can address their personal despair of being loved and understood, but you also have to address their collective despair of surviving. These kids don't *really* want to be carried off by UFOs. They want to live long, full lives on a beautiful planet. You have to convince them that that's possible and that they can do something about it. That isn't easy when so many of *us* are cynical and pessimistic. They pick that right up from their parents, and from the media.

"In the best of all possible worlds, I'd develop a program to treat them with megadoses of good news. I'd have experts come talk to them about the rebirth of democracy in the East bloc. I'd invite activists to come and tell them what's going on in solar energy and community land trusts and reforestation, and show them how to sign up. If I were President, I'd put them in a national service and let them plant trees or teach Headstart for two years. But I'm not, so I try to keep them alive long enough to inoculate them with an optimism I don't always feel." She smiled tiredly.

"Thank you," Sunny said, closing her notebook. "I hope I got all that right. Because you've made my article. I didn't know *anything* about hex until now, and I don't think many people know yet." She grinned and held out her sore hand. "We've got a scoop, doc."

Dr. Goodman had a good firm handshake. "Who knows," she said, rolling her eyes heavenward, "maybe somebody will even fund my proposals."

Sunny hesitated, embarrassed at what she was about to ask, but more afraid.

"Do you think someone from security would take me downstairs? I'm going to call my friend and ask her to pick me up, but I'd hate to, you know, disappear between here and the door."

"Go ahead, call your friend," Dr. Goodman said. "I'll see to it."

Sunny dialed. "Willa?"

"Sunny! Thank God. Do you know what time it is?"

Sunny had completely forgotten. She looked at her watch: 6:40

Twenty minutes till the shit hit the fan.

Sunny groaned. She'd never be in Burlington by seven. Sasha would worry. Sasha worried was an enraged bear. Oh well, it wouldn't be the first time she'd been late. Or the last.

"Willa, do me a favor. Pick me up in front of Holyoke Center? I'll explain in the car."

"Are you all right?"

"I will be when I see you"

Dr. Goodman and Sunny had a few minutes to exclaim over each other's pictures of children, dogs and cats before the security guard arrived to escort Sunny downstairs. He was short, stocky, polite, and Hispanic, and Sunny was relieved to see that he packed a gun. For a woman who'd successfully defended herself that afternoon, she was disgracefully jumpy.

"Did you help throw a fat guy in a tie-dye shirt out of here earlier? With a beard?" she asked the guard as the elevator descended.

"No, ma'am. My shift started at six."

Ma'am. It always jolted Sunny. Maybe she should dye the gray out, after all.

The guard held open the glass door for her and turned to go back. "Please, wait here till my friend comes," Sunny cried out, and then felt foolish when they stood outside on the busy sidewalk and there was no sign of Eddie/Sam. Luckily, Willa's white Toyota pulled up within two minutes, sparing her further humiliation. Sunny ran to the car, jumped in, and slammed the door. Willa responded by gunning the engine.

"I feel like a getaway driver," she said, driving fast up Mass Ave. "What are we getting away from?"

"I—oh, shit!" A tie-dye shirt leapt out of the crowd. Sunny shrank down, then saw that the shirt's wearer was much too skinny to be Sam. A student, probably, buying a hot dog by the gate to the Yard. She let out her breath.

Willa was looking at her. "You did it, didn't you," she said with affectionate reproach. "You got into trouble."

"Well, let's see. I almost took a dangerous drug, but didn't. I used my karate, successfully. And I escaped from a really scary pursuer. I'd say I got *out* of trouble, wouldn't you?"

"Oh, Sunny." Willa laughed, the laugh of someone watching an extreme skier hit a mogul, flip, and land on his feet. "Tell me."

So Sunny did. She had time; the traffic was terrible. It was almost 7:30 by the time Willa got off Route 128 and started searching the labyrinth of little suburban streets for Gary's. Sunny was too engrossed in catharsis to notice Willa's growing silence. She had to tell somebody, and it wasn't going to be Sasha.

"So I know a lot more about hex than I did a few hours ago, but I still have no idea where it's coming from. Is there an organized distribution network? Is there an Owsley behind it all, you know, as in Owsley acid?" Willa didn't know, but never mind. "I've got less than a month to try to find out, and I'm going to lose a week in Romania. We promised Sasha's mother, we can't postpone the trip. But as soon as we get back, I've got to go out to Berkeley."

It took her by surprise when Willa said, "I think you're expecting too much of yourself." She looked straight ahead, gripping the top of the wheel, peering for a street sign. "If the police haven't found the source of this drug, why should you? It's arrogant, Sunny. Your job is to report on the world, not to save it. You're going to get hurt playing hero. Is this where I'm supposed to turn?"

"Make a right here at the mall and a left at the bottom of the hill," Sunny said sullenly. "You sound just like Sasha."

"For a good reason," Willa said, looking at her now. "Both of us love you, and we want you around. No article is worth a hair on your head, hon. So just write about hex as an unsolved mystery, okay? Are we there?"

"Right up this driveway." Willa swerved to avoid a toppled tricycle, a toy bulldozer, and a pedal-powered Batmobile. At the end of the road, where the drive made a loop, was a large new house of pink New England brick with a plantation façade of four white pillars. The house didn't know it was postmodern; its ornaments had long since forgotten their origins. But it had presence. It sprawled at the top of the drive in an arc both welcoming and grand, like Gary's hug. The windows glowed. Inside was Sasha: life, safety, warmth…noise.

"Here we are." Sunny opened her arms to her friend. "Thanks," she said into Willa's silky hair. "And thanks for worrying. You're right. No more heroics." She held up her right hand like a drunk taking the pledge.

Her heart beat faster as she ran up the steps. Sunny braced herself and pressed the buzzer. The doorbell chimed a little tune.

CHAPTER 5

─────────────── ▼ ───────────────

"Tell the one where you stuck the stick of dynamite in the guy's mouth and lit it," Sasha pleaded, mopping away tears of laughter.

"God, 's like tha's gotta go back to '70, '71," said Bo-bo Badinsky, alias Bo-bo the Bad, stretching out his long ex-basketball-player's legs and sucking his fourth Budweiser dry. Bo-bo had aged some in the several years since Sasha had last seen him. His gut pushed at his shirt, and his thick brown hair, combed forward from a monkish bald spot, was graying. But his rugged Polish clown face was as red and merry as ever, and he was just as capable of mayhem.

Bo-bo trusted Sasha like a father. Sasha was flattered, as he would have been by the trust of a tiger. He respected Bo-bo's lack of certain inhibitions the way he would respect a tiger's power to rend and tear. He kept up the relationship by phone, really loving the crazy Polack, and never knowing when he might need someone to do what he would rather not.

"C'mon, tell us," coaxed Gary, tossing Bo-bo a fresh can of Bud. They had been swapping stories ever since Bo-bo landed at the airport. Sasha loved a good laugh, and nothing got him going like slapstick violence. Bo-bo's tales were better than the Three Stooges.

"It was at McVann's," Bo-bo said thoughtfully, popping his fresh beer. "We were goin' a McVann's, live music. Somebody threw a snowball and it hit one a us. So I went in and lined 'em up, five, six people, and slapped 'em, told 'em 'Who the fuck threw the snowball.' They told me, and I said 'I'll be back.'"

"Like Arnold in 'The Terminator,'" Sasha exulted.

"Well, I went and got a stick a dynamite. So I got this kid on his knees and put it in his mouth and lit the fuckin' thing. And I said, 'This is the countdown. Nine, eight, seven, six…'

"The whole joint emptied out! It was winter, and everyone ran out without their fuckin' jackets and everything. The kid is slobberin'. He thought it was gonna blow up in his mouth. They didn't know you gotta have a cap and shit. There was no blasting cap. They didn't know." Bo-bo waxed philosophical. "Fear is the biggest edge you can have. It's half the battle."

"June!!" Sasha howled to Gary's girlfriend, the number-one real-estate salesperson in the country, who had been sitting and enjoying the stories like one of the guys. "You got some potato chips or something? When he talks like this I gotta fuckin' eat, or I'm gonna go nuts."

"I'll cut up some cheese and pepperoni," June said, getting up. "Should I staht dinner? When's Sunny coming?"

"Oh, *shit.*" Sasha looked at his watch for the first time in half an hour. Twenty after seven. A sharp stab of worry, and then the puncture filled with anger. "I told her to be here by seven," he muttered.

"Ah, don't worry about her," said Gary. "The traffic's bad around heah. Give her another half hour, she'll show up."

"She'd better," growled Sasha.

"Speakin a traffic," said Bo-bo, "Sasha, I meant to ask you, you know anyone in New York has a connection with the Motor Vehicles?"

"Not offhand. Why?" Sasha glanced at his watch. The second hand moved maddeningly slowly, like Sunny.

"I have to get my license. I ain't had no license in years."

"Why not?"

"'Cause I went the wrong way on the thruway. I ever tell you *that* story?" Bo-bo was expanding in the warmth of an appreciative audience. "I was drivin' the wrong way on the thruway, getting' blown. This girl was blowin' me, a topless dancer, and I was so fucked up on coke, I went on the skyway the wrong fuckin' way. Trucks were comin' at me and everything, like in a fuckin' movie. The troopers finally pulled me over. They asked me to blow into the little thing, and I said, 'I ain't blowin' into that.' Girl says, 'Gimme that, I'll blow that, too.' Then they asked me to touch my nose. I missed it. I got home and my wife goes—she didn't know about the broad, right, or goin' the wrong way—but she says, 'How the fuck could you miss *that* test, touching your nose with your finger, with that big fuckin' nose?' I missed it. Hit myself in the eye. So they took my license."

"Jesus Christ," Sasha said, but his heart wasn't in it. He looked at his watch again. A helpless need for action was growing in his body; in a minute he'd have to stand up and pace, go outside to cool the sweat breaking out on his forehead. *Somebody got Sunny.*

"Jeez, I did so many stupid things I can't even remember," said Bo-bo, on his sixth Bud and on a roll. "Tell you about the time they got me in a room 'n' tied me up—"

Somewhere in the house a chime played a mellow little tune.

"Heah she is," said Gary. "What'd I tell you?"

Sasha was already out of the room. He strode to the front door and yanked it open, filled with relief and righteous indignation, ready to thunder like Jehovah.

*   *   *   *

Sure enough, Sasha came to the door with his big mouth open. Before he could make a sound, Sunny threw her arms around him and buried her face in his chest. It was only partly calculated; she'd planned to knock him off balance with a burst of affection, but it was so good to see him, and to *feel* him, the bulwark of his body between her and all the harm in the world.

He held her close for a surprised moment, and Sunny felt the vulnerable heart of his protectiveness. Then he fended her off as if she'd attacked him. "Don't try to con me," he said. "You know you're in the shithouse. Why are you *always* late? Hah?" His voice cracked into the rhetorical falsetto Sunny hated. "Did you learn from your WASP Daddy-o that it's fashionable to be late? Remember how you left me standing in the snow while you socialized with some old lady?" That was ten years ago. Sasha's anger always tapped into a deep well of old, unforgotten grievances.

Normally Sunny would have fought back, or made excuses. She wasn't above claiming that her watch had stopped. But this afternoon's fear had worn her down. She burst into tears.

"Sunny! What's the matter?"

Tears instantly took the fight out of Sasha. It would have been funny how simply this "woman's weapon" disarmed him, except that Sunny was sobbing in earnest. "You're—supposed to be—my friend," was all she could get out.

"I *am* your friend. I'm your best friend, you dummy. So when you say you're going to be home at seven o'clock *be* home at seven o'clock! You know I worry. Here." Sasha gave her the handkerchief from his back pocket. "Everybody's waiting for you. And if somebody bothered you," Sasha looked heavenward, "God have mercy on him. You got Georgie Patton's Third Army on your side, and you don't even know it."

Sunny was still sniffling and sighing as she came into the living room. "Hi, you guys," she said as brightly as she could. She hugged June and went over to greet Bo-bo. Sasha hadn't exactly told her about Bo-bo, but he'd hinted and implied. "Bo-bo is bad news," he'd said with a horror-movie chuckle. "Bo-bo is...*not nice.*" All Sunny knew was that the fabled killer always gave her the sweetest, shyest, gentlest kiss.

"We've been holding dinner for ya," Gary said as she kissed him on the cheek. "Want a beer first?"

"How about a rum and coke with some of that Captain Morgan?"

"I'll have one too," Sasha exclaimed

"Gimme another beer," said Bo-bo.

"All right," Sasha said, raising both hands for silence. "Sunny's gonna tell us about her afternoon. If anybody so much as looked at you wrong, Sunny, I expect you to know his name and address."

"What's this? Somebody gave her a hahd time?" Gary sat up straight. "On my territory? Oh, no. That doesn't happen," he said softly, with a fixed, bloodthirsty grin.

"Sasha. You're my man," Bo-bo said sentimentally. "Somebody messes with your girl, I'll kill 'em."

Sunny looked around with wonder at this roomful of undomesticated manflesh. She knew that Sasha had brought her into the presence of something primally male, a fire that had been all but doused in her class of law-abiding, reasonable men: the lust for a righteous fight. And it confused her. She'd been raised to disapprove of it—a very early memory was of her mother saying "Civilized people don't hit"—she knew all the pacifist and feminist arguments against it, and she believed the human race had to evolve beyond it. But Sunny yearned towards every kind of vitality like a plant towards light. And after a brush with Yosemite Sam, it was frankly warming to have some warriors on your side. The truth was, right now Sunny felt as safe and special as the queen of an army. She found it a shameful feeling.

The three of them were looking at her with happy expectancy. She could give them what they wanted. She could toss them Eddie Cole and turn them loose.

To do that would be to admit she couldn't fight her own battles. It would also be to behave in a shockingly primitive way.

"Nobody bothered me," she said breezily. "I talked to some kids, and one of them actually gave me a cap of hex. Look! I'll show it to you." Sunny had forgotten all about Ralph's gift till now. Her "in-gift," creepy Maria had called it. She took the blob of tissue paper out of her coin purse and gently ejected its contents onto June's coffee table.

It rocked to stillness, shining like a bullet, one little black-and-yellow-striped capsule as vivid and nasty-looking as a wasp. "Son of a bitch, so that's hex," Sasha said. Everyone sat looking at it in respectful silence—except Bo-bo, who picked it up between thumb and finger and made like it was going into his mouth.

"Bo-bo!" Sunny yelped. "Don't swallow the evidence! I need that!" She retrieved the capsule and put it back in its protective wrapping. "So that's what I got," she said. "I also had a great interview with a woman doctor at Harvard Health Services." She looked around at the waiting faces and shrugged. "It was a good day's work."

Gary and Bo-bo sat back, looking disappointed. Sasha looked suspicious.

"Sunny. I know you. You just don't walk in the door and burst into tears."

"I do when I'm tired, and I walk in the door and you start yelling at me before you even say hello."

Sasha gave her a skeptical scowl and turned to Bo-bo. "Go on. Tell the one about the time they tied you up—"

"Why don't we move it to the dinner table?" Gary suggested.

They carried their drinks into the dining room, except for Bo-bo, who disappeared, Sunny supposed to piss off some of that beer. She and Sasha helped June put the food on the table, and Sunny recognized Sasha's southern fried chicken. She'd wondered that afternoon what men friends do when they're alone together. She should have known that in Sasha's case the answer was, "Cook."

"For Christ's sake, Sunny, take your jacket off," Sasha said as they sat down. "Just looking at you makes me sweat."

"I'm a little chilly," Sunny said, and then, defensively, "You know I'm always hot when you're cold, and vice versa."

Bo-bo came back from the bathroom with a springy step and sat down.

Sunny hadn't realized how hungry she was. She apologized silently to the chicken and tore into the brown crust of a boneless breast.

"Was this guy, O.J., we used to call him," Bo-bo said with his mouth full. "Big Polish kid about six five, about two seventy-five. And it was, jeez, it was Christmas Eve. And he says let's go get a broad." Bo-bo dumped a huge mound of Sasha's fluffy mashed potatoes onto his plate. "I says yeah, fuck it. So we rode around, you know, like where the hookers hang out on Main Street, and we pick up a really nice, light-skinned off-yellow black girl. I had a convertible car, 1971 Chevy, it was a brand-new Chevy, almost. And I says, 'I'll go in first. Give me fifteen minutes, and you knock on the door and I'll let you in.'

"So I'm getting'—I'm naked, I got my Ban-lon socks on, and she's blowin' me—and a knock on the door. And I say, Jesus, he ain't smart, but he's fuckin' prompt. So I open up the door, it's three fuckin' nig-gers." Sunny flinched. "Broad" she could take—it was Sasha who hated the locker-room words for women—but she'd been brought up never, *ever* to use the N-word. It was one of the mysteries of Sasha's world that white people like Bo-bo, who hung out with blacks, used the word like pepper—"fuckin'" being the salt.

"Three fuckin' niggers," Bo-bo repeated. "They range in size, you know, little, fat, and whatever. And I says, 'I don't want no fuckin' shoeshine.' Y'know, I'm drunk out of my fuckin' mind. Says, 'I don't want no fuckin' shoeshine.' So I hit the little fat kid in his head, his Pandora hat flew off—that was it." Bo-bo suddenly sounded cold sober. "They put a razor to my throat, a gun to my head. They tied me up, and I said they're either gonna cut my prick off or fuck me in the ass. I said, I'm dead. I'm fuckin' dead."

"Aaaahhhh!!" Sasha roared with joy, grabbing two more chicken thighs.

"So now the little fat guy that I hit, cut his lip, he punched me. Now it took me about an hour to get out of—"

"That's *all* he did?" Sunny gasped.

"They left me tied up. They took my leather coat, my money, and my fuckin' car keys. Now it took me an hour to get out of it, right? Christmas Eve, now. So O.J.'s still in the fuckin' car. I say, 'O.J.,' I says, 'What the fuck you doin'?' He says, 'I fell asleep.' I says, 'That's smart a ya.' I said, 'I got rolled.' He said, 'I thought somethin' looked suspicious.' So now all I had was a fuckin' sweater on, it's fuckin' snowin' out, it's cold. I flagged down the cops. So I got home, 'n' Christmas dinner was gettin' ready, or breakfast or whatever, my mother says, 'Where were ya?' I said, 'I was tied up for a little while.'"

The punch line blindsided Sunny. Mouth full of chicken, she exploded with laughter that turned to coughing. "Hey there." Gary got up and pounded her gently on the back. She finally got it under control, tears streaming from her eyes.

"You okay now?" Gary leaned over to look into her face, grasping both her upper arms to steady her.

"Owwooo!!" Part yelp, part gasp, it escaped before Sunny could stop it. Her left hand had flown to her right arm. Gary had grabbed her right where Yosemite Sam had. Everyone at the table was looking at her.

There was a long moment of silence, and then Sasha stood up.

"Take your jacket off, Sunny."

∗   ∗   ∗   ∗

Slowly, with downcast eyes, Sunny shrugged out of her jacket. Sasha saw her wince as she drew her right arm out of its sleeve, and then he saw the huge purple bruise wrapped around her slim, muscled upper arm. It was the print of a man's hand; he swore he saw the finger marks. The sight struck him deep in his lower belly, where something began to groan and churn like a dragon awakening.

"Son of a bitch, look at that," said Gary.

"What fuckin' mother-fucker," said Bo-bo.

A dark sound came out of Sasha, a sighing growl. With effort he turned it into words, but his voice was thick, blood-engorged. "Who did that to you?"

Sunny raised her head and looked at him. "You would have been proud of me," she said, tears filling her eyes. "I got him with a *kin-geri* and ran. But he came after me."

"Who came after you, Sunny?" Gary demanded like a prosecutor.

Sunny sighed and looked down at her plate. "He's a drug dealer. Or I'm pretty sure he is. His name is Eddie Cole. He owns a head shop where the 'hexies' hang out. This weird girl took me there. I tried to sound him out, and it went sour."

"What did he do to you?" Sasha said in his unfamiliar voice. He braced for her answer, wanting the pain, like salt in a wound, trusting it to stoke his rage and burn out all pity.

Sunny started telling how she went into the store. Sasha stopped her and made her describe the head-shop owner. A sleazy biker type: fat, hairy, greasy. Wonderful! His hands squeezed closed, feeling the rolls of lard squelch out between his fingers. The creep had a reputation for sexually abusing young girls. Better and better—the type you could torture with a pure heart. Sunny told how the fat sack of shit had twisted her arm, dumped out her purse, taken her tape recorder, and…searched her.

"He *searched* you? Physically?"

Sunny nodded unhappily. Sasha felt Bo-bo and Gary go on full alert.

"You mean he put his filthy hands on you?"

"Yeah, and he…"

"Aiiiyaaaoooww!!!" A howl from Bo-bo, drumming on the table-cloth like a movie Indian on the warpath. "Lemme have him!"

"Go on, Sunny. What else did he do to you?"

"He didn't get a chance to do anything else. I kicked him in the balls and ran." She told how the creep had followed her into a building and tried to grab her. Sasha knew Sunny had been badly frightened. She'd been trained in the dojo not to show pain or fear—"Poker face, poker face," Sensei was always saying—but when she finished her story, she was shaking.

"Tell me exactly where this store is in Cambridge," Sasha commanded.

"I'm gonna marry this guy," Bo-bo crooned. "I wanna fuck him in the ear till his brains come out. Where is he? Take me to my bride!"

"No, no. This asshole belongs to *me,*" Gary said. "This happened on *my* turf, and I take it very personally. The timing couldn't be better. We're pouring the foundation of my new condos tomorrow morning." Sunny looked wide-eyed from one to the other. She thought Gary and Bo-bo were really contemplating murder. And who knew? Maybe they were.

"Hey, wait a minute," Sasha said. "What about me? This is *my* beef."

"And you're my guest," Gary said.

"And you're my fuckin' brother," said Bo-bo.

"Whaddaya say? Do we split him up, or do we cut the cahds?" Gary loved to gamble.

So did Bo-bo. "Cut the fuckin' cards!!" he hollered. "I feel lucky tonight. But no cheatin', you Irish son of a bitch. Gemme a new deck."

June got a cellophane-wrapped pack of cards out of a drawer behind the wet bar. She was smiling with serene amusement. A bright, scrappy blue-collar girl who'd tended bar before getting into real estate, she wasn't taking this anywhere near as seriously as Sunny.

"Sasha, please do the honors," Gary said, tossing him the deck. Sasha unwrapped the cards and shuffled clumsily, thinking of C.J. East. Pick a card, any card, Eddie my boy, your number's up.

"Aces high!" he declared, and thrust out the deck.

Gary got the king of diamonds. He showed it around without a word, grinning carnivorously, his face blood-red.

Bo-bo closed his eyes, mumbled what might have been the Hail Mary, opened his eyes, and shot out a long arm like a rattlesnake striking.

A blood-curdling howl: "The fat cocksucker is miiiiiiine!"

Bo-bo had cut the ace of spades.

✳   ✳   ✳   ✳

Sunny was scared. Excited, too, in a horrible way. And carsick. Gary's Lincoln floated nauseatingly free of gravity even at 80 miles an hour. The disorienting darkness, the smell of the silky leather seats, the boisterous, menacing bulk of the three men, the adrenaline in her blood, all made it worse. She pressed the window button and let the night air blast into her face.

Oh my God, what have I done? Sunny had the feeling that she was about to see something she shouldn't, to witness the male mysteries of violence. And yet, when Sasha had given her the choice to come along or stay home with June and Stevie, she hadn't hesitated. She might learn something about the source of hex. And she didn't want to be excluded or exempted from anything on the grounds of gender. If Sunny had been born in the seventeenth century, she would have bound her breasts and ridden with the soldiers. She might not share the men's jolly sadism, but she was tough enough to witness it.

And she was curious.

"I know. I know. You won him fair and square," Gary was saying as he took the Storrow Drive exit into Cambridge. "But you owe me a couple of clean shots at him."

"*Clean?* That filthy pig? Ya wamme to wash his face for you?" Bo-bo roared, taking another swig of beer. "You wanna clean shot, wear gloves. That prick shits his pants, they're gonna smell it in Providence."

Sasha whooped with laughter. He certainly had a strange sense of humor. And Bo-bo was working himself into a state like a Norse berserker. Sunny was beginning to grasp what Sasha had been trying to tell her: Bo-bo had an extra gear, something more than the normal human endowment, like a sixth finger. Sunny was prepared to see Yosemite Sam hurt and frightened to the extent that he had hurt and frightened her. She believed karma should be fair. But to drop *this* secret weapon on him made about as much sense as nuking a shithouse. She began to hope they'd find the store dark, that Eddie Cole wouldn't be there.

He was there. Or somebody was. A shade was pulled over the glass panel of the door, outlined in telltale light. Sunny's heart hit bottom with a thud. As if he'd heard it, Sasha reassuringly cupped her knee in his warm, padded palm.

The Lincoln crept soundlessly by the shuttered store. Even Bo-bo was quiet, though Sunny could hear him breathing through his mouth.

Gary turned into Mount Auburn Street, floated a half block, and parked. The blue glowing numbers on the dashboard read 10:49.

The four of them walked back towards John F. Kennedy Street. Bo-bo didn't seem worried about attracting attention. He wound up like Orel Hersheiser and pitched his beer can into a bush. It was starting to rain. The few students still on the streets hurried to get out of the wet.

"Randy's" banner hung heavily, darkened by rain. Sunny's heart was hammering. She watched the men hustle down the four steps with deadly purposeful athletic lightness.

Bo-bo banged on the glass with the flat of his hand.

A pause, and then the crack of light darkened. Eddie's voice said, "Yeah?"

"Pickup," Bo-bo mumbled.

A silence, and then the voice said, "We're closed."

"Eddie," Bo-bo pleaded. "Lemme in, I gotta talk to ya!"

"Who the fuck are you?"

"Peanuts sent me."

"Boston's crime boss." Gary whispered to Sasha. "He can't take a chance."

Metallic fumbling, and the scrape of a padlock being withdrawn from a hasp. The door opened a few cautious inches and then immediately tried to slam shut again, with the full authority of Eddie's weight behind it. But it met the immovable object of Bo-bo's shoulder.

Bo-bo's long legs pumped and quivered as he ran in place against the door. Gary dropped his shoulder like a fullback and slammed into Bo-bo. Their combined weight drove the door open easily. They didn't tumble forward, but stood up and sauntered into Randy's, with Sasha right behind them. Sunny tiptoed in last.

"What do you want?" She couldn't see Eddie, just heard his sullen voice from behind the mountain range of shoulders. "I paid you guys already this month."

"You didn't pay *enough*, Eddie," Bo-bo chortled. "You got expensive tastes. I brought you the bill for this afternoon's entertainment. Ta-da." He stepped aside, and Sunny's eyes met Yosemite Sam's.

Her guts contracted at the sight of him. His little eyes darted to the men and back to her. She saw recognition, astonishment, and—with a hot flash of pleasure—fear. *The boot's on the other foot now, Eddie.*

He had been backing slowly away from them. Now quick as a greased pig he darted around the end of the counter. Sunny heard a drawer opening—and all six feet four of Bo-bo sailed through the air, vaulting over the counter, ramming his hip back against the drawer as if he was dancing Da Butt with his Buffalo homeboys.

"Aaaaaagggghhhhh!" Eddie screamed. His hand wasn't coming out of that drawer till Bo-bo was ready, and when it did, it wouldn't be good for much.

"Eddie!" Bo-bo said with real pleasure, greeting a long-lost friend, sitting down to a delicious meal. *"Ed*die! I've been dreamin' about this moment, Eddie! I hadda see the prick who had the unbelievable fuckin' balls to put his hands on *my* best friend's girl!"

"I didn't touch her," Eddie panted through his pain. "I swear, I AaaaAAAAAH!!" A crunching sound as Bo-bo wiggled his butt against the drawer. Sunny winced.

"Oh yes you did, you fat lying slob. I seen the bruise you put on her arm. Where else did you put your stinkin' hands on her? Look at me when I talk to you, Eddie!" He grabbed Eddie's beard in both fists and yanked his face up with a ripping noise. Eddie was grunting and sweating and grimacing. "Yeccch," Bo-bo said. "I was plannin' ta fuck ya, but you're too fuckin' ugly. Shit. I'll have to think of somethin' else." His face lit up with joyous inspiration. "How 'bout this?"

Bo-bo reared back and slapped Eddie harder than Sunny had ever seen anyone slapped in her life. It really needed a new word, from the vocabulary of high explosives. But even more amazing than the blow was its effect. "Oh please," Eddie blubbered in a high, childish voice. "Oh please. Don't kill me." His nose was running snot and blood.

"Eddie, I'm disappointed in you," Bo-bo said sorrowfully. "I thought you were a tough guy. I heard you like to fuck with little girls. Show me some a that, Eddie. Pleeeeease. Get tough with *me."* *Whap!* Bo-bo blasted him again, snapping his head to the side, cutting his lip.

Eddie's left hand rose to his mouth. Bo-bo hooked him in the gut. "Uuuhhh." Eddie's hand went protectively to his belly. *Blap!* Another open-handed blast. "Ooooff!" Another body shot. It was developing a rhythm, like the Anvil Chorus. Eddie gagged and spat blood. Bo-bo smacked him again. His right hand was as bloody as a butcher's.

Sasha and Gary were laughing uncontrollably. Sunny felt like she was going to throw up. She grabbed Sasha's arm. "Stop him, Sasha, that's enough!"

Sasha looked at her as if he were coming out of a pleasurable trance. In an insight like a lightning flash Sunny saw Bo-bo as a rogue fragment of Sasha, something escaped from the dungeons of her lover's psyche. She didn't think Sasha could enjoy beating someone to a bloody pulp, even someone really evil. There were too many civilized and complex counterforces in him. But he could and did fantasize about it. Bo-bo was his fantasy come to life, a golem that, once set loose, would go into painless, endless spasms of revenge.

It was Gary who spoke, in the forcefully soothing tones of a lion tamer. "Hey, you don't have to kill the bastid! Remember, I live here. I'm the one who'd feel the heat. Cool it!" He put a restraining hand on Bo-bo's arm, something Sunny would not have hazarded any more than she would have tapped a feeding shark on the shoulder.

But Bo-bo stopped. "Aw fuck," he panted, his daubed hands hanging by his sides. "This was just getting to be fun." Eddie bowed whimpering over the glass counter, cradling his crushed hand, watching fat drops of blood patter down from his nose. Sunny felt involuntary pity. "Eddie's a tough guy, ya know that?" Bo-bo sang out. "I love tough guys." He made a sudden little run at Eddie, and Eddie cringed.

Bo-bo held up his hands in the T-sign. "Time out," he bellowed.

"Here. Wipe your hand." Sasha tossed Bo-bo his folded handkerchief.

"Aaah, it'll just get dirty again. I still might decide to kill this piece a shit. 'S too much garbage in the world already, right, Sasha?" A husky melancholy had crept into Bo-bo's voice. But his face brightened when he used Sasha's handkerchief to open the drawer and held up a large blue-steel handgun. "See what our boy Eddie wanted to play with?"

"A .41 Magnum," Gary murmured with surprised respect.

Bo-bo checked the clip. "'S loaded."

Sunny's knees weakened as she realized the import of Bo-bo's antic leap over the counter.

"Don't leave any prints on it," Sasha warned.

"Prints? Shit, I ain't leavin' the *piece*. I can *use* this." Bo-bo stuck the gun in his waistband. He reached into the drawer again and held up Sunny's tape recorder.

"My baby!" Sunny held out her hands, and Bo-bo tossed it to her. She caught it in mid-air and clicked it on and off. To her relief, it still seemed to work.

Bo-bo had his arm deep in the drawer and a beatific smile on his face. Out came a fat roll of money. "I stuck in my thumb and I pulled out a plum," Bo-bo crowed. Riffling through the roll, he made a face as if the plum was sour. "Tens, fives and ones," he said with disgust. "You gotta do better than this, Eddie."

"Over there," Eddie wept, pointing frantically at the floor in the corner. "Panel. Take it all. Just please go away."

Bo-bo was down on his knees, running his long spatulate fingers along the baseboard. He found the section that lifted out, reached his long arm into the hole, and swept out a cigar box and a mess of photos and magazines.

The cold, square weight of the little tape machine in her hand concentrated Sunny's whole professional identity into one authoritative sensation. Suddenly she could move again. She went over to see what was in the cigar box. She hoped it was full of hex. It was full of cash—neat stacks of twenties and fifties bound with rubber bands.

"Yeee-haaah!" whooped Bo-bo, stuffing wads of bills into every pocket. "There's gotta be at least ten thousand. We'll split three ways, right, you guys?" All the bills out of sight, he patted himself with satisfaction. "What's *this* shit?" He pawed the pile of magazines and photos with the toe of his shoe.

With a physical shock Sunny saw a very large erection pointing at the bare bottom of a very young girl. The girl might have been eleven or twelve. All the rest of the photos and magazines appeared to be variations on the same theme. Sunny had never seen "kiddie porn" before. It was an ugly sight.

"Why, you child-molestin' mother-fucker," Bo-bo snarled, striding for Eddie like a guided missile.

"It's business, man! It's just business!" Eddie screamed hysterically, trying to cover both his head and his stomach. "I never made it with a chick under eighteen!"

"Bullshit. You was lookin' at this shit beatin' your meat when we knocked on the door. Hell, I bet you took them pictures yourself. That your dick? Huh?" Bo-bo grabbed Eddie by the hair and hauled the blubbering man around to face him.

"Let *me* have a shot at that scum," Sasha growled.

"Hey, leave something for me, will ya?" Gary protested. "I got a beautiful little niece that age."

"Wait a minute!!" Sunny screamed.

Her shrill female voice sliced through the funk of gathering violence. All four men froze, looking at her. Bo-bo stood with both fists in Eddie's beard like a kid caught with his hand in the cookie jar. Sasha and Gary looked surprised, as if they'd forgotten she was there. Eddie Cole looked at her, too, with the wet, adoring eyes of a dog, as if she had the power to save his life.

Well, maybe she did. If so, he would have to pay for it.

*　　*　　*　　*

"I think I have something to say about this," Sunny declared. "I'm the reason you guys came here. At least, I thought I was." She looked from one of them to the other, shaking her head. "Now how about helping me do my job? This motherfucker owes *me* something." She jabbed an angry finger at Eddie. "As long as we're here, I'm going to get what *I* came for. And that's information." Sasha saw both Gary and Bo-bo looking at her admiringly, and his heart swelled with pride. His Sunny! She hadn't acquired that kind of guts at Radcliffe. He felt as if he'd given birth to her himself.

Bo-bo was grinning from ear to ear. He dragged Eddie around by the beard to face Sunny and shoved him down on the store's one straight chair. "Take it away, babe," he said fervently. "You ask the questions, I'll do the question marks." *Whap!*—a backhand blast this time.

"Aw, no, man," Eddie whine-mumbled. "Don't have to do that. I'll tell her whever she wans'a hear."

"That's just what I was afraid of." Sunny tossed her hands in the air. "That kind of information is worthless. I don't want to hear what I want to hear. I want the truth."

Bo-bo looked sincerely puzzled "She doesn't want to hear what she wants to hear? I'm confused. You're confusing me, Eddie!" *Slam!* "Wait, I think I'm getting' it. She wants the truth. Oho, you been lyin' to her, Eddie?" *Blap! Bam!* Eddie moaned, and his head lolled.

"Will you make him stop!!" Sunny shrieked to Sasha. "This is serious!"

Sasha kept a straight face, but his body shook. Bo-bo was bad. He knew he shouldn't laugh, but between his friend's comic-innocent expression and demented logic, he could barely contain himself. Sunny had never had such a research assistant. Bo-bo was like Dr. Frankenstein's overenthusiastic lab technician who kept running too much voltage through the monster.

"Hey Bo-bo, let her ask a few questions, will you?" He cleared his throat to disguise the laughter.

Bo-bo threw him a look of conspiratorial mirth. "Sure, Sunny. Be my guest." He yanked Eddie's ponytail, and Eddie's head came up like a marionette's. His eyes were white half-moons, his face swollen and dreamy. Sasha had seen that look on boxers out for the count. Eddie must have a nice concussion by now.

With a hopeless shrug Sunny clicked on her tape recorder. "Eddie. Eddie, can you hear me?"

"Uuuuuuhhh…"

Sunny actually stamped her foot. "Will one of you goons please throw some water on him or something?"

Gary was by the door, watching the street. He left his sentry post, went through the doorway behind the counter, and came back through the clicking bead curtain with a glass of water, which he splashed in Eddie's face. Eddie shook his head and blinked blearily at Sunny. She looked sick, but she held her tape recorder steady in front of him.

"Do you sell hex to students?"

"Uh…huh…" The ruined remnant of a nod.

Gary chimed in. "And you use it to get your dick into the girls. It gives you the power, right, Eddie boy?" Gary suddenly dodged in like a boxer and plunged his fist deep into Eddie's soft gut. A good shot. Sasha felt it from both ends, in his own shoulder and belly. Eddie was doubled over, retching. Bo-bo yanked his head up again.

"I feel better now," Gary said, grinning. "Sorry, Sunny, go ahead."

"Jesus *Christ,*" Sunny groaned, glaring at Sasha as if to say, now all I need is for *you* to get into the act. She started to pace. "Are you the main distributor of hex for the Boston area?"

"Uh…uh." A barely perceptible shake of the head.

"Cambridge?"

No answer.

"Eddie, I don't hear nothing, Eddie," Bo-bo warned, juggling his right hand. "You lost your voice, Eddie?"

"Nnnnnn." Eddie shook his head with more force.

"Don't hit him again!" Sunny said sharply. Eddie raised his eyes to her like a castaway sailor who sees a lighthouse but thinks he's hallucinating. Dim hope dawned on his swollen face. He sat up straighter, a retarded pupil eager to please.

"Eddie, listen to me. *Where does the hex come from?*"

Eddie shook his head, and his shoulders began to heave. It was impossible to tell if he was crying or laughing. "…kill me," came out in a falsetto croak.

"Who? *Who*'ll kill you?" Sunny leaned closer.

"What's the difference who kills you," Bo-bo hollered, "me or them? When you're dead you're dead, you slime!"

"*Sa*sha…" Sunny said, part appeal, part warning.

Eddie gargled and rasped. To Sasha's surprise, his normally fastidious Sunny grabbed the empty water glass and held it forward with a nurse's brisk solicitude. Eddie spat stringy blood. Still holding the glass, Sunny pushed the tape recorder closer.

"Special ways," Eddie said quite clearly.

Sunny shook her head. "Special ways of what?"

"Kill you." He shook his head violently from side to side and then groaned, paying for it.

"Who are you talking about, Eddie? The people who give you the hex?"

Eddie raised one finger, let it drop.

"One person."

A nod.

"Let me guess. Mafia?"

"Naah. The Mob won't mess with shit like this," Bo-bo broke in. "Too small-time."

"Don't be too sure," Sasha said.

"From California?" Sunny tried.

Eddie started to shake his head and then shrugged.

"You don't know where he comes from—it is a he."

Nod.

Sunny sighed and straightened. "And here I thought Randy Flagg didn't exist." She put the bloody glass down, walked in a circle and came back. "The person who gives you the hex said he'd kill you in some special way if you tell anyone?"

Eddie shook his head.

Sunny put a hand in her hair, scowling in bewilderment. "Wait...The person who threatened you is not the same one who gives you the hex?"

Eddie said, "Boss."

"Someone here supplies the hex and the boss comes in to threaten you?" A nod. "But you don't know where he comes from." A shake. "How old is he?"

A shrug.

"What does he look like? Short? Tall?"

A nod, and then Eddie struggled to remember how to say something. His brain wasn't working well at all.

"...orna."

"What? Can you speak up?"

"Horner," Eddie said more loudly. Or it could have been "Warner," or "Forner." His swollen lips weren't working, either.

"Is that his name? Did you say 'Horner' or 'Warner'? Just nod your head. Is the boss's name Horner?"

No response. Station Eddie was fading out. Sunny spun away with a groan of aggravation.

"You're not doin' so good, Eddie." Bo-bo pranced restlessly, cracking his knuckles. "You don't tell her all about this Horner guy, you'll *wish* he got to you before I did." He shoved his face close to Eddie's and screamed, "Ya wamme to bite your nose off, you prick?"

"He's not kidding," Sasha said with theatrical awe. "He bit a guy's ear off up in Buffalo. Right, Bo-bo?"

"Yah, but I don't have a nose in my collection."

Suddenly Eddie stirred. With a physical effort he lifted his head and looked up at Bo-bo. "Fuck youuuu, maaaaan," he said in a voice past all caring."

"Did you hear that!!" Bo-bo said with joyous outrage. "Eddie's a tough guy after all!"

Sunny clapped her free hand over her eyes like a child. She must have believed that Bo-bo really was going to bite off Eddie's nose—and Sasha wouldn't have put it past him. But he didn't. He just smashed it in with a fist dead center. The chair went over backwards, and Eddie's head bounced on the floor. He slipped over to the side and lay curled in fetal position, snoring, blood bubbling from his nose. "Talk, motherfucker." Bo-bo kicked him in the back. "I don't hear you talking."

"How can he?" Sunny cried. "You've half killed him."

"All right, all right," Sasha said uneasily. His treacherous fellow feeling for the underdog had suddenly flared up. *He* was the one on the floor, the sadistic Russian guard kicking his ribs in. It was a weakness of his imagination that kept him from being as ruthless as he should be with a scumbag like this. He forced himself to picture Eddie hurting Sunny, raping a defenseless college girl. Then he felt better.

Bo-bo stalked back and forth above the fallen enemy. "Put your fuckin' hands on my brother's girl," he was muttering.

"Let's get out of here," Sunny wailed.

Bo-bo prowled behind the counter. He seemed in no hurry to leave. "I'm hungry. Got somethin' for me to eat, Eddie?" he said conversationally to the unconscious form on the floor. He rummaged a white paper bag out of the wastebasket, reached inside and tossed out a paper cup and a crumpled napkin stained mustard-yellow.

"For Christ's sake, we got all that fried chicken at home," Gary said. "Let's vamoose before we have any visitors."

"Well, lookit this." Bo-bo was holding up a fat white paper package. He laid it on the glass counter and undid it like a baby's diaper. Little yellow-and-black hornet-striped capsules rolled in all directions.

"That's hex!!" Sunny squealed. "Where did you find that?"

"In here." Bo-bo waved the white paper take-out bag. "In the wastebasket. Musta hid it in there when we knocked. Last place you'd think a looking." He started to scoop up the capsules and put them in his pockets with the cash.

"Let's leave it," Sunny said. There was a tremor in her voice, and Sasha realized that her teeth were chattering. "The c-cops could never catch him dealing. I'll call them from a payphone. Eddie won't be p-preying on any more girls."

"Shit, this stuff sells, right?" Bo-bo kept on scooping.

"No, leave it." Sasha held up a hand. "She's right. At least leave enough for them to nail him." He put his arm around Sunny and felt her shivering violently, reaction setting in.

As they went to the door Bo-bo yanked a thick fistful of T-shirts off their hangers and wadded them inside his jacket. "Eddie wants us all to have a little souvenir of this lovely evening." He blew Eddie a kiss. "Sleep tight, shitbeard."

Gary signaled that the coast was clear. Sasha closed the door gently on Eddie's snoring and the tinkle of rocking, empty hangers.

$*$ $*$ $*$ $*$

"Guess you never saw anyone get a beatin' before," June said sympathetically, handing Sunny a snifter of brandy. June had on her trophy, a hex-sign T-shirt.

Sunny wrapped her hands around the glass and shook her head. "It's not that," she kept saying to everyone who thought the blood bothered her. "It's not that." They were all acting as if she'd passed some kind of initiation rite. She was sitting on June's soft couch, with a blanket and Sasha's arm around her, and she couldn't stop shaking. The glass clicked against her teeth, and the healing heat of the brandy bloomed in her chest.

"D'ja see the way the shit started blubberin' when all I did was slap him in the face?" Bo-bo was in a good mood. He was wearing a brand-new Joker T-shirt and working on a new six-pack. "'Oh, please,'" he mimicked in a high falsetto voice. "'Don't kill me.'" The impersonation was uncanny. Sunny shivered harder.

Sasha pulled her close and tried to change the subject. "Hey, we *know* what happened tonight," he said jovially. "I wanna hear some more of those crazy stories from your after-hours days."

"Christ, there's so many of 'em," Bo-bo said obligingly. "I was with a nigger hooker upstairs a one a the after hours in Buffalo, and she rolled me. Picked my pocket. She was runnin' down the stairs naked, I was runnin' after her, I grabbed her, and she had on a fuckin' wig. I fell down the fuckin' stairs. I tumbled down the stairs naked, and I started drinkin' and playin' dice naked. So I go out and say, 'Give all the white people a drink, and fuck the niggers.' And I was the only white guy in the place."

Sasha and Gary roared. Sunny sipped her brandy and let their voices blur into a roisterous, comforting sound, like a huge hearth fire in a medieval castle. The next words she heard clearly were Sasha saying, "I think it's time to hit the prone position."

"Awww. The night's young," Bo-bo coaxed. "There any action around here, Gary? We c'd take this money and go gamblin'." Bo-bo and Gary had offered to divide the spoils four ways, honoring Sunny's equal status in their raid, but she'd declined. Each of the men was $3600 richer.

"Haven't you had enough action for one night?" Gary marveled. "I'm ready for a good night's sleep. Jesus. You did all the work and I'm tired."

"Not me. I'd like to get fifteen coon broads and make 'em run around naked an' whip 'em with pussywillows. Hey, I got an idea. We could take some a these, see what happens." He brought a handful of yellow-and-black capsules out of his side jacket pocket. "Whaddaya think? Should I pop a few, find out what all the excitement's about?" Bo-bo looked trustingly at Sunny. All she had to do was say "Sure, why not?" and in they'd go.

She stared at him with appalled admiration. Bo-bo threw himself into life the same way he threw himself downstairs or into the air: he held nothing back. Whether it was the animal trust that protects drunks and babies, or a darker indifference to whether he lived or died—or a bard's compulsion to live tellable stories—he was missing the normal hesitation of prudence. And that recklessness of his had saved their lives. If he'd hesitated for a split second when he heard the drawer open, one or more of them could've been killed. But Bo-bo's nervous system knew no delay between stimulus and response. Maybe it was fear he was lacking, and that was why he was so feared.

Bo-bo on hex…now, there was a notion. Sunny tried to imagine a Bo-bo without interpersonal boundaries, and decided she'd better discourage him. "The doctor told me there are some side effects," she said. "Impotence, muscle weakness…um…panic attacks…"

"Forget it." Bo-bo poured the hex back into his pocket and shook his hand as if to rid it of contamination. "I'll stick to Bud."

"Come on, Sunny." Sasha pulled her to her feet. "These nuts can stay up all night drinking and talking. We gotta catch an early train. The kittens are waiting for us."

"I turned on the heater on the waterbed for you," June said. "It oughta be nice and wahm by now. You feelin' better?"

"Yeah. Much better, thanks." She wasn't shivering any more. She kissed June, thanked Gary, and finally went over to Bo-bo. What was she supposed to say to him? "It's been real?"

"Thanks for saving our lives," was what she said.

"You're a great girl, Sunny," Bo-bo said with husky sincerity.

"And you're a—a poet of chaos, Bo-bo," Sunny said, not sure he would understand, but he beamed with pleasure. "Do me a favor. Find out who's dealing hex around SUNY Buffalo. Okay?"

"Sure, Sunny." Bo-bo grinned. "C'mon up and we'll pay him a visit."

When Sasha lay down on the warm waterbed, it heaved and glugged like a captive chunk of the Gulf Stream. "Down to the ships at sea," he said, trying to adjust his bulk comfortably and sending Sunny on an undulating wild ride that made her giggle.

"I miss the kittens." Sasha pushed his lower lip out like a child's. His broad face was all wistfulness. The menacing Sasha who had marched into "Randy's" with Bo-bo was as gone as if he had never existed. Sunny marveled at the way he could wipe the slate clean. It must be a valuable survival tactic when you'd had to see—and do—a lot of ugly things. Only now was *she* beginning to leave "Randy's."

"What made you shake like that?" Sasha asked abruptly. "I hope you didn't feel sorry for that piece of shit. Or was it Bo-bo? You don't ever have to be afraid of him. He's on your side."

"It wasn't that," Sunny said for the eighteenth time.

"So what was it?"

She sighed. "I saw a film clip once, on a show about Amnesty International. 'Viewer discretion advised.' I forget where it was, Iran or Chile, one of those places. It was this grainy, jerky, out-of-focus color film of someone being tortured and interrogated. One of the torturers held the guy's head in a bucket of water, and the other one asked the questions." She fell silent.

"Get to the point."

"Don't you see? I was in that film tonight." Hot tears ran down from the corners of Sunny's eyes into her ears. "I was the one asking the questions."

"You jerk, you," Sasha scolded gently, rearing up on his elbow, setting the waterbed aflutter. "Don't you know what that creep was going to do to you? He would have raped your body *and* your mind. You could have been permanently damaged."

"Are you saying that one evil makes another evil right?"

"Sometimes you got to fight fire with fire. Next time Eddie wants to hurt a little girl, he'll remember Bo-bo and think twice."

"Well, maybe I'm just not a firefighter. I don't ever want to be in that position again."

"Then you never will be. C'mere." He pulled her into the crook of his body. "At least now you know something you didn't know before. You're looking for a guy named Horner. That could be the key to the whole thing."

"He stuck in his thumb and he pulled out a plum," Sunny murmured.

"What?"

"Nothing. It's just a nursery rhyme. 'Little Jack Horner.'"

"I'll ask Georgie if he's heard the name. Could be a made guy, or a free-lance. When you call up your California people, ask them if *they* know this Horner. Between the two of us, we'll find him."

"Mmmmmm." She wasn't thrilled with the lead. Eddie's enunciation hadn't been very clear, and Bo-bo had put his lights out before she could get him to repeat it. But she was too exhausted to worry about it right now.

Sasha curled around her back, "spooning" her. Soon his hands found the curve of her hipbones, and the waterbed began to rock. Sunny made a complaining noise. It stopped.

"What's the matter now?"

"Violence doesn't turn me on."

The waterbed registered Sasha's indignation. "Do you think it turns *me* on? *You* turn me on! But you're right. Let's go to sleep. It's better at home."

The waterbed subsided, and so did Sasha. In a minute he was snoring. Sunny lay with her eyes open for a long time.

CHAPTER 6

▼

"Blue!!"

Sasha dropped their overnight bag and swept the Siamese up in his arms. It felt as if he'd been away from the kittens for a month, not just a day. How was he going to survive a week in Romania? Blue was purring, with a fond, humorous, ever so slightly cross-eyed expression on his dark-brown face. Several more cats wound around Sasha's legs and complained about his absence.

He heard the answering machine twitter and clack as Sunny rewound the messages. As eager as he was to bury his face in Blue, she could never wait to get her hands on the answering machine and the mail. Now she had one hand on the machine and the other absently stroking Olly, the crooked-tailed tabby who loved her so much that he would escort her to the bathroom in the middle of the night and pee when she peed. It wasn't fair. She had a natural bond with animals that Sasha would have killed for, and she took it completely for granted. The kittens got in her lap, lay on her chest, as they never would with him, and she was always pushing them aside to read some stupid magazine. Sasha adored the cats and served them like an ancient Egyptian. Sunny treated them with casual equality, as if she were a cat herself. He'd seen her play chase with them, wrestle and bite them, express her displeasure by hissing, and even do her best to purr. He guessed grudgingly that she loved them as much as he did, in her own way.

A cough of static, and the answering machine said "Hi, Sunny." Sasha recognized Darlene's voice. "Just wanted to see how you're doing on the hex beat. Did you see the story in the *Times* this morning? The one about the two sixteen-year-old suicides in Colorado?"

"Shit," Sunny said under her breath.

"If you didn't, run out and get it. I'll clip it for you, too. I'm sure you'll want to follow up on that. In the meantime, it's total chaos up here. We're up against the June fifteen deadline, and Kalish comes in with last-minute rewrites again. Oh! And I met this man I'm dying to tell you about. I'm really worried—I can't find anything wrong with him! When do you leave for Romania? Lunch next week if you can make it. Love to Sasha. 'Bye!"

"Jesus Christ," Sasha grumbled. "Doesn't her jaw ever get tired?"

A beep, and the street roar of a payphone. "Sasha. Georgie. Call me." Beep.

"Now *that's* a message," Sasha said approvingly.

"This is Patty Woo's office calling Sasha. You have an audition tomorrow at 4:20 at Our Studios, 633 Broadway at Bleecker, fifth floor. The project is 'Fearful Symmetry,' a feature film, and the character is Pavlovich, 'a heavy-set, ruthless Russian general.' Please confirm. Thank you!" Beep.

"A *Russian* thug this time," Sunny commented.

"This is Armand at Destinations Unlimited," said a deep, accented voice. "Your tickets for Romania are ready. Why you want to go to such a godforsaken country I do not know. You are completely crazy. Come pick them up any time. Thank you, ma'am." Beep.

"That's it." Sunny rewound the tape. "I've got to go out and get the *Times*. Did you hear that, Sash? Hex killed two more kids." Her eyes shone with front-line fever. Next thing she'd want to fly out west to interview the grieving parents.

"You stay right here," Sasha said firmly. "The kittens need you, and you need some lunch. You're not going to save any lives by running out to buy the *Times* right now. Don't you think it's more important to find out what Georgie has for you?"

Sunny brightened. "So call him!"

Sasha looked at his watch. "He's sleeping at his mother's now. And he's not going to say anything on the phone. Tell you what. You were always bugging me to take you to the after-hours place. Tomorrow morning I'll get you up at five, with the help of some dynamite, and we'll go up there and see Georgie." What the hell. Now that she'd watched Bo-bo slap the shit out of that asshole, why shelter her any longer from the Grand Guignol of the night world? Let her see for herself.

Sunny admitted that she *was* hungry, so Sasha made them a couple of toasted bagels with cheese. Then they walked to the health club, Sunny buying the *Times* on the way and starting to read it on the street, so that Sasha had to guide her steps like a seeing-eye dog.

In the hot whirlpool bath, bubbling like a cannibal's cauldron, she told him about the story. A boy and girl, sixteen, had cut school, locked themselves in the girl's father's garage while their parents were at work, turned the key on her Camaro, and killed themselves with carbon monoxide. It wasn't so different from the rash of teen-age suicides in Texas and New Jersey a few years ago, except that these kids had left a strange note. The Earth was dying, they said, so they had become one and gone ahead, leaving their bodies behind because they wouldn't need them. Three capsules of hexamethylene had been found in the boy's pocket.

Sunny seemed to find this story tragic. To Sasha it was just bewildering, like so many things about his adopted country. Nearly forty years here, and he still couldn't understand how people could sit in the midst of such plenty and be miserable. "How old did you say these kids were?"

"Sixteen." At sixteen he'd been fighting to stay alive, without so much as a pair of socks, a bar of soap, or a warm jacket.

"This girl had her own car? What is a sixteen-year-old doing with her own car?"

"I suppose her parents gave it to her." Sunny sounded embarrassed. "It's a pretty typical suburban sixteenth-birthday present."

"She has her own car, a full refrigerator, a healthy young body, a horny boyfriend, and she kills herself because of some drug fantasy??" His voice scaled a peak of incredulity. "Who made them take that drug? Was somebody pointing a gun at them?"

"Keep it down, will you?" yelled an angry-looking fat girl at the other end of the whirlpool. "Some of us come here for peace and quiet." She glared at Sasha and then closed her eyes in pious meditation.

"Fuuuuck youuuu," Sasha gave her a sendoff into Nirvana.

"Come on, Sash," Sunny argued in a low voice, under the noise of the bubbles. "You're always talking about what we've done to the planet, saying no one should have kids and make them live through what's ahead. Dr. Goodman says these kids are feeling that despair. You wouldn't want to be sixteen years old now."

"Oh no? It's a whole lot better than being sixteen years old in Mine Twenty-eight," Sasha said. "Give me the full refrigerator, and let them dig coal in Russia if they're in such a hurry to die. They'll change their minds." He was sweating with anger now as much as the heat. He got up heavily out of the whirlpool and put his earplugs in his ears to go float in the pool. What this society needed was a good dose of reality to straighten it out.

But he admitted to himself as he sank into the pool that he felt sorry for those rotten spoiled junkie kids. They had everything, yes, except for the great thing he'd grown up with: clear values, black and white, and a strong father to divide them with a blow of his hand, like God dividing day from night. Without that you were lost in a wilderness of options. Sunny often told him he should run a camp for fucked-up kids, give them love and discipline. It wasn't a bad idea, but he'd rather help the animals. They were innocent. Sasha resented having to think about those kids and be confused by the confusion they faced. It wasn't his problem. He liked that line of Bogart's in "Casablanca": "I'm the only cause *I'm* interested in."

What he wondered as he floated on his back on the Styrofoam kickboard, the blue water cooling his mood, was whether there wasn't a score in this story of Sunny's. He'd been thinking about that ever since he saw Eddie Cole's cash stash in the cigar box. How much of a take did that $10,800 represent? A month? A week? Multiply that by every dealer in every college town…Or look at it another way. The girl who'd led Sunny to the head shop had guessed there were a hundred thousand users. Take that as a ballpark figure. If each of them took the drug once a week, at four to six dollars a capsule—he remembered Dan Rather saying that like it was yesterday—four to six hundred grand a week. Probably two, three times that. Even skimming off the street profit, where was the money going?

Eddie Cole had given them a clue.

Supposing Georgie got a line on this Horner/Warner guy. Sasha would ask for a meeting with Don Chaluch' and propose an operation. Take them off and split up a couple million. Now *that* was something worth doing. And Sunny could still have her precious scoop.

When the alarm went off at five the next morning it was still dark. Sunny groaned, rolled over and sank back into sleep. Sasha, as always instantly wide awake and cheerful, swung his legs out of bed and went to make Turkish coffee. He brought Sunny a cup and tried to wake her up kindly. It had taken him a while to understand that she didn't see the morning as a friend, bringing the astounding gift of another day of life. Morning didn't smile on Sunny, it scowled and shook its finger and dumped the day's load of obligations on the bed. So Sasha tried to be patient.

"Little Sunny."

"Mmmmmmmmm." A sorrowful moan.

"Here's your coffee, my baby."

"Pu' over there f'ra minute," waving a hand at the windowsill. "Jus' gimme a minute, pleeeeeease."

Three minutes later, his tone already crisper: "It's five fifteen, Sunny."

"Waaait. 'm trying to 'member my dream…"

At five twenty Sasha lost it. "You're a pain in the ass," he roared. "I'm doing this for you, for your story. Well, fuck you *and* your story. I'll go up and see Georgie, and we'll have a nice breakfast and some laughs."

Sunny scrambled out of bed and groped for her glasses. "I'm coming with you."

"Who, you? Sleeping Beauty? Go back to sleep. Dream."

"Why do you have to be so nasty in the morning?"

"I give up!" Sasha looked up at the skylight for help.

"The city's beautiful this early in the morning!" Sunny said with wonder as they rode up clean and empty First Avenue in a cab. She had enough caffeine in her to wire an elephant. "You should get me up more often."

"Not on your life," Sasha groaned.

They left the cab at 74th and walked the last block. A white Cadillac and a long black limousine in front of 475 East 75th hinted at the high life behind the blind façade. Sasha's practiced eye flicked over the cars. He didn't recognize the Caddy, but these wiseguys changed cars every year. Steam pulsed from the limo's tailpipe. It had DPL plates. Some Arab consul bringing his oil prince to gamble? Diplomatic immunity covered a multitude of sins.

Sunny was enthralled by the little sliding window in the door. "Just like a real speakeasy!"

"It *is* a real speakeasy." Sasha tapped, eyeballed Salvi, and the door opened to them.

"Ooooh," Sunny said, caressing her bare arms as the throbbing beat enveloped her. Sasha knew he wouldn't be able to keep her off the dance floor.

"Salvi, this is my girl Sunny."

"I've heard a lot about'cha," Salvi said, shaking her hand. Sasha caught the involuntary flick of the little guy's eyes down Sunny's body. Sleepy as she was, her vanity had been awake, and she'd put on a short, clingy black-and-white striped shift, white high-heeled sandals that showed off her taut legs, and dangly black-and-white earrings. In the after-hours club she wouldn't be judged by her I.Q.; okay, she was willing to play on that game board, too. She wanted Sasha to be proud of her. He was prouder than she knew.

"You know what 'speakeasy' is in German?" he yelled to her as they started up the red-carpeted stairs. *"Flüsterkneipe."*

"'Whisper tavern'!" Sunny squealed with delight. Sasha had never dreamed he'd find someone who got as big a kick out of words as he did.

As they reached the top of the stairs, two men in dark leather coats burst out the door on a gust of violence. "Watch it!" Sasha shouted at the two thugs, shielding Sunny with his body. "What the fuck you think you're doing?" But they weren't looking at him, they were looking up at the doorway, at the furious, flaming-cheeked face of C.J. East, the magician.

"The next time I see your ugly face, I'm going to kick your ass all the way back to Budapest," drawled C.J.

"You will pay for this, I pro-mice you," said one of the men in a cold, unpleasant voice, hurrying down the stairs with offended dignity. Close to six feet, big-boned, gaunt, damp-looking sallow skin, heavy black eyebrows, harsh lines slashed down beside the mouth, glint of metal teeth. No problem physically, Sasha thought, one good shot to the gut, but you'd have to move fast; the man was a snake, treachery smoked off him like cold off a reptile's skin. The other one was the muscle, a hulking pinhead, barely able to turn his head over his shoulder as he followed close behind his boss.

"Men'yo fekete vologabo," Sasha called cheerfully after them in his foulest Hungarian, and they were out the door and gone.

"What was *that* all about?" Sunny squirmed out from between him and the wall.

"You finished with them? Want me to bring 'em back for you?" Sasha said to C.J.

Margie appeared in the doorway. "Sasha!" she shrieked. "Did you see him? That's him!!"

"That's who?"

"Dracula!"

And there was Georgie. "Hey, Sasha," he said in his usual tired way. "Yeah, that was that guy that's been messin' with her, the asshole from your country."

"My country?" Sasha turned to C.J. "I thought you said Budapest." He almost had to shout to be heard over the disco music.

"Isn't Budapest in Romania?" C.J. yelled back.

"No, that's Bucharest. So that was Dracula! Why didn't you tell me? I didn't even call him a dirty name in the right language! Did he hurt you?" he demanded of Margie.

"Not with me around," C.J. interjected.

"Hurt me? He's the classic Continental lover," Margie shuddered. "He sends two dozen roses. Then he comes in and slobbers all over me and asks for my phone number. I've seen some creeps in my day, but— I don't know. This one scares me. Hiiii, Sunnnyyyy." The two friends shared a long consoling embrace.

"I only saw him for a second, but he scared *me,"* Sunny said over Margie's shoulder. "Sasha—he had on a leather coat!"

Sasha nodded. A lot of *securitate* agents in Romania wore leather coats or jackets, a status symbol that gave them away as surely as black shoes and white socks betrayed the F.B. I. The encounter was a chill wind from their forthcoming trip, a bad omen. Was it really nothing more than a coincidence? How could the man have known he was coming today? Was his phone tapped? But he hadn't called Georgie…

"Guess we'll hafta eighty-six the creep," Georgie said reluctantly. "He's a live one, though," meaning a big spender.

"Don't let him get away!" Sasha willed a heartiness to mask his forebodings. "I'll be in the mood to talk to him when we get back from Romania. Margie, keep him dangling a little longer if you can stand it. Then we'll arrange a tryst in the basement. C.J. can come along. Sunny, meet C.J. East, the best magician this side of Madagascar."

C.J. kissed Sunny's hand, and she yelped with surprise to find a carnation in it.

"Got something for me?" Sasha said aside to Georgie. Georgie jerked his head towards his office. Sasha pointed questioningly at Sunny. Georgie hesitated, then shrugged. In that half-second his eyes, too, had summed up Sunny's body. Sensual approval settled on his face.

"Hi, Georgie." She came over to give him a kiss on the cheek.

"Hey, Sunny. Good to see ya." They were two highly intelligent creatures from different planets who regarded each other with uncomprehending respect.

Sunny and Sasha followed Georgie as he cut a path through the crowd towards his office. Each time Sasha introduced "my girl Sunny," both men and women welcomed her with great warmth, like a member of the family. Later on he'd tell her she'd been kissed by a madam, complimented by a bank robber, and had shaken the hand of a contract killer. Sunny was as nosy as a cat about any world normally closed to her; it pleased him that acceptance into this one was a gift only he could give her.

Georgie closed the door of his office and set up folding chairs for them both. Sunny crossed her legs and took out her notebook. Her full attention was on Georgie, but her foot had a life of its own, jigging in time to the beat.

Georgie sat down and eyed Sasha cannily. "Whaddaya hear from Bo-bo? That crazy Polack." Before Sasha could say a word, Georgie said, "I heard he did a job on a guy up in Boston."

Sasha whistled. "Bad news travels fast!"

"*Good* news," Georgie said. "The people up there weren't happy with this guy. They say he used to move a lotta coke for them, but then he got into this new thing, *your* thing"—he pointed at Sunny—"and he started holdin' out on 'em. They were gettin' ready to lean on him. Bo-bo saved 'em the trouble." Georgie chuckled. "I heard there was a couple other big guys with him."

Sasha grinned. "Bo-bo sends his best. How'd you get the word?"

"Guy's lawyer's connected. They say the cops got a tip, found this drug and dirty kid stuff all over the place. Had to throw water on the guy to read him his rights." Sunny threw Sasha a triumphant look. "He wakes up in the prison ward squealing to his lawyer about some killer from Buffalo. Lawyer says surprise, pal, you ain't makin' bail. They let him take the fall and washed their hands. At least, that's what I heard." Sunny had observed that Georgie always distinguished carefully between what he knew only by hearsay and what he'd seen with his own eyes, a piece of preliterate savvy she said he shared with the grammar of Hopi. "I got a call on it 'cause I'd put out the word I wanted to know the score on this hex shit."

"What else did you find out?" Sunny asked. Sasha started to ask about Horner, but she waved him silent. No leading questions.

Georgie lit a Lucky and blew smoke out in a dissatisfied hiss. "Not too much," he said. "Yet. Nobody's seen a shipment. Nobody's been offered a distributorship. Shit seems like it's goin' from nowhere straight on the street. These people, whoever they are, they got their own pipeline to the street, like the fuckin' Colombians."

Sunny made a note.

"Now for the right price, the spics'll sell you a kilo or ten. They're stone fuckin' crazy, sure, but they ain't fussy. If your money's green…" Georgie shrugged. "See, none of our people tried to move in on this.

They ain't into hurtin' kids. But I got a *paisan'* owes me a favor, he's puttin' the word out he's interested. They smell top dollar, they'll come outta the woodwork. Then we'll see what we got. Gimme a week, tops.

"You ever hear the name Horner?" Sasha couldn't contain it any longer.

"Or Warner?" Sunny added. "Or even Forner."

"Mmmm." Georgie cocked his head, letting the names carom around in his memory. He shrugged. "Warner Brothers makes cartoons. 'That's all, folks.' All I watched, one time I was hidin' out."

Sasha told him about Eddie Cole's reference to the "boss" who had threatened him with death.

"I'll run the name past some a my people," Georgie said. "And I'll tell my man, shoot for a meetin' with the boss."

"If he gets a meeting with him," Sunny leaned forward, "can we tape it?"

"Slow down," Georgie said with lazy amusement. "We ain't even rung the guy's bell yet." Georgie didn't know from deadlines. In his world, too much of a hurry could make you dead.

"One thing's for sure," Sunny said to Sasha. "With a name like Warner or Horner, he isn't Colombian."

"Plenty of German blood in South America," Sasha warned. "Carlos Lehder's as Colombian as they come."

"I'll bet he turns out to be a garden-variety American." Sunny turned back to Georgie. "It smells like an old-hippie thing to me."

Georgie shrugged. He wasn't big on theories. "We'll wave the green flag and see who comes outta the bushes."

"If Georgie says he'll do it, it's done," Sasha said sternly. "When we get back from Romania, your mystery will be solved."

Georgie waved the flattery away. "Take it easy. I ain't Shylock Holmes." A laugh burst out of Sunny, and Georgie, unaware of his Brooklyn accent, chuckled too.

Sunny put her notebook away and gave Sasha her I-want-something look. "Can I dance now?"

Sasha clapped a hand to his head. "I was afraid of this," he groaned, playing to Georgie. "Now you won't be able to close the place. She'll still be going strong at three in the afternoon. Who are you gonna dance with out there?" he challenged Sunny. "A goombah from Staten Island or some drunk, fucked-up tourist from Jersey? What if he starts putting his hands all over you?"

"Why don't *you* dance with me, then?"

"Oh no," Sasha said. "You aren't getting me to dance to that horrible rock'n'roll. Give me goood jaazzz," he spread the word out like a soothing ointment. Privately he'd admitted to Sunny with surprise that he liked the energy of rock, but it wasn't part of his public image.

"All right." Sunny sighed. "Then I'll dance with Margie. How's that?"

And that was what she did. Margie got the other barmaid to cover for her, and she and Sunny worked their way out among the writhing bodies and went at it. Sasha watched from the edge of the dance floor. Margie was just a little bit better, he observed, feeling disloyal. She was inventive, bizarre, uninhibited, and her pelvis seemed hung on a well-oiled hinge. Her dancing never forgot seduction, while Sunny's was more self-contained and athletic; she seemed intent on getting on the beat, like a body-surfer catching a wave. When she caught it just right she'd spring joyously into the air, as if she'd escaped gravity.

As they danced on, though, Sasha could see her watching Margie and trying to imitate her, loosening up, moving her hips more. A mood of affectionate competition had possessed them both. The dance was turning into a sexual challenge match. Sasha was scandalized and aroused to see the Sunny only he knew in bed beginning to show on the dance floor, in this public place. He was sure that every man in the club was looking at her. He was as embarrassed as if she'd flung off all her clothes. He felt a strong need to get her home, to hide her and to have her. The next time the two girls looked his way, he scowled and made an angry beckoning gesture. Sunny came, looking crestfallen.

"Aww, you're such a spoilsport."

"Yeah!" Margie protested. "It was just getting good."

"You told me you needed to work all day today," Sasha scolded.

Sunny sighed. "Well, pal, it was great while it lasted." She and Margie fell into each other's arms, cackling like witches.

In the taxi going downtown Sasha said, "I don't like it when you dance like that."

"Like what?" Sunny was all innocence.

"You know exactly what I'm talking about. That's private, between you and me."

"But Margie dances like that." Sunny sounded genuinely surprised. "You love the way she dances. Why is it okay for her and not for me?"

"Margie's not my girlfriend."

"Oh." She seemed to grow taller. "Would you like to cover me from head to toe, like a Muslim woman?"

"Don't give me that libbie shit," Sasha said. "You're so dumb. You have no idea how sexy you are. You give every man in the place a hard-on, how is it not supposed to bother me?"

"Don't exaggerate."

"Is this an exaggeration?" He took her hand and plopped it in his lap.

"*Sasha!!*" Startled and prim. "We're in a *taxi!* This is a public place!"

"Uh huh! See how *you* like it." He craned and peered around the driver, willing him to move faster, cursing when he saw an opening the driver missed.

They had never made wilder love. Sunny sweated like she had on the dance floor, her flesh slippery, damp hair clinging to her forehead.

"Oh my God," she panted, stretched out on the bed. "How'm I ever going to get in the mood for work?" A moment later she struggled upright, slid off the bed naked and went to run a bath. Guilt and ambition never let Sunny luxuriate for long. Sasha knew he wouldn't see her for the rest of the day. She was worried about getting enough work done before they left; she had to do phone interviews with Colorado, and set up her trip to Berkeley as soon as they got back. She'd be on the phone and at the computer, all business, the wanton Sunny hidden away inside where no one would suspect its existence. She didn't even look up when Sasha left.

He went first to Armand's travel agency to pick up the tickets. Armand was a Balkan Robin Hood who loved outwitting the airlines for his friends. He always got them incredible deals. When Sasha pushed open the door, Armand came out of the back room with a velvety chuckle and an ash-flaking Salem hanging from his lips. Sasha was struck again by his resemblance to she short, stocky, gap-toothed character in the Charles Addams cartoons. Armand was hardly older than Sasha, but he looked well over sixty, with his silver hair, humor-seamed face, and stiff movements. Like Brooklyn Georgie's, his lifestyle might have had something to do with it: the ashtray on his desk overflowed with butts, and he opened his desk drawer and proffered a half-empty quart of Teacher's.

Sasha shook his head. His eyes had been drawn helplessly to the contour map of Romania on the wall, to his hometown at the knee of the Carpathians. Unpleasant feelings fought in his chest. He longed for that beautiful little town in his memory; he hated going there and seeing what had become of it.

Armand poured half a drinking glass of Scotch and tossed it down. His eyes followed Sasha's, and he shook his head. "It's a fucking tragedy," he said in his deep, smoky voice. "But what can you do?" The two of them contemplated the map like mourners at a close relative's coffin.

"Why doesn't somebody kill that crazy son of a bitch?" Sasha didn't have to say who he meant. Their unfortunate homeland had survived plagues, floods, wars, Mongol, Turkish and Tatar invasions, only to be destroyed by one man: its own president.

Armand rummaged in the mess of papers on his desk and handed Sasha a thick envelope "It's your funeral," he said, quickly adding "*Kinahora*"—the Jewish charm against the evil eye, followed by a morbid chuckle. "You heard about that *Newsweek* reporter who just got kicked out? You didn't? They questioned him for two days, roughed him up, took away his notes, and put him on a plane. Tell Sunny to be careful."

"They don't know she's a reporter."

"Come on," Armand scoffed. "They've got a file on you this thick. I love you, you big *goniff*. Don't do anything stupid, like change money with a *securitate* agent."

Worrying about the trip now, Sasha's mind wasn't going to be on the audition. He looked at his watch, striding toward the subway.

"'Scuse me!" a voice called behind him. "'Scuse me, sir?"

Sasha turned around and saw a bright-faced black kid on roller skates, wearing the winged cap of a messenger service. "Didn't I see you in 'Trading Places'?"

The look on the kid's face was so eager, Sasha's heart expanded like rising bread. He stuck out his hand, and the kid grabbed it with a big grin. "Wow! All right, mister! You got any more movies comin' out?"

"I'm going to read for one right now," Sasha said.

"Hey! Good luck, okay? I'll be lookin' for you!"

"Who loves you??" Sasha hollered, spreading his arms as the kid skated away. *See, Sunny? There's no excuse.* Here was a kid who had two strikes against him, because he was black, and yet he obviously wasn't on drugs. Spoiled suburban wimps threw their lives away. The winged messenger loved life, and Sasha loved him for it. It was a good omen. He felt confident now that he would get the part.

The casting agent's waiting room looked like the back ward of a state mental hospital. People of a grotesque assortment of sizes and shapes sat on hard benches around the walls, moving their lips and mugging as they studied pages of script. It was easy to spot the competition for the Russian general. There were three other fiftyish men in the waiting room. They had foreign faces and the soft bodies of character actors. None of them had military presence. It would be a breeze. Sasha signed in, took his "sides," and read through his lines without moving his lips. It was a matter of pride. The Brooklyn Georges of the world moved their lips.

The director was a middle-aged Englishman in wire-rimmed glasses. He looked up from Sasha's resumé, in which Sunny, over Sasha's protests, had included "Prisoner in Russia—escaped." "Have you ever been interrogated by the K.G.B.?" It sounded ridiculous in that British accent.

"Yes," Sasha answered curtly, his heart sinking at the uselessness of his experience. What good was reality if the director wanted a Hollywood-fantasy Russian general? Oh, well. The script was surprisingly good. Sasha put on his glasses and began to read. As he imagined being General Pavlovich, the authority of his military forebears flooded into him.

The Brit was impressed; Sasha saw it in his face. He hadn't given the man enough credit. "Veddy, veddy good," the director said. "Will you be available in two weeks?"

Sasha said he would, and the director said he'd be in touch. The general's scenes would be shot in a studio in Toronto. As he walked home, Sasha realized that if he got the part, he wouldn't be able to go out to California with Sunny. Well, if necessary, he'd just have to send Bo-bo along to protect her.

Packing for Romania was always a pain in the ass. Sasha took the bare minimum for himself—two pairs of pants, two shirts. He made Sunny take more clothing; she couldn't shatter their friends' fantasies about Americans by wearing the same thing every day. But three-quarters of their suitcase space was filled with chocolate bars, toothpaste, cans of coffee and tuna, dog and cat food for their malnourished animal friends, cartons of cigarettes, vitamins, Levis, Nikes.

Sunny, working frantically on her article, made Sasha do all the shopping. He could barely drag her away to the dojo; then after class she got into a long huddle with Pierre, of all unlikely people, and he had to drag her back home to finish packing. By the night before their departure they were screaming at each other.

"What did you just put in the suitcase?"

"My tape recorder. And some notes, and paper. I have to transcribe my interviews with the Colorado Springs police chief and the boy's mother."

"Take it out. All of it. Are you trying to get us arrested?"

"Sasha, I can't stop working on this for a whole week!"

"So work on it in your head! You know anything like tapes or papers makes them suspicious." Sunny sullenly lifted her work out of the suitcase, but he had a feeling she might try to sneak it in again when his back was turned.

By Wednesday Sunny was starting to get excited about the trip, in spite of herself. Sasha was starting to get seriously apprehensive, as he always did. At four P.M they double-checked their passports, tickets, and cash, said a mournful goodbye to the kittens, who stared at them with hurt reproach, and lugged the heavy suitcases downstairs to the Train to the Plane. Sasha sweated like a bitter fountain. "This is the last time," he swore to himself.

As he always did.

CHAPTER 7

━━━━━━━━━ ▼ ━━━━━━━━━

"Look at the faces," Sasha muttered to Sunny as they sat down in the little bus that would take them from the Pan Am plane to the terminal at Otopeni Airport.

"Look at the machine guns," Sunny murmured back. The bus was being guarded like a prison transport by very young, very serious soldiers in dull green uniforms. Their contemporaries in America were swallowing hex, smoking crack, toting boom boxes, spiking their hair. This was a different world, and as if in recognition of that fact, the new arrivals were isolated and herded along as if they bore some decadent virus.

Sasha was exhausted and wretchedly uncomfortable. He hadn't slept all night on the transatlantic flight, nor had he been able to sleep in the big black lounge chairs in Frankfurt International Airport. At the gate in Frankfurt, where they'd boarded the smaller plane for Bucharest, he'd begun to be oppressed by the faces: sly, sensual, corrupt, complacent, unmistakably Balkan, incurably Communist. It was mostly big shots and spies who could afford to travel, and there they were, waiting for the plane in their leather coats and shiny shapeless brown suits, with their well-fed paunches, manicured hands and amused, opportunistic little eyes.

Now, packed together on the bus, Sasha smelled the body odor in their badly-cleaned suits and felt Romania closing in on him. His dread always focused on the passage through Customs, even though, as Sunny reminded him, he wasn't carrying anything illegal and had nothing to fear. "You still have a guilty conscience from your black-market days," Sunny astutely guessed. After he'd escaped from Russia, he'd crossed too many borders with contraband watches in his pockets, saccharin pills strapped to his ankles, and adrenaline screaming through his veins. Sunny knew these tales from reading his second book, *Black Market Blues.*

She was bright-eyed now, looking all around. Of course she didn't share his insomniac fear. How could she? To her this trip was an adventure. He didn't know which he envied more, her unscarred psyche or her small body. While he'd struggled in vain to get comfortable in his plane seat, she'd curled up like a cat and read every hex story in the *Times, Post* and *Newsday.* She'd exulted to Sasha that nobody had a clue yet where the drug was coming from, so maybe she'd have her scoop if Georgie came through. Then she'd eaten her veggie meal, drunk a glass of wine, and gone to sleep. She'd slept some more in Frankfurt. As a result, she was as fresh as anyone with jet lag could be, while Sasha felt heavy, sour and sandy-eyed.

"I recognize the smell," she said as they were shepherded into the gloomy airport. Sasha recognized it, too: a damp, brown, disconsolate smell, the night-sweat smell of poverty and fear that hung over this country like a pall.

At Otopeni Airport, with typical Romanian logic, you went through a security check when you got *off* the plane. As they waited in line to put their bags through the old X-ray machine, the uniformed security officer stared at Sasha with suspicion. He and Sunny were the only Americans on the flight, except for a nervous new citizen who had fled Romania eight years ago and had come back to visit her elderly parents for the first time. Sasha knew he and Sunny stood out in this drab line, that a waft of prosperity and freedom came off them. It was all summed up in the two smart blue-and-silver passports he slapped down on the counter. Even the officer looked at them with envy. Those little booklets were concentrated power, magic fragments of the United States. Sasha would clutch his, like a cross against vampires, even when he went to his mother's outhouse in the middle of the night.

After they walked through the metal detector, Sasha lost sight of Sunny for a moment while she went into a separate curtained booth to be searched by a security matron. A uniformed male guard felt his armpits and the insides of his legs. The guard's hand suddenly stopped, feeling a small, square box in his side jacket pocket.

"Aveti tigar?" the guard asked in a low, avid voice.

Sasha reached into his pocket and handed the guard the pack of Kents. American Kent cigarettes were Romania's black-market currency. No one was immune to their allure; they could melt the sternest policeman into a wheedling panhandler. *It still works,* Sasha thought, and he began to feel a little better.

They were standing in line for Passport Control when they heard the scream.

"No, no, oh my God!!!" Every head in the sparsely populated airport turned towards this shocking rip in the dull fabric of regimentation. It came from the frail woman in the black fake-fur coat who had come back to visit her parents. She launched into a flood of imploring, scorching Romanian.

Sunny grabbed Sasha's arm. "Is she crazy? What's she saying?"

"They've refused her a visa," Sasha murmured. "Her parents are outside waiting for her, and they won't let her see them. They're sending her back on the next plane."

"But *why??*"

"She defected. Now they're punishing her."

The woman had switched back to accented English. "Please, you must let me see the parents!! They are waiting me! My father is not well, you will kill him!...At least bring the parents here to me! Oh, please, I want to see my father before he die!...Criminals! *Criminals!!*"

Sasha felt cold in the pit of his stomach. Here it was, the power that had framed *his* father in the tiny window of a boxcar and decreed that that should be their last sight of each other. The boxcar had jolted into motion, sixteen-year-old Sasha had fallen away from the window sobbing, and his fate had begun. His father had died almost twenty years later, before *détente* made it safe for Sasha to return.

Sunny was tugging at his arm. "Should I go talk to her?" she asked in a horrified whisper. "At least I could get her story in the American press."

Compassion briefly fought self-preservation in Sasha, and lost. "We better mind our own business," he whispered.

The woman was still wailing like a siren, broadcasting words that are never even whispered in Romania. Damage control had already begun. Two bulky men in sports jackets came through a partition, walked briskly up to the woman and pinioned her between them. The three then appeared to walk away together arm in arm, but the woman's feet weren't touching the ground. She was still screaming as the men shouldered aside the partition and carried her into the off-limits area of the airport. The woman's voice grew muffled, and then a door slammed and it was still. Sunny burst into soundless tears, burying her face in Sasha's jacket.

"Control yourself," he said coldly.

The silence in the dingy airport was embarrassed, full of the rustle of forbidden thoughts scurrying for cover. But the border guard who took Sasha's and Sunny's passports into his booth seemed unperturbed. Sasha hoped that they, too, would be turned away. He wanted to go home.

"Vorbiti romaneste?" The guard had spotted his accursed place of birth and was asking if he still spoke the language.

Sasha shrugged with his broadest American smile. "I forgot."

The captain appraised Sasha with his eyes, but made no further attempt to communicate. Probably he spoke no English. He looked down and busied himself with his papers again. Then he spoke on the telephone. Finally he stamped something, wrote something, and shoved their passports under the glass.

They were in.

At least they were in another grimy room, where suitcases hobbled slowly around on an antiquated conveyor belt and customs inspectors waited at low wooden benches. Now came Sasha's ordeal. "You pick one," he whispered to Sunny, pointing at the inspectors. "You always have good luck."

Sunny hauled their two suitcases off the belt, shrugging off the help of a frail, aged porter. Sasha palmed the old man a 100-*lei* note anyway, and he trembled with gratitude. Sunny scrutinized the customs inspectors and settled on a plump woman. Sasha hoisted their bags into line.

"Domnule! Veniti aici." The stocky little inspector at the next bench waved them over, grinning. *"Ati fost boxeur, nu?"* The little guy mimed boxing motions. Sunny's eyes widened in alarm, but being recognized in this friendly way didn't scare Sasha. It reassured him to see the old convivial Romania shining through the threadbare fear. He lifted their bags onto the little guy's bench. The inspector directed him to unzip the suitcases, went through the motions of looking, and waved them closed again. Sasha thanked him with two packs of Kents, which vanished with a speed C.J. East would have envied. Exuberant with relief, Sasha shook hands with the little guy. The inspector exclaimed over the size of his hand and his calloused karate knuckles. As they carried their bags through the barrier, he cocked his fists again. "Archi Mur!" he cried. "Maik Taison!"

Sasha scanned the airport lobby for a weeping, clinging old couple, the parents of the woman who had not been let in. He didn't know what that would do to Sunny. But they must already have been hustled away. What he saw was the glowing eyes of a dozen hustlers and thieves, like hyenas around a campfire. He began to feel at home.

"Taxi?"

"Taxi, *Domnule!*"

"Taxi? Hotel Intercontinental?"

"Hotel Nord," Sasha said to the one whose conniving face amused him the most. The winner beamed and grabbed both suitcases out of Sasha's hands. Outside it was overcast and sultry. The air smelled of dust and trees and crude petroleum.

"Any minute he's going to ask me to change money," Sasha whispered in Sunny's ear as the battered black cab shot along the road to the city. Like all Romanian cabs, it was missing its window handles and windshield wipers—either stolen, or removed to keep them from being stolen. Sasha offered the driver a Marlboro. The driver accepted and lit up.

"*American?*" he asked, with the accent on the last syllable.

"New York," Sasha said.

"New *York!*" There was a pause. Here it came, desperately casual: "*Vreti sa schimbati?*"

"How much?"

"Feefty."

Sasha knew he could do much better, but he also knew what a score he represented to the cabbie. Let a poor thief hope. He took down the man's phone number while Sunny jabbed him with her elbow. Now that they were safely through Customs, he relaxed, and she became the paranoid one. She saw *securitate* agents everywhere. He saw only people struggling to get by.

The taxi dodged through the labyrinth of Bucharest with breakneck speed and dexterity. Everything in this city was gray: the delicate old rococo buildings caked with grime, the square Socialist high-rises still cracked from the last earthquake, the ponderous monuments to the President's glory, the open pits of rubble with yawning steam shovels standing idle in them, the overcoats and head scarves of people standing in long lines for chicken's feet or cardboard shoes. The Hotel Nord was gray, too. It still bore the rating of *Categoria Lux,* but those days were long gone. Sasha and Sunny stayed here because, unlike the hypocritical hothouse hotels most foreigners stayed in, the Nord was honestly sleazy.

"*Sa traiti, Domnule!* May you live, sir!" The fat doorman saluted when he saw Sasha. The desk clerk, too, gave him a hearty welcome. The Nord's whole staff regarded Sasha as a veritable money tree. Sunny filled out the registration forms that would help the police apparatus track their movements through the country. The desk clerk gave them a key hooked to a heavy Bronze Age chunk of metal with their room number crudely stamped on it. An undernourished bellhop dragged their luggage to the tiny elevator.

"Alone at last," Sunny said when Sasha had dismissed the bellhop with an outrageous tip. She looked around at the lumpy twin beds, the heavy maroon drapes, the black-and-white TV with its one state station. "Isn't this the same room we had last time?"

"Of course." Sasha pointed at his ear, then at the walls. The bugged rooms were specially reserved for foreigners. "We'll have to talk 'Mobese.'" He and Sunny used gangster slang as a code in Romanian hotel rooms. Sasha loved to think of puzzled secret agents, trained in Oxford English, poring over a tape that said, "The geezer slipped me twenty-five balloons."

"I need a bath," Sunny moaned.

"Call the embassy," Sasha ordered. He ran a bath in the big old-fashioned tub while she jiggled the phone cradle, waiting for an outside line. The smallest act in Romania was surrounded by a halo of hassle. At least there was hot water. In winter, when you really wanted it, there wouldn't be.

Sunny finally got a line, dialed and asked for the deputy chief of mission. Ever since becoming good friends with an earlier ambassador—whose Siamese cat was Blue's mother—Sasha and Sunny always touched base at the U.S. Embassy before venturing deeper into the country. It probably made the Romanians think they were CIA, but it protected them. And a couple of career diplomats had joined the actors and gangsters in their irregular circle of friends. Sunny made a lunch date for the next day. Then Sasha grabbed the phone.

"Harold! There's an American citizen stuck in the airport. They won't let her in, and she hasn't seen her parents for eight years. Her father's sick. You can take care of it, can't you?"

Harold said cautiously that he would try, but relations were not the warmest right now—he phrased it with diplomatic understatement over the tapped phone—and it was the Romanians' prerogative to decide whom to let or not let in. "We'll send a staffer to the airport right away. Thank you for letting me know about this."

"State Department wimps," Sasha growled after he hung up. "Where is Georgie Patton??" Privately, he felt a little chill. He was suddenly not so sure of the embassy's power to protect them.

No sooner had he and Sunny bathed than the jet lag hit like a sack of cement. It was 6 P.M. They stretched out on their separate, uncomfortable beds, and Sasha sank into unconsciousness. At two A.M. he woke with a start to find the light on. He looked across at the other bed and saw Sunny scribbling in a pocket notebook, frowning.

"A black guy was dealing hex in the park," she said out loud when she saw that he was awake. "Then there's Eddie Cole in Cambridge. And Pierre tells me there's a Hispanic type dealing around Queens College. There's no pattern."

"Talk Mobese," Sasha warned, pointing at the ceiling.

"They won't have any idea what I'm talking about."

"What's this about Pierre? Ah hah! So *that's* what you were talking to him about in the dojo! You've been running around behind my back again." Sasha shook his head. "Why don't you listen to me?"

"I have to do my...thing, Sasha." She'd remembered not to reveal her job to the hungry microphones.

"Like you did in Cambridge? See what happens when you go out there without me?"

"I asked Pierre for help *before* we went to Cambridge. I've told him to drop it now."

"I don't believe you."

"Why don't we just have a nice fight for our lovely audience?" Sunny said sourly. Sasha put on his glasses and got out his Elmore Leonard novel. They withdrew into their separate silent pursuits until the light came and it was time for breakfast. By then, the argument had faded.

Sasha led Sunny yawning into the Nord's dim, nearly empty dining room. At a few tables, in a haze of smoke, early blackmarketeers conferred over cups of Turkish coffee. They all looked like something that had crawled out from underground. Their clothes were black or dark brown, their skins rough, dirty and unshaven. Only their eyes were bright and darting in the shadow of their Russian-style fur hats.

Sasha spotted a waiter he recognized. The little man was skulking in the shadowy corridor to the kitchen, nervous and abject, like Peter Lorre in "Casablanca." A moment after Sasha saw him, he saw Sasha and reacted as if he'd been struck by lightning. He picked up a teapot and came scurrying over. When he had set the pot down on the table, he stood twisting his hands together.

"How are you, sir," he said in his quavery Peter Lorre voice.

"Very good! How are you?" Sasha boomed.

The little man winced and edged closer. "You change?" he said in a stage whisper, looking fearfully around.

"Maybe," Sasha said. "How much?"

"*Sasha!!*" Sunny hissed, shaking her head so hard her hair flew. But Sasha knew his man.

The waiter briefly showed six fingers. Sasha was unmoved. "I can get eighty on the street, easy."

"Yes, but…" The little man looked around again and then made a snatching motion with his hand. "*Tsap tsarap.*"

"Seventy," Sasha said firmly. "I'll give you four hundred." Sunny shot him a venomous look.

"Please, meester. My children…sick."

"Oh? Your children were sick two years ago, too," Sasha said cheerfully.

The waiter agonized for a few moments. Then he nodded, raised a finger, and fled. Sasha fished openly in his pocket and brought out a wad of bills.

"You're so obvious," Sunny groaned sotto voce. "You want us to get…*tsap tsarapped* before we even see your mother?"

"Don't worry," Sasha scoffed. He felt invulnerable, like a gambler on a roll. "Everybody does this."

"Yes, but you're not everybody!"

The waiter was back, with a plate of rolls and something wrapped in a napkin. He placed both items on the table, and Sasha palmed him four new hundreds. Terrified and triumphant, the waiter bobbed his head, backed away and scuttled into the kitchen.

"How do you know that's not newspaper?" Sunny seethed.

"Shut up and stick it in your pocketbook." He passed her the package under the table. "Relax. Have some breakfast."

Sunny sighed and dispiritedly picked up a roll. "Yuck!" The underside had a bite taken out of it. She dropped it. "Let's just get out of here, okay?"

"Okay."

He was still laughing at her when they got back to their room, locked the door, and unwrapped four wads of filthy blue hundred-*lei* bills, worn soft and pale as toilet tissue, and not worth much more. Sasha started counting them.

A sharp tap on the door.

Sunny's hand flew to her throat, and she gave Sasha a frightened look. He commanded her with his eyes to get the money out of sight. Hands shaking, she stuffed it into the bottom of her purse. Sasha unlocked the door.

There was the waiter, holding a bottle of mineral water. "You change more?" he whispered.

"No, no. Maybe later." Sasha accepted the bottle of mineral water, relocked the door, and collapsed against it, weak with relief and laughter.

"What's so funny?" Sunny scowled. "It could have been the fuzz."

"Well, it wasn't. You see? You're safe with me."

But later on he had to admit that that was when things started to go wrong.

$$*\qquad*\qquad*\qquad*$$

Sunny first noticed the man in the brown leather coat as they waited for a taxi near the embassy after lunch with Harold. She nudged Sasha, and he followed her gaze. The man was standing fifty yards away, staring straight at them. He was tall and broad-shouldered, with wavy fair hair. They got into a cab, and Sunny looked through the back window as they drove away.

"Sasha, look!"

He craned around and saw the man actually running after them, pumping his arms and legs.

"I think we were supposed to see him," Sunny said when they had left the man far behind.

Sasha warningly indicated the driver's back with his eyes. "What do you mean?"

"There are two kinds: the ones you never see, and the ones you're meant to see."

"Who told you that?"

"I read it." She got a defiant look. "In a thriller."

"God help me the day I need advice from John Le Carré."

"I think they're trying to spook us," Sunny persisted. "To send us a message."

Sasha was silent the rest of the way back to the Nord. He could see his mother right now: cooking, putting fresh sheets on the bed, in a happy fever of preparation. He'd turn around and go back to New

York, but it would break her heart. It was probably just a bluff. He didn't think the *securitate* would dare to mess with them; the American ambassador himself had walked them to the embassy gate. Still, before they checked out of the Nord, he took one last precaution: he had Sunny call Harold and tell him on the open line that they'd call him every day from Sasha's home town. If one day he didn't hear from them—send the Marines!

They took their bags down in the crackerbox elevator and waited while the elevator operator's cry of *"Serviciuuuuu!"* echoed through the empty lobby, forlorn as a coyote's howl. After ten minutes a bellhop appeared, but after twenty more minutes, their taxi still hadn't. Sunny was jumpy, convinced that every hustler in a leather jacket was staring at them. And of course they were, covetously eyeing Sasha's watch and Sunny's designer jeans. Then Sunny confessed that she was hungry. She'd turned down the good goulash soup at lunch to pick at a stupid salad.

"You can't eat now. You'll have to go to the bathroom on the train."

"Oh, God! You're right." Sunny had tried to use the bathroom on a Romanian train once, ten years ago. Clogged toilet bowls overflowing on sloshing floors and walls fingerpainted with shit were unlikely to have improved in a decade when the rest of Romania had alarmingly deteriorated.

The taxi finally came and bounced them through dusty streets to the station. Sasha paid the driver to buy their tickets. No way was he going to stand in those long, drab lines, pressed close to people who smelled sad and probably had fleas and lice. The station echoed with depriva-tion. While they waited in the shuffle of stooped shoulders and trudg-ing feet, a gypsy urchin, startling blue eyes in a dirty face, came up to them with her hand out, whining like a fly. On impulse Sasha whipped out a 100-*lei* note. The kid's eyes got huge, and then she snatched the bill and ran like the wind.

Their tickets were first class, reserved seats in a relatively clean com-partment. Several tired-looking people crowded in with them. Sasha helped them put their suitcases up on the rack, and each one thanked him with the unaffected humility that made ordinary Romanians so heartbreaking. Sunny was watching the aisle outside the glass door fill up with working men and young rowdies. Suddenly she gasped.

The man in the brown leather coat who had so ostentatiously run after them was shouldering his way past their compartment. As he passed, he stared straight into Sasha's eyes. His glare was wildly, theatrically angry; in any other setting it would have been ridiculous. Here, it was so plainly a threatening message that Sasha's heart actually stopped for a second. By the time it resumed beating twice as fast, the messenger had moved down the aisle and out of sight. In those two seconds, their compartment-mates had stopped smiling and withdrawn into themselves as if Sasha and Sunny had the plague.

"Is he still there? No—don't look." Sasha pushed Sunny back down in her seat. "Look out the window. You're right, they want to spook us. So don't let them." He put more assurance into his voice than he felt.

The train started with a jerk.

Sasha disciplined himself to look out the window. The land around Bucharest was flat and monotonous. Even though it was spring green, it looked defeated gray. The first time he'd brought Sunny, she'd observed that crossing the Iron Curtain was like Dorothy's return to Kansas at the end of "The Wizard of Oz": everything changed from color to black-and-white. A friend who'd escaped said the same thing in reverse: when he'd crossed into the West, suddenly the world bloomed into color. Now the color was starting to leak into Hungary and Poland and even the Soviet Union—at least, they looked like colorized movies—but Romania, if anything, had *blackened*. The country looked blasted, curling around the edges, like a land under a curse.

Yet no human curse could rise above a certain altitude. Like a sick mist, it clung to the ground. Mountains broke through and soared above it. As the train passed the glittering peaks by Sinaia, everyone in the compartment gazed at them with something like thirst. Sasha tugged the window down, and the air that rushed in was fresh.

Sinaia itself was a different story, a kitsch town, its villas stuffed with the privileged and corrupt. It was the Party's premier resort. The President and his wife had a palatial hideaway here. There was something particularly evil about a place so pretty and so rotten. At least Bucharest had the decency to be as sad and ugly as its soul.

Fifteen minutes past Sinaia, Sunny looked at Sasha and bit her lip.

"Oh God," Sasha said. "You have to pee."

Sunny nodded shamefacedly.

"Can't you wait?"

"I have waited."

Sasha grabbed his head. "Ooh. You and your goddamn bladder," he groaned fatalistically, as one might complain of rain in spring or heat in summer. "We shouldn't get separated. Our smiling friend could be waiting down there. But if I come with you, I have to leave the luggage."

"Ask these people to watch it for us."

Sasha looked at their traveling companions. The heavy old woman with the sorrowful face kept her eyes fixed on her crocheting. The young professional was absorbed in cutting a gray sausage. The nondescript middle-aged man was reading a smeary newspaper. Sasha hated to ask anything of them, after bringing the serpent of *securitate* attention into their journey. But he made the formal request in Romanian.

"*Sigur, Domnule,*" the grandmother said without looking up.

Sasha stepped into the corridor first and looked up and down it. There were so many men standing and smoking in the aisle that he couldn't see if the man in the brown leather coat was there. He signaled Sunny to follow him and started shouldering his way past coarse young men with badly-cut hair to their collars and badly-cut gray-brown pants legs to the floor. The train smelled of empty beer bottles and bad tobacco and increasingly, as they approached the end of the car, of sewage. Sasha glanced into each compartment, but he saw only drinking parties and domestic vignettes. Maybe the man in the brown leather coat had gotten off the train, his message delivered.

The stench was strong and the floor was wet outside the WC. The noise here was deafening; a broken door between cars let in the rhythmic racket of the tracks. Sasha took his handkerchief out of his back pocket and pressed it into Sunny's hand. They both knew better than to expect toilet paper. "Don't sit down!" he hollered. Sunny wrinkled her nose, opened the door and tiptoed gingerly in. Sasha stood guard, looking left up the aisle, right into the empty maw of the next car.

The bathroom door opened. Sunny came out, closed the door behind her and took several deep breaths. "How was it?" Sasha yelled. She made a horror-movie face. "I'll go too," he shouted. "Wait right here! Don't fuckin' move!" She nodded. Sasha held his breath and went in.

He'd seen worse. It stank, and the plugged-up bowl sloshed over with each jerk of the train, but the problem was more fluid than solid. Sasha unzipped and took aim. At that moment the train plunged into a Carpathian tunnel: blackness and blasting noise. Sasha swayed in the dark, trying to keep his balance without touching the walls. Just as abruptly the tunnel ended, light burst back and the noise fell off. Sasha zipped up, congratulating himself on staying unsmirched. He opened the bathroom door.

Sunny was gone.

Panic exploded in Sasha, almost tearing his chest open. For an instant he wanted to run in five directions at once. Then his terror planed like a good speedboat, leveling off at a high pitch of functioning. The engine of his brain sang with high-octane adrenaline. Sunny wasn't stupid. She wouldn't just wander off. Therefore, she'd either gone back to check on their luggage, or she'd been snatched. Either way, she wasn't far. There hadn't been time. Sasha ran up the aisle, shoving startled Romanians aside, expecting to see her in their compartment. Of course. Good girl. She'd worried about the luggage

He arrived breathing hard in the compartment door. Their three companions were sitting there. No Sunny. The bags looked untouched. *"Ati vasut sotia mea?"* he panted. The grandmother and the young professional glanced up fearfully and shook their heads.

Shit. Now he'd lost a precious minute. Sasha ran back, bowling through the same men in the aisle, churning up a wake of raucous curses. "Run! Run into your mother's cunt!" He wouldn't waste time asking them. If they'd seen something happen to Sunny, they wouldn't say The Orwellian compact was that such things don't happen. Anyway, it had happened in the dark.

He knew for sure that she was still on the train. It hadn't stopped. He stepped into the next car and forced himself to stride, not run, up the aisle, looking into each compartment. His eyes registered nothing of the people inside. He would see only Sunny, or some bright feather of her: her purse, her jacket…Nothing.

Into the next car, his heart sinking: No Sunny, no Sunny, no Sunny. Outside the familiar landscape streamed by, peasants working fields in some famous painting, oblivious to the man falling into the sea. Halfway up the aisle a closed compartment door was jerking and rattling, as if someone was trying to get out. A muffled female scream! Surrealistically, no one in the corridor was looking. As Sasha shoved by, a young dude in a shiny suit dropped his cigarette butt and crushed it out with his heel, deliberately.

The curtain had been drawn across the compartment door, but the voice was Sunny's, sounding mad, thank God!—"Let me out of here!!"—and he could see her little white-knuckled hands on the door handle, the thick chain looped through it. As he grabbed the outside handle with both hands, she yanked the curtain back and he was looking into her face, white with fear and fury. Her eyes got huge as she saw him, and he saw the uniformed conductor sitting behind her, his cowed apologetic look, no one else in there. He threw his weight against the door handle one, two, three times, and the inner handle snapped off, the chain clattered to the floor, the door slammed open and Sunny was sobbing against his chest.

"What the *fuck* are you doing?" Sasha boomed over her head at the frightened conductor.

The old man shrugged, a servile, self-excusing gesture, and whined in Romanian, "They told me I had to keep her here for fifteen minutes."

A blank moment in Sasha's brain, like the pause between lightning and thunder, and then it hit. "The luggage!" He grabbed Sunny by the wrist and towed her up the aisle, past turned backs, lowered eyes and furtive glances. He'd been decoyed, but good.

They ran through the second car and into their own car. The bold young men who had cursed Sasha now shrank away from him as if he was cursed. Their traveling companions had vanished from the compartment. In their place, two black leather backs bent busily over Sasha's and Sunny's open suitcases. Sasha saw gifts, personal things, even Sunny's underwear piled haphazardly on the seats. He felt a savage spasm of violation, as if their hands were in his guts.

He tore the door open and grabbed each leather coat by its collar before the men could turn. With a shove he flung the two against opposite walls of the compartment. One sprawled back over an open suitcase, the other struck the luggage rack and sat down hard.

"What do you think you're doing?" Sasha roared. He'd remembered to use English. He glared down on the two, who slid each other uneasy glances. "Sunny, close the door. And pull the curtain." These two might be demigods in the eyes of a terrorized populace, but in this small space with his rage, they were nothing.

"What gives you the right to search my luggage? Or did you plant something? Hah?" He grabbed them by their coat fronts, shook them and let them fall back. By their stunned expressions, this was outside their experience

"Ce spune?" the dark agent with the low forehead and widow's peak muttered to the one with the pale narrow face and colorless hair. The second agent shrugged. They didn't even know English.

"Ai gasit ceva?" the pale agent murmured to the dark one. *"Hirtie, aparate? Camera, casetofon?"*

"They're looking for papers and tape recorders," Sasha said to Sunny. "I hope to hell you didn't smuggle your work along."

"I'm not stupid," she hissed.

"Numai un fotoaparat," said the dark one, and reached over to pull their Polaroid Sun camera out of a pile of clothing. Sasha struck the man's wrist a nerve-numbing blow.

"Be nice," he warned. The agent was cradling his hand with an expression at once cringing and vengeful. "Say please." Sasha picked up the camera and handed it to the man as if training a child in manners. As the agent turned it in his good hand, his mouth gaped open like a retarded child's. He had never seen such a wonder before.

"Pare rau, Domnule, trebuie sa confiscam aparatul," the pale agent apologized in a nasal voice. They'd decided to be polite.

"There goes our camera," Sasha said to Sunny, and then to the agents, "Why? I'm not allowed to take pictures of my mother? Is she a state secret?"

The two cops looked at each other and shrugged. *"Doamna nu poate sa face fotografie,"* warned the pale one, wagging his finger from side to side. The two of them stood up slowly, keeping a wary eye on Sasha as they straightened their leather coats. *"Scusati pentru neplacerea. Am avut ordine."* They edged by him, pulled open the door and left.

For the first time Sasha focused on the world outside the window. The train was already on the outskirts of Brasov. He swore and started throwing their things back in the suitcases. "We've got to get off in five minutes," he said. "I wanted to look through this all carefully. They could have planted some drugs or something, and be waiting to arrest us when we get off."

"What did they say?"

"They said sorry, they had orders. And...strange! They said *you* weren't allowed to take pictures." Sasha paused and stared thoughtfully at Sunny. "Like they know you're a reporter." He resumed throwing things into the bags, Sunny helping. "Who grabbed you and locked you in, anyway? Why didn't you scream bloody murder?"

Sunny gave a trembly laugh. "With a hand in a leather glove over my mouth? The train goes into the tunnel and wham! Arms go around me from behind. I almost had a heart attack. I did try to bite him, though. We come out of the tunnel and I'm in the next car. It's the scary-looking guy with the brown coat and the pale eyes. He says in English, 'Keep quiet if you want to see your husband alive.' So of course when he takes his hand off my mouth I keep quiet. He hustles me another car down and orders this poor terrified conductor to lock me in with him. Stands outside while he does it, giving me this menacing stare. Then he goes off towards the front of the train."

Sasha locked the suitcases and put them on the floor. The train was slowing into Brasov's main station. "We'll have to take our chances that there's nothing in them. Come on. Keep your head down and walk fast."

Sasha helped Sunny down onto the platform and scanned the crowd. It was drab as a flock of winter birds, except for the gypsies in their full flowered skirts and bright kerchiefs. Sasha didn't see the two men who had searched their luggage or the man in the brown leather coat. That didn't mean they didn't see him. He hurried Sunny downstairs and through the dark, muddied corridor to the exit.

Outside the spring sky was bright, and the local people squinted vitamin-starved eyes. With his size and American clothes, Sasha felt more conspicuous by the moment. Thieves, informers, and gawkers circled closer like buzzards. The taxi stand was deserted. Sasha dropped some coins into Sunny's hand. "Go call the big guy."

Sunny ran back to the station. Sasha kept his eyes on her as she pushed through the wood-and-glass doors and struggled with the primitive payphone. He wasn't letting her out of his sight for another second. From now on, they were going to the john together.

"He's on his way," she said when she got back.

Sasha *felt* watched. It wasn't just the open stares of the curious and greedy. It was a sensation on his skin, a nightmarish feeling that inanimate objects had eyes, that the trolleybuses and the station building were looking at him. Apparently he and Sunny were no longer meant to see their watchers. Intimidation was accomplished; surveillance had begun.

Wasn't that the big guy's grayish Dacia turning into the parking lot? Yes, there was his big, rugged head behind the wheel. Sasha felt a surge of relief, spiked with regret for luring Omar into the sights of the hunters. Now he'd be questioned for hours after they left. Luckily, he was an old hand. Whenever they made him report on what he and Sasha talked about, he'd say, "Memories of how we slaved together in Russia." It was Omar who had dug Sasha out, shoveling for four hours, after Mine 28 caved in. *The Seventeenth Level* was dedicated to him.

Omar pulled up in front of them and got out. "Hallo! Sasha!" The two were virtually the same height. "The big guy" grabbed his hand in a crushing grip, and Sasha felt reunited with his twin. The bond forged by savage labor side by side was as strong as ever.

Sunny threw herself into Omar's arms, and he lifted her off the ground. They wasted no more time on public hellos, but slung their bags into Omar's trunk and took shelter in his car. As he left the station behind, Omar blasted his horn at a shabby pedestrian who limped across the street inches from their front bumper. "Hey! Asshole! Why are you wandering around like a fart in a lantern?" Sunny giggled in the back seat.

"There's the vegetable market!" Sasha said. "Jesus, it's empty." A few years ago, there had been tomatoes, potatoes, eggplants, big pale cabbages, bright peppers. Now the stalls were gray and bare.

"There is nothing to eat, nothing, nothing, nothing." Omar spoke in a rapid, turbulent stream. "He's brought the country to its knees. It's over.—Watch out, you stupid goose, or go to your wild grandmother! You want a foot in the ass?" He hit the horn again. They turned into the street that led towards Sasha's home village, twelve kilometers away. Sasha wondered if they were being tailed. There was no way of knowing if one of the Dacias behind them was *securitate*.

"How's the factory?" Sasha asked. "Still making those plastic bags?" Omar nodded, and then snorted with laughter. Even his twenty-year-old daughter believed he made plastic bags, but once, when the two of them were alone, he'd told Sasha the truth. He was a supervising engineer in a chemical plant that produced plastic bags as a front, and chemical weapons for sale to the Third World in a top-secret, behind-the scenes facility. The weapons violated international accords, but the Romanian President didn't care. The trade brought hard currency into his Swiss bank accounts.

"Look at that. Such a beautiful land," Omar said. "Too bad they've shit all over it." They were driving through a valley like a bowl, surrounded by soft blue foothills of the Carpathians. Mountain peaks shone gold in the six o'clock sun. Sasha had walked into this view every day on his way home from school. Its contours were engraved on his memory, like his mother's face. What was surprising was how Sunny had fallen in love with it.

"There's the fortress!" she exclaimed.

One of the foothills had a bare, rugged crown, like the stump of a rotten tooth: the ruined fortress where Sasha's village had taken refuge during invasions from the Asian steppes. An ancestor of Sasha's mother had led the defense up there in the fourteenth century—a defense that had not been entirely successful, as witness Sasha's Mongol cheekbones. But he could point out the tumbled walls where his family had lived under siege. His roots here went bone- and bedrock-deep. On that hill the wild boys of his childhood had clambered in summer and sledded in winter, with him as their leader.

They drove into the village itself, with its beautiful old heavy-walled houses painted light blue, lime-green, peach and melon, each builder's family name and date inscribed on the ornamental cornice above his heavy wooden gate. The houses, proud and immaculate in Sasha's childhood, wee in sad disrepair after fifty years of Communism, foundations cracked and mossy, plaster scabbed. Sasha's mother's house stood at the pivotal corner of the village. It was a dignified house even in decrepitude, big-boned like Sasha's family, painted a rust-pumpkin orange. The big guy stopped in front of the brown wooden gate. Sasha looked at the house, remembering the first time he'd come home after 22 years, the first sight of his mother's face in the window, altered by age and sorrow.

"Shall I open the gate?" he asked Omar. "You should bring the car inside. They'll take down your license number."

"They can stick my license number in their ass," Omar said. "I don't want to intrude. I'll just say hello and leave."

Sunny quivered with excitement as they unloaded the bags and carried them through the gate. Inside the courtyard, once bright with flowers, now gray and strung with wash, Sunny ran up the steps to his mother's door. It didn't matter who went in first, because she was almost as dear to his mother as he was. When he came into the dim, familiar rooms, the two of them were already in each other's arms.

Memory overwhelmed Sasha's senses. In this room he'd eaten every meal with his parents and his older sister, lost in Russia. In the next room he'd come into the world. These two unchanged rooms and the little kitchen were an island out of time—all that remained to his mother of the old extended family home surrounding the courtyard.

"Bubi!" His mother called him by his childhood name and came over to embrace him. She had to reach up, but not that far: she was a tall, strong woman even though time had stooped her. Her wool sweater had a harsh honest texture, which was like her: she was not given to soft, fluffy things. Sasha felt her iron bones, so like his own, and her fine-textured skin, so like his own, her old-fashioned upright-ness, her tremor of emotion. He remembered running to her as a child, the sense of absolute security and affection, reliable as rock and sun.

"Come see what we've brought," he commanded.

"Come taste what I've cooked," his mother ordered simultaneously. They both laughed at their likeness—and the likelihood of a battle of wills.

"Excuse me." The big guy cleared his throat in the doorway. "I'm on my way. You're all invited for dinner tomorrow." A little bell rang in the house as he exited the courtyard. That would serve as a warning if…someone else came to visit. It must have rung when they came for his father. Sasha pushed that thought away.

"Get the basket!" he told his mother. While Sunny unloaded gifts from the suitcases, Sasha checked for anything missing or planted. On quick inspection nothing was wrong, but they'd have to go through the bags more carefully. His mother brought in a big old basket that she used to bring potatoes up from the cellar, and Sasha and Sunny piled it high with toothpaste, soap and hand cream, kitchen gadgets like can openers, chocolate, vitamins, and cigarettes. Mama exclaimed over the chocolate bars, tried out the gadgets, and opened up a pack of Kools. She looked quite jaunty with a cigarette in the corner of her mouth, even though it was the only time she smoked.

After "Christmas," it was time for dinner. Sasha's mother brought out a dish of tender cornmeal *mamaliga* baked with cheese, and then a pot of delicately sour soup in which parsley, golden drops of fat, and bite-sized pieces of meat and potatoes floated. It must have been hard work to find the makings of this meal, but it was his mother's pride. She watched them eat with a spark in her berry-black eyes, hooded and keen.

After dinner, over cake and Romanian rum that tasted like caramel, Sasha and his mother told funny stories from the past while Sunny listened raptly. "Do you remember the time you tried to climb into the honey barrel and tipped it over?" his mother asked. "And your father came after you, and you his behind the tile stove in the bedroom, all sticky?" She laughed with a rasp from her chronic bronchitis, and with the droll expression of a cat playing. Sunny thought his mother had the best sense of humor in the world.

"Do you remember the time you were in the swimming pool and I jumped in right on top of you?" Sasha chimed in.

"Do you remember…"

It was dark outside. Sasha's mother had stoked the woodstove against the mountain chill, and gradually the dining-room table became a glowing island of laughter and safety in a sea of darkness. Sasha had decided to wait till morning to go in search of a phone, call Harold, and report the incident on the train. He knew he was taking a chance, but the hell with it. Danger seemed strangely unreal here at the heart of the world. He wasn't going back out into the night.

Except to the outhouse, of course.

"I have to pee first," Sunny said when they couldn't fight off sleep any longer.

"I'm coming with you," Sasha said immediately.

"Oh Sash, don't be silly."

"Silly? For the rest of my life I'm gonna associate going to the bathroom with losing you. I won't even be able to piss unless I can see you. Get the flashlight."

Sunny took his mother's American flashlight, the roll of coarse gray toilet paper, and the old iron key, and they went out into the courtyard. The air was cold and fresh, and Sasha realized just how dark it was. To save energy, Romanian towns and cities didn't burn their streetlights. This was the old mountain night, the land black and the sky dense with stars. He could hear the tired clip-clop-rattle of a horse and cart in the street outside.

Sunny grabbed his arm and pointed upward. "Look! The Big Dipper," she whispered. Then, to his surprise, she began to sing in a low, pure voice:

"Follow the drinkin' gourd

"Follow…the drinkin' gourd

"There's an old man there a waitin'

"For to carry you to freedom,

"Follow the drinkin' gourd."

"It's an old slave song," she explained in a whisper. "If you escaped, you followed the Big Dipper to the Underground Railroad. I'll be out in a sec." She took the flashlight and shut herself into the outhouse

The song echoed in Sasha, standing in the black night of his enslaved country. He knew what it was to lie in the open, hunted by your fellow man, and look to the stars for direction. At this moment, he was sure, people were slipping through the woods, following the Drinking Gourd across the border into Hungary.

The outhouse door opened. "Come in with me," Sasha insisted, pushing the giggling, protesting Sunny back into the dank little space to wait beside him while he took a leak. Then, shivering, she ran ahead of him back to the house.

His mother had made her own bed for them, the bed where Sasha had been born. She would sleep out on the couch. She tucked them in and kissed them both goodnight as if they were children. After she closed the door, Sasha heard the sounds of her presence in the next room.

Sunny wrapped herself around him. The sheets smelled starched and clean. "Know what I think?" she murmured in his ear.

"What?"

"Maybe I was your sister in my last life."

Sasha half-sat up in indignation. "Don't give me that New Age crap. Are you trying to tell me I'm screwing my sister?"

"Is that all you can think about?" She sighed. "It's just so weird how at home I feel in this house, with your mother."

"It's because she loves you," Sasha said. "Now shut up and go to sleep. We've had a rough day."

"Know what else?" Sunny said minutes later, dragging Sasha back from the edge.

"Mmf?"

"It all seems to far away…New York, *Metro,* my story. Hex. It's so unreal. *This* is real." She moved against him. "Let's make a baby," she whispered, so softly he barely heard it.

He was suddenly as wide awake as if cold water had been thrown on him. "First you tell me you're my sister, now you want us to have a kid?"

"Oh, fuck you," Sunny said, flouncing around with her back to him. "Just try to get me to say that again."

"Shhhhh." Sasha put his arms around her. She was rigid. "We'll have a kid if that's what you want," he soothed. "We'll live in the country and have lots of animals, and bring my mother over, and we'll travel. You can write articles if you feel like it, and not if you don't." A coaxing note crept into his voice. "Let's just make it first."

"I'll be too old by the time we 'make it.'" Sunny's voice was hoarse. He touched her cheek and felt hot tears. Was this his fiercely ambitious Sunny, who cared only for making her name?

"All the more reason to make it quick," he said. He wanted to comfort her, but he couldn't give her what she wanted. Not yet. How could he explain his fear of being a father? It went back to the look on his father's face the last time he'd seen him, through that boxcar window. He'd never seen his father powerless before. It was his worst nightmare: to see what he loved in trouble and have no power to protect. Sunny wasn't afraid because she didn't know what could happen to you. She didn't know you could be brought so low you cursed your own mother for bringing you into the world.

But maybe—at last—she was turning away from causes and towards her own life. Their life. If bringing her here had worked that magic, it was worth the trouble.

Still…

He wasn't ready for her to forget about hex quite yet.

Not before he found out if there was some money in it.

CHAPTER 8

▼

A hand in a leather glove clamped over Sunny's mouth.

She tried to scream, but no sound came. She bucked and struggled with all her strength, slamming against her leather-coated captor, trying to break his grip. The hand over her mouth only tightened. Now it crept up to cover her nose as well. Sunny began to suffocate. Terror swelled in her chest with the need for air. She must not black out—

She sat straight up in Sasha's mother's bed, gasping for breath.

It wasn't pitch dark out, it was a white, overcast morning. She could hear Sasha and his mother laughing, talking and clinking dishes in the next room. Now she remembered Sasha trying to wake her, and his mother reproaching him to let her sleep. She wished she had gotten up. Then she wouldn't have had the dream.

They had been in the village four days, and nothing had happened. No one had come looking for them. No one had visibly followed them. Yet every night, Sunny had had the nightmare. Was her mind just replaying her terror on the train, or was it the poisonous tension in the air as they walked around the village visiting friends? Sunny had never had this feeling before—a sense of malevolence directed at them personally, like a beam of radiation. Sasha felt it too. "We're waiting for the other shoe to drop," he'd muttered to Sunny late one night.

The morning after they arrived, they'd walked to the post office and public telephone center, and there, under the eyes of the president, who watched from every official wall like Big Brother, they had made a very public phone call to Harold. It was possible that that ritual, repeated every morning like a prayer, was all that held back the hostile forces around them.

That first morning, Sunny had known that her little pocket note-book was missing. Sasha assumed she kept it in her purse, but she'd happened to toss it into the suitcase in the Hotel Nord before they took the train, and it was the first thing she'd thought of when she saw the two men rummaging. Not that there was anything to interest Romanian agents in it: some scribbles and diagrams about the hex mystery, and the fantastic doodles she did when she was thinking, in which flowers, leaves, breasts, and bubbles often sprouted from a pair of big feet. It seemed safe enough not to mention this minor loss to Sasha. It would *not* be safe to admit to him that so much as a scrap of her handwriting had fallen into enemy hands.

They'd both done a good job of hiding their forebodings from Sasha's mother. The night Sunny woke up screaming, they made up a story about something she'd eaten on one of their visits. In fact, the nightmare was worse that night because of something she'd heard, from Ana the gypsy.

*   *   *   *

The tiny old woman adored Sasha; she called him her "luck child." She had been his wet-nurse after he drank his mother dry, and hard as it was to believe now, her withered fig of a body had been full and bountiful. Sasha had grown straight and strong, and who knew, maybe he'd imbibed a little of her psychic power, too.

The first time he brought Sunny to her, Ana had spread Sunny's hand in her strong brown work-calloused ones and studied the palm. She'd read Sunny's sensitivity, stubbornness, imagination and independence as easily as a literate person reads words off a page. And then she'd adopted Sunny, like his mother had. Despite the fifty-year difference in their ages, the two of them would whisper and giggle together like girls. So it was very noticeable that this time Ana was somber and subdued. She hugged them tight and stroked their cheeks and gazed into their eyes with her wise little black ones, but as she drew them into her parlor, she seemed unhappy.

Ana's parlor was the most amazing room Sasha had ever seen. Ana had turned it into a cross between a carnival tent and a rabbit warren. Standing screens and fringed shawls draped over clotheslines created tunnels where there had once been open space. The ceiling was blackened by smoke, and the walls were covered with sentimental pictures, old religious calendars, and garish embroidery. Polaroid instant pictures of Sasha and Sunny were clipped up here and there with bobby pins. Every surface of the dusty old furniture was cluttered with empty teacups growing gardens of mold, coffee cups encrusted with brown hieroglyphics, eggshells saved for the calcium, lockets, crystals, clocks, religious statuettes, and chipped china figurines.

In the center of the room was a square table, covered by a sensible piece of oilcloth and a hand-crocheted doily. On this table Ana kept her crystal ball—she actually had one—a dirty old pack of cards, dried roots and flowers, and some weird-looking amulets. Sasha, with his orderly nature, was faintly repelled by this room, through it made him feel disloyal. Sunny had been enthralled at first sight.

Ana sat them down at the table and insisted on stirring up a Turkish coffee on her little wood stove. She shuffled over with a cup and saucer rattling in each hand, and then sat down and stared at them. Her gaze was objective, with an unnerving penetration. Sasha always said Ana's look could strip the paint off a battleship.

"You have trouble," she said.

Sunny almost dropped her cup.

"Enemies are around you," Ana said darkly.

Sasha burst out laughing. "Tell me something I don't know, Anica." It didn't take a witch to say "You're wet" in the middle of a rainstorm. But Sunny had turned white.

"Be serious." Ana shook her finger at him. "Ana knows you are not careful here. You talk loud—ba, ba, ba. You do tricks with money. You walk around like a big American." She pushed herself to her feet and did a fair imitation of a John Wayne swagger. Standing over him, she suddenly closed her eyes and thrust four fingers against his chest. "Watch your heart," she croaked. "Shield your heart."

A sharp pain pierced Sasha from front to back, taking his breath away. Goddamn overactive imagination! He swept Ana's hand off him. "Tell us about our life," he said heartily. "Are we going to make a lot of money this year?"

"What about my work, Ana?" Sunny asked. "What I'm doing now—will it be a success?"

Ana's eyes opened. She looked from one of them to the other, as if coming back from a distance, and then she nodded toward Sunny's coffee cup. Obeying, Sunny inverted it and turned it, deftly rotating her wrist as she'd been taught. She placed the cup upside-down on its saucer. When it had dried a little, Ana picked it up and squinted at the rippled brown pattern.

"Two men," she said. "Two men and a third. Coming into your life very soon now. They mean you harm. See, this one's arm is raised." Sasha leaned over to peer into the cup and saw only meaningless squiggles. Suddenly inspiration struck him.

"The three men on the train!" he said to Sunny. "She's telling us about something that's already happened! It's the one thing psychics never get right—the time frame."

Ana shot him a silencing look. "The letter D, or P..." she went on, frowning. "A cross...There is sickness here. And a death. Not yours, but your heart is heavy." She looked up, into Sunny's eyes. "This is a hard cup. You have accepted the fight with evil, and evil is powerful."

"I *told* you to leave it to Georgie," Sasha broke in.

"Look." Ana pointed an arthritis-crabbed finger at a black smudge in Sunny's cup. "Here is darkness, at the point where the past meets the future. If you choose to go into it, you may be lost...or you may become stronger. I cannot see the other side." She put the cup down and stared sorrowfully at Sunny. One thing Sasha had never understood about Ana: she didn't try to protect you from your fate.

"You're not going into any darkness while *I'm* around," he said with finality. "Okay—now me." He picked up his cup and turned it in a clumsy circle. Half the grounds slopped out; the rest coated half the inside of his cup with impenetrable black. "I fucked up," Sasha said sheepishly.

Ana waved a hand at him in an affectionate "Oh, go away" gesture, and drew her crystal ball toward her. She stared into its center with intense concentration. All Sasha could see in the ball was an upside-down image of Ana's crazy room. But Ana evidently saw something else.

"A suitcase," she said slowly. "A suitcase...stained with blood."

"Oh, no. More trouble with suitcases," Sunny moaned under her breath.

"Around this suitcase, I see...great trouble. And great joy."

"We'll be really happy when we get home safe," Sasha the optimist interpreted.

But it was with foreboding that they lifted their suitcase (unburdened of gifts, the little one fit inside the big one) onto the train for Bucharest the next morning.

✳   ✳   ✳   ✳

All her life Sunny had hated saying goodbye. She and Sasha's mother had embraced and kissed in the train compartment, and now Mama stood outside on the platform next to Omar, every line of her fallen face and shoulders expressing desolation. As the train jerked and started to slide out of the station, she raised one hand in a lost child's wave. Sasha blew her a kiss, sat down, and resolutely got out his Elmore Leonard thriller. He had survived, Sunny thought, by not looking back. She waved until the two tiny figures dwindled out of sight. It was always wrenching, leaving the old woman to another year of loneliness, not knowing for sure if they'd see her again.

As the train came down out of the mountains, the weather turned oppressively humid. A young mother in their compartment opened the door to let the air circulate. Soon Sunny heard a high, unearthly wailing. A small gypsy woman came in sight, dressed in a kerchief and full skirt. On one arm she carried a heavy baby; with her free hand she held up the cupped hand of a ravishingly beautiful young girl, who was blind, or pretending to be blind, singing with her eyes closed. The girl's song was haunting and wild, devoid of any Western sentiment. Some of the people standing in the corridor tucked bills into her upraised hand. The little caravan moved on, but Sunny heard the alien melody for a long time. It gave her the same shivery feeling old Ana's eyes did. There was an ancient strangeness here, an almost reptilian fatalism. Perhaps only on a total lack of hope could such despotism thrive, like those toxic bacteria that prosper in the absence of oxygen.

When they made it all the way to Bucharest without incident, Sunny's spirits began to rise. Their plane left early the next morning. The nightmare was almost over. Her real life was already brightening the horizon of her mind. As soon as they got home, she'd make her reservations for California. "California"—the word was a golden talisman shining through the gloom of Bucharest's North Station.

There were no taxis.

"Let's walk," Sunny said, full of nervous energy. "The suitcase is so much lighter now."

"We're not going to the Nord," Sasha said.

A man in a dark-blue suit was hurrying furtively toward them. Sunny's heart started to hammer. When the man got close he said in a low voice, *"Aveti nevoia de masina?"*

Sasha nodded, and the man walked off toward the parking lot. "Follow him," Sasha said. "He's a private citizen moonlighting as a gypsy cabbie."

"Are you sure?"

"I'm sure," he said firmly. "A lot of people do it to make money. Hotel Flora," he directed the man when they'd climbed into his shabby black car. Sasha handed him two folded 100-*lei* bills. The driver thanked him and floored the accelerator.

He drove fast, in grim silence, dodging around the rear of overburdened trolley cars, cutting out of a bus-clogged avenue, plunging into a labyrinth of shadowy side streets.

"*Unde mergeti?*" Sasha asked indignantly. "This isn't the way to the Flora."

"*Constructie,*" the man explained, pointing off to his left. Sasha and Sunny looked at each other, bouncing around in their seats as the car caromed off potholes and loose cobblestones. Suddenly Sunny noticed that the inside door handles were missing.

They weren't getting out of this car until the driver wanted them to.

They burst out of a warren of old buildings onto another avenue. The driver jerked his thumb rearwards. Looking back, Sunny saw a huge gray crater where a part of Bucharest had been.

"*Face un palat,*" said the driver.

"He's building himself a palace," Sasha translated, with a slight tremor in his voice.

A few moments later the car turned into the green park surrounding the tourist hotels Parc and Flora. The driver got out and opened the door for them. "*Scusati,*" he apologized with a shamefaced shrug, pointing at the missing door handles. "*Fura.*" They steal.

When Sunny stepped out of the car, her knees would hardly support her. The driver took their suitcase out of the trunk. He thanked Sasha again and, with a nervous glance at the hotel, got into his car and took off.

"Whew. I thought—"

"Shut up," Sasha said. "We're going home."

The Flora catered to foreign clients of Dr. Ana Aslan's anti-aging clinic. It was one of those hotels Sunny hated, but when they got to their room she had to admit it was nicer than the Nord, in its phony way.

They called Harold. "I'm glad you're safe and sound back in Bucharest," he said heartily. "Dinner tonight? Oh, I'm sorry. There's a shindig at the Nigerian ambassador's that I can't get out of. But if you need anything, just call my staff at home. They'll know where to find me. And come visit us again soon."

"Fat chance," Sasha said after they hung up.

They took turns soaking in the tub, their first in a week. Drying herself in a huge towel, Sunny said, "I'm hungry."

"Me too." Sasha was looking at her appreciatively, also for the first time in a week.

"Gotta feed me first, mate, or I won't be no good to ya."

"Let's go down to the dining room and celebrate," Sasha said. "I've still got some *lei* to get rid of. We'll buy a bottle of wine."

At the door of the room Sunny hesitated, looking at their deflated suitcase, Ana's warning on her mind. "Think we should stay here and have room service?"

"Nah," Sasha scoffed. "We won't be that long." He double-locked the door and put the key in his pocket.

"I know you. You're too cheap to order room service," Sunny said, trotting to keep up with him in the dimly lit hall.

The menu was elaborate, but the kitchen didn't have most of the things on it. Sasha settled for meatball soup and a cutlet. Sunny ordered chicken. After several minutes of chewing she said sadly, "I think this chicken had a hard life."

The dining room was nearly empty. The waiters slunk around and watched them eat. The French fries were greasy-soft, and the wine tasted chemical. Sasha wolfed his meal down; Sunny left hers half untouched. They were suddenly eager to get back to their room, to sleep and make tomorrow come more quickly.

Upstairs, Sasha went into the bathroom to take an Alka-Seltzer. Sunny stripped off her clothes and opened the suitcase. She took out one of Sasha's big T-shirts to wear to bed, and was about to pull it over her head when she froze, barely remembering not to cry out.

Her little pocket notebook was back.

Her mind scrambled for a benign explanation. The notebook had been there all along, hidden in the folds of that T-shirt…No. She'd searched thoroughly that first morning at Sasha's mother's. She reached for the notebook, hesitating as if it might burn her, then snatched it up and flipped through the pages. It looked the same. She sniffed it, and thought it smelled strange, but that could be her imagination. She put it in her pocketbook.

Trouble with a suitcase…Had they taken anything else? Put something in? She'd better search quickly and quietly. If she told Sasha the notebook was back, she'd have to admit it had been missing in the first place. She began to rummage through their clothing with clammy, trembling hands.

The knock on the door was no tentative tap, but a heavy, authoritative pounding. "Who is it?" Sunny cried in alarm.

A male voice: "Hotel security. Open up, please."

The other shoe had dropped.

*   *   *   *

There were three of them: their old nemesis in the brown leather coat, with the pale eyes popping out—must have something wrong with his thyroid—and two goons in black leather coats whom Sasha hadn't seen before. "Hotel security," my ass. They were *securitate,* state security, and they were being as stern and chillingly polite as a doctor bringing a terminal diagnosis. Popeyes radiated blame; Sasha could feel his righteous disapproval like heat. A technique to induce guilt, when it was Popeyes who should feel guilty for grabbing Sunny and giving them the scare of their lives. Sasha burned to hit him. Instead, he went for the phone. "I'm calling my embassy."

Popeyes bent and pulled the phone cord out with the snap of a vital artery being severed. "That won't be necessary," he said in an unpleasantly high, nasal voice. "We only want to ask you a few questions. If your answers are satisfactory, you will be free to go." In his mouth, these words of reassurance were oily with menace. He jerked his head at one of his associates and barked, *"Hai cu valise."* The goon zipped their suitcase shut with his black-leather fingers and picked it up. The other one grabbed Sunny's arm and pulled her up out of the chair where she'd been sitting since she got dressed. Sunny jerked her arm free. That little flare of temper made Sasha feel better.

They were hustled down the stairs and out a side door to a waiting black Soviet-made Volga. Popeyes and Goon One pinned Sunny between them in the back seat and directed Sasha to sit in front beside Goon Two, the driver. He touched his pocket, feeling for his passport, a foolishly superstitious gesture. No one on earth knew where they were.

They didn't drive far. Bucharest had police stations and interrogation centers the way American cities have McDonald's. A uniformed sentry let the Volga through a gate in a high wall topped with barbed wire. Sasha and Sunny got out, and their three guards, squeaking with leather, herded them across a small cobblestoned courtyard where a few official vehicles sat at random angles in the dark. One weak light bulb above the door splayed long shadows behind them. Inside, too, energy was being conserved. The light was sour and dim, the walls a chalky green. The desolate smell of the country was strongest here, compounded of lime and mold and wretched sweat. Sasha wondered if that smell pulsed out from buildings like this one, broadcasting an animal message to surrender.

Popeyes went to a little window in the wall and said something to the man behind it. Over Popeyes' shoulder, Sasha saw the heavy-set man pick up a telephone and speak rapidly into it. Hanging up, he gave Popeyes a significant nod and opened a thick ledger full of hand-written entries. Popeyes thrust out his gloved hand.

"Your passports, please."

Sunny threw Sasha a stricken look. He had taught her Rule One in Romania: never be separated from your passport. "Don't we have a right to refuse?" she asked in a small voice.

"You are not in the United States, madame," Popeyes said. "You are a foreign national suspected of criminal activity on Romanian soil. It is I who have the right to demand your passport."

Sunny's mouth had fallen open in shock.

"Criminal activity?" Sasha heard his own voice crack. "What are you *talking* about?"

Satisfied, Popeyes returned to soothing mode. "It is possible that this is all a misunderstanding. We, too, wish to settle the matter quickly. Now, please, give me your passports. It is procedure. After the numbers are recorded, they will be returned to you."

Sunny fished in her purse and slowly handed over her passport. As Sasha let go of his, he felt oddly light and insubstantial, like a prisoner stripped of his street clothes, belt, and shoes.

Popeyes tossed their passports through the window and signaled to Goon One, who unlocked a door with a big bunch of keys. Sunny and Sasha followed Popeyes through a series of sparsely furnished offices, Goon Two bringing up the rear with their suitcase. Somewhere in the labyrinth of rooms, Sasha heard a sharp shout trail off into a moan, as if someone had been hit in the body. People disappeared into places like this and were never seen again. But not Americans! If they weren't on the plane tomorrow, they would be missed. At least Sunny would. He clung to her arm like a life preserver.

Down a long green corridor and into a bare room with only a wooden bench, two chairs, and about a 45-watt light bulb. Goon One closed the door behind them.

"Please sit down," Popeyes said, like a good host who had something prepared to serve them.

That something, evidently, was their own suitcase. Popeyes signaled Goon Two to put it up on the bench in front of them and unzip it. Goon One stood over it, hands poised, like a chef about to toss a salad. At a nod from Popeyes, he began delicately leafing through their clothes.

The search went on in silence, while Sasha and Sunny sat side by side, walled in their own thoughts. Sasha knew they could have planted something while he and Sunny were down in the dining room. Or they were brazen enough to slip something into the suitcase right in front of them. But what? A gun? A Bible? Money? A scrap of microfilm? Three grams of cocaine?

Goon Two shook his head and backed away from the suitcase. Relief welled up in Sasha, then sank as Popeyes angrily motioned for the search to continue. Goon Two shrugged and resumed. He unzipped Sunny's little pouch of earrings, shook it out on the bench, poked the earrings around with a forefinger, and carefully put them back. The next item he came up with was a small box of Tampax. He held it up, turning it curiously this way and that. Suddenly he held the Tampax box to his ear. He shook it. A small, hard rattling.

He opened one end and tilted the box. Six black-and-yellow capsules slid out into his gloved palm.

∗　　　∗　　　∗　　　∗

Sunny would never forgive Sasha for his first reaction. Here he was, surrounded by what he said were the most treacherous people in the world, and what did he do? He turned and glared at *her*. As if the hex could have come from noplace else, as if the Romanians hadn't read *Newsweek* (and her notebook), as if they didn't have agents in the U.S…as if *she* were that reckless and stupid! She forced down tears of rage and betrayal and stared furiously back at Sasha. Almost immediately his face softened with doubt and remorse. But it was too late: the Romanians had seen his accusing look. The one with the scary eyes wore a smug expression.

"The problem is in madame's personal effects," he said in his nauseating accent. "So madame will tell us: what are these capsules? A medication? Or could it be one of the illegal drugs that are so popular in your country?"

"I don't know," Sunny said. "You put them in there. You tell me." Sasha squeezed her knee in support and apology. She didn't look at him.

"Cauta geanta," the pale-eyed chief snapped at one of his lieutenants. The man lifted Sunny's purse strap right off her shoulder and started pawing inside. *"Da-m caietul,"* the chief said, snapping his fingers impatiently. Ah hah. Black-coat handed over her little notebook. Brown-coat flipped through it. What a farce.

"'Hex,'" the chief read out loud. He looked from the notebook to the little pile of pills in his other thug's hand. Then his eyes snapped back to Sunny. "You are lying." He stabbed at the notebook with his finger. *"This* proves that you know very well what the capsules are. We have heard about this new drug that is corrupting the youth of your country." His voice rose. "You have smuggled it into Romania with the intention of corrupting our youth!"

Sunny laughed out loud. She couldn't help it.

"This is not a laughing matter," pale-eyes warned. "Drug smuggling is a very serious crime if you are a private profiteer. It is far more serious if you are an agent of the United States Government."

"For Christ's sake," Sunny said, "I'm a reporter on a story!" Pale-eyes smiled, and she saw how neatly she'd been trapped.

"Then why bring the drug here? To—how do capitalists say—try the market? Or to learn if a chemical engineer in Brasov can make it?"

Oh no, were they going to drag the big guy into this frame-up too? Sunny couldn't breathe. She felt too small to contain the outrage that was growing in her, straining her ribs, closing her throat.

"Of course, six pills is not so much." Pale-eyes paced, savoring his power, a cat slowly maiming a mouse. "It would be interesting if we find more. *N-ai gasit nimic in geanta?*" he snapped at his sidekick, who was still holding Sunny's purse. The man shook his head. *"Poate ca ascunde unde-va pe corp. Chiama Aurica."* Sidekick dropped the purse and left the room.

"You bastard," Sasha muttered lethally.

"What did he say?" Sunny felt the flame of fear and anger leap up, licking for fuel.

Before Sasha could answer, a woman in a dark-blue uniform came in, middle-aged, thick-bodied, keys at her waist. *"Cauta Doamna,"* pale-eyes commanded her. The woman looked at Sunny—her American clothes, her danger-signal eyes—and glanced hesitantly back at her boss. *"Hai, hai,"* he snapped with a hurry-up gesture. *"Are in acelas loc ca si romanca."*

"She's supposed to body-search you," Sasha said in a congested voice. "You know what that means? He said you have it in the same place as Romanian women."

Sunny had a vivid tactile image of the matron's fingers invading her, and her whole being convulsed in rebellion. The swelling bubble of outrage burst, flooding her with warm and welcome adrenaline. She felt strong enough to blast through the clammy walls of this place, out into the starry sky.

Sasha had struggled to his feet, compelled by ancient genetic chivalry to defend her body with his to the last. "Don't worry," he said, braced like a bear at bay. "Nobody's going to touch you."

"You're goddamn right they're not," Sunny said.

*   *   *   *

Sasha looked at her, surprised by a new note in her voice. She was standing up, fists clenched, eyes blazing. A moment ago he'd been down to his last, poor trump card—his physical strength, not worth much in any police station. Now it seemed that Sunny had an ace up her sleeve.

"You tell that fat bitch to keep her hands off me," she hissed at Popeyes, walking right up to him and jabbing her finger in his face. Sasha felt a surge of terror and joy. He got ready to leap if the agent touched her, but Popeyes was frozen with astonishment.

"Do you have any idea who I *am?*" Sunny spat into Popeyes' face. "Do you have any idea who I *know?* Do you know what will happen to you if you don't let us go *right now?*" She was still pointing her finger straight at his nose. "This is a catastrophe for your government, and *you* will be held responsible!"

Popeyes looked like man who'd reached for a garden hose and closed his hand on a cobra. They had little or no experience with defiance. In their book, such confidence could not possibly come from principle. It could only come from power. Sunny actually had him intimidated.

"I"—she jabbed her finger at her own chest—"am one of the most respected journalists in my country!" Sasha could have drowned in bliss. For years he'd built up her ego, fighting her ingrained New England modesty. Here at last was his reward, her pride unsheathed like a sword. "I have interviewed *two* presidents of the United States," she said, crackling with authority. "I write for the *New York Times.* And you think you can have your flunky search my body? Think again! When I get through with you, you'll be lucky to be mopping floors in the train station! Give me your name!" She thrust out her hand, palm up.

Popeyes stared at her. "My *name?* My name is—is not important!"

"Oh, of course not! All that strutting around like a big shot—that's just when the boss is away, right?" Sunny stalked back and forth like a hunting heron. "Well, you call your master, and tell that moron who he was dumb enough to take on. My father is an international banker. He and the chairman of the U.S. Senate Foreign Relations Committee went to Yale together. And you know who else was in their class? Bill

Lowell, the chairman of CBS. Push this scam one inch further, and the three networks will be crawling all over this country. The U.S. Senate will mount a full investigation. The international banks will call in their loans. And *you* and *your boss* will have to explain it to your president! Do you understand?" Popeyes blinked. Sasha suspected he understood the music better than the words. And what sweet music it was, jubilant as John Philip Sousa.

"First of all," Sunny seethed, "I want you to drive us back to our hotel, right now."

"I cannot do that, madame," Popeyes said physically shrugging off responsibility, "until I have authorization."

"Don't 'madame' me," Sunny said. "I want us out of here in five minutes."

"I do not know if that is possible. The General may be sleeping."

"Then wake him up!" Sunny grabbed her purse, turned to the bewildered matron, and commanded, *"Telefoane!"*

The matron risked a fleeting glance at Popeyes. As much as she feared his wrath, Sasha thought she might have enjoyed his humiliation. He gave a grudging nod, and the matron ushered Sunny gingerly to the door. Sasha followed, not wanting to let her out of his sight. "Wheeew," one of the goons whistled behind him. *"Ce cainoasa.* What a bitch!"

Sunny was talking rapidly into the phone in an office, the matron hovering over her. Sunny covered the mouthpiece. "Where are we? *Unde?"* The matron answered, and Sunny repeated the information into the receiver. She put it down and came to Sasha, looking unhappy.

"I had to give the message to Harold's maid," she said. "And you know she's one of *them.* He's still at that stupid Nigerian party." But when Popeyes came into the room, she drew herself up and announced, "The Deputy Chief of Mission of our embassy will be here in a few minutes."

Popeyes answered with another evasive shrug. "Please. Wait here." He evicted the occupants of a small office with two padded swivel chairs, and motioned Sasha and Sunny to sit in them.

"Oh. Now we're the guests of honor," Sunny said bitterly when they were alone.

"You're a pisser," Sasha said, keeping his voice low. "I didn't know you had it in you."

She shrugged. "You always wanted me to play the heavy American," she whispered. "I hit him with all the clout I could think of. Did I leave anything out?" She wrinkled her nose. "I hate people who say things like 'My father is an international banker.' Yuck!"

"Ahh, you're an asshole," Sasha said sadly. "It just saved your skin, and you hate it."

"Hey, do I have to like it? I did it, didn't I?"

"Shhhh!" He pointed at the walls. "You did it magnificently, but you couldn't do it again if you tried."

"Oh yeah?" Good, she was mad again. "If Harold isn't here in a few minutes, watch me." A quizzical frown crossed her face. "Actually, I enjoyed that quite a lot."

"Whew!" Sasha sagged in his chair with exaggerated relief. "You had me worried."

They sat in silence, except for the squeak of Sunny's swivel chair as she fidgeted. Sasha studied her, wondering how much more she had in her. You needed a real fire in your belly, and life had treated Sunny too gently; grievance was not her native tongue. She'd gone far, but not far enough. They were still here, entombed in soundproof walls of chalky despair, in the middle of an indifferent night.

Their plane left in the morning. Would they be on it, or would they be held here, used to create some kind of scandal? Traded for a spy? Of course, such a move would cost the Romanians dearly; everything Sunny had said was true. The trouble was, it would cost Sasha, too. Even a few hours of being treated like a criminal had cut to the hunted quick of him. Confidence that took years to build could crumble like sand.

He dozed, feeling sweaty and ill, like a thief in a detention cell. When he was startled awake by the commotion in the hall, he knew they had come for him.

"What seems to be the problem?" said Harold, coming briskly into the room.

He was dreaming. No, this was real! Help had arrived.

Sasha wouldn't have picked J. Harold Allen to personify the power of the United States. He wasn't Georgie Patton, or John Wayne. He was a mild, baby-faced diplomat with a paunch, a retreating hairline, and glasses. But at this moment, in this place, he was a sight for sore eyes.

*   *   *   *

Suddenly the little office was crowded with people: Harold in a three-piece suit, cheeks rosy with wine from the Nigerian ambassador's dinner; his amiable *securitate* chauffeur, in a black vest and cap; Sunny's kidnapper with the scary eyes, acting all deferential; and a small, leathery, expressionless man with lots of gold braid on his uniform. Everyone was talking at once.

"You cannot detain U.S. citizens without very serious provocation," said Harold.

"Get us the fuck out of here, *now,*" said Sasha.

"This man and woman are accused of smuggling a forbidden drug into Romania," said the general.

"Harold, they're trying to frame us!" Sunny yelled above the din.

"Hold it, hold it." Harold made calm-down motions with both hands. "One at a time, please. These people are personal friends. You say there are charges against them?"

The general jerked a come-hither hand at the pale-eyed agent the way an impatient man might summon his dog. It was the same gesture brown-coat had used on his own subordinates; he was clearly familiar with both roles. He stepped forward, military-prompt, and presented an envelope containing the six wasp-striped capsules and a bureaucratic form in quintuplicate, sandwiched with carbon paper.

"*This* was found in madame's luggage," said the general.

Harold peered into the envelope. "What is it?" He turned to Sunny. "Looks like a prescription medication."

"Why are you looking at *me?*" Sunny cried with exasperation. "I told you, they planted it!"

Harold turned back to the general. "If that's true, it's a very serious charge. I should warn you—"

"Wait till the media get hold of this story," Sunny broke in, addressing the general, who was hardly taller than she was. "Innocent tourists come here and you plant drugs in their luggage—"

"These people are not 'innocent tourists,'" the general said coldly to Harold over her head. "They are traveling under false pre*ten*ses. To begin with, the woman is a journalist." He said it with the loathing Westerners reserve for "terrorist." "She did not register with us as such. And she has introduced a dangerous drug into our country. For what purpose, or on whose instructions…" he let the insinuation linger "…is a matter for investigation." He signaled sharply to brown-coat, who produced Sunny's notebook on cue. "Look at this. Many re-*fer*-ences to 'hex.' This is the same drug we have found in her bag." Clever bastards. Even Sunny could see that it looked fishy.

"Hex," Harold said with interest. "Is that what this is? I've read about it." He looked at Sunny for an explanation.

"I'm writing an article on it," Sunny said, furious that she was the one on the defensive. "When they searched our bags on the train to Brasov, they stole my notebook." Out of the corner of her eye she saw Sasha gaping at her. "They had time to find out what hex was while we were in the village. And I guess somebody—" she drilled her eyes into the general—"saw a chance to screw us *and* our government. They must have flown the pills in on Tarom. Too bad they could only come up with six. It makes a lousy case for smuggling. But they're no match for New York's drug dealers."

"A very complicated story," the general said to Harold. "We have a saying in Romanian: 'The liar takes the long road around the truth.' We would not bring that drug here for any reason. We do not want your vices in our society."

"But Ms. Randall is quite right," Harold said. His voice was a ray of sweet reason slicing through the mad totalitarian murk. "Six pills make no case for drug smuggling. First of all, no one has proven that these things actually are 'hex,' as you claim." That had never even occurred to Sunny. Her shocked recognition had functioned like guilt. The capsules could be fakes. "Second, supposing they *are* hex, and even supposing that she *did* bring them in—which I have no reason to believe," Harold said hastily, intercepting Sunny's glare—"six pills could be for...ah...personal use. If your allegations were true, she would be guilty of being unwise, nothing more." He turned to Sunny. "Do you have your passports?"

She shook her head.

"Bring me their passports and their luggage, and this incident will end right here."

"They should be tried before a tribunal of the people," the general said. "We will make a formal protest to your embassy in the morning."

"That's your privilege," Harold said, collecting their passports from the man in the brown leather coat. "Good night." And he turned and simply walked out, Sasha and Sunny following him like Hansel and Gretel through the dark woods. Harold's driver came last, with the wretched suitcase.

"You'd better stay the night with Nancy and me," Harold said on the way out. "I'll get you an embassy car to the airport in the morning, as soon as all this is cleared up."

"From rags to riches," Sunny murmured, remembering the formal vastness of diplomats' mansions. You couldn't travel further in one night.

Outside in the courtyard a long black car was waiting among the stubby Volgas and Dacias. A little flag flew on its antenna; its lines sang of Detroit and power and freedom. Harold handed Sasha and Sunny their passports, his driver opened the door, and they got in. "Oh, God," Sunny groaned, sinking into the silken leather. "It smells American."

*   *   *   *

The Tarom jetliner did not smell American. It was a Soviet-made Ilyushin IL-23, and the stewardesses had heavy legs and too much lipstick under their moustaches. To Sasha, this was the final indignity: to be forced to endure the atmosphere of Romania all the way back to New York. But they had missed their Thursday morning Pan Am flight while Harold negotiated with the Romanians, who had the gall to insist on filing charges, but grudgingly agreed to forgo a trial. Sasha and Sunny had sent their cat sitter a telegram and slept a second night under high-class house arrest at Harold's. And on Friday there was only the Romanian airline. Harold had accompanied them personally to the airport, where a scowling officer stamped their passports with a black-bordered ban that would prevent them from entering Romania again. Sasha had beamed like W.C. Fields being eighty-sixed from Philadelphia.

"Take a good look around at the faces," he said to Sunny at 33,000 feet. "It's the last time you're ever going to see them."

"Not counting all the cab drivers and hot-dog vendors in New York," Sunny said.

"They're already a higher class," said Sasha. "They had the brains to get out."

"D'you think the seats are bugged?" Sunny peered nervously into her ashtray.

"Ah hah. You're starting to think like a refugee." Sasha looked around. "What I wonder is which of these creeps is assigned to keep tabs on us." The stewardesses were handing out plastic trays of sausage, cheese and tomato and plastic cups of warm beer and mineral water. A little fat guy with the world's shortest thighs sighed with gluttonous complacency as his food was put in front of him. He could be the one. Or the professorial type two rows up, with the thinning greasy hair, glasses, and no lips. A high-ranker, the stewardesses were fawning over him.

"I hope Georgie's onto something," Sasha said to Sunny. "Your fuckin' hex just took ten years off my life. It owes me."

"I wish I'd never heard of it. I feel like it's my fault we're cut off from your mother."

"My mother will just have to get a passport if she wants to see us again," Sasha said heartlessly. He shifted in his seat in a futile attempt to make his legs comfortable under his dinner tray. In his state of aggravated stress, he ate too much and then regretted it. He dropped an Alka-Seltzer into his mineral water. Sunny drank two cups of bitter beer and slept. Sasha couldn't. He cursed the prevailing winds. Why did it have to take so much longer to get home?

At long last they banked in over the shore of Long Island. When the plane touched down, all the spies clapped like schoolchildren. Sasha was out of his seat and dragging Sunny up the aisle before the plane had finished taxiing. They were the first ones out the door. Sunny had to run to keep up with his stride down the neutral corridor that led onto safe ground. There it was: the long line of foreigners forming by the booths to the left and the uniformed guard waving all U.S. citizens to the right, through the world's most wonderful wide-open door.

Sasha beamed at the guard, a very black woman with myriad little braids and a plastic Immigration badge clipped to her navy vest. "Hi there," she smiled back. "Welcome home."

They were the sweetest words Sasha had ever heard.

*   *   *   *

Waiting for their accursed suitcase, Sunny found she'd become hypersensitive to the sound of Romanian. Every time she heard its aggrieved, minor-key music near her in the crowd, the back of her neck prickled. Most Romanians from the plane had enormous amounts of luggage, cheap sets of five or six matching bags, bulging and strapped with rope or belts. There was also a group of dazed refugees, whose suitcases had been sealed into white muslin sacks at Otopeni in some strange ritual of banishment.

A harried customs inspector rushed up to Sasha and Sunny in line, looked at their declarations, and scribbled his O.K. without so much as a glance at the suitcase. Sunny scampered after Sasha through the glass doors into the arrivals area. People thronged around the aisle of metal railings, holding up hand-lettered signs with foreign names. Flights from Germany and Spain had come in at the same time, but Sunny felt sure she could pick out the Romanian faces. In fact, there was one she recognized: a tall, gaunt, sallow man with a beard shadow. Sunny felt a start of confused fear. Hadn't she just seen that man in Bucharest? No—it was *before* their trip! She grabbed Sasha's arm, braking his headlong stride for the exit.

"Look! Isn't that Margie's creep from the after-hours club?"

"Come *on,*" Sasha roared. "Let's get out of here."

Sunny looked back. For sure, it was the man Georgie called Dracula, the one who'd burst out the door of the club as they came up the stairs. She even recognized his thick-necked companion, bending to lift an army-green canvas duffle bag off a luggage cart, SAC DIPLO-MATIC crudely stenciled on its side. Sunny tugged on Sasha again. "Look at their diplomatic pouch!" she giggled. "Like something out of the Flintstones!"

Sasha glanced briefly back. "Oh, yeah. The guy from the U.N. mission." Then he did a double take. Sunny knew what he was thinking:

that guy might have been involved in the operation against them. Someone in New York must have sent the hex to Bucharest—if it was real hex. Had the Romanians known she was a reporter? Had "Dracula's" appearance at the after-hours club been no coincidence? Had everything that happened on their trip been planned in advance?

Would they ever get over this paranoia?

"Dracula" wasn't looking their way. He was embracing a bespectacled man from the plane, kissing him on both cheeks. Sasha pulled her outside, into the exhaust fumes of the ground transportation stop.

"I suppose they've been wanting to get something on you for years," Sunny said. "I feel bad that my work gave them the opening."

"Forget it," Sasha said. "If it wasn't that it would've been something else."

"I guess you're right," Sunny said as they climbed into the bus to the train to the city. "The important thing is, we're home safe."

*   *   *   *

Sasha lay stretched out on the bed, completely covered with rejoicing cats. Sunny, true to form, was going through the mail and playing back the messages. His face buried in Blue, Sasha listened with half an ear. Darlene, saying goodbye…a Greenpeace fund-raiser…bla bla bla…some women's-magazine editor, wanting an article on lipo-something…*there* was one that got his full attention: "Georgie. I got somethin' for ya."…the Radcliffe Club…"Sasha, it's Patty Woo's office. You're cast as General Pavlovich in 'Fearful Symmetry,' at twenty-five hundred a week, and they want you in Toronto Tuesday. Sorry for the short notice! Come pick up your ticket. Bye!"…Sunny's mother Harriet, hoping they were back safe…Sensei, now *that* was unusual, growling, "Sasha-san. Purease terrephone me. Impotant."

"Call him, see what's up," Sasha murmured.

Sunny punched the buttons and handed him the phone. "You talk," she said. "I'm too tired."

"Harro," Sensei growled. Sasha could picture him sitting at his desk in the dojo. Another large part of their life he'd completely forgotten about this past endless week.

"Sensei! OSU!" he hollered. "We're back!"

Silence.

Sasha tried again. "How are you?"

"Sasha-san. Aaahhhhhh…" A sound of pure reluctance, dragged out of him.

"Is something wrong?" Sunny asked.

"I have bad news," Sensei said formally. It was rare for him to utter such a complete, correct English sentence. Sasha pushed the speaker-phone button so Sunny could hear it too.

"Aahhhh," Sensei's sigh came into the room. "Pierre dead."

CHAPTER 9

▼

"Even the sky crying," said Sensei of the gray drizzle that fell softly outside the Bon Dieu Funeral Home.

That set Sunny off again, sobbing into a wadded Kleenex. Sensei looked concerned, and touched by her grief, but Sasha knew she was crying more out of guilt, though she'd been genuinely fond of Pierre. Guilt was a driving force with Sunny. If something went wrong, she assumed first that it was her fault. Sasha thought it was healthier to pin the blame on somebody else if you could. So when she got hysterical at the news that Pierre had been found in a room at the Washington Hotel on Twenty-Third Street, tied to a chair with his throat cut, Sasha had pointed out that there were things far likelier to have killed him than asking a few questions about hex. Like a coke deal gone bad, or a Caribbean turf war. The cops were already speculating that he'd burned some Jamaicans or Colombians, and they'd taken revenge. The knife-happy M.O. was typically Latin, but some of Pierre's friends had said he'd been dealing with Jamaicans.

Sunny would have none of it. "Special ways," she'd wept.

"What are you babbling?"

"Eddie Cole said they—they had special ways of killing you."

"What's so special about getting your throat cut?"

When she kept carrying on as if she'd killed Pierre herself, Sasha had gotten annoyed and said, "See, if you didn't run around doing things behind my back, this would never have happened." She misunderstood, thinking he blamed her too, and got even more desperate. It dawned on Sasha that she really wanted to be talked out of it. So he said, "What I mean is, if you hadn't bothered Pierre, you could be a hundred percent sure the poor bastard got himself killed. This way, you can only be ninety percent sure." It didn't help.

By the time the body was released by the police and fixed up by the undertaker, it was Sunday. Sasha had no desire to see a friend in the clutches of death, but Sensei felt strongly that they should pay respects, and Sunny, thoughtful and wan, insisted on coming too. So they had taken the subway a very long way into what Sunny called "darkest Brooklyn."

The scene at the funeral home was eerie. The three of them were the only mourners; Pierre's mother and sister were staying away. A sign at the door announced "Mr. Pierre Coquillon" as if he were the current attraction in a hotel ballroom. Inside, Pierre lay alone in an open coffin, indifferent, self-enclosed, stiller than stone, his golden-brown glow doused to ash. Sasha had that helpless feeling of being unable to get his attention. It was confusing, because the karate calluses on Pierre's knuckles looked so familiar. The funeral parlor was empty the way that deadly tollbooth was silent and empty in "The Godfather": as if all the living had fled before a squall of slaughter. This ominous loneliness had prompted Sensei to invite the sky as a mourner.

"I...*hate*...death," Sasha ground out, squeezing his fists, as they stood under the canopy waiting for the rain to slow. Sunny's face was the color of flour. Sasha didn't think she'd ever seen a dead friend before.

That night he made her stay in bed while he went up to the after-hours club to find out what Georgie knew. He could not wait another night to learn whether there might in fact be a link between Pierre's death and hex. He needed to know if Georgie's friend had made contact with Horner/Warner or his pushers, and if so, how he read them. If they were killer cowboys, it would take a different strategy than if they were just scum like Eddie Cole.

Georgie wasn't there.

At first this struck Sasha as a sinister coincidence. But then Fat Joey waddled over and said, "Ah, Georgie, ya know him, he's lyin' low."

"You know where?"

Joey's shrug rippled through his huge body like Jell-o. "Somewhere the shylocks can't find him." The loud red night pulsed obliviously around them, the inside of a heartless heart.

Sunday, a slow night, was Margie's night off, so C.J. wasn't around either. Sasha had planned on setting a trap for "Dracula," to repay the shit they'd gone through in Romania. It would just have to wait till he got back from Canada. "If you hear from Georgie, tell him to give me a call, will ya?" he asked Joey, and then he went down into the warm spring dawn. He scat-sang jazz to himself as he walked. He was happy: happy not to be in Romania, happy not to be in that coffin.

Sunny didn't wake up when he came in, just turned over, whimpering. Sasha sat on the edge of the bed and put a gentle hand on her to wake her. She bolted upright with a gasp.

"Don't scare me like that! I thought you were—" She broke off, shaking her head.

"The nightmare again?"

She rubbed her eyes with the heel of her hand. "The guy from the train was lying in Pierre's coffin in his brown leather coat. I wanted to get away quick but I couldn't, and those horrible eyes popped open and stared at me, and he *smiled!*"

"C'mere." Sasha wrapped her in his arms and put one big hand on her head, a cap of comforting.

"What'd Georgie say?" she asked into his chest.

Sasha explained that a bad debt had driven Georgie into his burrow. "He'll probably call while I'm up in Toronto. Make sure you get a number where I can call him back."

Sunny pushed away from him. "Can't I set up a meeting with him myself? This is my last week for research."

"No. Georgie won't give you the information he has, and I wouldn't trust you with it if he did. I know you. You'll be prowling around the park five minutes after I leave for the airport. I should get Bo-bo down here to watch you."

He expected a defiant outburst, but all she said was, "Jesus, Sash. Don't you think I've had enough adventures?" She slid off the bed, combing her wild hair with her fingers. "Well, maybe I'll find out something in California."

"You don't have to go to California."

That got a look of alarmed indignation. "What do you mean, I don't have to go to California? Professor David Szlacter is the grand-daddy of designer drugs. I can't write this piece without talking to him."

Sasha held out the telephone.

"Oh, great. 'David Szlacter, U Cal Berkeley Professor of Psycho-pharmacology, is sixty-two years old and has a soft voice. Sorry, but I can't tell you if he's tall, short, fat, thin, bald, has wild white hair like Albert Einstein, or gestures when he talks.' That's real vivid journalism. Besides, this guy's been working in a legal gray area for thirty years. He probably thinks the FBI has his phone tapped, and he's probably right. He's not going to talk on the phone."

"So have Darlene fly him here! It's the same plane fare. The streets of California are full of crazies killing each other over drugs. You want to end up like Pierre?"

"You're the one who told me Pierre couldn't have gotten killed over hex! Look, I'm not messing with any more street people. One Eddie Cole is enough. I'd interview the professor and come home."

Sasha sighed. She was as agile and maddening as a mosquito. "Look, Sunny. I want to do this part with peace of mind. I don't want to be constantly worrying about you. I want you home, where I know you and the kittens are safe." *And where someone can keep an eye on you,* he thought again, but didn't say it.

"What am I supposed to do?" she yelled. "Sit on my ass for a week?"

"Start writing the article!" he roared. "Enough research already! You've got plenty of material. If you need more, use your imagination!"

"Oh, Sasha. You're hopeless." She was laughing in spite of herself, shaking her head. "I give up. It's no use arguing with you."

Sasha took that to mean he'd won.

*   *   *   *

"Got your ticket? Your passport?"

Sasha held open his jacket and showed her.

"Alka-Seltzer? I know you and those movie-set buffets. Aspirin? Q-Tips? Toothpicks? Your new Spenser book?"

"I got everything, little Sunny."

"Okay. Take good care of yourself. And don't worry about us. We'll be fine." Sunny stood on tiptoe to kiss him. He got into the cab, looking forlorn, as he always did when he left her. She felt the same emptiness as she watched the yellow cab dwindle up the avenue.

When the cab had blended into traffic, Sunny stood there for a moment, shoulders drooping. Then she turned decisively and strode back to their building. She took the stairs two at a time, flung herself down in her desk chair, grabbed the phone, and punched in a number.

"American Airlines, how may I help you?"

"What time tomorrow do you have flights to San Francisco?"

Sunny had it all figured out. Tonight Sasha would call from his hotel in Toronto and give her his phone number. She'd offer to call him from now on, because it would be cheaper. (Sasha could never resist an appeal to thrift, a scar of Russia as real as those on his legs.) She knew he wouldn't go bar-hopping with his fellow actors; he'd rather spend evenings in his room, reading or watching a B thriller on

TV. She'd just call him from the Coast and pretend to be home. As extra precautions, she'd forbid the cat sitter to answer the phone, and she'd call the answering machine often to intercept and return any messages from Sasha. She'd only be gone for a day and a half. She'd made the appointment with Professor Szlacter for Thursday morning. She'd fly out Wednesday afternoon, have the rest of Thursday for follow-up, and take the red-eye back that night.

It bothered her to lie to Sasha, but what other choice did she have? To leave him in an agony of unnecessary worry? Unless Professor Szlacter was himself the mastermind of hex, or a co-conspirator, she had nothing to fear. This wasn't Romania.

That was a thought that struck her with renewed force early Thursday morning, as she walked up Telegraph Avenue towards the professor's house. Romanians walked their gray streets with the intense focus of privation and fear, alert to the possible threat or the next crude pleasure. Berkeleyites strolled or jogged their sun-gilded streets with an air of dreamy distraction, lost in their thoughts and sometimes the extra diversion of a Walkman. Even more than New Yorkers, these Californians wore a layer of psychic fat that Sunny could *see*. And in Berkeley, most people lived in a dream within the Dream: women Sunny's age in long skirts and long earrings, blue-jeaned men whose radical beards had grayed.

A tall, thin street dweller stood like a sentinel on the corner of Telegraph and Dwight Way. Sunny recognized uneasily that he, too, was her contemporary. His grease-black jacket and drooping pants were the uniform of homelessness everywhere, but his long prophet's beard and hair marked him as the Bay Area's unique breed of derelict: a mad Magellan of LSD, an Ancient Mariner gone adrift from the Haight-Ashbury two decades ago. As Sunny waited for the light, he fixed her with a stare that shouted silent apocalyptic warnings. He was the only one she'd seen whose eyes were as urgent and present as a Romanian's.

A wind chime dangling on Professor Szlacter's front porch made sounds like a Beatles sitar. His house was dark-green frame, with white trim on the windows and a dense evergreen hedge grown tall around the back yard. Sunny heard the doorbell ring far back in the house, and then she stood there. She was beginning to think nobody was home, that Professor Szlacter had forgotten the interview or thought better of it, when she heard the shush of bare feet, and the doorknob fidgeted.

The woman who opened the door looked Mexican Indian, and not much more than 25 years old. Sunny took in her bright embroidered dress and gold coin earrings, her dusky skin and long straight black hair, the flat planes of her beautiful but impassive face. Student, housekeeper, adopted daughter—or the professor's Gauguin fantasy?

"I'm Sarah Randall from *Metro* Magazine. I have a nine-thirty appointment with Professor Szlacter."

Holding the door open with one hand, the girl twisted her upper body like an otter and called back into the house, "Daa-*veeed!*"

The house was aquarium-dim. Sunny saw rioting houseplants, piles of magazines, walls of books, old dark tables, overlapping ethnic rugs like the floor of a seraglio, a primitive wooden flute resting on a music stand. Fierce but dusty masks glowered from the walls. With a start Sunny remembered going to the Museum of Natural History after her first mescaline trip, understanding the agony of revelation on all the carved faces: Zulu, Iroquois, Inca, Haida. She was sure these masks were no mere collection, but tokens of membership in a brotherhood beyond space and time. Her heart quickened. She felt close to the secret of hex.

From the back of the house she heard the squeak of old stairs, accompanied by the scrabble of a dog's nails on bare wood. The dog came first, a bullet-sleek Doberman, loping down the central hallway to launch itself through the air at Sunny—and lick her face. Grappling with the dog, she heard David Szlacter's voice before she saw him: "Down, Saba. Good girl! Now get down." It was the same high, husky voice she'd heard on the phone, strained through some sort of obstruction. The dog dropped to its haunches, and Sunny was face to face with the granddaddy of designer drugs. A lean saturnine man, around five nine, baggy work pants, halo of unkempt gray hair around a balding crown, thick black-rimmed glasses, and an accordion grin that collapsed deep creases into his cheeks.

"You passed the acid test," he said, not much above a whisper. "Saba kissed you. It's the opposite of the Judas kiss. If someone doesn't mean us well, she bites 'em. Government agents are her favorite meal. Call me David." He stepped forward and held out his hand. He had a firm dry grip, and his skin radiated heat like a desert animal's. Something in Sunny went *Oh-oh.* Sure enough, as the professor squeezed her hand, his magnified eyes raked down her body in a move at once practiced and hungry.

She sighed inwardly and prepared for a difficult interview.

"And this is my wife, Socorro," the professor went on without missing a beat. Sunny shook the woman's cool, passive hand, only now noticing the wedding ring on it. "Socorro is a Mazatec, from Huautla de Jimenez," Szlacter said proudly, as if his wife were an acquisition no more sentient than a Ming vase. "In fact, she's a grandniece of Maria Sabina." He darted his eyes at Sunny to see if she grasped the significance.

"The mushroom shaman, the one with the chants," Sunny said, displaying her psychedelic bona fides. She saw the spark of pleasure in his eyes and knew she'd passed his second acid test.

"Have you ever heard them? They're extraordinary. They can put you into an altered state of consciousness all by themselves. Come on, I'll play one for you." Szlacter went down two steps into the sunken living room to the left and turned coaxingly.

"Thank you, but I think we'd better get started," she said. "I have about a thousand questions to ask you. I'll tell you frankly that this interview is very important to my piece."

The professor came back up the steps. "I get a good feeling from you," he said to Sunny's body. "I've had a few wise-guy reporters come around asking about hexamethylene. I didn't like 'em, I didn't trust 'em, and…they'd never traveled. You know. I gave them the official Berkeley-professor rap, psychopharmacology of hex, bang, finished." He eyed her like a chess master challenging a worthy opponent. "Ask me the right questions, and you might learn more."

"You're on," Sunny said, feeling the thrill of the chase. She was glad she was female and that she'd taken mescaline, even if it was just twice. Those two keys could unlock this story. But she'd have to use them very carefully.

"Let's sit out back, why don't we? Want something to drink? Make us an iced Red Zinger, would you, Sokey?" Without waiting for his wife's reply, Szlacter turned and led the way towards the back of the house, Saba skulking beside him. Sunny followed, checking her watch.

A quarter of ten: quarter to one in Toronto. They'd be breaking for lunch on the movie set, and Sasha might call her. The night before, from her room at the Willows bed-and-breakfast inn in San Francisco, she'd managed to convince him she was home. He'd wanted to hear one of the cats, but she'd told him they were all asleep and she didn't want to wake them. So far so good. As soon as this interview was over, she'd check her messages and leave one for him. She'd have to fool him once more, from the airport tonight. By morning she'd be in New York, and the brief deception would be over.

✳   ✳   ✳   ✳

"How's Sunny?"

There was a pause. "Then she's not with you," said Billy Baines.

"With *me?* What are you talking about?" Sasha roared. Two lighting technicians setting up the next shot glanced over at him.

Another pause. "I lost her." Billy sounded gruff and sheepish.

Sasha almost dropped the receiver of the pay phone. "You *what?*"

"Hey, man, take it easy. I'm goin' right over there. I'll call you the minute she shows up."

"You idiot." Sasha pulled at the tight collar of his Russian general's uniform, feeling the sweat break through his makeup. "You weren't supposed to let her out of your sight if you had to sleep on the door-step. Were you drunk?" If only he'd called Bo-bo. But the time had been short, and Billy—musician, carpenter, former regular in Sasha's bar—had been available and eager to repay old debts. He was one of many talented Village vagabonds Sasha had helped, and one who'd turned out all right, thanks to Alcoholics Anonymous.

"No, man. Come on. Six years sober, and you think I'm gonna pick this moment to fall off the wagon? That really hurts me. No, yesterday afternoon around two-thirty, she comes out with a little bag and gets in a cab. And you know how it is, you need a cab there aren't any? I got the license number of hers, but it was ten minutes till another one showed up."

"You lost her *yesterday?*" Sasha's mind raced. "But she called me from home last night. Or—wait a minute." He was beginning to guess what had happened. The spotlight of his anger swiveled off Billy, stabbed in search of Sunny, then shot back. "Why didn't you tell me this last night?"

"Hey, I didn't want to scare you for nothing! I figured she'd proba-bly gone uptown on business. When she wasn't back by eight, I called the cab company, got the night dispatcher, and tracked down the driver at home in Queens. Took me an hour and a half, but I found out she went to the airport. Okay, I figured most likely she flew up there to surprise you. Anyway, I was gonna call the airlines, try and find out where she went before I got you all upset."

"I know where she went." Sasha was breathing hard. "She left the kittens. That dirty bastard." He pictured them lonely, hungry, their kitty litter lumpy and their water bowl dry. It wasn't like Sunny to leave them neglected, but he wanted to imagine this betrayal as total.

"All right. It's not your fault," he said to Billy Baines. "You've got the keys. Go up and make sure the cats have food and fresh water. And keep watching the place. When she comes back, call me immediately."

If she comes back, he thought as he hung up the phone and pressed his forehead against its metal, drawing cold from its cold. It would serve her right if something happened to her.

He started towards the set, then turned back and viciously punched the buttons for their home number.

"Hi! Sasha and Sunny can't come to the phone right now, but you can leave a message after the funny little beep..."

Her voice wrung Sasha's heart. He waited grimly for the message to end, then left one telling her in no uncertain terms what he thought of her.

He hung up, hesitated, then punched the number again.

"Hi! Sasha and Sunny—"

Sasha interrupted, pressing the code for collecting messages. He wasn't sure he'd done it right, but the machine beeped three times, and he heard the twitter of rewinding tape. The first two messages he ignored, bullshit for Sunny.

"Sasha. Georgie. Call me at 718-439-6266."

Sasha laboriously wrote the number down. Christ, these little tasks cramped his big hands. Sunny normally did them for him, with her clever fingers. It was one of the many ways he felt her absence.

Fuck her.

He wondered if somebody was doing just that

It was an ugly suspicion, and he hated himself for it. But he hated her more for the lie that forced him to feel it, as if every lie between a man and a woman came down to that.

The assistant director was signaling him, five fingers held high. "Positions! Rolling in five!"

Sasha hurriedly dialed Georgie.

"Yeah." The voice that answered was soft and wary, slurred to elude recognition.

"It's me. Sasha."

"Hey!" Georgie's voice came into focus. "Where are ya?"

"Up in Toronto, on the movie set."

"Got some news when I see ya."

"Oh yeah? Would Willie Sutton like it?" The famous hold-up man had liked banks because "that's where the money is."

"We-ell…There's a Hispanic connection."

Sasha's blood froze. He saw Sunny out there exposed like a doe in the cross hairs. He made a decision.

"I'm coming down tonight. There someplace I can meet you?"

A long pause. "Call me when you get in," Georgie mumbled.

Sasha hung up and strode toward the hot lights, trying to get back into General Pavlovich. Hopeless. His lines were gone, blown clean out of his mind. He plucked a script out of a startled script girl's hand and leafed through it. The shooting schedule gave him tomorrow off; then came the weekend. Time enough, with luck, to catch Sunny and bring her up here with him. While he ranted in Russian for the cameras, she could sit and write her article in the Parc Hotel.

✳   ✳   ✳   ✳

Sunny followed Professor Szlacter through a messy sky-blue kitchen, with an old stove and sink, strings of dried chilies draped around a poster of a Tibetan mandala, and bunches of yellow straw flowers in night-blue glasses. Socorro worked clinking at the sink, her back to them; a large tortoise crawled around free on the floor. Saba pawed it, then darted outside when Szlacter unlatched the back door. He ushered Sunny out onto a small, cracked flagstone patio, sheltered by a latticework arbor twined with grapevines and morning glories, their soft blue trumpets still open. Another wind chime danced and tinkled in the breeze.

Sunny pulled out a white metal chair and put her notebook and tape recorder on the glass-topped table. The morning was cool, and the chair chilled the underside of her thighs. The professor sat down across from her and smiled at her with too much warmth and intimacy. Sunny felt an uneasy stir in her lower belly. She'd run into this type of man before, and while their regard was so impersonal as to be insulting, it was also so intense and knowing that you had to respond. She looked away, out into the yard, and saw there, like an erotic emblem, a golden faun of a young man, naked from the waist up, digging in a garden beside a small greenhouse. As he swung the shovel, smooth muscles glided under his skin: Sunny's Gauguin fantasy. Feeling her gaze, the boy looked up like a startled animal, a flash of black-and-white eyes under a wing of black Indian hair. Sunny began to feel as if she was tripping.

Szlacter followed her look with too much understanding. "Socorro's brother, Fernando," he said. "We're sponsoring him as a student here." His voice dropped. "Beautiful, isn't he?" The words were right in her ear.

Sunny shook her head angrily. The trance broke, and she was sitting here with a dirty old man and his yard boy, who was probably planting marijuana or worse. "Beauty is truth, truth beauty," she said, and clicked on her tape recorder. "So how about some truth, Professor? I bet you know more about hex than almost anyone in this country. And with kids dying, I think you have a responsibility to tell what you know."

Socorro appeared like a shadow, set down a tray with two tall red glasses of iced tea, and was gone.

Szlacter wore a Sphinx's smile. "We'll get to that," he said. "But I'll start with a little history of the neuroconsciousness frontier." He lifted his glass to Sunny, and she reluctantly reciprocated. Was there something in the tea? She'd heard there were people who could hypnotize you without your knowing it; she was pretty sure Szlacter had been doing that to her. Would he stop there? True believer, seducer, maybe even criminal that he was, with his greenhouse and his Doberman? She took a tiny sip. Part of her began anxiously monitoring her own state while another part listened to him.

"You may already know that I was Tim Leary's grad student at Harvard, in the psilocybin project. Spring of 1961. There were, oh, two dozen of us. Most of them came out of academic psych or soc sci, plus a couple of artists and poets.

"I came at it from neurophysiology, sticking electrodes in rats' brains. I was the good Newtonian scientist who scoffed at this psychologist friend of mine raving about love and the ecstasy of consciousness. He dared me to try psilocybin. I took it to prove him wrong." He chuckled. "Next time I went to wire a rat, he looked at me with his little red eyes, and damned if he wasn't my brother. I put him in my pocket and took him home."

Sunny began to like him in spite of herself.

"I was smart, though. When Leary got his ass thrown out of Harvard, I stayed. Tim was mutating into a poet, a prophet, a guru. I was still a scientist—still am, for that matter. I subscribe to Huxley's axiom: don't abandon scientific principles, transcend 'em." Szlacter leaned forward, his eyes glowing. *Thank God,* Sunny thought, *the blood's going to his brain now.* She was also relieved to find that she felt normal. Emboldened, she took another sip of tea.

"You see," Szlacter said, "I believe the psychedelic drugs have more to teach us about the mind-matter interface, the quantum cosmos and its creator than any other tool discovered by woman or man. The better we understand the chemistry of the brain, the more we can refine the tools; the better the tools, the more we learn about the brain and its cosmic context. So I hung in there and got my doctorate in the new field of neurochemistry. My thesis was on neurotransmitters and schizophrenia, a subject much illuminated by LSD."

His sharp eye caught Sunny squirming in her chair. "All right. Cut to Berkeley in the late Seventies, and my"—wry grin—"justly celebrated seminar, 'The Chemistry of Consciousness.' Turn it off." He jerked his head abruptly at the tape recorder. Sunny, startled, complied.

"What I'm about to tell you now is off the record." Szlacter leaned close to her and lowered his voice even more than usual, though there was no one nearby to hear. Sunny could feel the heat from his skin.

"I've decided to trust you with information that could compromise my career. I've made this decision on two grounds. One is, as I've said, I have a good feeling about you. And I have one of the finest bullshit detectors on the planet. The other is that if you betray my trust, and quote me, I'll sue the hell out of you and your magazine for libel, and you'll lose. You'll have no proof that I ever said any such thing, and no corroboration, because the few people who know the truth have as much to lose as I do.

"I've kept my academic position and my private research interests scrupulously separate. I will have to live this schizoid life for just as long as the medieval laws of this country lump an exquisite tool like MDMA together with a blunt instrument like heroin. There is no middle ground in this culture between total prohibition and total excess. No room for wisdom. What's happening now with hexamethylene is a scandal. I've seen those kids, over on the campus. It's tragic. A drug that powerful should never have gotten out of the laboratory, or at least not beyond a circle of adepts, like the few thousand people who use 'Vitamin K.' But that doesn't invalidate the beautiful work therapists were doing with Ecstasy. Now it's a street drug, and you don't know what you're getting. The spirit of responsible inquiry has been driven underground by irresponsible lawmakers and irresponsible profiteers. And that, alas, is where it's going to stay. Agreed?"

Before she could answer, he cocked a warning finger at her. "If you refer to any of this, it's in the vaguest, most general terms—temporal and geographical. You show me those references before you go into print, and you print only what you've shown me and I've okayed. If anyone can identify either me or the former members of my seminar, your ass is sued. Got it?" He softened the tough talk with an engaging grin.

Sunny solemnly mimed pricking her finger and signing in blood, and the grin widened.

"Okay! The 'Chemistry of Consciousness' seminar.

"I had twelve hand-picked graduate students, my twelve apostles, the best scientific minds I could find—brilliant, rigorous, but venturesome. We'd learned from Tim Leary's mistakes. Oh, had we learned! We covered our asses. Officially, the seminar was a sober look at neurotransmitters and alertness, making rats sleepy and waking them up again. Informally, we were tinkering with some new compounds that bore a significant resemblance to natural brain chemicals. And then we met in this house at night, like a witches' coven, and tried the results on ourselves."

Sunny waited for him to go on, but he was silent, looking at her from under half-lowered lids with a come-hither smile. *Oh no,* Sunny thought. *Here comes the part where I have to give something to get something.* But then she remembered him saying *Ask me the right questions,* and she thought maybe he was one of those people for whom intellectual fencing is almost as sexy as sex. The right questions...*Did you invent Ecstasy?* wasn't one of them. He wouldn't answer it, even off the record. As for hex, from the disapproving way he talked about it, and his convincing air of curmudgeonly integrity, she doubted he was the mastermind. But she thought that he knew who was, even if he didn't know he knew. It had to be one of the students from his seminar. Had to be. Sunny felt very, very close. She almost held her breath to keep from blowing away the downy feather of truth.

When she spoke, it was barely above a whisper. This might not be one of the right questions, but it was the one she needed to ask.

"Was there someone in your seminar named Horner? Or Warner?"

$$*\qquad*\qquad*\qquad*$$

At nine thirty-five that night, Sasha cleared U.S. Customs at LaGuardia Airport. He went straight to a pay phone and called Brooklyn Georgie, who, from the area code, must be close by, in Brooklyn or Queens—if he hadn't moved his den. The phone rang for a long time, but finally Georgie picked up.

"Was on the can," he apologized.

"Where can I meet you?"

"Uh…grab a cab, tell him to head for Sheepshead Bay." So Georgie was deep in home territory. His old man had owned a café in Sheepshead Bay where a lot of big mob guys hung out. He gave Sasha directions to a candy store on a particular corner.

Sasha didn't know Brooklyn, so he entrusted himself to the Trinidadian cab driver and tried to feel where Sunny was, what was happening to her. He drew a blank. It was a creepy sensation, like having half your face lost to Novocain. A big chunk of him was just gone.

When he got out of the cab in front of the tiny candy store and newsstand, he smelled the sea and fried fish. In Manhattan you had no sense of how very close you were to the ocean, but Sheepshead Bay was a place where working-class people had boats in their back yards.

He stood there pretending to look at the newspapers for a few minutes before he heard a whistle and saw Georgie's rotund figure waiting at the edge of the light. Georgie was dressed for shadows, in a gray jacket and gray pants. Black leather Italian shoes, though; he wouldn't wear sneakers even to sneak. He looked tired, but Georgie always looked tired.

They walked a few blocks in silence, and then Georgie led him up onto the porch of an old three-story wood frame house, unlocked the front door, and continued up a narrow stairway, wheezing. He rested on the second landing, then struggled on up the last flight. He let Sasha into a little attic apartment with a hot plate, a gray carpet, a claw-footed tub, and one old armchair with a head-grease stain, facing a black-and-white TV. The TV was on without sound. A big bowl of popcorn sat beside the armchair, heavily buttered and half-eaten.

"Pain in the ass," Georgie said by way of apologetic welcome. He waved at the armchair.

"No, no. Go ahead." Sasha settled his butt on the windowsill and watched Georgie collapse gratefully back into the armchair. Georgie held out the bowl of popcorn. Sasha shook his head, and Georgie's eyebrows went up in a sleepy owl's surprise.

"I never seen you say no to somethin' ta eat."

"As soon as I turned my back, Sunny ran off—"

"Ah hah."

"—chasing this assignment of hers out to California."

Georgie rolled his eyes. "Whaddaya gonna do with these broads. I says to my mother, God bless her, she says why don't you get married? I says, Mamma. They don't make 'em like they useta." He tossed a handful of popcorn into his mouth.

"I'm worried about her running into those Latinos you mentioned. What's the story?"

Georgie finished chewing. "Dominick made contact," he said, wiping his mouth with his hand. "Street dealer was pushin' a few pills a the stuff around Erasmus Hall High. Dominick wanted to beat the shit out of him an' kick his ass outta the neighborhood, but he followed instructions. Made a lotta noise to the guy about how he wanted in, but in a big way, none a this nickel-and-dime stuff. Dealer seemed real nervous. Dominick kept on him. Finally the guy gives him a little slip a paper says 'Junior's,' for Chrissake, 'Tuesday, 10:30 A.M.'"

"Junior's? The cheesecake place on Flatbush Avenue?"

"Yeah. Big joint, real public place, but empty in the morning. Dom's sittin' there, drinkin' a cappucin', and this spic walks in."

"A Colombian?"

"How the fuck do I know? Dominick don't have no idea. A spic! Joo know? One a them guys talk like thees, looks half Injun, half *muliyam*"—meaning black, the Sicilian word for "eggplant."

"Part black?" Sasha leaned forward "Could be Dominican, Puerto Rican, Cuban…probably not Colombian, though."

Georgie shrugged. "Who the hell are you, El Exigente? What's the difference if they fuckin' shoot you?" Sasha had to laugh in spite of himself. "Dom says this guy's their enforcer." Georgie shook his head. "Bad news."

Sasha felt an icicle go through his heart. "How so?"

"Guy's maybe thirty and his face's all cut up. Knife scars. Jailhouse tattoos on his arms, skulls and stuff. Comes on quiet-crazy. You know how some psychos talk real soft, but their eyes are goin—" Georgie made spirals with both forefingers in front of his eyes. "Right on the edge, Dom says. The type cracks, they got no control at all.

"The wild part is, he tells Dominick to stay away from hex! Dom says, 'Don't you wanna make money?' The guy laughs like he's Donald Trump on coke. Then he says, 'We got our own operation, man. We don't need your money. We don't want your kind.'" Georgie looked hurt. "Joe Columbo oughta be around to hear about this anti-Italian prejudice. Says 'Stay the fuck away,' quiet like a close shave. Dom gets the definite feeling he means it."

Sasha frowned. "Nothing about Horner, or Warner?"

"Nah. No names named. So then he leaves, and Dom has his nephew Petey outside, and Petey tails him." Georgie rubbed his eyes and yawned. He was a man of few words, and the strain of narration was getting to him. "This might be what you call the Willie Sutton part. Petey gets in his car, follows the guy several blocks to *his* car, which surprises the shit out of him, 'cause it's a black limo with low-number plates. This guy don't look like no limo driver. But he gets behind the wheel, far's Petey can tell with the tinted windows, and Petey tails him onto the BQE, from there onto the Van Wyck, and then the spic pulls a fast one, cuts across three lanes in that fuckin' limo, damn near starts a pileup, but gets off near JFK and loses Petey. Petey circles back, cruises around the airport terminals and some a them back roads with all the parking lots and warehouses, but he don't see no limo."

"So where is de money, *hombre?*"

Georgie shrugged. "Maybe a guy like that could disappear on the Upper West Side, or in Spanish Harlem, but in Howard Beach?" Georgie snorted. "I got him. Just a matter of askin' a few questions."

He stretched painfully. "I could use a score. Get them fuckin' gorillas off my back."

Sasha stood up. "First I've got to get Sunny off the street. This is nothing for her to be involved in. You gonna be here?"

"Far as I know," Georgie said. "If I move on, or if I hear the heat's off, I'll call ya."

"When I get hold of Sunny—"

"Smack her," Georgie said sagely. "I told ya. Put some respect in her or you'll never have nothing but grief."

"I'm gonna take her up to Toronto and sit on her. I got one more week up there. Try to track down that spic. You find their base, see how tight security is. When I get back we'll move on 'em."

Georgie turned up his palms. "I got nothin' but time."

Sasha took the train back to Manhattan. It was after midnight and the subway belonged to the predators, but one glance at Sasha told them he wasn't Bernhard Goetz, and he traveled undisturbed except by his own thoughts. If the hex network had a dangerous enforcer here, why should it be any different on the West Coast? What if that professor was a major player, with Hispanic muscle working for him?

He hurried upstairs to the apartment, hoping to find Sunny safe in bed. No one was home but the kittens. They had plenty of food and fresh water, whether from Billy Baines or from some arrangement Sunny had made. Sasha looked around for a clue to her whereabouts. The answering machine was blinking. He tried to remember the right buttons to push to rewind and play messages. He listened to the first three without interest.

"Hi, Sa-sha." Margie's spacy singsong, in a melancholy minor key. "I need to talk to you when you have a chance. Okay? Thanks, cousin. Sunny, are you there? Call me, will ya? By-e!"

The fifth message was the one he'd been waiting for. It was Sunny, and she was crying. "I'm sorry, Sash," she said, and then a lot of stuff he couldn't understand, even on the third playback. A terrible, roaring connection, sounded like a pay phone in a truck depot. He thought he heard her say, "…you won't believe," and he thought he heard "tomorrow." Then her voice was cut off by the sound of the coin being collected, and came back to say, "I love you."

Sasha didn't know what time she'd called or from where, whether she was alone on a street corner or a hostage with a gun to her head. "Tomorrow" could mean she was coming home tomorrow, but why was she crying? She'd sounded scared.

He called the Toronto hotel. Four messages from Sunny, starting in the afternoon, the last one around midnight. No return number.

He stomped around the apartment swearing, looking for something, anything that would tell him where she was. He finally found it in one of the little scrunched-up balls of paper she threw for the cats to play with. He uncrumpled it and read "Willows Inn, 14th St.," and a 415 phone number.

He called in an eager rush of relief. An obviously gay voice told him that Ms. Randall had checked out at five.

It was eleven now in San Francisco. Two A.M. in the east. Sasha dialed Bo-bo.

The phone rang and rang.

*   *   *   *

"I'm sorry, Sash," Sunny wept into the staticky pay phone. "I shouldn't have lied to you. I just didn't want you to worry."

His brief message on the answering machine had frightened her. "I know where you are," he'd said, "and I know what you're doing." She heard him breathing. "I'm glad I found out that you're capable of treachery." That was all.

It wasn't the words that upset her. It was the ugly tone of absolute, cold hostility. She hadn't been able to find a mote of warmth in his voice. She'd seen Sasha that way only a few times in their twelve years together, and it was terrifying. When he felt betrayed, he "went underground"—his words, chilling ones given his background, as if only at the lowest point of his life would he be safe. Then Sunny saw what he'd had to become to survive: a being without need, pity, or attachment. Those moments were a nightmare to her—less of fear for herself than of wild grief for him, lost in that frozen loneliness. She'd gotten hysterical, and in a kind of miracle, her tears had melted the permafrost. He'd become human again, seeming dazed, like an Ice Age hunter thawed out of a glacier, coming all the way back from Mine 28 in a few minutes.

So she cried on the phone, afraid that this time she'd gone too far and he wouldn't come back. How did he know she wasn't in New York? What did he mean, "I know what you're doing?" That was creepy.

"I found out something so incredible," she said with a catch in her voice. "You won't believe it. And I couldn't have found it out without coming here." That was for sure. "I'll keep trying you in Toronto. I'll be home tomorrow. I'm taking the red-eye—" The phone swallowed her coin. Just in case the connection was still good, she added, "I love you."

The Ancient Mariner, still on the corner—maybe he lived there— was staring at her with appalled sorrow. She gave him a little smile and wiped her eyes and mouth with her sleeve. Then she walked slowly up Telegraph Avenue, consoling herself by imagining telling a different Sasha what she'd learned from Professor Szlacter (though not how she'd learned it), imagining his reaction.

When she'd asked, "Was there someone in your seminar named Horner? Or Warner?" the light of recognition she'd hoped for had not dawned in his eyes. He just blinked.

"No," he said. "The names of the participants in my seminar are a matter of public record. Here, I'll save you the trouble of looking 'em up. Campbell, Gray, Friedman, Santucci, Sikorski"—Sunny scribbled in frantic shorthand—"Manea, Greenberg, Fernandez, Harris, Sung, Dyckman, and Schwartz." He looked at her noncommittally, an electron of mischief dancing deep in his eyes.

Sunny's heart sank with her one clue. "Where are they now?"

"All of them?" He laughed. "Scattered to the four winds. Most of 'em have quite respectable academic positions—following in the old man's footsteps. Sikorski's at Harvard, just made full professor. Marcia Friedman's at Stanford. Karen Sung at Ohio State. Dyckman—University of Hawaii. Santucci," his shoulders shook, "works for NIMH." This seemed to be a huge private joke. Sunny supposed he could still picture the sober public servant rolling around on his Kilim rugs in the throes of Ecstasy. These people really were experts at covering their asses, if one of them had landed a government job in a decade when a joint could disqualify you for the Supreme Court.

"Campbell...poor Colin Campbell was our casualty," Szlacter said regretfully. "I picked 'em for brains, but there was, as yet, no way to select for neurochemical stability. Once they nail the genes for susceptibility to schizophrenia, we'll know who has to stay away from this kind of research."

One of them went crazy! Hope leapt in Sunny. "Where is Colin Campbell now? Do you know?"

"Mmm-hmm. McLean's mental hospital, outside Boston. On permanent suicide watch. Sends me a homemade Christmas card every year." So much for that. "Let me see. Fernandez went home to Argentina..."

Sunny held up her hand. "Wait a minute. We're talking wild goose chase here. I can't track down each of these people, interview them, investigate them. Give me a hint."

His eyebrows went up in mock innocence. "A hint of what?"

"Come on, Professor." Sunny's Arien directness came out with her temper. She was losing patience with this foreplay. "You know better than I do how likely it is that one of those people created hexamethylene. And I'm sure you have an idea which one—who was unstable, or...grandiose, or greedy enough to do such a thing, for profit, or power, or revenge. I know you feel a loyalty to all of them, and that's admirable. But there are considerations that should override your loyalty. This drug is killing people! Knowing something about it and keeping quiet is the same as harboring a criminal."

Szlacter was silent for minutes, letting Sunny know she'd broken the rules of the game. Then he stood up. "Come on," he said. "I want to show you something."

Sunny followed him reluctantly over the grass toward the greenhouse, the Doberman romping beside her. She didn't want to be alone in an enclosed space with this cerebral billy goat. He knew something, no question—and his whole demeanor said, "How badly do you want it?" It was outrageous. But she wasn't his student; there was no committee on sexual harassment she could report him to. *Now I know how a starlet feels on the casting couch,* she thought wryly. *How badly* do *you want it?*

Szlacter exchanged a silent signal with the Indian boy, who caught Saba by the collar and led the ebony dog toward the house. He had the decency to avert his eyes from Sunny, but that made her wonder how many times he'd witnessed this little scenario. Her face flamed.

Szlacter opened a heavy padlock on the greenhouse door and stood back to let Sunny in first. Inside, they were on another continent. The air was moist as warm fog, condensate dripped from every leaf, and somewhere water gurgled steadily. The green smell was overwhelming. The professor had created his own tiny tropical jungle, and Sunny knew before he began to introduce her to the plants that it was a psychoactive jungle. Hidden in the drooping heads of the flowers and the potent coils of the vines, visions waited to spring out like jaguars.

"I don't grow marijuana here," the professor said in his high, hoarse voice, "because everyone, including the cops, knows what it looks like. But no one can object to an innocent passion for tropical orchids." He pointed to a delicate, freckled spray perched on a dead tree branch. "I've held benefits for the endangered tropical forest right here! And no one recognized these little fellows as *psilocybe mexicana,*" indicating a cluster of phallic mushrooms, "or this decorative vine as *Banisteriopsis caapi,* the principal visionary ingredient in *ayahuasca,* or these dramatic flowers"—slack, pallid trumpets straight out of Poe—"as belladonna, or deadly nightshade, which Yaqui shamans use to fly." His voice was stealthy and soothing. It reminded Sunny of a cat stalking a bird.

"The plants themselves teach us." He touched her sensitive inner arm, apparently to guide her along the narrow boardwalk. Sunny jerked away and walked ahead, making profane clomping noises with her shoes to ruin the mood. "In my seminar," he went on, unperturbed, "we first apprenticed ourselves to these natural teachers. Then when we began to create synthetic chemicals, we returned frequently to the plants as guides." He squatted to finger a mushroom with a bright red-orange head. "Amanita muscaria," he said. "You see, nature is wise. Man can go wrong. Man can create great evil, even by accident." He stood up. "That's what happened in the case of hex."

He sauntered over to face Sunny, taut as Clint Eastwood before a quick-draw contest. "I'll give you what you want," he breathed, "for a kiss."

Sunny turned away. "Oh, how *childish,*" she said in a loud, sad, disgusted voice. A pulse was hammering in her throat.

Szlacter turned her face back toward him with one finger. "You compliment me," he whispered. "The child is the source of all wonder in us."

God, what a tough hide his ego had. "That's all, then," she said, part question, part warning.

"That's enough." He was actually trembling. "Such a beautiful mouth."

"Get it over with," Sunny said through gritted teeth.

"Of course I know who created hex," said David Szlacter. "We did." And he grabbed her head and plunged his tongue into her mouth.

Sunny's mind spun. The blow of what he'd said had cut clean through her defenses; she wanted to think, not struggle. The taste of another human being was shockingly intimate. His hands swirled over her breasts, then down to her buttocks and pulled her, hard, against his erection. Hey, no fair! She got the heels of her hands against his chest and bucked like a coiled spring. It made enough space between them. She slugged him in the mouth.

David Szlacter staggered backward and bent over, clutching his face. After twelve years of karate, Sunny was still surprised by her own strength. She backed away, feeling behind her for the door. The professor straightened up and looked at the blood on his fingers. He looked at Sunny with complete astonishment, and then he began to laugh.

"I've kissed a lot of girls," he managed to say, "and I've been scratched and I've been slapped, but you're the first one that ever punched me!" He seemed proud of it, a perverse trophy for his collection.

"You owe me," Sunny said with venom. Then she turned and walked haughtily out of the greenhouse and across the lawn. She was sitting at the white table, bouncing a pencil angrily on its edge, when Szlacter sat down opposite her, blotting his split lip with a folded handkerchief. It was already swelling. Sunny wondered what he was going to tell his wife.

"You're right," he said, regarding her with amusement and respect. "I do owe you. So collect."

"You invented hex," she said with contemptuous wonder. He nodded. She found that she felt an unwilling physical connection to him; she could still taste him. That had been forced on her. She felt raped. "You mean your seminar?"

"That's right. In October of 1978."

"But then who—are you—"

"We created it," he said calmly, "and we destroyed it."

It was Sunny's turn to stare with astonishment. "What do you mean? It's all over the place!"

Szlacter let out a bleak hiss. "Over our dead bodies, so to speak," he said. "This is exactly what we hoped to prevent by destroying the drug and all records of its creation. Hex wasn't the only molecule we sent back where it came from. But hex was the worst."

"Come on, Professor. You're a scientist. You know technological advances are irrevocable. Once the cat's out of the bag, you can't put it back. It's like trying to unsplit the atom."

Szlacter fixed her with a steady gaze. "The Japanese had the gun in the sixteenth century," he said. "They got it from the Portuguese. When they realized that it was going to destroy their culture, they banned it for three hundred years. They deliberately forgot how to make it."

"That's the Japanese," Sunny said with exasperation. "They're crazy. No such thing has ever happened in the history of the West. Don't tell me your seminar is the exception. Maybe you destroyed the records—"

"We burned them. In a solemn ceremony. We went around the circle, and each of us fed his or her copy into the flames."

"—but I'm sure all thirteen of you remember that formula like it was yesterday. Somebody probably even kept a Xerox. And now one of you has decided to cash in on it. Or maybe more than one."

Szlacter shook his head. "No," he said. "You see, hex was the drug that pushed Colin Campbell over the edge. The rest of us saw what it did to him, and we know what it did to us. The total loss of boundaries. The...seductive sense of fusion." He chose his words carefully, using his hands to help sculpt a precise description. Sunny flipped open her notebook and wrote it down. "The telepathic suggestibility. The abject eagerness to surrender to a more powerful mind. It made you feel your individuality was a prison, and unison with others was a Nirvana you desperately craved. The potential for abuse, for mind control, was terrifying. Totalitarian. We knew we'd created a monster, and we agreed to smother it in its cradle." He gave her a sad smile. "Isn't that the moral of every horror movie?"

"And then the monster comes back anyway. For the sequel." Sunny stared at him thoughtfully. "Through someone's greed, or Faustian pride. But whose?"

"I'm quite sure it's not one of us," Szlacter said.

"Give me a break," Sunny said. "You don't take this 'twelve apostles' bit seriously, do you? Are you telling me you're all saints? Look, it
doesn't have to be a bad person. Maybe someone's in financial trouble;
they've got a sick kid, or too many debts. Or...well-meaning messianic
fantasies. The world's in a terminal mess, and they think somehow the
power of this drug could turn it around." She shrugged. "I don't know
your people. You tell me."

He was shaking his head again. "When the bad news broke that hex
was out of the bag again, we met. At least the ten of us who are still in
the States, and sane. If someone hadn't shown up, I agree, it would
have been highly suspicious. But they all came. We got caught up on
each other's perfectly ordinary lives: jobs, kids, grants. And we renewed
our vows, you might say." Szlacter drank the last of his tea and put
down the glass with a conclusive clunk. "I told you, I've got a good
bullshit detector. A lot of us do. The hallucinogens sensitize you to
interpersonal nuances." He smiled, touching his lip. "Though they
don't always tell you when to duck. No, I would have known if someone was lying. We came to the conclusion that it was most likely independent   re-invention.   According   to   Sheldrake's   theory   of
morphogenetic fields, when something's been done once, it becomes
much easier to repeat it, even without any knowledge of the first trial."

"But wait a minute. You said two of them aren't in the States. What
about them? Are you in touch?"

"The foreign students. Brilliant boys, both of them. I've had an
occasional postcard from Fernandez, on his collecting trips to the Ama-
zon. Manea, I guess, went back to Romania. I never heard from him
again."

Sunny stared at him blankly. Szlacter didn't seem to notice that the
world had come to a stop.

"Sure, I've wondered if it could be one of them. But I don't see how.
Fernandez was a romantic, more poet than scientist, intuitive, but
completely disorganized. He couldn't mastermind getting himself to
the airport, much less a major drug operation. An innocent, really."

Sunny's throat was dry. She swallowed with effort and said, "Tell me about Manea." It came out in a dusty croak, like Szlacter's own.

"Ion Manea's a little more of an unknown quantity. Extremely bright, off the scale, I'd say, but very quiet, very shy. He wouldn't say much until we got stuck. Then, often, he'd come out with the elegant solution to the problem we'd all been bashing our heads against. We'd roar and pound him on the back and try to get him drunk—yes, alcohol's still the substance of choice for celebrations. Manea would just smile this little sad, superior smile. He was a sort of waif who made some crucial contributions, though not, as I recall, in the case of hex. I got to be fond of him." Szlacter's eyes were distant, reminiscent. His nuance detector wasn't picking up the fact that Sunny was totally blown away.

"It was hard for him to open up. I remember times when everybody was sprawled all over the floor, laughing and crying, and Manea sat there with his back against the wall and that little smile. Finally once I got him alone on Ecstasy. Apparently I'd gained his trust. It was like a dam breaking. He sobbed and told me he didn't want to go back. There were some family horror stories. Mother died very early. His father was distant, authoritarian, a big-shot Communist from the Thirties. He'd never gotten a kind word from his father, and never had an identity apart from his father. He was 'old Manea's kid,' the sapling in the shadow. Getting sent to study in the States had been his first big break, and he didn't want it to end. I guess I was a kind of alternative father for him.

"He never said another word about it, but I tried to help him. I convinced the department to offer him an assistant professorship. We went through months of paperwork and actually got him labor certification, proved he was more qualified than any available American. And then Immigration wouldn't let him in. Some bullshit about Communist Party membership. Real McCarthy era, witch-hunt stuff. It was a bitter disappointment for him. But there was nothing I could do."

"There's a motive right there," Sunny said softly.

"What?" Szlacter focused back on Sunny, and for the first time noticed her agitation. *"Manea?* Impossible."

"Why? You're the one who called the drug totalitarian."

"Way over there, locked up in some little Balkan country? How could he do it, by remote control?" Szlacter frowned. "Even if he was back here without my knowledge, how would he put together a national distribution network? Manea was no leader of men. And his English sucked."

"His government has motives, too," Sunny whispered. She was seeing, over and over again, the six vivid capsules of hex sliding out of her Tampax box. More than an attempt to frame or intimidate her, had it been a brilliant diversion? All that puritanical ranting about capitalist decadence—meant to point the finger in exactly the wrong direction?

Had they thought she'd come to Romania on the trail of hex?

David Szlacter made a gesture of disgust. "Reagan promoted exactly that kind of paranoia about cocaine. 'Narcoterrorism,' he called it. Anything as bad as our drug problem must be a Communist plot. Couldn't possibly have anything to do with poverty and despair, right? Convince us Nicaragua's a transshipment point for coke, and you've finally got a justification for the contras—big dope dealers themselves, but never mind. It's the good old Red herring, designed to disguise the fact that our government's the biggest oppressor on this planet."

Ah. The Berkeley blind spot.

Sunny looked at him, hearing herself twenty years ago. At least she'd had the excuse of youth. *You may be a world-class scientist and seducer, Professor,* she thought, *but politically, you ought to wind your clock.* She wondered what Sasha would say. She knew: "Punch him again."

She couldn't wait to tell Sasha. He'd freak. He'd just freak. The incredible part was that no other reporter would beat her to it. Even the cops were probably looking in all the wrong places. The two of them were uniquely qualified to blow this story wide open—

Which, of course, was exactly why the theory appealed to her. Slow down, girl, watch out for bias. Don't chop up the foot of fact to force it into your glass slipper.

She'd need evidence. Proof.

Sunny gathered her things together and stood up. David Szlacter stood up too, seeming startled that the interview was over. He held out his hand, a peace offering. Sunny hesitated and then took it. "Did you get what you wanted?" he asked, not letting go. She didn't miss the *double-entendre.*

"More than I came for," she said acidly. "Goodbye, Professor. Is there a gate out of this yard?" She didn't think she could face his wife.

Szlacter escorted her to the gate, and she promised to send him a draft of the article. She felt him watching her walk away. She did not look back.

And then she'd gone to the corner, called the machine, and heard Sasha's message. Already badly shaken by the kiss and the bombshell, she'd fallen apart.

Now she walked slowly up Telegraph, trying to think. So far this Romanian lead was only a theory. How could you prove…To track this Manea's Romanian career would be impossible. There was no *glasnost* in Romania. So go at it from this end: check with Immigration. Had a Ion Manea come in? When? It would strengthen her case to learn that Manea was here, especially if hex had cropped up shortly after his arrival.

All right. How would he distribute the drug? According to Joint Task Force Chief O'Brien, it wasn't being made all over the country. Famines pointed to one source, or very few. But where was the lab? And how did hex find its way from that point to Washington Square Park, Cambridge, Ann Arbor, Boulder, Berkeley? How did an Eddie Cole get hold of the drug? From a middleman named Horner?

Sunny froze in mid-step, remembering something she'd seen at "Randy's" after Bo-bo had beaten Eddie's lights out. As she stood still, a lot of little pieces pattered into place, a jigsaw puzzle magically assembling itself.

It was crazy, but it was possible.

Sunny started walking fast towards the U Cal campus. She didn't have to be at the airport till nine. Plenty of time to check out her hunch. If she was right, she wouldn't move on it here. She'd do that in New York, where Sasha could help her.

If he would help her.

She put that thought aside, and kept walking. And as she walked, she said "Ahhhh." Another image had come into her mind, alongside six black-and-yellow capsules spilling into the *securitate* agent's palm, and the neat white package of hex in Eddie's store.

It was the image of Eddie Cole, dark-red blood and snot running from his nose, trying to put his swollen lips together and say, "Foreigner."

CHAPTER 10

▼

When Sunny came upstairs from the airport subway, the Village looked somehow unfamiliar. It took her a minute to realize why: the angle of the light. On a normal morning at this hour, she'd still be in bed.

But nothing was normal about this morning. Her body had just been hurled across three time zones, and she'd hardly slept on the plane, between the intense excitement of her story coming together and her painful worry about Sasha. She'd called the Toronto hotel again and again yesterday. He'd still been out at midnight.

So when she unlocked the apartment door and saw his overnight bag, unzipped, with his shirts sticking out of it, her first reaction was joy—instantly followed by dismay. Where was *he?* The apartment smelled of him, his distinctive clean smell like baking bread. The bed had been slept in; he hadn't made it, and she knew it was because the cats had nested in the folds of the blanket. She thought of the kindness of the Prophet Mohammed, cutting off the sleeve of his robe so as not to disturb a sleeping cat.

So Sasha was here! He'd gotten her message and come back to wait for her. Then he was probably more worried than angry. Sunny felt an exhausting wave of relief and remorse. Suddenly she wanted only to sleep in the hollow left by Sasha's body until he came back and woke her up. First he'd be loving, and then he'd remember to be mad and mean, and he'd yell, and they'd fight, and she'd cry, and he'd hold her, and then they'd make love and go back to sleep. When they woke up, he'd be ready to help her with hex.

She'd never known predictability could be so comforting.

Sunny took off her clothes, crawled under the covers, pulled a cat into every angle of her body, and breathed in Sasha's scent.

✳   ✳   ✳   ✳

Sasha had told Margie she could meet him at the health club. Sunny hadn't called home this morning; he hoped that meant she was on her way. Even the earliest flights from L.A. wouldn't get in till mid-afternoon. Rather than sit around worrying, he might as well take a soothing soak in hot water and try to deal with Margie's problem, whatever it was, at the same time.

Margie was waiting for him in the health club lobby, dressed in dance-class clothes, the long legs in tights and leg warmers, a scarf thrown round her neck. No makeup, pale beneath the freckles, blue smudges under her eyes. She stood up tall to kiss him—Sasha was aware of the surprised, speculative looks of club regulars, wondering where Sunny was—and Sasha told her to change and meet him in the whirlpool.

She came down in a high-cut black bathing suit that made her legs even longer. They seemed to take a long time vanishing under the water. Margie sat down in the thick of the bubbles and closed her eyes.

"Are you all right?" Sasha asked her.

"Yeah. I had a scare, but I'm okay. It's C.J. I'm worried about." She opened her eyes. "Where's Sunny?"

"You tell me and we'll both know."

"Wha-a-at? Is she in trouble?"

"I hope not." Margie gave him a questioning look. "I don't feel like talking about it. Tell me who scared you. And what's with C.J.?"

"We-ell…That creep Dracula came to the club again a few nights ago—you'd left for Toronto. He was real polite, hands-off, sorry I upset you, I want to show that I really respect you, all this crap. He just wanted to buy me a drink so there'd be no hard feelings, right? Okay, I let him buy me a drink, it's good for the house, but it's just ginger ale. He's bragging about this fancy house he's remodeling out on Long Island, and how he'd like me to see it, and in between serving drinks I'm pretending to listen.

"So I pick up my ginger ale to take a sip, and damned if old C.J. doesn't pick that moment to get carried away doing a trick, bump into me and spill the whole thing down my front! I was ready to kill him, but ol' Drac was ready to *kill* him. He turned white as a sheet, and the two of 'em glared at each other like 'Duel in the Sun,' ya know?

"For a minute I thought they were gonna get into a fight. Then Drac marches out, and C.J. grabs me and says, 'Margie! Run after him and give him your phone number. I'll explain later. Don't worry, I'll protect you. Trust me.'

"I can't believe what I'm hearing, but C.J. is saying 'Go on, go on, we're gonna get him,' so I scribble my number on a napkin, run downstairs and catch him getting in his limo, shove the napkin in his hand and run back inside. He probably thinks I'm overcome with shyness. Actually I'm trying not to puke. I run back upstairs and say, 'C.J., what the fuck's the idea? Now I'm going to have to change my phone number.' And he looks at me real serious and says, 'He put something in your drink.'

"I go, 'Wha-a-at? *What* did he put in it?' C.J. says, 'I don't know, but he was trying to drug you.' 'You sure you're not imagining things?' He says, 'Marge, hon, if you know how to fool the eye, your own eye can't be fooled.' And he says, 'You got an answering machine?' I say yeah. 'Put it on. Don't answer the phone. If he calls, in a couple of days bring me the tape. I'm gonna get the son of a bitch.' He won't say how.

"I've got the tape in my purse. Sasha, he must've called twenty times. I don't know, 'cause I stopped listening after the first two. It scared me too much. I'm terrified that with my phone number, he's gonna find out my address. And meanwhile, *C.J.* has *disappeared!*" she wailed. "He hasn't been in the club since that night. Now I'm scared to go to work myself!"

Sasha swore. "C.J. couldn't wait for me. The stupid bastard."

"I brought a few things down with me in my bag. Could I stay with you for a few days? Would Sunny mind? I thought she'd be here alone, and I'd stay with her."

"Of *course*, baby," Sasha said. "That's exactly what I was going to suggest. When Sunny gets back, I'm taking her up to Toronto with me. You can stay here and feed our cats. Nobody'll know where you are."

"Oh, God, I feel so much better." Margie collapsed back into the bubbles and closed her eyes again. "Hope C.J.'s okay," she murmured.

"One of the things I've learned in life," Sasha said bitterly, "is that you can protect people from just about anything but themselves. So relax. In a couple of hours we'll go home and wait for Sunny."

"Okay, cuz, if you promise me one thing."

"What?"

"You'll let me treat you to a big lunch."

He really should stay home with the kittens and wait for the phone to ring. But eating *would* make the time go faster.

"Chinese?" Sasha said.

✳   ✳   ✳   ✳

Sunny woke up with a start and looked at the clock. Almost noon. The other side of the bed was empty.

"Sash?" When he wasn't in bed with her he was usually in the bathroom. But there was no answer.

Then it all came back to her, and she remembered that there was still an unhealed wound between them. She'd been dreaming that everything was all right.

She sat up and swung her legs over the edge of the bed. If Sasha was so worried about her, why wasn't he here waiting? Hadn't he gotten her message?

The messages! She wriggled off the bed and went over to milk the answering machine.

"Hi, Sa-sha. I need to talk to you when you have a chance. Okay? Thanks, cousin. Sunny, are you there? Call me, will ya? By-e!"

Oh. So maybe he was with Margie.

"I'm sorry, Sash—"

Sunny hit the "Off" button. She couldn't bear the sound of her own weepy voice. She spun her Rolodex to Margie's number and punched it. The line was busy.

She couldn't stand around waiting for these people. She had work to do.

Sunny fed the cats, showered, and pulled on a pair of snug jeans and a black turtleneck. She tied her comfortable old New Balance running shoes, pulled a brush through her hair, and put the tape recorder in her purse with its tiny mike clipped just inside the opening. She started to leave, hesitated, came back and stabbed REDIAL. Margie's line was still busy. Sunny grabbed a pad of paper that said HELL RAISER: MOTHER JONES MAGAZINE and scribbled a note to Sasha. Then she kissed Olly, murmured "Wish me luck" into the fur on top of his head, and left the apartment, striding towards Washington Square Park.

She'd seen what she was looking for in Berkeley. Now it was time to clinch it. She'd wanted Sasha as backup, but what the hell.

The day was fresh and sunny, and the park swarmed with people. Sunny noticed a group of haunted-looking teen-agers huddled on two adjoining park benches, murmuring like spies. The plague was spreading. She scanned the happier part of the crowd, ignoring the flying Frisbees, the skateboarders, the musicians, the puppeteer, the brown-and-white umbrella of the ice-cream vendor. There it was.

She strolled up the walkway and sat down on the bench closest to the hot-dog cart. Then she took a fat paperback out of her purse and pretended to read.

The idea had come to her out of nowhere as she was walking sadly up Telegraph Avenue. That package of hex in Eddie Cole's store had been in the wastebasket, in the bottom of a white paper bag. Bo-bo had found it scavenging for something to eat. They'd thought Eddie was smart to hide it in a food vendor's bag, under a Coke cup and a mus-tardy napkin, when he'd finished his hot dog. But *all the hot-dog sellers in the park were Romanian*—it was her and Sasha's private joke.

If the Mob could sell heroin through pizza parlors, why not the Hot Dog Connection?

And then Sunny had remembered the smell of sauerkraut as she came out of Harvard Yard after her unnerving encounter with the "hexies." There had been a cart hovering right by the entrance. Sunny tried to remember the vendor. A teen-age boy; she'd assumed he was Hispanic. But he could have been a Romanian gypsy.

What could be more innocuous, more ubiquitous, than a hot-dog cart? What had more opportunity to get right in among the kids?

Sunny had hurried to the UC Berkeley campus. There had been a hot-dog cart in front of the steps of Sproul Hall, where Mario Savio had delivered the eloquent defense of free speech that kicked off the Sixties. Now the steps had their own hive of "hexies," clean, too-thin kids in tie-dye and Big Brother T-shirts, with empty identical eyes, all quivering and buzzing like an airplane about to take off.

Sunny had bought a hot dog. The vendor was a woman in her twen-ties, small, thin and swarthy. She would easily have been taken for Indian or Middle Eastern. *"Esti romanca?"* Sunny had asked casually as she accepted her change.

The woman recoiled as if Sunny had thrown acid in her face. *"Cum ati stiut?* How did you know?" she gasped. She was certainly not delighted, as most immigrants would be, to hear her mother tongue so far from home. But she'd recovered quickly and asked Sunny with cold politeness, *"Si Dumneavoastra sinteti romanca?"*

"No, my husband's from there," Sunny had said. "Well, *la revedere. Noroc in Statele Unite.* Good luck in the States." She'd sat on the steps and fed her hot dog, bun and all, to somebody's black Lab with a blue bandanna around his neck, while she watched the procession of customers at the cart. The Romanian sold hot dogs to a variety of students—jocks, hexies, punks and straights—as well as to bearded junior-faculty and old-radical types. All the transactions looked disappointingly routine. If the vendor was passing hex, Sunny couldn't spot it. She'd have a better chance in Washington Square Park, where she at least knew who the likely drug dealers were. In Berkeley almost everybody looked fashionably disreputable.

And in Berkeley, she wasn't about to follow the cart back to its source.

But here, in the Village, she *knew* where the vendors gathered at the end of the day. How many times had she heard their carts rumbling in or out of the garage on Thompson Street?

She glanced up over her book and saw a young mother with a stroller buying a hot dog. Behind her was a tall, jittery black man in a leather cap. He looked all around and popped his joints like a marionette while he waited.

The young mother moved off, munching. The tall black man put his palms on the cart and leaned forward, placing his order. Sunny watched the vendor carefully. She recognized him: one of the Thompson Street Romanian regulars. He prepared two hot dogs and capped a cup of soda, set them down, reached behind the cart, brought up an open white paper bag, and immediately dropped two napkins in it. He held one hand under the bag; Sunny couldn't see whether there was a weight in the bottom. Then he carefully packed in the two hot dogs and the drink, curled the top of the bag, and handed it over. The black man palmed him some folded paper money. There was no change.

Sunny suspected that she'd just witnessed a hex transaction.

She sat there transfixed, watching a pale old man, a grungy guitar player, the Chinese juggler, and a long-haired student stop at the hot-dog cart. She discovered that the vendor's motions never varied, unless the customer didn't want a bag. However many hex deals went down in a afternoon—Sunny spotted three possibles in a couple of hours—they were hidden in among scores of ordinary hot-dog sales.

She looked at her watch. Almost three-thirty! And Sasha hadn't come looking for her. Well…time to swallow her pride, go home and look for him. They had some things to thrash out, and then she could ask for his help.

She was heading for the chess players' corner when she saw him walking along the bottom of the park. The shape and size of him was unmistakable: the massive but somehow vulnerable shoulders, his small head struck blond by the sun. Joy and fear fountained up in Sunny's chest. She cupped her hands to her mouth to yell "Blon-*die!*", like Eli Wallach in the Clint Eastwood spaghetti Westerns.

The word died in her throat when she saw that he was walking with Margie.

They were walking towards the apartment.

Margie had her arm through Sasha's arm.

Margie was carrying what looked like an overnight bag.

Sunny took two steps backward, as if she'd been hit. Normally she'd think nothing—well, almost nothing—of seeing Sasha with Margie. She'd go up to them, make some funny crack about crashing the party, and Sasha would say, "What's the *matter* with you?" and Margie would give her a hug. But that was the world that had ended yesterday, when she had violated his trust. Margie was much more from Sasha's world. It was natural that he would turn to her.

But in our *bed?* That seemed so final.

Sunny's throat burned, but her eyes were dry. She hadn't spent twelve years with the master for nothing. She too could "go underground," become cold and self-sufficient.

She found a pay phone and called Darlene.

*   *   *   *

Sasha and Margie walked past the apartment and up Avenue of the Americas to Charlie Mom's Chinese restaurant. Margie treated him to everything he liked best: fried dumplings, cold sesame noodles, fried rice and shrimp lo mein. While he ate, he told her about Georgie's discovery of the deadly Latino, Sunny's big lie, his fears for her safety, her evident disdain.

"It's not her fault she led a sheltered life before she met you," Margie observed with her mouth full.

"It *is* her fault that she hasn't listened to a word I said for twelve years!"

"Is everything all right, sir?" The waiter had hurried anxiously over. Sasha hadn't realized how loud he was talking.

"Fine. Bring me another order of cold noodles." He was eating too much, too.

"You could try calling that professor in Berkeley," Margie said.

"Call him, my ass. I'm going to send him Bo-bo."

"When you care enough to send the very best," said Margie. "Come on, let's go. The suspense is killing *me*. I bet you find a message that she's on her way home."

He found more than a message. He opened the apartment door and saw her overnight bag cheek to cheek with his.

"Sunny's *here!* Where the fuck *is* she?" Sasha exploded with relief and frustration. She'd slipped through his fingers *again!*

"She left you a note," Margie said, handing it to him.

"'Working in the park. Come find me near the hot-dog cart. I've got a surprise for you,'" Sasha read out loud. "I'll be right back," he said to Margie, already on the stairs.

"I'm coming with you," she called after him.

Sasha ran towards the park, puffing. He really should lose some weight. Margie caught up easily. In the park they split up, and he pushed through the crowd, swiveling his head. The hot-dog cart was there, all right, but Sunny was not. He had a few false leaps of hope at the sight of a dark head, but three times around the park and he hadn't seen her. When he rejoined Margie, she shook her head.

Sasha wanted to scream. "What is she up to now?"

"I think the best thing is to go home and wait for her to come back, or call."

"Oh, shit!" Sasha clapped his hand to his head. "I forgot to turn on the answering machine!" He grabbed Margie by the wrist and towed her back toward West Fourth Street.

$$* \qquad * \qquad * \qquad *$$

Sunny looked at her watch. "I'd better go back," she said, and gulped down the rest of her coffee. "They'll be heading in soon now. If I see what I think I'm going to see, it'll be the biggest scoop *Metro* ever had."

Darlene signaled for the check. "I don't want you putting yourself in danger," she warned. "You're accident-prone right now. Why don't you go home and make up with Sasha? He must be frantic with worry."

"Worry," Sunny snorted. "He's with this irresistible dancer who always has men hanging all over her. That's how worried he is."

"That doesn't sound like Sasha," Darlene said. "If he is with her, he's probably sitting there fully clothed, talking about you."

"You only know Sasha's sweet side," Sunny said. "Ever heard him on the subject of revenge?"

"Revenge for *what*, Sunny? What did you do that was so terrible?"

"I lied to him, and you know why? Because I didn't have the guts to stand up to him. It was cowardly and stupid. I *know* he goes crazy when he catches me in a lie. It shakes the whole foundation his world is built on. He thinks…" She shrugged.

Darlene gave her a shrewd look. "Is there something else you're feeling guilty about?"

"No." Sunny felt the blush spread beyond her control. "Nothing that wasn't in the line of duty," she said softly to the tablecloth.

"Want to tell me about it? He'll never know."

"I've got to go." Sunny jumped up. "You should hear from me tonight with exciting news. But if you don't…"

"I tell Sasha you think it's Romanians. A chemist named…" She looked down at her notes. "Manea. Hot-dog sellers as couriers." She shook her head with an amazed little laugh. "And then I call Chief O'Brien." She stood up to call to her friend, already halfway to the door: "Sunny, be careful!!"

As soon as Sunny was out of sight, Darlene went to the coffee shop's pay phone and dialed Sasha. There was no answer; the answering machine wasn't on. She'd try again when she got back to the office. She didn't believe Sasha was screwing some dancer for one minute. And she wasn't going to wait till Sunny was in trouble to let him know what was going on.

✳   ✳   ✳   ✳

Sunny's timing was perfect. As she walked back towards the park, she heard a familiar rumble behind her and turned to see two hot-dog carts, coming from St. Mark's place or Cooper Square. She stopped to look in a store window and let them pass. The vendors were shouting back and forth in vulgar Romanian, confident that no one understood. It disoriented Sunny like a drug flashback to hear the language so near home.

"Ce ai facut astas, eh Ioane?" (How'd you do today, Johnny?)

"Ziua buna, ma. Acum sunt un om bogat." (A good day, man. Right now I'm a rich man.

"Da, si in zece minute est iares nenorocit." (Yeah, and in ten minutes you'll be a poor bastard again.)

"Vai, futui mama mati, e adevarul." (Fuck your mother's mother, it's the truth.)

"Hai, frate, pune ceva in busonar pentru tine. De ce nu? Nimen nu stie." (Hey, brother, put something in your pocket for yourself. Why not? Nobody will know.)

"Numai tu, prapaditule." (Except you, you son of a bitch.)

They rumbled westward towards the park to pick up their colleague. Sunny cut south down Broadway, almost running. She had to get to the garage five minutes before they did. At Third Street she turned west and ran the six blocks to Thompson, blessing her karate workouts for keeping her in shape.

She dropped to a walk past the parking garage, looking it over. The first entrance was the platform elevator where the carts would go in, its metal jaws closed now. Next came the main entrance to the garage, opening on a public area with a glassed-in cashier's booth and a ramp leading upward into darkness. Third was a separate ramp exit with its own door, also closed. If a car would just come out now, that would be the best way to slip in; otherwise she'd have to try to sneak past the attendant on duty. A couple of old neighborhood guys sat out on chairs near the main entrance. Sunny was friendly with one of them, the super of the building across the street, a man the size of a retired jockey with a sourly amused, seen-it-all face.

"Hey, Skip, what's new?"

"Hey, Sunny." He shrugged. "Nuttin'. What's new wit' you?"

"Not much." *I may just have stumbled on an international narcoterrorist plot, that's all.*

"Where's your better two-thoids?" It was what Skip always called Sasha, and his own wit always cracked him up.

Sunny felt a physical pain in her heart. "I don't know. He'll turn up," she said lightly.

She tried to make small talk with Skip, while looking to her right to see if the hot-dog vendors were coming and to the left to watch for a car leaving the exit. Here they came, a slow flotilla of square silver carts, five or six of them rumbling down from the park. Sunny glanced quickly at the exit ramp. The door was still closed.

"Skip," she said, "would you do me a favor?"

"Sure, Sunny. You're a *paisan'*, ain't you?"

"I'm honored. Listen. I want to slip into the garage and, uh, surprise a friend who's coming for her car. It's her birthday. Could you get that guy's attention for a minute?"

He shrugged. "Sure, why not?" As the super of a building like a soap opera, whose tenants ranged from junkies to Italian grandmas, Skip was professionally incurious. "Hey, Albie," he shouted. "C'mere a minnit."

The young black attendant sauntered out into the light. Skip drew him into animated conversation, and Albie laughed. Sunny faded into the shadows of the garage, turned and sprinted for the ramp. For this she'd put on dark-colored clothes.

It was dark in here before your eyes got used to it. *Here is darkness,* old Ana said in her mind. *If you go into it, you may be lost.* "Or I may become stronger," Sunny said under her breath, and forced herself to go on up the slope. The dead air was soaked with motor oil. She stopped at the top of the ramp and peered out at the dim forms of the cars. Her eyes were adjusting already.

This was the first floor. There were four more. She could see the exit from the platform elevator across the garage in the gloom. She didn't know what floor the carts were stored on, and she couldn't explore, in case whoever came to collect the take was already here, waiting.

No sign of life on the first floor; no voice, footstep, or idling engine. When she had watched and listened long enough to be sure, Sunny edged out of cover, hating the moment of exposure, and ran around into the welcoming dark maw of the next ramp. She cat-footed up the slope without a sound, grateful to her running shoes, and peeked out onto the second floor.

Nothing.

Then the third.

Nothing.

On the fourth floor she saw a tall, gaunt man in a dark suit leaning against the trunk of a black limousine, smoking. He appeared to be alone; the ember of his cigarette brightened and sank like the single taillight of his mind on a dark and winding road. Sunny was too far away to see his face clearly, but she saw the harsh angles of it, upswept eyebrows and down-carved furrows, lit demonically from below by the cigarette's glow each time he dragged—

Dracul was Romanian for the devil. "Dracula" meant his son. It was him. It was Dracula—Margie's suitor, the man from the Romanian mission.

For a confused moment Sunny wondered if it was a coincidence, and he was down here stalking Margie. She hadn't expected her net to catch such stunning quarry—not a shy, embittered scientist, not some nondescript middleman, but a high-ranking diplomat and spy. If Dracula himself was the "foreigner" who made threats and collected money, it meant Bucharest was not just sanctioning the hex operation, but running it. It took Sunny's breath away.

And now she heard the groan and rattle of the elevator. Under cover of the noise, she dropped to a crouch and ran low behind the row of cars. Her heart was racing. She had to get closer, close enough to catch something on her tape recorder. She crept along the back wall, the cars' grilles grinning in her face, and squatted by the front wheel of a maroon Lincoln three cars shy of the limo. She slipped a hand into her bag. When she heard the rasp of the elevator door and the clank of the carts bumping out one by one, she activated the tape recorder.

"*Sa traiti, Domnu Dima,*" several voices mumbled.

"I told you always to speak English, you idiots," said a voice Sunny found "clammy"—nasal, affected, full of false culture and cold loathing. "You are in the United States, not in the slums of Bucharest. I want you to speak English even when you fuck your wives or your whores, do you understand me?"

"*Da*—uh, yes, sir." A shuffle of feet.

"All right, let's have the money. Branco! Get your fat ass out here." Sunny heard the impatient thudding of a fist on metal, and a car door yawned. "Where is the bag?" An apologetic mumble. "Get it *out* of the trunk, moron, are you asleep? Move!" The voice cracked like a whip, brandished in an old tradition of military abuse—the same tradition, Sunny realized, that Sasha's tirades came from. He must have drunk those contemptuous cadences from his officer father's canteen when he was still a little boy.

"Step up, step up! Simeon!"

"Twenny-four hundred, sir." Sunny heard a prolonged whisper of bills being counted, then the plop of the wad into a canvas bag. That wasn't hot-dog money. But would she get something on tape to prove it?

"Calinescu!"

"Two thouthand."

"Moldovan!"

"One—"

A slap like a pistol shot rang in the bare garage.

"You are cheating me, Moldovan!" A falsetto jabber of protest. "Don't even try to lie to me. I know every time you steal, and how much. How do I know? I read your little mind. Branco, go in his pockets." A pause. "His underwear too, if the peasant wears any." More squeals of protest and injured dignity, then a ghastly silence.

"Ah hah," Dracula said. "Your poor old mother in Bacau. She will be so disappointed in you."

There was a whimper of fear. So that was how they controlled them.

"Mieranu!"

As Sunny listened, Dracula took in over ten thousand dollars. If that was an average day's take, he could be making between fifty and a hundred thousand a week from this neighborhood alone. The Village was the drug supermarket for kids from the Jersey and Westchester suburbs.

When all the money had been counted and bagged, there was a long pause. Then Dracula said in a louder voice, "Which of you has some hex that he did not sell?"

Sunny could hardly contain her exultation as these words wound into the heart of her tape recorder. She had her proof. Now her job was done, and the feds and the cops could take over. She just had to lie low till they were out of here—

A tiny sound behind her.

Sunny spun around, instinctively throwing up an arm to shield her head, and deflected the canvas bag coming down like a butterfly net. The man with the bag dropped it, grabbed a handful of her hair and slung a tattooed python arm around her neck. She started to scream and he cut her voice off, his arm hardening to brown steel against her windpipe. Useless to scream anyway. Her voice wouldn't carry outside. Who was going to save her, Dracula? Stupid, stupid, stupid. Stupid to think your enemy is stupid.

Her assailant was whipcord strong but not very big. He was dragging her backwards out from between the cars, clamping down on her throat at the slightest resistance. She'd had the chance to see that he wasn't Romanian. Short dreadlocks, coffee skin, bad purple scars, crazy eyes. Some kind of Latin? What was *he* doing here?

"Well well," said Dracula as the Latin set her on her feet in front of him. "So we meet again. You've been following me for some time, you and that big brute. But you're the one who caught me." He spread his skeletal hands with a humorless smile. His gums were prominent and bluish. He had all the warmth and charm of a three-day cadaver. Sunny stared stonily at him. She was discovering something else Sasha must always have known: when freedom is gone, dignity is all you have.

"Give me her bag," Dracula said. A bull-necked bodyguard, bulging out of his maroon jacket, yanked the bag off her shoulder and handed it to Dracula, whose name apparently was Dima. He looked inside and his nose twitched with disgust. He dropped the bag on the floor and held up the tape recorder in front of her, its wheels still serenely turn-ing. With ritual deliberation, Dima popped open the little door, hooked a finger through the ejected tape, and ripped yards and yards of its guts out, looking straight into Sunny's eyes. *This is what I'm going to do to you.* He stuffed the disemboweled tape into his side pocket and, in a sudden spasm of power and fury, smashed the tape recorder against the cement floor. Little parts rolled in all directions, as if scut-tling for cover.

The hot-dog vendors stood looking at their shoes, a mute, hangdog Greek chorus.

"Get her in the car," Dima hissed to Sunny's captor.

The forearm rightened across her throat. "Let me go," she said in a choked whisper. "I'll come with you. I'm not stupid." *No, I'm a fucking genius,* she thought, *now that it's too late.* The Latin cautiously with-drew his chokehold and quick doubled her arm behind her, pushing her down into the back seat with the triumphal sneer of a man forcing a woman to give oral sex. He swung into the plush back seat beside her, slammed the door, and worked something shiny out of his tight jeans pocket. Smiling at her, he made it click, and Sunny gasped as a blade leapt out of his hand. He panted with silent delight and started clean-ing his nails with it. Dima was giving some last instructions or threats to his dealers. Then he got into the front passenger seat, and the bull-necked man squeezed behind the wheel and sparked the ignition. Someone rolled up the tinted partition behind the driver, sealing off the rear from the garage attendant's view.

As they turned and rolled down ramp after ramp, Sunny desperately figured how to signal Skip. The limo's windows were tinted; she'd have to throw something at a window hard enough to shatter it. But what? And how, with that blade so close? As the limo eased to a stop and Bull-Neck paid for the parking, the little Latin assassin tickled Sunny's neck with the point of his knife. She thought helplessly of Pierre, and her mouth filled with fresh, sour fear. They rolled out into the sun. Skip was standing right there, sizing up the limo, looking skeptical and unimpressed, as out of reach as a character in a sepia silent film. As they drove away down Thompson Street, Sunny felt the despair of a space-walker whose cable has been severed, watching Earth tumble silently away.

She had never been in a situation before where she had no ideas. It was as if her mind was shut in a smooth black box. It could exhaust itself beating on the walls, and still no door would appear.

Out of the corner of her eye, she saw a little light go on. A cellular telephone was built into the left armrest. Up front Dima had picked up the phone and was talking to someone. Probably a lieutenant in the hex trade, or a colleague at the Romanian Mission. But Sunny saw her last thin line to the outside. If she was going to die, at least someone should know. She grabbed up the phone and screamed into it, "Help! This is Sarah Randall and I—"

"Shut her up, you crazy Cuban!" Dima's scream of rage came over the intercom.

The wiry little cowboy's elbow slammed into Sunny's temple, and the phone receiver fell uselessly to the floor.

Sunny sighed, and snored. Hector Alvaro hung up the phone and went back to cleaning his fingernails with his switchblade. The limousine sped east, across the Manhattan Bridge.

*   *   *   *

When the phone rang, Sasha jumped as if he'd been shot, almost overturning the ashtray. The apartment was layered with haze;' they'd both been chain-smoking Margie's cigarettes, something Sasha had vowed never to do again.

"HELLO!!" He answered so ferociously a stranger would have hung up in fright.

"Sasha, it's Darlene. Has Sunny come home yet?"

Sasha listened in silence. Margie watched his face change, the deepening scowl of disbelief and alarm turning him into a vulnerable gargoyle.

He hung up and said, "We got to get back to the park."

This time Margie had trouble keeping up. Forget about asking questions, it was all she could do to catch her breath. Sasha shoved through the thinning evening crowd to the place where the hot-dog cart had been. It was gone. He took off running towards Thompson Street.

When Margie caught up with him, he was questioning a little old guy in janitor's overalls who had his chair tipped against the wall of the garage.

"What time did Sunny go in to surprise this…friend?"

"Oh, half, three-quarters of an hour ago."

"And you didn't see her inside any car that came out."

Skip shrugged. "Nah. I ain't seen her since. Sure, some cars came out. She musta been in one of 'em. I didn't see her, that's all."

"Did the hot-dog carts go in for the night?"

"Oh, yeah. Not too long after Sunny, matter a fact."

Sasha turned and ran into the garage. "Hey, mister! Can I help you?" called the attendant. Sasha ran on up the ramp.

The garage was shadowy and echoing. An occasional clank or the sound of a motor roaring to life made Sasha start the way a creaking brace had in the mine. He prowled quickly around the first, second, and third floors, and flattened against the ramp wall to peer into a descending Bronco, whose bespectacled driver, alone, gave him a cold look. Across the fourth floor he spotted a little huddle of trash on the cement. He went over to it and, like a sucker punch in the gut, recognized Sunny's smashed tape recorder. It lay there like her little body after a long fall. He had to stop himself from sinking to his knees and groaning.

He was too late.

The hot-dog carts, six of them, were padlocked and chained together in a corner. Sasha went over and rattled them. They felt light and empty. No names or addresses posted on them. The vendors must carry their licenses in their pockets.

He stumbled out of the garage, blinking in the light. Margie was waiting beside Skip. "They got her," he said.

"*Who* got her?" Margie wailed. "What is going *on!*" Instead of answering, Sasha went back to the cashier's booth. "Do you take down the license numbers of the cars you park?" he demanded of Albie.

"Yeah, we do. Why?"

Sasha thrust out his hand. "Give me the tickets for all the cars that left in the last hour." Albie quickly obeyed.

Sasha fanned the tickets. The license number DPL-455 leapt out at him.

He took it to Margie. "Recognize this?"

She shook her head.

"Could it be Dracula's?"

"I don't know! I never saw his license plate. What would he be doing down here?" Her eyes got big. "Does he know where I am?"

"You got that tape in your purse?" She nodded. "Come on. We got to play it."

On the way home he told her the incredible theory Sunny had entrusted to Darlene: that the *Romanians* were behind hex. It would explain where Dracula got the bankroll he flaunted at the club; it would even account for his presence there, fancying himself one of the city's drug kingpins. "There's just one thing I don't understand," Sasha puffed as he ran up the stairs. "Georgie's man rang their bell and got a whacked-out Latin. That seems to point in a whole different direction."

"Why?" Margie rummaged in her purse. "They could be working together. Maybe he's a Cuban or something. Here's the tape." Sasha snapped it into Sunny's "ghetto blaster," where she'd so often popped in Phil Collins or Fleetwood Mac to dance alone in the center of the room. He pushed "Play."

"Margaret, thees is your frand, Liviu. I am so glaad you have geeven me your number. I am sorry, you cannot call me here, but I will try to call you later. I keess you."

Beep.

"Margaret, it's Liviu again. Are you there?...Margaret?" A sigh. "I am waiting to see you. I keess you." Beep. The man had a nasty nasal voice and an unpleasant accent, and he spoke what Sasha called "spy-school English."

"Margaret?" The voice had become peremptory, warning. "Margaret...I hope you are not playing games with me. Are you seeing someone else? I expect you to be home at ten o'clock in the morning." The voice softened, became unctuous and caressing. "I am thinking now of your beautiful long legs...your leeps..." Raspy, masturbatory breathing. "The way your hair totchess your cheek..."

Sasha heard a sound from Margie. "Excuse me," she said in a small voice. "I can't listen to any more of this." She fled into the bathroom.

Sasha listened to the rest of the messages, following their descent into obsession. The nauseating voice recalled scenes of lovemaking that had never taken place, threatened to kill "the magician" or any other man who touched Margie, and finally, promised to hurt her if she betrayed him. "I will put my hants around your beautiful nack and squeess out your brath..." Now Sasha knew why Margie was frightened, not just annoyed. The man who called himself Liviu was one sick motherfucker. Most terrifying was his attempt to use hex—that must have been what he'd put in Margie's drink—to take control of a girl and bend her to his will.

If he had Sunny...

She wasn't the object of his obsession. But she was something he *should* be taking far more seriously—a threat to his whole operation.

Where *was* she??

Sasha was afraid she was a prisoner in the Romanian Mission on East 38th Street. That building was a fortress, rendered off limits to police by its diplomatic status. It was actually considered Romanian territory. He'd never get her out of there. But where else could she be? There wasn't a clue on the tape.

Or was there?

He rewound it and listened again, trying to focus on background noises. Some of the calls could only have been made from at home, in bed. There were no background sounds, only repulsive foreground ones. Other calls, less intimate, might have been made from an office. Once Sasha heard a faint female voice, once the tick tick of a typewriter.

On three calls, the voice was almost drowned out by the roar of an airplane.

Georgie's man, Dominick—no, his nephew Petey—had lost the spic in the limousine out by JFK.

Sasha grabbed the phone and dialed Georgie's hideout. He let the phone ring thirty times.

There was no answer.

CHAPTER 11

▼

Sunny had a horrible headache. And she couldn't seem to open her eyes, or to move. Except for the headache, she recognized this state: it was the struggle to wake up from a nightmare. She could remember, as a child, lying just under the surface of sleep, as if in shallow water: if she could open her eyes, if she could just sit up, she'd break the surface and reach the air.

But she *was* sitting up.

Her hands were pinioned behind her, so that her inner arms pressed painfully against the wooden back of a chair. When she tried to move her feet, something bit into her ankles. Something also covered her face, making it impossible to see and hard to breathe.

With a start she remembered her tape recorder smashing on the garage's cement floor.

It was the last thing she remembered. She heard voices now, murmuring and shouting in Romanian, scuffling footsteps and sounds of activity. Where was she? The sounds had an echoey ring, suggesting a large, bare space. Sunny was cold.

The blindfold over her face was loose. She made faces under it, working her nose and eyebrows until it began to slip. Letting her head hang forward as if she were still out cold, she peered out between her bangs and the top of the cloth.

What she saw was puzzling. She had guessed she was in a warehouse, but this looked like an office. Carefully raising her eyes, she saw that the walls were only partitions, and the ceiling above was lost in darkness, from which an industrial lamp hung down on a long cord. Sunny was bound to a chair in one corner. Near her were a dusty desk with an old black telephone and a battered green filing cabinet. A worn gray couch sagged against the opposite wall. Beside it was an open door, through which Sunny heard echoing footsteps coming and going on metal stairs.

The man called Dima sat on the couch, a gray canvas bag beside him, frequently licking his long fingers as he counted and bound stacks of money. In front of him on the floor was an open suitcase of cheap oxblood leather—Romanian, from the look of it—almost half-full of bricks of cash. Two more suitcases stood closed and strapped by the door. As Sunny watched, the bull-necked bodyguard appeared in the doorway, tossed in a full canvas sack, and muscled both suitcases out the door.

Sunny suppressed a laugh that might have been a sob. Drug dealers really *did* carry around suitcases full of money. Sasha hadn't made that up.

At the thought of him, the whole weight of her aloneness swooped and struck.

An airplane roared close overhead. Sunny had a dim sense that it wasn't the first she'd heard. Her mind was full of fuzzy memories of the sound, like fading vapor trails.

"Hai da repede," Dima snapped at his bulky bodyguard. "Hurry up. *Zbor pleaca nu chiar in dou ore.* The flight leaves in less than two hours."

They must be somewhere close to the airport. And they were flying all that cash home on Tarom! Millions of dollars from the marrow of America's young.

Apparently they assumed she was still out. They were ignoring her in their rush to get the cash shipment packed. Out of the corner of her eye she saw movement way over to the left, at the far end of the room. She strained to look by moving only her eyes. It made her head throb harder, but she saw two of the hot-dog vendors working at a card table, making white-paper packages. From time to time they dipped a black-and-yellow handful out of an army-green duffel bag on the floor.

She'd seen a bag like that before, at the airport—their diplomatic pouch.

The hex wasn't being made here! It was being flown in from Romania, under the official seal of the government itself!

"She's awa-ake," said a lazy, warning voice from the doorway. Sunny jumped. The dreadlocked little scarface who had caught her was lounging with his hip against the doorframe. He was pointing straight at her with his knife; he also had a large machine pistol shoved sideways into his waistband.

Dima looked up, tossing another packet of bills into the suitcase. He glared at Sunny and she closed her eyes, heart pounding, stomach sick. The afterimage of his strange eyes floated in darkness. His irises were so black that they looked like they were all pupil, two big black holes.

"*Vai de mine, a vazut tot,*" squeaked a high voice. "My God, she's seen everything." This voice came incongruously from the big bodyguard.

"If you had put the focking blindfold on right, she wouldn't haff," Dima snarled in English.

"Doesn't mat-ter," said Scarface in a mocking playground singsong, "we're gonna kill her any-way."

"Not yet," Dima snapped. "First we must find out who she has told."

Scarface sauntered smiling towards Sunny, wagging his knife in front of him. Dima caught him by the arm, and Scarface whirled around, eyes blazing. Dima drew back as if he'd touched a live wire. Sunny saw that he needed Scarface's savagery but could not control it. "*Futu-s mama ta,* all you can think is cutting, cutting, cutting," he spat.

"This is almost the twenty-first century. To get information we do not need to use the knife." He gestured sharply to the big one. "Get Manea."

Sunny's eyes went wide.

The man Dima's bodyguard led through the doorway was in his forties, pale, bespectacled and blinking. He was a nondescript, fade-into-the-wallpaper type, but Sunny thought she recognized him from their Tarom flight; he was the one Dima had embraced and kissed on both cheeks outside Customs. His shirtsleeves were rolled up, and he wore a white apron and wet rubber gloves. He looked at Sunny as if she were a lab specimen.

"Ce faci cu laborator?" Dima fired at him.

Manea wrinkled his nose. *"Foarte murdar."* He had a soft, weary voice that refused to be hurried. *"Ma simt ca o servitoara. Dar merge.* It's filthy, I feel like a fucking maid, but it's going."

What was going? Something about a laboratory.

It dawned on Sunny that she had stumbled into this operation just as they were setting up the first hex lab in the United States. The reporter in her rejoiced uselessly. It was like feeling proud you were pregnant on the abortion table. The knowledge would die with her, and soon police and parents would notice an ominous quantum leap in the blight of hex.

"What is the usual dose for her body weight? Speak English," Dima said to Manea. He wanted her to know.

The chemist shrugged. "Fifty milligrams," he said in his dreamy voice. "One small capsule."

"At one hundred fifty to two hundred, what will happen?"

Manea shrugged again. "Hallucinations. Ataxia."

The locomotor-ataxia hootchie-kootchie, said Sunny's mind, a line from some Beat poem in lieu of a definition. There were maybe a dozen words in the English language that Sunny Randall did not know. "Ataxia" was one of them, and it didn't sound good. She started clenching her teeth. They wanted to chatter.

"Will she be capable of telling the truth," Dima wanted to know.

"You will see everything that is in her mind," Manea said with faint indignation. "You know it was cited at the '84 Warsaw Pact convention as *the* drug for humane interrogation and reeducation." He recited proudly: "'Full disclosure and significant value change without the need for physical pain or damage.'"

"Adu patru capsuli," Dima commanded. *"Si o sticla de apa."*

Bull-neck and Scarface converged on her, Bull-neck with a carefully cupped hand, Scarface with a glass of water.

Sunny bit down hard. Bull-neck clamped a huge hand over her face and dug his thumb and fingers into her cheeks. She resisted and the pain spiraled skywards. He got the heel of his hand on her chin and pushed down. With a sudden jerk Sunny wrenched her face free and whipped her head from side to side too fast for them to catch it. Finally Bull-neck captured it under his arm like a football, and squeezed. Sunny felt as if her skull would burst. She began to whimper.

They tried again. Bull-neck wound a hand into her hair and jerked her head back. With his other hand he pinched her nose shut. Sunny tried to breathe through her closed teeth, but the struggle had made her need more air. This time, when Scarface squeezed her cheeks, her teeth parted and snapped shut again. *"Coño,"* he swore, "I'm gon' break your teet' if you don' open up for me." He wrapped his fist around the handle of his knife and feinted driving the end down on Sunny's front teeth. She flinched; fear of pain and (for what?) vanity loosened her jaw. Scarface quick forced the knife handle between her teeth while Bull-neck wrapped her brow in a hammerlock and tipped her head back.

One, two, three little capsules pattered onto her tongue. She was frantically trying to push them out when the fourth one touched down. Scarface bent over and came up with the glass. He poured water between Sunny's teeth, around the knife and down her front. She was succeeding in shoving the capsules forward with her tongue—there, one fell out of the side of her mouth! Scarface swore and stuck his finger in to push the others back past the point of no return. The knife fell out and Sunny bit into knuckle and capsule, tasting blood and flesh and bitter, nauseous hex.

"Owoooooo!" Scarface howled. "Bitch!" He yanked his mangled finger free and slapped her.

Surprised by the slap, Sunny swallowed, gagged, spat, retched. The taste was awful, but she wasn't going to vomit. Goddamn cast-iron stomach. How much had gone down? She began to cry in defeat.

Dima had been banding money throughout this operation. Now he looked at his watch, stood up, and kicked the open suitcase. *"Mai tine inca o suta de mii,"* he said to Bull-neck. "This one will hold one hundred thousand more. *Ascunda si mergem.* Put it in the safe and let's go." Bull-neck zipped the suitcase and picked it up.

Dima looked Sunny up and down. "By the time we come back, she will be ready." He speared Scarface with his eyes. "You do not touch her. She is mine. Do you understand me? None of your games." Dima jerked his head at the two men wrapping hex at the card table. "They will tell me."

"*Okay! Okay!*" Scarface placated, hands up.

Dima and Branco went out and shut the door.

The lock clicked.

Scarface looked at Sunny and smiled.

＊   ＊   ＊   ＊

"Mrs. DeSimone?"

"Yes…" Georgie's mother, normally cheerful, sounded like a wet Kleenex.

"Is Georgie there?" Is something wrong?

"Who is this?" Wary.

"His friend, Sasha."

"Oh, Sasha! My God! You haven't heard?"

Sasha's blood froze. "Heard what?"

"My poor Georgie is in the hospital," she wailed. "In intensive care. God forgive him, they don't think he's gonna make it."

Oh Jesus, the shys finally got him. Poor Georgie. And now of all times, with the key to Sunny's life locked behind his lips. The double blow made Sasha stagger. "What happened? Can you talk about it on the phone?"

"A *heart* attack!" Georgie's mother wept with indignation. Death with his boots on she could accept somehow; a natural cause was an outrage. "Everything was all right, you know what I mean? An old friend of his father's fixed it. He came home. And I come in from my Thursday afternoon card game and he's lying on the kitchen floor, on his face, in front of the refrigerator! The paramedics told me his heart stopped! They got it going again, but he gotta breathe with a machine…"

"What hospital is he in? I want to see him." Sasha felt terrible, needing something from his friend when Georgie was in mortal need.

"Mother Cabrini. I'm going back there now myself. Pray for him, Sasha, promise me!"

"I will." *You pray for my girl…*

"We're going to Cabrini Hospital," Sasha said to Margie. "I don't know if Georgie's conscious, but I got to try."

"It's right near my apartment," Margie said.

Darkness had fallen. They rode the cab in silence, except for Sasha's muttering "Moron!" whenever the cab driver passed up an opening.

They ran up to the doors of the intensive-care unit just as visiting hours were ending. "I'm sorry," the nurse said. "Only immediate family after eight P.M." It was two minutes of eight.

"I'm his brother," Sasha said. She gave him a long look—*I'm nobody's fool*—but let him in. In New York, nerve is thicker than blood.

The unit was right out of "Star Trek." The beds were arranged in a crescent, if you could call them beds; they looked like, and were, high-tech battle stations, with blipping screens, beeps, and the hiss-toc of half-a-dozen respirators. In each bed was a mound, motionless except for the jerky rise and drop of mechanically pumped lungs. The nurse pointed at the mound in Bed 5.

He wouldn't have recognized Georgie. His color was waxy, his face slack, his eyes gummed shut. From his taped mouth sprouted the respirator hose, like a blue elephant's trunk. The little running line of blips on the screen looked more alive than he did.

Sasha leaned close. "Georgie," he whispered into the hairy ear. "Georgie, my man. Who loves you?" There was no response. Georgie lay in his fastness, already impervious as Pierre. Only the blood-red numbers on the digital heart monitor fluctuated with the struggling flame of his life.

Sasha had never prayed, even in Russia. It wasn't exactly that he didn't believe in God; he thought God believed in strength. He wished he could give Georgie a Transylvanian blood transfusion, rich with the will to live.

Georgie's hands lay on top of the cover. Sasha squeezed one. It was cold and inert. He spoke out loud, as if explaining to Georgie: "I got to go to the Don."

"Can I come with you?" Margie pleaded as they hurried down the hospital corridor.

A short laugh came out of Sasha. "No. But I'll take you home."

"Oh, Sasha. I'm scared to be home alone."

"I think your friend has his hands full tonight," Sasha said grimly. "Besides, I'd like you to answer the phone if he calls. If you want to help Sunny, lead him on, keep him talking, try to find out where he is, try to lure him away, ask for his phone number—anything. I'm gonna call you every half hour or hour. Keep your door locked and you'll be all right."

He saw her to her door and waited while she let herself in. They both heard the final beep and click of the answering machine cycling off.

"Rewind it. Maybe he called again," Sasha ordered.

Three messages skittered backwards. The very first one was from "Liviu."

"I saw you." The voice was harsh and choked almost beyond recognition, but the accent was his. "I was driving through Green Witch Village. I saw you with *him.* Now I know why you have not answered my calls. Well. It is a very strange stroke of fate that he hass you, and I have—"

Another voice erupted like hot lava in Sasha. "HELP! THIS IS SARAH RANDALL AND I—"

"SHUT HER UP, YOU CRAZY CUBAN!"

They heard the thud-bump of the receiver falling, the hum of a car in motion, and then someone hung up.

*   *   *   *

"I thin' we better introduce ourselves. We gon' be spendin' some time together," said Scarface, strutting back and forth in front of Sunny like a bantam rooster. "Fac' is, we gon' be innimate frens. I'm Hector." He mockingly held out his hand and pretended to be hurt when she didn't take it. "Not very fren'ly of you. Oh, es*cu*se me! I din' realize you were tied up."

Ma, I was tied up for a little while. God, would she be glad to see Bo-bo.

Sunny didn't want to talk with her executioner. She was bracing herself for the onrush of the drug. What horrible karma for her curiosity: *You want to know what hex is like? You got it!* She had a few minutes left to dig up the lessons of a long-dead drug culture. What had the "guides" in their phony yogi robes said? "Set" and "setting" were all-important. State of mind, preparation, expectation were your set. Setting should be safe, soothing: low lights, soft music, trusted friend. What a laugh. She was in for one screaming horror of a trip.

But fear would be self-fulfilling, self-augmenting. At least she had some control over the set. What had she told herself when she took mescaline? The three R's: *Relax, roll with it, remember it's only a drug.* If you're holding your friend's hand and you feel her arm fall off, if the little boy crossing the street turns into a monster, it's okay because *it's not real.*

The problem was, Hector and Dima *were* real. The ropes tying her to this chair were real. And so was her approaching death.

Okay, try another tack. *That which can die is not real. Only that which does not die is real.* Who had said that? *To be beneath the blade when swords are crossed is hell; one step forward and you're in heaven.* She knew who'd said *that:* Sasha's friend Mas Oyama, the great karate master. There was grinning Hector with his blade. Sunny closed her eyes and tried to meditate.

She couldn't calm her breathing. It came fast and shallow, and her heart raced like rain driven against a windowpane. Was it the hex, or just adrenaline? The thought that it was beginning frightened her and made it worse.

She was trembling uncontrollably. Her teeth chattered, her jaw tightened. All her muscles were stiffening and jerking. As her arms went straight and rigid, the sides of the chair back bit into her flesh, and the pressure on her shoulder joints was excruciating. She was terrified that she would have a convulsion and her body would be torn apart, her arms broken, shoulders dislocated, a live dog in the Philippines trussed up for the meat market.

"Untie meeee," she said to Hector through her locked teeth. "I'll pass...out...pain..." Her voice sounded blurred and echoing; had she spoken out loud?

Hector looked at her and cocked his head, a giant robin about to stab for a worm. Eyes bright shiny unfeeling a bird's. Hey, you crazy, callin' me Big Bird? He had a metal heart. She felt it in her own chest, light and cold, no problem. Better than a meaty maggoty heart that hurt. Contempt. Nice tits, jiggle when she shake like that. Tie her legs apart. Shit, they watchin'. She pass out, spoil my fun, anyway she s'posed to talk. Ain't makin' no sense now, tha's for sure. The blade shot out. Sweet answering throb in his groin every time. A whistle of wind between her wrists and the arms sprang free, rising by themselves, a cross, a tree, still rooted to the chair.

"Sunny" was not in the chair. There were two hot centers of her at the card table and another one vis-à-vis her body, posing with the knife. Actually she didn't see the room so much as feel it, like a pit viper's infra-red world or an Einsteinian landscape of space warped by mass: each living mind a hot spot or a spike. She could shift to the card table and inhabit two variations on appetite and cunning in Bucharest's gypsy ghetto; she had, if she wanted it, access to the slaughterhouse of Hector's memories, his bloody crowing survival atop the dung heap of Havana's slums; or she could examine, with the dispassion of a doctor, Sunny's stiff-necked pride and naked fear of love. She itself felt no more fear, only immense and equal pity for all four human beings, locked less into their gauzy bodies than their iron minds, their shackling stories. And there were others here; that came as no surprise. The air was thick with their murmuring. She strained to see them, to hear what they were saying; they had the answer, but she was still too crude a receiver to tune in. Because Sunny, out of stupid fear, had spat out the fourth capsule. The saddest thing about humans was the way they clung to that pathetic five per cent of their brains.

The body couldn't move very well, but that meant nothing. She itself was lucid, free, and powerful. She wanted the others to know this, that they were this. Freedom! She had to be careful how she explained it, because if she said "Join me," the one called Hector would take it sexually. There he went already, squeezing his crotch. Had he heard her thoughts or was she talking out loud? 'Course you talkin' out loud, mami, don'tchoo know dat? I never heard so much bull-shit in my life, till you say freedom, till you say seck-shuwally. Yeah, *now* you talkin'. I know something 'bout freedom, did life under the mother-fuckin' Revolution, twelve years till old Fi-del put me on the boat at Mariel. Hey, *he* like freedom too, squeezing his crotch, looking quickly twice over his shoulder at the card table, getting his back to them, unzipping.

They know, but fear him as much as Dima and won't tell. His cock sprang out and squinted at Sunny with its one eye, just like a Robin Williams routine on HBO. Whaat, choo think it's funny?! See, comedy sometimes brushed close to what the Others were so urgently whispering.

She wanted to hear them. She was so close. She could sort of see them now, little squat dark beings with eyes of light. The other thing was such an annoying distraction. Should she do something about it? It really didn't matter. In fact she discovered that she longed to be touched, it was so achingly *lonely* out here alone in between, but touching the body wouldn't help unless the other was out here too. And Hector was locked in himself, and Sasha, locked in his great self with all its tunnels and levels and mines—it would matter to Sasha. Out of pity for Sasha, she should try to stop it.

She wondered if Sunny could move her arms. The fingers seemed to be working all right.

The one-eyed thing was leering right in Sunny's face now, going in and out of its sleeve and Hector's hand. She was bathed in the cold flame of his mechanical pleasure, and she knew it—she knew she was going to feel—

Sunny retched as she socked Hector in the balls and he doubled over. Gagging nauseous pain spread upward, turning the world a luminous red-green. Such pain as no woman had ever known, part payment for childbirth. Through it she felt ripples of suppressed laughter from the other two.

She wasn't about to tell him the karate trick of jumping sharply to bring his balls down, but it seemed she already had. He was doing it: jumping, doubling over with a groan, jumping again. How many guys had she watched do that in the dojo after a stray groin-kick—poor Pierre. She saw blood vomit out of the fresh grin in his throat. He was tied to a chair.

A mushroom cloud of rage boiled up in Hector, driving the pain ahead of it like clouds in a high wind.

He could stand straight now, thanks to her involuntary advice. He walked up to Sunny and slapped her hard, forehand, backhand, forehand. *"Bitch! You! Bitch!"* She must have been shouting it joyously with him in perfect unison, because he suddenly backed off looking scared. Sheesh, how you do that? Maria Yemaya, *protejame!* An image from "The Exorcist," Regan-demon grinning, her head grinding round. He fumbled at his neck, pulled a leather amulet in African colors out from under his T-shirt and made the cross with it. Tiny Hector sucking his thumb, flies an umbilical hernia old woman with herbs funny smell.

Poor simple, superstitious killer. Hector meat and muscle for Dima, that's all. She was infinitely, ridiculously more powerful. She could scare him, and had. His manhood had only one recourse. The knife flicked open and nicked Sunny's chin. How you like to die, bitch? Like this? Tracing the knifepoint over her pulses, hard enough to scratch. C'mon, off her, shit, can't do it yet, want the bread, but she don' know that, this almos' as good as doing it, like a taste of wha's cookin' for supper. Or like this? This blow the back of your head off. The pistol was out of his waistband and the muzzle pressed against her left I, a camera lens looking into her as she looked into it, darkness calmly regarding darkness. A rich oiled metallic click as he cocked the gun. His nerves were erect electric hairs, firing in a rhythm jittery as jazz.

There was a sound, a metal echo of feet on stairs.

Hector took one step back, in the same motion pointing the pistol skyward. Sunny understood how very close he had come to firing. But that was of no consequence. Not compared to what was at the door, making Hector hurriedly click the safety and stick the gun in his pants, and making Sunny feel terror for the first time out here.

There were deaths worse than that of the body. That was what she knew as the black hole called Liviu Dima walked through the door.

*   *   *   *

"Don Chaluch', I never asked you for anything."

The silence in the little room was broken only by the buzzing of the fluorescent light. It could have been the hum of a power generator. From here, the back room of a Village social club, invisible cables of influence and intelligence radiated out into every borough of the city and beyond. Somewhere within its reach lay Sunny, still alive. Sasha had to believe that.

The Don looked at him and inclined his head very slightly. The elegance of power impressed Sasha even in his distress; the insecure and insignificant gesture big—Hey, look at me!—but for the Don, the smallest movement was sufficient. The tiny nod of encouragement reached Sasha as a wave of warmth. He cleared his throat and continued.

"You told me years ago if I ever had any kind of problem, to come to you. I treasure the friendship you've given me, and I never want to abuse it. But now I got noplace else to go. I must ask for your help. They've taken my girl."

The Don's eyebrows went up, and he shifted in his chair, waving two fingers at one of his omnipresent entourage. *"Due espressi,"* he said, and a strapping young soldier threw his cards face down on the table and hurried into the front room. "Sunny," said Don Chaluch'. "Wasn't that her name?"

"Yes, Don Chaluch'. And Georgie's probably told you about this assignment she has with the new drug, hex. He was looking into it for me."

"Ah, Georgie." Don Chaluch' touched his fingers to his forehead, a masculine vestige of the sign of the cross. "God protect him."

The young soldier came back in and placed a tiny cup of espresso in front of each of them. Sasha sipped his, taking strength from the bitter medicine, and went on.

"Sunny found out that the people pushing this drug are foreigners, spies from…a Communist country. She got too close, and they snatched her. We know they got a bad spic enforcer on the payroll, a crazy Cuban. Georgie's friend Dominick, his nephew tailed him, lost him out near JFK."

"I heard about it. What time was she taken?"

"Around five-thirty today. I got to talk to Dominick. He might know where they got her. I went to see Georgie, but…" He shrugged sorrowfully.

"Hey Tommy." The Don beckoned to the next table. "Bring the phone. And get me Dominick's number. Dom Acocella, in the Colombo family." Before he finished speaking, a heavy-set man with black wavy hair and bulldog jowls was on his feet, coming round the table with a black dial phone on a long cord. He set the phone down in front of the Don and fished in his inside jacket pocket, bringing out a handful of little folded pieces of paper. As he licked his fingers and thumbed them open one by one, Sasha felt worse than he did when he rode in a slow cab, but the Don did not express impatience and so he kept his to himself.

"Here," said Tommy.

"Call him. Tell him I want to talk to him."

Tommy whipped the dial around with his thick forefinger, waited, said "Put Dom on the phone, willya?" Waited some more covered the mouthpiece with his hand and said in a gravelly stage whisper, "He's out. Wife don't know where he is."

Sasha's heart went into a bottomless fall.

"Tell her I want to talk to him," said the Don.

Tommy did.

He hung up. "He'll get back to us," he said.

They waited.

Sasha knew Dominick's wife was placing urgent phone calls to candy stores, bars, bookies, strategic points on the grapevine, putting out the word: Don Chaluch' wants him. The message would travel like a spark of grassfire. Wherever Dominick was, it would find him—soon.

Soon enough to save Sunny's life?

They waited. The Don sipped his espresso with graceful, unhurried motions. His control helped Sasha not to fly apart.

The phone rang.

Tommy snatched it up. "Yeah." He put his hand over the receiver. "It's Joey, from Newark."

The Don waved a dismissive hand. "Tell him to call tomorrow at six." Tommy conveyed the message and hung up.

They waited. The telephone radiated a black, malevolent silence.

After what seemed like an hour, but was seven minutes, it jumped and rang.

Tommy listened, nodded significantly to the Don and handed him the receiver.

"Dominick." The weight of command was in the Don's voice. "Brooklyn Georgie had you tailing some Cuban in the hex trade…Yeah, too bad about Georgie…Georgie's friend Sasha is here. They snatched his girl." The Don listened. "Yeah?…You sure?…" He met Sasha's eyes and nodded. Sasha's heart leapt. "Oh, Sally Salvatore rented it to them?"

The Don made angry writing motions. Tommy produced pencil and paper like a magician whose life depends on his trick. "Old hangar…warehouse. Mmm hmm…Mmm hmm…Thank you, Dominick. I'll remember this."

He handed a slip of paper to Sasha. Rather than write out the instructions, as a conventionally educated person would have, the Don had deftly sketched a map. He explained that it represented the Van Wyck Expressway, a particular exit, an old service road, and a maze of back roads bordering on the darkness of the Jamaica marsh. Sunny liked it out there; she always remarked on the sweet smell of the reeds as they stood on the platform for the airport train, coming home from Romania.

"I'm gonna send a couple a my boys out there within the hour," said the Don. "You want to get a head start, I don't blame you, but you should have a piece." He said something in his subtle sign language, and Tommy disappeared through the back door. Sasha heard footsteps going down wooden stairs.

"Don, I can't—"

"'Eyyy," the older man said gently and challengingly. "I would be very disappointed if you went to the cops. I *expect* you to come to me."

The sound of feet on stairs, and Tommy came in carrying a brown paper bag. He handed it to Sasha. It was heavy. "A clean .38 and some shells," the Don said. "Go on, take a look."

Sasha looked in the bag and saw a thick chunk of machined blue steel and a nest of little missiles.

"I have one last favor to ask of you," he said.

The Don cocked his head.

"Bo-bo from Buffalo is on his way down. I can't wait for him. With your permission, he'll come to you for directions and hardware."

Don Chaluch' nodded assent, and the hint of a smile touched his sensual lips. "That crazy Polack likes a sawed-off shotgun, if I recall," he said. "I almost feel sorry for them *schiffos'.*" Sasha stood up, and the Don reached out his hand and gripped Sasha's in the seal of alliance.

"Get outta here. Sunny's waiting for you."

*   *   *   *

As Dima walked through the door, words came flapping like warning crows: *Black tornado. Black Niagara.*

What had entered Sunny's perception was a being of another order, qualitatively different and terrifyingly more powerful than anyone else in the room. Humans, even Hector, were spikes or bumps in the energy field; the entity called Dima plunged bottomlessly downward, a sucking drain. It was "attractive," in a horrid way. With a silent roaring, like the great falls thundering off into space, it skewed the whole fabric of reality toward it, making a slippery slope on which Sunny scrambled in terror.

Shocked by its naked force, she was even more astonished by the thick shield body and mind could be. There were things like this walking around in the world and nobody noticed! Maybe a few hairs stirred on the back of the neck, no more. This…force had come so close to Margie, and all she'd felt was "the creeps"! That made it easier for some to resist the "psychopath," but also for others to be fooled and sucked in. Hidden behind the human mask of Charlie Manson and Ted Bundy, of Hitler and of Ceausescu, Dima's boss, was this roaring vortex. Absolute hunger, like absolute zero. And it swallowed souls. A couple of dozen, many millions—it made no difference to the hunger.

As the thought of Margie the roaring had intensified. It was in unimaginable, unappeasable pain, so extreme it became sadistic joy.

Sunny felt as frail as a butterfly in a hurricane. The only refuge was in her own body. She shrank back inside, only to find that it had become transparent. He saw her cowering there. Dima laughed at her. He knew, he was a master. She would be sucked into his empty eyes, down through his sex center and out into a blackness that made the gun muzzle seem sweet as the womb. She clung for dear life.

"Not yet," he said in human words. "First the information. We want to see who knows. Whom she has told."

Sunny squeezed her eyes shut an instant too late to blot out the image of Darlene: delicate, dignified, funny, blond ringlets and neat little teeth, little hat, bolero jacket. Dima snatched the image right out of her mind, and Sunny felt guilt and mourning as intense as if she'd thrown her friend to the wolves.

"Who is she? Who is the blond? Ah! Your editor." She didn't know if he'd spoken or interrogated her directly, wordlessly; she didn't know if she was babbling or silently emptying out her mind. All she knew was that she couldn't withhold anything. When she tried to resist, he applied the roaring vacuum like a blowtorch of cold. The image of Sasha tore loose from her—far more than visual, a beloved ball of touches and tastes and sounds—and spun off into space, dwindling to a speck. Goodbye, goodbye.

"*E foarte rau,*" Dima said to dull, bull-necked Branco. Then for Hector's benefit: "It's very bad. The editor has probably already blabbed to her boyfriend. Fortu*nate*ly for us, the boyfriend has had certain experiences that incline him to distrust the police. He will tell the editor not to call them until further word from him. That gives us time to find and kill them both, but very little time." Dima paced, deploying his forces like a chess player, Hector the knight, Branco the fat rook, someone on Thirty-Eighth Street the suave and deadly bishop, the hot-dog sellers dumb pawns.

He whirled on Sunny. *Where is Sasha now?* Was it his question or hers?

An inner shrug. So alone, tired of the futility of resisting. She'd been stripped of so much already. It was starting to feel good. Lightening for a journey, like a quote she loved: *I never had happiness nor anything of peace till divested of all.* He could have whatever he wanted, now that Sasha was gone.

Last I know he was fucking Margie.

To her surprise, his attention released her. Sunny felt the strength surge back tingling into her as Dima writhed like a corpse in fire. So he could be hurt: there was pain past absolute pain. She saw it. That his power could not give him a soul he wanted made him want it more and more, till all his emptiness focused on a single point. A way to fight him, or at least distract him, but dangerous. The pain first weakened him, brought him closer to human, then in a backlash spun him harder, blacker, *added* power. She could divert the tornado towards Margie, but it would come back to her with a vengeance. At best she'd gain a little time. But for what?

To come with us, whispered the Others. *To come with us where he cannot reach you.*

She was flooded with grateful warmth.

Like Scheherezade, Sunny made Margie dance in her mind as a go-go dancer in Vegas, wearing only a blue sequin G-string. She enhanced the image with all the sensuous envy one woman can feel for another, adding a luster to the skin and a perfection to the legs that they didn't quite have in real life. Somehow she knew she had the power to infect Dima's imagination. Sure enough, "Margie" pulsed her hips and Dima groaned, sweat breaking out on his forehead. The image brightened and Sunny knew Dima was creating it with her, that he believed it was his own. She quickened the dance, pumping "Margie's" hips harder, using her own sexuality without shame to inflame his.

And then something happened that sickened Sunny. At the moment when he should have reached orgasm, some natural valve closed, and all the molten lava of desire poured off into hate, like red-hot iron plunged gasping into ice water. For him there was no fulfillment, no release, not even in fantasy. There was only the cold joy of destroying.

She felt his dead desire congeal into a plan and set hard. He sprang for the telephone.

In that moment Sunny dived up out of her body, passed easily through the high, thin metal ceiling, and found herself free in the night air.

Immediately the Others gathered around her, thick and soft as feathers, gently urging her upwards.

*   *   *   *

Goddamn sonofabitch. I'm lost.

Sasha stopped and looked around in the dim light of the quarter moon. Frogs shrilled spring songs in the marsh all around him, and the smell of the rushes was thick and sweet. Must be close to midnight. The cab driver had let him off at the entrance to the service road with a strange look. Probably figured he came out here on a drug deal, but being a New York cabbie he'd shrug and mind his own business.

A plane roared low overhead, its landing lights winking. A zone of frog silence swept after it like the shadow of a cloud.

Sunny must be very close, and he had to go and get fucking lost. He had the .38 in his right hand, the Don's map sticking to his damp left palm, but he couldn't read it in the faint moonlight, and he didn't want to strike a match. He'd taken what he thought was the second left off the service road, but maybe he'd missed one and this was the third. The dirt road didn't seem used much, he'd tripped over weeds growing tall between the ruts. But to retrace his steps would lose precious time.

If he couldn't find it, how the hell was Bo-bo going to? At least he'd grown up in the country. Bo-bo was a city animal. He could find his way around the South Bronx or Little Italy blindfolded, but the Jamaica marsh might as well be Borneo. He hoped the Don's boys had better instructions. Was he going to have to stand here waiting for the sound of gunfire?

It might already be too late.

Sasha's system was jacked up on adrenaline. He had to take a piss. He unzipped and aimed off into the reeds, listening to the sound of his stream mingle with the chiming of the frogs.

Suddenly Sunny was with him.

The conviction came as a warmth and certainty in his chest. It wasn't just that taking a piss had reminded him of the train and the outhouse and the Drinking Gourd. She was really here, not just beside him but inside him; he could feel the radiance of her smile like an inner sun. Relief swept him, because now he was sure she was alive.

And then cold dread hit. Maybe this meant she was dying. Maybe she was saying goodbye.

As he thought that, she was gone, leaving a cold hole in his chest. Wind whistled in it, the starlight shone through.

He looked up and saw the Big Dipper.

Somehow now he knew which way to go.

*   *   *   *

Hey, wait a minute, Sunny said, this is neat! I want to look around.

Apparently her curiosity was independent of her body.

Come with us come with us, the Others chanted. They were insistent, not so gentle now. They were pushing her upward towards a light that was very beautiful. The light was pulling her, too, like Dima but just the opposite. No fear. Like a mother's arms. So easy to drift into it, so safe.

Yes, but first I want to look around! Okay? What's the big hurry, if we're all going there anyway?

Sunny wrenched free.

She was floating—whatever "she" was—about twenty feet above a large humped silvery building. Beside it was a long black car, and another car. Building was…Quonset hut? No. Airplane hangar! Airplanes kept passing over, big shadows. Something around the building, an old fence. Two spikes of heat in opposite corners, guarding it, she guessed. Dip into their minds, one like diving into Romanian rum he wanted it so bad, the other one half asleep, dreaming a mountain meadow. She was getting good at this.

A sharp yank from Dima made her gasp, just as if black hands had fastened on her ankles. Something bad was happening to her body. Killing it now, or hurting it to bring her back? She struggled like a trapped diver.

Hurry hurry. The Others closed around her again. *Come with us where he can't reach you.*

Who are you?

We are the children at childhood's end. This cradle will fall. Come, where the pain of earth can't hurt you.

Eh, Sempai Sun-nee, don't be scared! One step forward and you're in heaven.

Pierre!

Gladness caused a rocket-like rush toward the light, pulling her free of the dark grip. But wait.

There was another one moving out there. No, two.

She had once made a vow to her curiosity. If something caught her eye, say passing a store window, she would always go back and investigate. What a drag right now—dangerous, too. But a promise was a promise.

She felt toward the life and found herself with Sasha.

Not with him, *in* him. In his heart, with a sense of such delirious safety and homecoming that she forgot all about the stupid light. He was in a rage of worry about her, he was lost, he was taking a piss, and sure enough, he was hungry. Sunny laughed with joy. Their separation had been pure stupidity, and now it was over. She wondered if he knew it too.

Then she realized that he was walking into terrible danger.

He was alone. There were two armed men ahead of him, maybe another one behind him, and inside the hangar, Hector and Branco had guns, maybe Dima and Manea too. They had her, and she felt in his bones that he wouldn't stop till he got to her, even if he was dead on his feet. She couldn't stop him. She couldn't help him. And she knew, being in Sasha, what he knew: that life on this earth, in this strong, hungry, destructible body, is real life.

With that realization, in a dizzying rush, she was back in the chair with Hector's knife at her throat.

*   *   *   *

Sasha crouched in the shelter of the reeds and looked across twenty yards of bare space at the warehouse.

With its hutch-shaped aluminum roof, it looked like an old hangar for small planes that had been converted. It probably dated back to when Kennedy Airport was Idlewild. Sasha guessed this area was too marshy for jet runways and hangars, and so had been gradually abandoned. A Sally Salvatore still held title to the building; God knows what the crime families had used it for over the years, or how the Romanians had come by it.

Around the building wavered a drunken chain-link fence that had fallen in places. Security was provided by the remote location and by two dark figures at opposite corners of the fence, on either side of a closed gate. One paced on the left, smoking a cigarette. In the corner to the right the other was propped motionless, maybe—with luck—asleep. Sasha stared for minutes and saw no sign of life. The biggest collapse in the fence was beyond him, towards the back of the building along the right side.

The warehouse had no windows that Sasha could see. It revealed no more of what was within it than a tomb. Between it and the fence sat a long black limousine and a smaller, dark-colored car.

Sasha slipped the gun in his pocket and searched the ground with both hands. The curve of a beer bottle. No good, it would whistle as it flew. No stones here. He tore loose a dried clod of soil and roots and slowly rose from his crouch. He waited till the glow of the sentry's cigarette was eclipsed, cocked his arm and threw the clod as hard as he could over the fence, over the sentry's head. Even without desperation he was good for forty or fifty yards.

He heard the small sound of the clod landing and the sentry's growl, "*Cine acolo?* Who's there?" *Don't wake the other one up!*

The guard waited, head cocked, listening. Then he walked cautiously down the left side of the warehouse to investigate, just as Sasha wanted him to. The other one hadn't moved.

Sasha took the gun out of his pocket and sprinted soundlessly to the right. Big as he was, he could run lightly as a cat, a gift of karate. He ran past the guard in the corner, hearing his snore, and down the fence to the fallen section.

The fence was about seven feet tall. At the part lying flat, it was a seven-foot broad jump. Sasha chose speed over caution and leapt. He fell just short, landing on the metal rail that had been the top.

The whole fence shivered with a tinselly sound.

Sasha dived for the black limo and crawled under it, pressing the gun and his hammering heart to the ground.

In a moment the feet of the first sentry ran right past between him and the black, open doorway. "Radule! *Ai auzit ceva?*" he shouted softly. "Did you hear something?" The fence shook again, and an angry voice said, "*Tu* ai fost! *De ce dorm, tampitule! Scoalate!*" Sasha pictured him shaking the sleeper awake, shoving him upright against the fence. He heard a groaning yawn.

"*Am auzit ceva, dar cred ca a fost numai un glotan,*" said the first one. "I heard something, but I guess it was just a rat."

"*Tu est glotan. M-ai sculat din un vis formidabil.* You're the rat, waking me up from a nice dream like that."

"*Da, eo vad, inca ai pula sculata.* Yeah, I see you've still got a hard-on. *Sta cu ochi deschis.* Keep your eyes open, will you?"

"*Nimic de vazut.* There's nothing to see," grumbled the other.

"*Nooooooo-o-o-o!*"

A screaming wail, coming from inside the warehouse, echoing in the high metal vault, Sunny's voice, stretched to the limit by horror. Still alive, but not for long. Sasha dug his fingers into the ground, panting with frustration. Shoot these two and run in! No! They'll kill her for sure.

"*E mai mult de vazut inauntru,*" one guard's voice said wryly. "Guess there's more to see in there."

The other one gave a verbal shrug. "Not our business. *Salut.*" The first guard's feet crunched past.

Sasha counted to ten, chest heaving, slid out from under the car and crawled on elbows and knees across two yards of moonlight, hoping the car covered him as far as the shadow of the warehouse. He made it into the shadow and scrambled gratefully into the deeper shadow of the doorway.

Pitch black in here. With an effort, Sasha held his breath and listened for the sound of another man's breathing, the scrape of a shoe. Nothing, but there were sounds upstairs—muffled voices.

And now voices, shouts from outside again! Had one of them seen him?

He groped his way quickly to the left-hand wall and along it. Half-way down the length of the building he banged into vertical iron. A stairway. He climbed it, blind, fast and awkward, gun in hand.

At the top he pushed open a flimsy door, and dim light welcomed his eyes. He was in a corridor lit at intervals by weak light bulbs, some burned out. Every ten yards or so was an old door, painted dirty green. One door was open, bright light spilling out. The voices were further down.

Sasha crept up to the open door.

The room inside was fluorescent-lit, empty except for a lot of labo-ratory equipment: tubes, flasks, gas burners, plastic vats.

Was this where they made the hex?

He moved on and put his ear to the next door. Nothing. It was the one after that. Light leaked under that door. Behind it, men's voices, arguing.

Over Sunny, or what was left of her. God, let me hear her voice. But he didn't. He heard noises downstairs.

Don't turn the knob. Don't give them an instant to think.

Sasha stepped back till his back touched the opposite wall.

$$* \qquad * \qquad * \qquad *$$

The cold steel that had recalled her to her body still pressed against Sunny's throat, stopped by an unlikely rescuer: Manea.

The scientist stood with his back to the door, arguing with Dima in Romanian. Sunny couldn't understand it all, but the gist was: Why kill her? With one more dose of this drug, you can send her back out there and she'll work for *you*. The nightmares will make sure of that.

It wasn't compassion that had brought Manea when she screamed. It was a fastidious distaste for primitive methods and an arrogant faith in his brainchild, hex. The quiver in Hector's arm, on the other hand, was pure bloodlust, barely held back. The knife blade transmitted the vibration to Sunny and picked up her answering tremor of fear.

She hadn't screamed for help. She'd meant to keep quiet, to let Sasha save himself. A cry of hopeless terror had torn out of her anyway, because it was over. God bless Margie, she'd kept Dima on the phone as long as she could. It must have made her sick, pretending to sweet-talk him. But he hadn't bought it. He'd told her she was a whore for Sasha and C.J., that he knew she was working with Sasha, that he had Sunny on Thirty-Eighth Street and would kill her in the morning—an obvious ploy to lure Sasha there. Finally he'd slammed the phone down and shouted to Hector, "We are *not* waiting till morning! I am finished with her now"—Branco had yanked her head back, Hector put the blade to her throat "—*almost.*"

Looking into his eyes, Sunny had screamed.

Manea was losing the argument. But it hardly mattered. Either way Sunny was lost. If she lived, it would be in a madhouse, like Szlacter's friend. Emptied out. She should have listened to the Others, she—

CRASH!!!

Manea flew across the room, propelled by the door, which had not opened but exploded. Sunny saw Sasha burst through the side of the world, breaking the black vacuum so life, air and motion rushed in. He hit the floor, losing his gun, rolled on his shoulder, and came up on his feet, empty-handed. Hector was already behind him. He'd leapt aside, dropped the knife, had his pistol out, both hands on it. "Watch out!!" Sunny screamed, but Sasha saw Branco's hands on her and went for him. He drove a shattering pillar of muscle and bone right through the big slow Romanian's jaw, and Hector shot him.

Sunny lurched forward as if a horse had kicked her in the back. *"Nooooooo-o-o!"* she screamed for the second time. Sasha got a wistful look on his face and crumbled like a building in demolition. At the far, indifferent borders of Sunny's attention, Dima scuttled out the door. The center of the world was the red patch spreading on Sasha's back. Sunny was having trouble breathing. Hector leveled his gun at her, smiling. Hey, this like shootin' fish in a barrel! She wrenched her chair over and fell on top of Sasha, feeling the bullet's breath on her cheek.

"Heyyy, *spic!*" came a joyous greeting from the doorway.

Bo-bo lounged there grinning, eyes alight, a muzzle resting on his arm like a snout with two nostrils. Hector spun round and BOOM! Bo-bo blasted him in mid-turn, an explosion of flesh and blood. A fine hot rain pattered down for a long time. Hector's body had crumpled and Sunny felt the dust devil of his life spin away, but Sasha was still here.

There was a gargling snore from Branco, asleep with his jaw stove in. Manea was out too, knocked cold by the door.

Bo-bo jacked another shell into the shotgun and pointed it at the two hot-dog sellers cowering in the corner. "Don't fuckin' *move,*" he said. They twittered like rodents. Bo-bo went through Hector's pockets and put a thick bankroll, keys, and another knife into his own. Then he lifted Sunny off Sasha and set the chair upright.

"He shot Sasha," she whimpered. The hex was fading but she could *feel* Bo-bo, rage and humor thickly intertwined, and behind that something unexpected, a baffled decency. He dropped to one knee and felt Sasha's neck, then cradled his friend's cheek with amazing gentleness.

Sasha moaned, coughed blood, and tried to clear his throat, a conscious, familiar sound.

"Sash, we're here," Sunny cried. "You're gonna be all right. It missed your heart." She didn't know how she knew

"Shit, he's bleedin' too much," Bo-bo mumbled. "Fuckin' bullet went right through him."

"We've got to get him to a—"

They heard quick footsteps pattering down the metal stairs.

"Dima," Sunny said.

"He ain't goin' nowhere," Bo-bo grinned, and raised a finger with two sets of car keys dangling from it. He picked up Hector's open switchblade and cut through the ropes tying Sunny's ankles to the chair. He put Sasha's gun in her hand, took the safety off, and made her point it at the two terrified Romanians. Then he cradled the shotgun and set off after Dima.

Sunny heard his feet go lightly down the stairs. At the same time, a car trunk or door slammed outside. Then she heard Dima's high scream of rage.

"Blue!" Sasha said suddenly, blowing a small bubble of blood.

"Shhhh," Sunny said. "We're going to see Blue."

Two shotgun blasts from outside.

A minute or two later, feet trudged up the stairs.

"I got him in the thigh," Bo-bo reported. "Motherfucker limped off into them bull-rushes. He'll bleed to death out there. Fuck him. Let's get Sasha to a hospital."

Sunny stood up for the first time in hours and almost collapsed. "You all right?" Bo-bo said. "What'd they do to you? The scumbags. They rape you?"

First thing men think of. Sunny shook her head. "Drug. I'm—I'm coming down." Her legs were asleep, her butt sore, the seat of her pants wet, no memory of when that had happened. She felt light and hollow.

Bo-bo gently rolled Sasha over and stripped off his own jacket and shirt. Sasha's eyes were open. He looked at Bo-bo with bewilderment, then his eyes moved frantically till they found Sunny. She tried to smile, and an expression of peace came over his face. He lay with his eyes fixed on her while Bo-bo tore up his shirt and made a hasty pressure bandage.

Manea stirred and groaned.

As casually as swatting a fly, Bo-bo picked up the shotgun, racked it and blasted him. A great hole torn in his back, Manea's shoes jittered against the floor. Sunny buried her face in her hands and sobbed.

"Somebody's gotta clean up," Bo-bo shrugged. "C'mon, let's get outta here." He put on his jacket over his T-shirt and put Sasha's gun and Hector's knife and pistol into the pockets. Then he got one arm under Sasha's knees, one under his back, and lifted his huge friend like a baby. "Christ, how'm I gonna get him down those stairs."

"Walk," Sasha said.

"Are you fuckin' crazy?" But Bo-bo gently let his feet down. Sasha's knees sagged, then locked. Sunny got under his left arm, and he leaned heavily on her. Pain stabbed through her chest: his. She didn't know if love or the hex made her feel it. Bo-bo picked up the shotgun, and the two of them supported Sasha to the door.

At the top of the steep metal staircase Bo-bo gave Sunny the shotgun. It was shockingly heavy. "Go ahead. Take this down, then help me. Shit, this's gonna make him bleed more. What can ya do." He held Sasha under the arms and slowly lowered him down the stairs, grunting, while Sunny placed his feet on the steps.

At the bottom the wavery trio reestablished itself, moved towards the door, and stopped.

Two dark figures in the doorway.

Bo-bo turned to steel, his finger on the trigger.

"Hey, Bo. Take it easy," one of the men called softly. "We're from the Don."

"Whew." Bo-bo lowered the shotgun. "C'mere and gimme a hand. Sasha's hurt."

The three men took Sasha's weight off Sunny and hustled him towards the limo, Sunny right behind them. The Don's men felt to her like well-made guns, greased precision mechanisms with no waste motion. They got the back door open and lay Sasha on the seat with his knees slightly bent. Sunny put up a jump seat, sat down by him and took his hand. It was cold for the first time since she'd known him.

"I gotta drive him to a hospital," Bo-bo was saying outside.

"Any more business to take care of here? We heard shots."

"It's a mess. Them two by the gate," Bo-bo said. "I said 'Fire Department' an' flashed a kid's badge. That confused the dumb fucks, an' I got 'em with the gun butt. Three more upstairs. And one out in the weeds somewhere, hurt bad. I don't want no witnesses, but in front a her…"

"We'll take care of it," one of them said quietly.

Bo-bo got behind the wheel of the limo, slammed the door, and drove through the gate and down a dark lane of reeds, lights out.

After a couple of turns he suddenly said, *"Shit!"*, wrenched the wheel and drove off into the marsh. The jolt and bouncing brought a bubbling cough from Sasha, and Sunny cried, "Bo-bo!"

"Shhh!" He killed the engine, and the car crunched to a stop.

Sunny heard a low sound of motors.

"Cops," Bo-bo said with disbelief. "How the fuck…"

"How do you know?"

"The Don only sent those two. Besides, I c'n smell 'em."

The sound came closer and then receded, going back in the direction they had come from.

"Gotta let the boys know," Bo-bo said.

He counted to twenty, started the car, and backed carefully out of the reeds. "Lucky it ain't been rainin'," he said.

Where the dirt road joined the old service road he got out, leaving the motor idling, and fired his shotgun once into the air. Then he got back behind the wheel and fishtailed squealing into the service road.

"Bo-bo!" Sunny cried again, holding Sasha down. "They'll come after us!"

"Naah," Bo-bo said. "Time they get back here we'll be long gone. It'll give those boys a chance to protect themselves." He shook his head. "Shitty timing. What hospital we goin' to?"

"The nearest one! He's passed out!"

"Yeah, but I don't know where that is, and I don't wanna be stopping and asking with a gunshot case in the back seat. What's near you in the Village?"

"Saint Vinnie's, but will he make it?"

They were shooting up the ramp to the expressway. "We'll be there in twenny minutes."

"Hurry!"

*   *   *   *

When they got to Fourteenth Street Bo-bo said, "Can you drive this thing?"

Sunny was wiping the clammy sweat off Sasha's forehead again. He was so cold. He hated being cold. She was shivering with him. "Aren't you taking us to the hospital?" Her voice cracked with panic.

"Look. I'm carryin' so fuckin' much I feel like a fuckin' hardware store. I come in with him all shot up, the cops'll be all over me in a minute. Anyway, I got to go see the Don. Lemme off in the Village, wouldja? I'll come see him in the morning."

Sunny started to cry. "Yeah, I can drive it. I'm just so scared he's gonna die." She was walled up in her body again, and she couldn't reach Sasha, closed up in his. She had no idea what he was going through. It was so lonely. How do we live like this?

"Aw, he ain't gonna die," said Bo-bo. "My man Sasha ain't that easy to kill. The fuckin' Russians couldn't do it, and they tried for two years."

Sunny laughed through her tears.

Bo-bo pulled over to the side of deserted Greenwich Avenue and started wrapping the shotgun in his raincoat. "Give you some advice," he said. "Drop him off and get rid a this fuckin' car. Save yourself a lotta trouble."

"But I have to stay with him," Sunny protested.

"They take him in the operating room, whatcha gonna do, sit in a chair? He'll be in good hands. Be smart, Sunny. Get rid a the car. I was you, I'd take it to an airport. Say LaGuardia. Wipe it down and leave it in a parking lot."

It sounded like climbing Mount Everest, but Sunny said, "Okay." Bo-bo got out and she stroked Sasha's forehead, climbed out and got in the driver's seat.

"God, you're a mess," Bo-bo said admiringly. He handed her his handkerchief. "You got blood on your face. Spit on this and wipe it off." He took her head in his big basketball-player's hands and kissed her forehead. Then he walked eastward with long, bouncy strides.

Sunny wiped her face, wondering whose the blood was, put the limo in gear and drove the block and a half to the emergency entrance of St. Vincent's Hospital.

She got out on shaky legs and pushed through the ambulance doors. "Somebody help me," she called. "I've got a man here with a chest wound."

Two strong young attendants and a nurse came running on rubber soles, pushing a wheeled stretcher. Sunny showed them the open back door of the limo, and the two men struggled to get Sasha's dead weight out of the car and onto the stretcher. His face was gray and his shirt was bright red.

"Gunshot," said one attendant.

"Pulse rapid and shallow," said the nurse. "Lost a lot of blood. He's in shock. Type him and get two units going, stat." The medical words were reassuring and competent, impersonal and desolate.

"Stay right there, miss," the nurse called back as they rolled Sasha rapidly away from her. Goodbye, goodbye. "We'll need his name and insurance, and your name. And the police will be here to take your statement."

"Of course. Just let me move the car out of your way. I'll park it and be right back." Before they could protest, Sunny was behind the wheel and backing out of the ambulance driveway.

Had they noticed the DPL license plates? When the cops arrived, they'd start looking for the limo. She wondered how much time that gave her.

She wanted to go home. She needed to touch someone, something warm and living. More than anything on earth, she wanted the cats. They held healing for all the evil she'd seen this night.

She drove down Seventh Avenue and across West Fourth and parked the limo in front of their building. Sasha'd always had fantasies of arriving in a limo. What a ghastly parody, empty as a hearse with his blood in the back.

She got out and had what seemed like a bright idea: she could slow the search for the limo by taking off the plates. It was a screwy, druggy idea, because crouching behind a Cadillac limousine at four in the morning unscrewing the plates—not to mention driving to the airport without any—was a great way to attract unwanted attention. But to Sunny at that moment it seemed like highest reason. She squatted by the rear bumper to see if she'd need a regular screwdriver or a Phillips.

The lock on the trunk caught her eye. Maybe there was a screwdriver in there.

She got the keys from the ignition, went back to the trunk, and unlocked it. The lid rose.

When she saw what was in there, Sunny suppressed a scream and then burst into tears.

CHAPTER 12

▼

"Oh, Sasha. Not *another* hot dog. That makes seven."

He rolled his head on the hospital pillow and gave her a rebellious look. "What's better than six million dollars?"

Sunny groaned. "You can't apply that logic to hot dogs. Seven hot dogs is *worse* than six! Hot dogs can kill you!" He saw her eyes darken. "Take it from me."

"Dr. Pearson says I need protein because I'm healing." Sasha had made friends with his chest surgeon, a serene, mischievous WASP from Iowa with wavy white hair and a bow tie. "That's why I have this terrible craving for Zion kosher all-beef franks." He waved a hand and Bo-bo, a willing pusher, handed him number seven, with extra sauerkraut.

Bo-bo looked into the bag he was holding. His jaw dropped and his eyes widened with horror.

"Oh, no! Sunny, you'll never guess what's in here!"

Sunny put her hands over her eyes. "Stop it. Just stop it. It's not funny."

"HA HAAAA!" Sasha tried his heartiest roar of laughter. It cost him a coughing fit, and he frowned with pain. Sunny rushed over.

"Take it easy! You're going to start bleeding again!"

"I can't help it." To his chagrin, his eyes filled with tears. They'd been doing that often and easily ever since he woke up in this stupid bed. "When I look at you, I feel so good, I got to eat, I got to laugh, I got to get up and walk home and cook for you." He struggled to sit up. "Let me outta this fucking hospital," he bellowed. "I wanna see the kittens."

The redheaded nurse, Kelly, poked her head in the door to see if something was wrong. "Gettin' rambunctious, huh? Well, the doctor says in just a couple more days, if your X-ray looks good, you can go home."

"X-ray my ass," Sasha grumbled.

"We can do that, too," Kelly laughed. "Dr. Pearson says he's never seen a patient heal so fast," she said to Sunny. "Or eat so much."

"Yeah, he has an amazing constitution," Sunny said. "He escaped from Russia with gangrene in his legs. Every doctor he's told about it says he shouldn't have survived." Sasha scowled. He got embarrassed when Sunny bragged about him.

"He has some pretty amazing luck, too," said Kelly. "Do you know that bullet missed his aorta by less than an inch? Makes you believe in miracles. Well, see you later, guys."

"Speakin' a miracles," said Bo-bo, shaking his head, "how about that Brooklyn Georgie."

"Tell me again," Sasha said, pressing the button to make the head of the bed rise. "He was sitting up, and what did he say?"

"'Bypass,'" Bo-bo growled in imitation. "'Bypass my ass. I'd a been fine if I coulda just made it to the refrigerator. I almost died a hunger.' His mom brought a spaghetti with sausage to the hospital, and they wouldn't let him have any. Was he pissed!"

"I love the fat little son of a bitch." Sasha's eyes filled again. "It's ten thirty," he said gruffly to Sunny. "Put on 'Wheel of Fortune.'"

The TV, a little black-and-white one, hung over the bed on an extending arm. Sunny pulled it closer and clicked it on. She held Sasha's hand through the first two puzzles.

"We interrupt this program for a special news bulletin," said Dan Rather. "The FBI and the Drug Enforcement Administration announced this morning that a high-ranking foreign diplomat, Romanian—"

Sunny gasped.

"—Mission to the United Nations Counselor Liviu Dima, has been arrested on charges of importing and distributing the drug hexamethylene for sale in the United States. This first major break in the deadly mystery of 'hex,' the designer drug that has infected high schools and colleges across the nation and that is linked to nine deaths, may also prove to be the first substantiated case of 'narcoterrorism'—the deliberate introduction of a dangerous drug into American society by foreign agents or terrorist groups. Dima, here in the custody of DEA agents—"

There he was, the ugly bastard, in a wheelchair being pushed by an athletic young agent, his wrists braceleted together, his dour face forested with beard stubble. Sunny moaned and covered her eyes.

"Shit," Bo-bo said. "I shoulda aimed higher. Those fuckin' cops saved his life."

Dan Rather was talking about how Dima had been wounded in a style suggestive of drug gang wars, and was being held in the Rikers Island prison hospital pending the decision to prosecute or deport. The strapping young black-haired agent pushing the wheelchair turned his head towards the camera for a moment. Even in black-and-white, you could see that he had rosy cheeks.

"Je-sus fucking *Christ!*" Sasha roared, nearly leaping out of bed. "That's *C.J.!*"

"Who?" Sunny peeked between her fingers.

"C.J. East, the magician! From the club! The son of a bitch! He's a *DEA* agent! Ow*oooo!*" Sasha whooped wonder at C.J.'s greatest magic trick. "What the eye sees, the heart must believe!"

"So he wasn't after Margie," Sunny said. "He was after Dima all along!"

"Gimme the phone." Sasha dialed Margie's number. Dan Rather was speculating on Romanian government involvement, calling the Romanian president "the last Stalinist, with known ties to Palestinian and Libyan terrorism," and promising live coverage of the FBI/DEA press conference later in the day.

"She's not home," Sasha said.

"She's probably on her way here," said Sunny. Margie had been a faithful daily visitor.

"Now I understand why C.J. made her give Dima her number," Sasha said. "He put a trace on her phone! That's how they finally tracked him to the warehouse! Thank God you warned the Don's boys, Bo. They were pretty muddy when they got back, but that's all. Jesus, how am I going to repay Don Chaluch'?"

"Wait a minute. Listen to this," Bo-bo said. "I don't believe this. Are they talkin' about lettin' that creep go?"

Dan Rather was explaining the concept of diplomatic immunity. It seemed that a diplomat could commit murder or another felony and suffer nothing worse than deportation back to his home country. Sunny turned pale.

"Fuck *that,*" said Bo-bo. "They got to fry the bastard."

"You should've aimed higher, Bo-bo," Sunny said grimly.

"He says it's not decided yet," Sasha tried to reassure her. "And maybe your article will have an influence."

"Oh God, the article," Sunny groaned. "I don't ever want to hear the word 'hex' again."

"Don't say that. It's important," Sasha said. "Important for you, for your career, and for…" He groped for words. "For people to understand how a drug like that can suck in so many bright kids. And hardly anybody here knows as much about Romania as you do. Rest, forget all about it for two weeks, and then I'm gonna make you write the story."

Sunny was staring at him with disbelief. "Are you sure he didn't shoot you in the head?" she said softly.

That afternoon Sasha had a procession of visitors. Margie came, and Darlene, who was the first face Sasha had seen when he came out of anesthesia, having responded to Sunny's frantic four A.M. phone call from LaGuardia. Other visitors ranged from the famous woman sculptor Sunny had profiled, who swept into the hospital room like a shy empress in inch-long false eyelashes and a fur-lined brocade coat, to a black hit man from Baltimore who asked Sasha seriously, "Can I kill somebody for you?" Everyone who knew and loved Sasha brought him something to eat, and by five P.M. the room was littered with empty Kentucky Fried Chicken buckets and Dunkin' Donuts boxes.

The visitors had tired him out. He didn't want to talk or laugh any more, just lie there holding Sunny's hand. He was even too tired to get a hard-on, which had happened to him that morning when she walked in, as easily and involuntarily as the crying. He felt too peaceful now.

One thing kept nagging at him, though.

"What pisses me off," he said to her, "is that they got all that cash on Tarom. They got away with it. The dirty bastards. How much do you think they got on this trip?"

Sunny shrugged. "I saw them take two suitcases. How much would a big suitcase hold?"

"It depends on the size of the bills," Sasha said indignantly. It was just like Sunny not to think of that. His obsession with numbers spun in his head. "I'd say one to three million."

"I wouldn't know," Sunny said.

Sasha sighed. "Boy, I'd have loved to get my hands on one of those suitcases. You know the first thing I would've done? Dumped it all out on the bed on top of you and Blue. You'd have had a bath in hundred-dollar bills."

Sunny sighed too. "Too bad," she said with studied sorrow. But Sasha caught the note of indifference in her voice.

"You don't give a fuck, do you?" he bellowed, propping himself up on one elbow and wincing. "You have no idea what a million dollars is.

The kind of freedom it gives you. The clout. Well, you know what?" He flounced back on his pillow and stared at the ceiling.

"I don't really give a fuck either," he said in a softer voice, touched by wonder.

He turned and looked at her. *"You're* my big score," he said. "And the next time I forget that, kick me in the ass, will you?"

"I will," Sunny said.

*   *   *   *

"Hurry up," Sunny giggled. She seemed to be beside herself with some private glee.

"I'm coming as fast as I can," Sasha said. He had paused on the second landing to catch his breath. The stairs made him puff, and his chest hurt. Dr. Pearson hadn't wanted to let him go until tomorrow. "Don't you think I'm in a hurry to see the kittens? Whaddayou got, ants in your pants?"

"I've got a surprise for you." She scampered a flight ahead of him, turned, and made coaxing motions, her eyes sparkling.

"What is it?" He hauled himself up five more stairs.

"If I told you it wouldn't be a surprise, would it?"

"Is it something to eat?" He rested, breathing carefully.

"Not exactly," Sunny giggled.

"A new kitten!"

"No! Isn't nine enough?"

"A pair of shoes?" Sasha asked forlornly. There were so few things he really wanted. They were the things he hadn't had in Russia, simple things that had become so infinitely precious he couldn't get enough of them. He already had twenty pairs of size 15EEE shoes.

"No. Come on, you're almost there."

"Give me a hint."

"It's heavy," Sunny said. "You know I'm pretty strong, and I could hardly get it up the stairs."

That stopped him. He frowned. "A new air conditioner?"

"Oh, come on! Everybody's waiting for you." She unlocked the door.

Sasha labored up the last flight and walked into his little paradise. *"Blue!!"*

The Siamese turned and looked at him, his big dark ears cupped to catch Sasha's voice, his azure eyes full of love.

He was sitting on an oxblood-colored suitcase of cheap Romanian leather, its sides bulging almost more than the flimsy straps could hold.

THE END

0-595-29872-9

Made in the USA
Monee, IL
20 July 2021

73974228R00169